W9-BTT-056

THROWAWAY GIRLS

THROWAWAY GIRLS

BY ANDREA CONTOS

KCP Loft

Kids Can Press gratefully acknowledges the financial support of the Government of Ontario, through Ontario Creates.

Published in Canada and the U.S. by Kids Can Press Ltd.
25 Dockside Drive, Toronto, ON M5A 0B5

Kids Can Press is a Corus Entertainment Inc. company

www.kidscanpress.com
www.kcploft.com

The text is set in Minion Pro.

Edited by Kate Egan
Cover design by Jennifer Lum

Printed and bound in Altona, Manitoba, Canada, in 6/2020 by Friesens Corp.

CM 20 0 9 8 7 6 5 4 3 2 1

FSC
www.fsc.org
MIX
Paper from
responsible sources
FSC® C016245

Library and Archives Canada Cataloguing in Publication

Title: Throwaway girls / Andrea Contos.
Names: Contos, Andrea, author.
Identifiers: Canadiana 20190095733 | ISBN 9781525303142 (hardcover)
Classification: LCC PZ7.1.C65 T47 2020 | DDC j813/.6 — dc23

To my daughters, Evangeline and Josephine, who will always be my greatest inspiration.

And to my brother, Andrew, who was always meant to live amongst the stars.

THE EDGES OF THINGS: AN UNNAMED GIRL BY AN UNNAMED LAKE

Everything started with the body at the edge of the lake. I know that now.

But back then, all I knew was the rush and gurgle of water where the stream fed into the lake, the gentle sway of yellow irises as the wind lifted their downturned petals. And the way the body's legs bobbed in time with the lap of water against the shore, like part of the girl's spirit was still trying to run from whatever had brought her there.

Left her there.

Hastily pulled half onto the shore.

Eyes closed. Mouth open. Full lips a watercolor blend of pink roses and the sky before a storm.

I knew what dead bodies looked like — even then. I'd been the one to find Edna Drake's body when she collapsed from a heart attack on the way to her mailbox when I was seven. By twelve, I'd seen two of Mom's boyfriends OD.

But this girl wasn't like the others.

I inched closer, careful to avoid the soggy spots where I might leave a footprint, and my shadow fell over the girl's face, shielding her from the blaring sun. Her dark hair fanned in a halo around her pale skin, mingling with the grass.

I didn't know her. Hadn't seen her around the estates.

The estates. I choked back a snicker, and tears followed right behind. Leaning in, but not too close, I whispered, "Sorry. I'm sorry. That was wrong. Defense mechanism. Sometimes I laugh when things are terrible, like —"

Like a beautiful girl with a necklace of bruises.

I sucked in a shuddering breath. "Really though, who was the first idiot to tack 'Estates' on to the name of every trailer park?"

My knees hit the ground before I realized I was moving, cold mud coating my jeans and seeping through the fibers. I whispered, "Who did this to you?"

I wasn't expecting an answer, but it felt right to ask. Like maybe some part of her would have the chance to scream out a name in a final shout of justice from her spot in the heavens. Instead there was only the creak of a heavy branch on a twisted tree.

Her thin arm lay outstretched, her inner elbow marked with faded scars.

I scooted toward her legs and yanked the sleeves of my shirt down to cover my hands, then I pulled her all the way onto the shore.

She was still then. No more running.

No more running. No more wanting. No more pain.

Just a beautiful girl lying on the shore in a forever dream.

I could've called the cops, but I'd seen the shows. How they'd stick her in a drawer after they cut her up. Gather their evidence even though no one would look too hard for a girl no one wanted to find.

For some people, life begins too far behind the starting line to have any hope of crossing the finish.

I closed my eyes and whispered a prayer — and an apology. Then I left her there to dream.

At the time, I saw the peacefulness of death. A quiet slip into blissful stillness. A relief.

I couldn't have been more wrong.

I know that now too.

CHAPTER ONE

Sometimes I try to convince myself Madison isn't really missing.

I decide she was brave enough to do what I couldn't and left everything behind.

But the delusion never lasts long, because I know she wouldn't leave.

I know she never *wanted* to leave.

She loved everything about her life.

She's never been the girl who wanted to escape. And she isn't the girl with all the secrets.

I am.

But it's Madison's mom on stage, positioned against a backdrop of fog-drenched hills and clustered trees, the sun blanching what color she has left in her face. She looks paler every hour, and it's been thirty-six.

She tugs her coat tighter against the rain-scented burst of wind as she says, for the third time, that someone must know something.

Mr. Bentley isn't up there with her. He's not even on campus.

He answered the phone when Mom called the Bentleys' house the night Madison disappeared. She suggested this vigil. A showing of support, she said.

His response carried through the phone and spilled into the hallway, because Mr. Bentley knew vigils wouldn't bring Madison home.

They're nothing but a way for all the parents and students on this lawn to hide their fear behind the illusion of action. And to hide their guilt over how grateful they are it's Madison and not them. Not their family.

Mom called back the next morning, when she knew Mr. Bentley would be gone. And now I'm standing at a vigil in broad daylight, holding a flameless candle so there's no threat of melted wax on the new football field turf, and plotting to get my mother off campus before she has a chance to talk to anyone.

Projected pictures of my missing best friend flash behind Mrs. Bentley as she says, for the fourth time, that someone must know something.

Every time the words strike the air they feel less like a statement and more like a plea.

I hold my breath, begging for someone to announce they know exactly where Madison is. That she's not missing at all. Because there are moments when I can't stop my thoughts from sliding into the horrors of where she could be. Places where she isn't fine. And futures where she doesn't come back.

Mrs. Bentley is alone up there, bookended by cops and faculty but no one who actually cares, and pressure builds behind my eyes, caging the tears I've forgotten how to let fall.

Madison would know what to do if she were here. She's the daughter Mom wanted but definitely did not get. The one who felt at ease in any room, who always knew the right thing to say and the right people to talk to during the outings, the fundraisers, the brunches and the dinner parties. When conversations turned to grades and accomplishments, futures and prospects, Madison always knew to turn it to me:

Caroline's in the running for valedictorian, you know.

Her team won last year's National Speech and Debate Tournament.

Caroline's already been recruited by Ivy League soccer teams.

We made up for each other's weaknesses.

Not today though. Today I'm alone, wishing, just for a moment, that it were Madison's feet frozen to the million-dollar turf that looks like grass but isn't. Her hand strangling this ridiculous flameless candle whose light no one can even see because there's a reason candlelight vigils are held at night.

It's the darkness and shadows, the way they hide the pain you don't want others to see, and the way they shield you from the truths you don't want to know.

Like the way Mrs. Bentley's fists clench every time her gaze finds mine.

I need to leave. Right now. But Mom's fingers dig into my arm, her elbow jabbing where my skin is still raw from the tattoo that will always remind me of Willa.

Mom doesn't speak, but in my head, I hear every syllable of my name. The way her tongue slides over every consonant of "Caroline" with a practiced ease that doesn't sound like the reproach it is.

It's a language only the two of us understand.

I planned this vigil. We're in the front row. You are not leaving.

Never make a scene. That's one of Mom's unbreakable rules.

St. Francis is a family — that's what all the brochures say.

The trouble with families is they know your weak points. Mom makes sure we never show ours.

Dad rubs my back, but it's a false comfort and my skin prickles with the need to shrug him off.

His arm falls when Mom glares at him.

A gust of spring wind draws rhythmic clangs from the flag-pole, and the crowd surrounding me stirs, like they're grateful to focus on anything other than Mrs. Bentley.

Her sobs are replaced by the soft notes of whatever song my mom picked for Aubrey Patel-Brennan to sing. Apparently, no vigil is complete without entertainment.

It's impossible to ignore Aubrey's voice, but I'm doing my best. By the time it fades into the clouds, the field is filled with tears and sniffles.

In an hour, all the cars will leave the grounds and all the students will be back at class. Restoring normalcy, they call it. Giving kids the comfort of routine. Besides, it's not like she went missing from campus. She was on a home visit and told her mom she was going shopping. She was only twenty miles from St. Francis, only six miles from home. They still haven't found her car.

That all adds up to St. Francis being officially free from responsibility. But not from response, especially when news of Madison's disappearance sent shocks through the community and the police launched searches right away.

Rumors of a temporary St. Francis shutdown followed close behind. So even as tears fell to tile floors and stares remained vacant, there were phone calls to Headmaster Havens.

It's a terrible thing that's happened to that poor girl, but …

We pay a lot of money to attend this institution.

My son shouldn't be denied his education.

My daughter has scouts scheduled to watch her next game.

The resident-assistance council, the yearbook club, the party-planning committees, they've all set up shrines to Madison in their offices. Their members still stumble through campus with red-rimmed eyes, but in every one of them, someone has offered to step into Madison's place. Just in case.

They never say the rest. *Just in case she never comes back.*

Headmaster Havens finally escorts Mrs. Bentley off the stage, the dome of his bald head catching in the glow of the sun, and then she's gone, disappearing into the car Mom has waiting to escort her back to Olivet Hall, where trays of salmon tartare and chocolate truffles await. Like maybe hors d'oeuvres are the trick to bringing Madison back safely. She'll just follow the fucking trail of smoked trout blinis straight from Grandmother's house in the woods.

Detective Brisbane steps toward the mic, his scuffed shoes thudding against the stage.

I've watched those shoes clip against St. Francis's marble floors every day since Madison disappeared, each echo a reminder that the world outside the manicured campus grounds can infiltrate ours.

But the other set, the ones that belong to Detective Harper, remind me of far more. Fake smiles and false assurances.

Detective Harper is a liar. That score to settle goes back nearly three years.

And if there's one thing I'm sure of, it's this: if things are ever going to be right again, it's not Detective Harper who's going to get them there.

I wrench my arm from Mom's grip and step back, making it impossible for her to recapture me without making it obvious.

I mumble, "I forgot to take my vitamin," and her jaw snaps shut, a flush coloring her face.

I walk away, and when a voice whispers my name, I move faster.

I'm nearly to the edge of the crowd when Jake Monaghan catches up to me and whispers, "Hey, wait up," even though we're standing in the same square foot of space.

I glance back to my parents and find Mr. Monaghan sandwiched between them, arms draped around their shoulders, like they're old friends and not just acquaintances who exchange pleasantries at St. Francis fundraisers. Mom's practically beaming — the delight of garnering attention from one of the school's most influential parents more than she can smother — and my anger toward her rivals my gratitude for him.

The screen behind Brisbane and Harper pauses on a shot of me and Madison, our faces pressed together, her blond hair tangling with mine — we're always the most extreme versions of ourselves when in contrast. But our smiles matched, because neither of us knew then what we know now.

I remember that picture.

Madison took it at the beginning of our fall outreach soccer camp for disadvantaged youth. She came with me in her official capacity as head yearbook photographer, and, as official co-captain of St. Francis Prep's soccer team, I made sure she got on-field access.

I know why my mom chose that picture, and it's got nothing to do with Madison.

It's because of me. Because it's been years since I've smiled like that in my mom's presence.

I want to tell her that smile wasn't just for the kids we taught that day. I want to shatter all my mother's delusions and tell

16

her the other reason was because, after years of waiting and wondering, that was the morning I saw Willa again.

But I'm too close to ruin everything now — only months away from graduation and leaving this version of my life behind forever. I've spent years giving each of my parents the part of me they can accept. All the rest is mine. And when I'm finally free of them both, I won't have to pretend for anyone.

A collective gasp rises from the field as the whine of a drone slices the sky — some desperate reporter trying to fill a five o'clock news segment. Then another drone joins the fray — from the team Mom hired — and they twist and tangle until they both whiz out of sight.

The crowd murmurs, uncomfortable coughs a clear indication that no one knows the protocol for a drone-crashed vigil. Even Mr. McCormack looks confused, and he's never confused about anything. He's the most decent and competent teacher St. Francis has.

A second later he regains his composure, murmuring something to the crowd of students surrounding him: Kids whose parents live too far, or couldn't make it. Kids who feel more comfortable with him than with their families. Whatever he said, they all look calmer for having heard it. I should've stood with them.

I shove my flameless candle into Jake's hand while he's still too stunned to question it, and then I'm gone.

He's two steps behind, silent the entire walk past the dorms. I grab my vape from my coat pocket and take a long vanilla-flavored drag. All the happy-making chemicals hit my bloodstream in a dizzying swirl of relief, muddying my thoughts for a few blessed seconds.

At least until Jake says, "Are you vaping?"

"Clearly. But it's embarrassing enough to watch myself do it, so please pretend you don't see me."

"Then why —"

"Cigarette smoke smells."

"No, why do it at all?"

Self-destructive tendencies, my therapist says.

I extend my arm, letting the vape dangle from my outstretched fingers. "Why did you follow me?"

Weight lifts from my fingertips as Jake grabs the vape and narrows his eyes, like a single inhale will lead to his rapid descent into rampant addiction and a lifetime of broken dreams. "You seemed upset."

There's nothing Jake Monaghan can do to fix all the things making me that way, so I say nothing, leading him past the chapel and around the back of Pearson Hall before he thinks to ask where we're going.

I say, "I am going to see Dr. Hern. I don't know where you're going."

"Why are you going to see Dr. Hern?"

When I don't answer, he slides in front of me so I have to stop, raking grooves through his mussed blond hair. "We're friends, right?"

The question hangs in the air as the wind sends leaves skittering across the cobblestone walk between us.

We *are* friends. Have been from the moment I broke away from Headmaster Havens's exceptionally condescending speech at freshman orientation. Jake found me on the soccer field and challenged me to score on him. When I said no, he assumed I sucked, so he promised he wouldn't even move from his spot in the middle of the goal.

He didn't think I'd aim for his nuts any more than I believed he'd actually refuse to move. It was a good lesson for both of us, to never underestimate the other.

We *are* friends. But we're not friends who fill each other's weaknesses, because we have the same strengths. And the one time mine faltered, my weaknesses on display, he never looked at me the same again.

So now we're friends who are the other's biggest fans on the field and biggest opponents in the classroom, constantly knocking each other out of valedictorian contention.

We're the kind of friends who have had plenty of conversations but none of them the right kind of honest.

We are *not* the kind of friends who talk to the school's head counselor together.

My gaze drops to the e-cig in his hand and I tell myself I'm not daring him to prove he's more than his Snapchat photos and lacrosse trophies, to say the words he always holds in when we talk. But when he tilts the vape onto its side and focuses on the amber liquid as it levels itself, I know I'm a liar.

He brings it to his lips and his eyes flare as he wheezes, cheeks puffing. He makes two hard coughs, his voice strained as he says, "Why does it taste like I'm smoking a cupcake?"

I shouldn't laugh, but I do. "It's vanilla, you asshole, now give it —"

He smacks away my reaching hand. "Wait your turn. I'll do it better next time."

If I had a gold star I'd stick it to his forehead.

I pull my coat tighter, but my tights do nothing to stop a rash of goose bumps over my legs. Because maybe I've been too afraid to be honest too. With everyone. And now Madison isn't here to listen to all the things I should've said. "I'm going to see Dr. Hern because we have an agreement. She understands it causes me 'undue hardship' to have my mother on campus, so she sort of … makes her go away."

Behind him, the green and yellow ribbons hugging every tree and lamppost flicker in the force of the wind, a few already reduced to a knot instead of a bow. No one could find a final answer on which color represents missing children, and everyone pointed out that Madison hates the color yellow, but no one listened until the grounds crew had already tied half the campus.

We're not allowed to participate in the searches. St. Francis Preparatory Academy released an official statement. *Our foremost concern is the safety of our students, and with the high concentration of boarders, we're unable to guarantee that safety outside of school grounds. We have the utmost faith in the ability of law enforcement to bring Madison home safely.*

Jake takes another hit, and true to his word, he does better. "It could be worse."

"Doubt it."

I've barely finished speaking before I want to take it all back. Jake's mom died when he was barely old enough to remember her. "Shit. I'm —"

He shrugs a single broad shoulder. "It's okay. I went to boarding school for elementary too. I had to with how much my dad travels. Then I was just like everyone else — no one in

20

boarding school has parents." He gives me a crooked smile, and it's obvious I'm not the first idiot he's had to deflect comments from.

We're nearly to the door when he hands me back the vape, but when I reach for it, he doesn't let go. "Did you really use taking your vitamin as an excuse to bail?"

This will be impossible to explain. "It's a code word."

My hand curls around the frigid handle as I swing open the door to Henson Hall, the brass placard beside it proclaiming the famous Maryland explorer it was named for.

I step inside, the soft hiss of radiators carrying musty heat, its warmth battling against the chill.

"Are you gonna tell me what for?"

I drop my voice to avoid the echo, my wet saddle shoes squeaking on the polished floors. "I take meds for anxiety."

"Really?"

"Yes."

"I didn't — I mean, you don't seem like you have anxiety."

I raise an eyebrow that I hope translates to "do you not see a correlation there?" so I don't have to say it and sound like a bitch.

"Is that why ..."

He waits for me to fill in the blanks from the night we don't talk about — when I led my team to nationals and scored the winning goal, when they carried me off the field and Jake ran on to help. There are pictures of that moment — pictures taken by Madison — that, years later, still hang in St. Francis's halls. Me, smiling, radiating all the joy that propelled me to tell my mom the things I'd been holding back.

Jake found me on the roof late that night, one of my last in the dorms, and I fell asleep sobbing into his arms.

He never asked why. I never told him.

I shake my head. "No. That's not why."

This kind of honesty may be what I need, but right now, it's more than I can handle. "Anyway, my mom has depression and she takes meds too, but my dad doesn't know about any of that because he thinks big pharma is trying to turn us all into chemically dependent zombies, when instead we should be searching out our mind-body balance through holistic means. My mom claims she and my dad were never closer to divorce than when the subject of childhood vaccinations came up."

What I don't say is my mother would never stand for divorce, not when she married Dad against *her* mother's wishes — a fact Grandma Caldecott has never let her forget. And my dad would never be able to undergo the confrontation long enough to try it, not to mention it's Mom's family that has the real money.

Sometimes I'm convinced they both want to keep me home forever because they're terrified of being left alone with each other.

Jake says, "Jesus, Caroline," but I don't hear any of the rest, because I'm frozen, steps away from Madison's locker.

I've autopiloted through this walk more times than I can count. Madison let me use her locker because mine is four buildings over, in a hall where I've had exactly two classes in four years, because I got last dibs on placement after Mom yanked me from the dorms middle of freshman year.

But I can't use Madison's locker anymore, and not just because there's a rainbow-colored collage of notes and messages tacked to the door. Or because of the haphazard mound of flowers and plushies covering the space beneath it.

It's because her locker is empty, off-limits now. I know, because the coat and books I had in there when Madison went missing were confiscated by Detectives Brisbane and Harper.

The next day, identical versions appeared on my desk, like replacing them might make me forget the reason they were gone.

Jake whispers, "Do you think it's true? What Madison's mom said?"

I should say something. Point out I don't even know what part of what Mrs. Bentley said he's talking about. But I can't stop the vision of the cops with their hands in Madison's locker, pulling out pieces of her life one by one. Searching for secrets she didn't have, like it's her fault she's not here right now.

She's not even supposed to have a locker. Only day students are eligible since lockers are limited and St. Francis is 95 percent boarders. But when your family name is etched into the stone of the campus's newest building and generations of your family are proud graduates of the academy, locker rules don't apply.

Jake finishes, "About someone out there knowing something but not saying it?"

My gaze snaps to his. "Do you?"

He doesn't answer, but my thoughts are too busy tripping over each other to listen. And then I'm walking before I can put together the reason why.

Madison knows my combination as well as I know hers. If she needed a place to hide something no one would find, my locker would be the perfect spot.

It's barely a theory, but I don't slow down when Jake calls my name, and by the time I burst through the doors, I'm in a full sprint, racing through the hushed campus.

He has no problem matching my speed, and neither of us let up, even as we climb the stairs to the second floor of Barton Hall.

Our breathing fills the silence, my fingers trembling over the ridges of the lock I haven't opened in months, and it's all I can do to remember what number comes next.

The metal creaks open and even the air smells empty.

Empty.

Just like the locker with the shrine around it. Like the parking spot she used to claim, right next to mine, so we could leave each other stupid notes beneath the windshield wipers.

Heat washes over my back as Jake steps closer, peering over my head and into the locker.

He reaches inside but I block him, hoisting myself higher with the help of the locker's bottom edge. Cold metal greets my palm as I run it over the top shelf, expecting a layer of dust and finding none.

My finger snags on a sharp corner and I grasp tight to whatever it is, tugging it free from where it's lodged along the shelf's edge.

I'm still wedged in the locker, my body shielding my discovery from Jake, which is good, because I have no idea how to explain this.

The matchbook from The Wayside sits heavy in my palm, black background fraying at the worn edges to reveal papery white.

This isn't mine. My second life at The Wayside isn't something I risk mingling with the one I have here. Too dangerous. Too many chances of someone seeing the wrong thing.

The Wayside is my secret. The one not a single living soul at this school knows about. Not even Madison.

Jake says, "What did you find?" and I hear myself respond that it's nothing, but my hands are sweaty where they grip the edge of the locker, and I hold my breath as I flip the cover open to reveal a phone number I don't recognize scrawled in handwriting I do.

Looping, scripted. Madison is the only person I know who writes every number like she's practicing calligraphy.

Madison went to The Wayside. She talked to someone there, wrote down their number. And now she's gone.

A deep voice calls, "Ms. Lawson," and I jump so hard my head cracks against the top of the locker.

I stumble back and Jake catches my shoulders, propping me upright so I have no choice but to look at Mr. McCormack instead of running away.

Mr. McCormack carries himself with the kind of confidence that comes from rarely being denied anything, and the kind of self-esteem that comes from being born with phenomenal genetics and the kind of pedigree St. Francis Preparatory Academy salivates over.

I'd hate him for it if I didn't owe him for more mercies and favors than I can track.

He's also the person I've worked the hardest to avoid the last few weeks.

He's planning to force me into a conference. I've learned the signs from the teachers that came before him. If he succeeds, it'll be my fourth "I'm worried about you, Caroline" conference of the semester — holding at a steady two-per-month pace. The others were easy enough to pacify, but Mr. McCormack will be a challenge.

And by challenge, I mean he won't believe me when I lie to him. Which is a problem, because he could ruin everything for me. A single meeting where he tells my parents what he knows — *everything* he knows — and my years of planning toward escape will crumble.

I rub my throbbing head with the pad of my finger, hoping I'll need a few stitches so I can avoid this conversation.

But I freeze when Mr. McCormack's eyes narrow on what's in my hand.

He says, "I'd like to speak to you for a moment."

I was wrong about the whole "not a single living soul at St. Francis knows about The Wayside" thing. There is one person.

Jake edges closer to me, his spine straightened to full height. "Caroline and I were in the middle of something."

Mr. McCormack raises an eyebrow and puts on his teacher voice. "Mr. Monaghan, I'm fairly certain 'loitering in the hallway' appears on neither of your schedules for third period. You're dismissed."

I need Jake to stay so I don't have to have talk to Mr. McCormack, but if Mr. McCormack is going to force the issue, I don't want Jake around for whatever he's going to say.

I'd pray for divine intervention, but the smarter bet is to walk away and hope they'll both be so busy staring each other down they won't notice I'm gone.

But my escape route collapses under the clip of familiar foot-steps that draw closer with every second. When I turn, Detective Brisbane flashes me a shiny badge and says, "Are you Caroline Lawson?" even though he knows I am.

Mr. McCormack's voice sounds over my shoulder, cutting through the empty hallway. "Ms. Lawson is a student on her way to class. And a minor."

Except I wasn't on my way to class, and sometimes the devil you *don't* know is the lesser threat.

I step toward the detectives. "What is it you need from me?"

Detective Brisbane rocks on his heels. "Ms. Lawson. We'd like to speak to you about the disappearance of Madison Bentley."

CHAPTER TWO

Well, that went well.

St. Francis doesn't offer a ton of criminal justice classes, but I'd bet lying in a missing persons investigation is grounds for prosecution.

I didn't lie about anything that mattered, just about the things that would stop me from figuring out exactly what Madison was doing at The Wayside, and who the number in the matchbook belongs to.

I've tried to call it, three times. Not a single answer. Generic voice mail.

This entire morning has been a stream of questions without a single answer.

Rain batters my windshield, cocooning me in the safety of my car as I let my head thud onto the steering wheel.

My breath escapes slowly, almost a sigh, and I force my knotted shoulders to relax. Heat blasts from the vents, drying my clothes much too slowly. My tattoo throbs, but since my ibuprofen is in my backpack, which is inside the school I can't go back into because I'm not *that* much of an idiot, I take another hit from my vape.

I should go to class. I should've gone yesterday too. My sporadic attendance and generally sucky homework performance since Willa left means I'm handing over valedictorian and I can't even bring myself to care.

I *should* go back inside.

Though that could mean running into Mr. McCormack again. Questioning me about my school performance will just be his warm-up. Then he'll ask about the matchbook from The Wayside.

That's where things get tricky.

I don't know why he stood up for me years ago when everyone else looked the other way. Or why he didn't tell my parents right away when he found me, with my girlfriend, in a bar. I'll owe him for both those things forever.

But he's still my teacher, and I'm walking the finest of lines, with no way to tell when I might step a fraction too far. And if he tells my parents what he saw that night, I may never get to leave the house again.

For my own good, of course. And I can't figure out why Madison was at The Wayside if I'm confined to my bedroom.

So. That's settled.

I slam my finger into the start button and the engine fires to life, fogging the glass within seconds, and I take one last hit.

My passenger door flies open and my scream gets tangled in my lungs. I cough out mist and all the air in my body until my eyes water, while Jake Monaghan mumbles apologies for jumping into my car without warning or invitation.

I blink the tears from my vision and glare at him. "So ... what the fuck?"

"Sorry. It was raining." When I stare at him, he adds, "I wanted to talk to you, and I would've knocked and waited, but —"

"It was raining."

"Yeah." He pauses. "I can't be in there anymore. Everyone's crying or gossiping."

He nods toward the vape. "How often do you use that thing?"

"Not often enough for this day."

This, too, is the detectives' fault. It was like they knew I was headed toward the nearest exit after our "interview," because they hand-delivered me to my next class, which gave gossip time to spread and Jake time to track me down. And now he's in my car asking questions while I'm supposed to be leaving.

I try to mask the impatience in my voice. "Why do you want to talk to me?"

"What did those detectives ask you about?"

"Shit that's none of your business."

"C'mon, Caroline, my dad's a judge and ..." He holds out his hand until I drop the vape into it. "She was my friend too. I want to help, not just hold a fucking candle, you know?"

"Flameless candle. In broad daylight."

"Yeah, what the hell was that about?"

His look of genuine confusion is enough to put me over the edge, and all the stress of the last few hours comes out in the form of highly inappropriate laughter. "It was supposed to be last night, remember? But it rained so it got moved to this morning."

Mom moved it because she couldn't bear a low turnout for her event, and she couldn't get canopies set up in time.

"The logical thing to do would've been to nix the candles, but my parents got into a huge fight over them. My dad wanted locally sourced, organic beeswax — if you're going to save the girl, you might as well save the bees too, I guess — and my mom disagreed because I don't think she knows how to do anything else. And then everything fell apart because we had to move it to the new field since it's farthest from the entrance and therefore inaccessible to lurking media."

It takes Jake several tries before he finally forms words. "So, she went out and bought a thousand flameless candles on some sort of principle?"

I shrug, because I'm not sure I have the words to fully explain why my mom does the things she does, or if I even understand enough to explain them.

It's a full minute before Jake says, his voice low, "Do you know something, Caroline? About Madison, I mean. About her disappearance?"

The question hangs in the closed-up silence of my car, the steady stream of rain pinging off the roof and draping us in curtains of glass and water.

I didn't an hour ago, but now I might. Except I'm not ready to share yet. "The detectives asked all the expected stuff. My name. Where I live."

"And?"

"And they asked me where I was the night Madison disappeared."

That was my first lie. I barely made it through the first five minutes.

Jake hands me the vape and rubs his palms down his thighs, like he's afraid of my answer. "Where were you?"

Truth: Starting the first phase of my tattoo at a place that doesn't get hung up on legalities like age restrictions or parental permission. "Out. Madison's calendar showed I was supposed to meet with her to start our chem project."

I *was* supposed to meet her. And I bailed.

Not because I *had* to start my tattoo that night, or even because I *wanted* to, but because I knew exactly how the night would go if I met up with Madison.

We'd make it less than thirty minutes before Madison would start to twirl her hair and then say, "So what's *up* with you, Caroline?"

She'd been building up to it for weeks — sharp inhales at the first lull in conversation that I had to cut off before she could call me out on breaking the promise we made to each other when we were fourteen, when we swore we'd never lie to each other. Never hold back the important stuff.

That night we sat on her balcony, moonlight straining against a wall of silver clouds, and sipped at Dixie cups filled with the vodka we replaced with water after breaking into her parents' liquor cabinet. We vowed not to sleep until the sun trickled into the sky and scared away the dark.

We talked about boys and I was *just* drunk enough to talk about girls, and then I froze, head spinning too fast to run. But then her cold fingertips found mine beneath our shared blanket and I didn't try to stop the tears that dropped to my cheeks. We spent the night huddled in the corner, until our breath turned white and then disappeared with the dawn.

She never told anyone, and I tucked her acceptance into my heart and let it convince me my spaces were safe. Then, that night after my game, I told my mom who I was and those spaces collapsed. I never quite found my way back.

So when I found Willa again, I didn't tell Madison. This time, I protected my safe space with everything I had, even from the one person who'd never betrayed me.

I broke my vow to Madison. I lied to her. And Willa left anyway.

I gave everything, and it still wasn't enough. *I* still wasn't enough.

Then I didn't know how to tell Madison I'd pushed her away for someone who left me behind.

And even now as I sit here in this car, with Jake staring at my temple like he can pull the thoughts from my head, I can't stop remembering how Madison seemed quieter lately, her smile a watt dimmer.

And not once did I ask why. Or what was up with *her*. I did to her what so many others had done to me.

I walked away.

Since then, all I've done is hand out flyers and wait.

"What'd you tell the cops?" Jake stares through the windshield to the blur of trees struggling against the wind.

"That I was sick." I avoid his gaze when he turns to me, but I can feel the accusation in it like a scrape across my skin. "What difference does it make, Jake? My answer isn't going to bring her back."

I want there to be more conviction in my voice, but my words fall flat and quiet, closer to a question than I'm willing to admit.

But there *is* something I can do — I just have to get Jake out of my car to do it.

My phone buzzes in my cup holder and an email notification from Mr. McCormack lights up the screen. My phone case fogs with the sweaty heat of my hands when I press my thumb to unlock it.

The screen shifts and I've barely read the first word when

Jake's hand darts out to grab my phone. I lunge for him and my fist connects with the side of his head, sending stabs of pain through my knuckles.

He yells, "Jesus, Caroline! You didn't need to concuss me with your douche flute." He rubs the spot on his head that has only the smallest smear of blood.

"Next time don't try to steal from me! And I didn't mean to hit you with it anyway. It was just in my hand."

His brows are furrowed. "Why is Mr. McCormack emailing you?"

I click the locks. "Get out."

"No. You shouldn't be emailing him. Or texting him. Or hanging out in his class after —"

"Mr. McCormack emails everyone. And I don't think I asked for your opinion."

"You don't —" He shakes his head, his eyes not betraying his thoughts.

"What?"

He shakes his head again, lips pressed so tight they've lost all color. "Just ... trust me."

"Not good enough, Jake. If you know something, tell me, otherwise get out so I can leave."

He presses his palms together, fingertips to his lips, then peels his hands apart so he can rake them through his hair. "Preston Ashcroft's brother is on the new task force for Madison's case."

"Preston Ashcroft is also the biggest gossip in the entire school. Why would anyone tell him anything?"

"I know, but just ... Just listen, okay? Madison had this burner phone she used sometimes to score weed."

I raise an eyebrow, but it's more to cover the guilt weighing heavily on my chest. At some point, it seems Madison started lying too.

Jake's face is splotched with red, his jaw clenched so tight I take pity on him and say, "Relax, Jake, I'm not the NCAA coming to drug test you for eligibility."

He nods toward my vape. "You wouldn't exactly be setting the right example."

I flip him off and his laughter fills the car before he says, "I don't smoke, and Madison didn't much either. You know that. Just for parties and stuff. But that's not the point. Preston says they found out about the phone because they got a warrant to search Mr. McCormack's earlier today, and Madison texted him from her burner the night she went missing."

I fiddle with the heat so I won't look as rattled as I feel. "So?"

Mr. McCormack converses with plenty of his students. He does movie nights and chaperones overnight trips. He's got an insufferably enthusiastic open-door policy for any student who wants to talk. But he's always professional, never letting anyone slip past a line. He talks with lots of students, all the time. By email *and* phone — his St. Francis–supplied cell phone.

If he was trying to hide something, he'd be smarter than that.

Whatever the cops are thinking, they're wrong.

Jake says, "So he called her after the text. And she answered. And then no one heard from her again."

My face flushes hot, blood prickling beneath my skin. "He's the most popular teacher on campus. Kids call him all the time.

He probably gave her the 'I don't think about my students like that' speech."

My brain scrambles to predict where this goes next, and I'm about to say Mr. McCormack will just provide an alibi for that night to clear himself. Except, I happen to know who his likeliest alibi would be and I doubt it's going to work in his favor.

I take a long hit off my vape, because self-destructive tendencies define me today. "Since when does talking to someone mean you kidnapped them?"

"It doesn't. But it makes you a hell of a suspect when you're the last person to do it before they disappear."

The wind gusts, battering my car and sending a funnel of leaves spiraling across the grass, and there's this pause in time where I wait to hear Madison yell, "Leaf tornado!"

But there's only silence.

I throw the car in reverse. "I have to go."

"What did you find in the locker?"

If I tell him, he'll insist on coming with me. If I don't, he could march right into school and tell Preston Ashcroft. Or Headmaster Havens. Or the idiot detectives.

There is no winning in this situation. "A matchbook. From a bar I know in West Virginia."

"A matchbook from a bar you know in West Virginia."

"That's what I said, yes."

He clicks his seat belt into place. "I'm coming with you, for whatever it is you're about to do."

Whatever I'm about to do.

I'm going to stop holding candles and start doing what the cops aren't — find my friend.

There's no way Madison spent time at The Wayside. She's meant for cocktail parties, not dive bars set along the side of the road. She wouldn't fit in there. People would have noticed, and talked.

I would've heard about it.

Except the matchbook with her handwriting is real, and I *didn't* hear about it, and that means whatever Madison was doing, it was a secret.

The Wayside is *my* secret — mine, and then mine and Willa's — but never Madison's.

There's only one way to find out when that changed.

And the whole drive to The Wayside, I'll try to make myself forget it's a place where Willa's presence is permanently soaked into the air, where I can close my eyes and still hear her voice.

If she were here, if she hadn't run for California, she'd wrap her arms around me, her fingers threading through my hair, and this fog in my head that makes it hard to think straight would vanish. The tremble of panic in my blood would calm. Willa was quiet strength, endless optimism, the girl everyone told their secrets to because they knew they'd be safe with her. That she would understand, free of judgment.

If she were here, I'd kiss her and the world would be right again.

Instead, she's gone and every minute is more wrong.

I jam the car back into park, toe off my shoes and raise my hips, ignoring Jake's hard exhale as I slide my damp tights down my thighs. "We'll go through the service entrance since the media are all out front. Are you allowed to leave or do I have to hide you under a blanket in the trunk?"

It takes him a moment of stunned silence before he manages, "Why do I feel like you've actually done that before. I can leave. Special Senior privileges."

Of course. How could I have forgotten the enormous honor of being awarded Special Senior privileges: "seniors with high academic and social standing who've demonstrated consistent adherence to St. Francis's guidelines for personal conduct." See also: students whose parents hold enough influence.

I look Jake over, and he's every bit the Special Senior. And nothing like a Wayside patron. "Do you have anything else to wear?"

"Not *on* me."

"Give me your tie, and ..." I survey him and he frowns. "I don't know, roll up your sleeves, I guess? Hold on."

I run my fingers through his hair, mussing it the best I can, the strands tickling my palms. It'll have to do. Jake is gonna look like his Uber dropped him on the side of the road when his daddy's credit card got declined no matter what I do.

After a quick forage in my landfill of a back seat, I come up with a jean jacket and a pair of black Chuck Taylors to fix my prep-school girl ensemble.

I loop Jake's tie around my neck and leave it sloppy. "You're just trying to get out of our calc test next period, aren't you?"

He gives me a crooked smile. "You're my only competition in that class anyway."

I throw the car into reverse, but not before I sneak a glance at Mr. McCormack's email.

It reads simply:

Ms. Lawson,

I'm requesting an immediate meeting to discuss your atten-dance and academic performance. Failure to comply will result in a demerit and an official letter to your student record.

Mr. McCormack

CHAPTER THREE

It's only a ten minute drive until we pass the border from Maryland to West Virginia. Ten minutes past the carefully manicured grounds of St. Francis, where rows of trees fence our world off from the stretch of open fields, insulating us from anything that hasn't been purposefully curated for our developing minds.

Not that I'd admit it to Mom, but I actually love St. Francis. The feel of it, the history, the challenge. The nights spent talking, discussing, planning.

I have yearbooks filled with pictures and shelves lined with trophies, walls covered in awards and certificates. I can't deny what the school has done for me — even if I wanted to.

But there are days — *were* days, even before Willa — when everything felt too close. Too *small*. When this pressure on my chest told me if I didn't leave, didn't remind myself there was a world outside those 689 acres, it would cease to exist.

I-81 is my gateway to freedom, to a life beyond this place. To the world I created to balance the one given to me.

It's twenty minutes from the freeway entrance to Martinsburg, with old farmhouses sitting a leap from the road, rusted railroad tracks that cut through town and quaint little dress and fabric shops lining each side of WV-9.

I can't go through Martinsburg without thinking of Willa, even though she's nearly three thousand miles away.

I should've gone with her.

I should've done what I wanted and left everything but her behind. Instead, in a display of emotion I can't call to memory without a wave of embarrassment, I begged. *Just a few more months. Just let me graduate.* I said *please* more often in that single conversation than in my last twenty.

I did *not* cry.

Maybe things would've ended differently if I had. If I could.

But even as she stood there, tears shimmering in her gorgeous blue eyes, she'd already decided. *I have to go. You need to stay here.* Those are the words she said more than any others.

And when I reached for her, she stepped away.

Even at the lowest part of that conversation, I didn't think she'd actually follow through. Or that she'd refuse to take my calls. Ignore my emails.

But then she was gone and her first letter, postmarked from sunny California, hit my mailbox one week later.

Letters. Pages of memories in her dainty cursive. And never with a return address.

I've been accepted to twelve different colleges across the country and I can't commit to a single one. I tell everyone I'm planning visits before I decide, but the truth is part of me is waiting for the letter that invites me to join her. And then my decision would already be made.

But that's a truth I barely admit to myself.

Rain fills the pockets of the parking lot where gravel hasn't, and my car rocks as I splash into a space near The Wayside's front door. No one paints neat white lines on the asphalt here, but no one needs to. If you have to ask, you don't belong here.

The Wayside is set far from the road. High windows. None of it is welcoming to outsiders. It's not supposed to be.

It's barely noon so there isn't much company, and by the light of day, The Wayside is a place you'd only stop if you had no other choice. Its closest neighbor is the gas station at the corner, the one that ends a series of empty storefronts and overgrown parking lots.

There's no neon Open sign in the window or vinyl schedule of hours affixed to the front door. That would require glass, and if there's one thing The Wayside provides, it's privacy.

It's definitely not a place for a teenage girl. Definitely not a place for a man like Mr. McCormack.

Jake drums his fingers on the center console and narrows his eyes at the dark brick building. "You come here?"

"Sometimes."

"Alone?"

"Sometimes."

The color bleaches from his knuckles where he's strangling the door handle. "A girl like you shouldn't come here alone, Caroline."

Before I can use my douche flute to knock out his front teeth, he flings open the door and storms toward the entrance.

I scramble to follow him, yelling, "What the hell does that mean?"

He sidesteps a wayward beer bottle, then turns and points to it, waiting until I catch up to say, "This." His arms fling wide in what I can only assume is meant to encompass the entirety of what The Wayside *is* and everything it stands for. "All of this. You're too good for a place like this."

St. Francis Preparatory Academy claims they're grooming tomorrow's leaders, preparing us for the future, but it's like walking a tightrope — it only works if you don't look down. *Down* holds the world outside the reality Jake grew up in. Outside *mine*, or at least the one Jake and I shared until I fought my way free.

Down is where you learn life is unfair and it only changes for people who need it the least.

Down is all Jake's seeing right now. The trash piled along the two-lane interstate, the graffiti scrawled on the gas station down the street.

I hold out my hands. The scars on my palms are healed, but the sun is just bright enough for the patches of shinier skin to stand out. "You remember when I missed a week of school freshman year? I wasn't there for our first debate club competition?"

He takes a tentative step and his fingers close around my wrists, pulling my palms nearer. "Yeah. Your family went to Cabo."

"My *parents* went to Cabo. I went to camp." I can't stop the shudder that works through me from the ground up, and Jake's fingers tighten.

I toe the gravel and expose a soggy line of dirt beneath it, shivering against a slice of wind that sends drizzle burrowing beneath my jacket. "Conversion camp."

His Adam's apple bobs and I'm grateful he's tall enough I don't have to meet his eyes. "Why?"

"Do you not understand what conversion camp is, Jake?"

"Don't make jokes about this. I meant why would they want to convert you?"

"Because my mom's built her entire life around the St. Francis social circle? Because she can't stop trying to win the approval of my grandma? Who doesn't give approval to anyone, by the way. But my mom, she's old-money St. Francis, and she's, I don't know, *scared*. That if I'm not perfect — if I'm not successful and pretty and marry the right guy and say the right things — it means she's not a perfect mother and everyone will judge her and everything *her* mom has said about her is true."

Jake is confused. It shows in every inch of his face. "I don't get it."

"It's like … your dad was an awesome lacrosse player, right? And then let's say little Jake comes along and the only thing he can play is the piano."

"My dad wouldn't care."

I sigh. "Pretend your dad has low self-esteem and needs the approval of others to validate him."

"Wait. You're saying she's like those pageant or dance moms on TLC who force their kids into shows so they can achieve things the parents couldn't?"

I *really* want to know how much TLC Jake watches. "Close enough."

"But why does she think anyone would care? Nobody cares that Michael Hughes is gay. Or Ella Ferris. Catalina Hunter has two dads and your mom made them co-chairs for the annual fund drive."

"Yeah, see, my mom doesn't exactly have a problem with *people* being gay, she has a problem with *me* being gay — because then I'm not a replica of *her*. I can't fulfill her expectations. Though she might not be as nice to Catalina's dads if they didn't get her tickets to their Broadway shows."

He shakes his head, droplets springing from the ends of his hair to land on his upturned palms. "But it's not a secret. People know."

"Yes. People know. And that's why my mother being on campus causes me 'undue stress.'"

The furrow in his brow grows deeper, and he grabs my wrist, tracing over the scars on my left hand with a wide fingertip. "What are these from?"

"Fire."

His eyes flare wide. "They set you on fire?"

"No. I set the building on fire."

He's too stunned for speech, so I give him what he's looking for. Maybe if I'd done the same with Madison, we'd all be tucked away in the classrooms of St. Francis right now. "I spent days being starved and held down and … They weren't going to let me go, so I made them. The kitchen door handle got a little hot. Skin and hot metal don't play well together."

I pull my hand away because his fingers around my wrist feel far too much like restraints.

His eyes glass over just long enough for him to blink the emotion clear. "What they did was torture."

"Felt like it, yeah."

"Can they do that? Legally?"

"Ha. Who's monitoring the private organizations people pay to send their kids to? It's still legal in two-thirds of the states."

"Fuck."

"Basically."

"Wait. Your dad was okay with that? Because he tried to sell my dad a lifetime package to a holistic healing resort once and —"

"I really didn't need to know that." Now I have to apologize to Mr. Monaghan without dying of embarrassment first.

"I'm just saying, your camp doesn't sound very holistic."

"He doesn't care who I date. But he'll never tell my mom that. Just like she'll never tell him the truth about my 'vitamins.'"

I tried to tell my dad what anxiety is like for me. Once. It earned me a lecture about the efficacy of chamomile tea and rhodiola root extract, along with a weekly acupuncture and meditation class. Followed by, *You're allowing your mind to control you, rather than you controlling your mind, Caroline. You're stronger than that.*

I'd love to shove him into a room full of chemo patients and have him tell them they're stronger than that. To mind-over-matter their cancer.

"Did —" Jake sucks in a breath. "Did it work? The camp?"

This time I *do* laugh. "Hell no. Sorry, Mom."

"Did you *want* it to work?"

"I don't want to change who I am, Jake. I *like* who I am."

Rocks scatter with the force of my footsteps, and I secretly hope a sharp edge finds its way into Jake's shin, especially after he made me think he could possibly understand.

But then he's in front of me again, making me pull up short.

I glare at him and he holds his hands high, palms out. "I'm sorry. I'm just —"

His hands fall, his voice quiet. "I'm sorry that happened to you. Everyone always feels sorry for me, because of my mom. But my dad, he always tried to make up for it, you know? He's always been there for me, whether I was at home or away at school. Anyway —" His breath hitches. "I'm sorry you didn't have someone like that."

He meets my gaze, no hint of a whisper in his voice now. "I'm sorry no one was there for you. And your parents are assholes."

I smile despite myself because my parents *are* assholes.

But he's not right about everything. I *did* have someone.

I had Mr. McCormack.

He was the only person who questioned what happened to me. Not even Madison mustered the courage to ask.

I still don't know what he said to my mom during the meeting he summoned her to the day after he confronted me about the scars on my hands. I can't even be sure he figured out what they meant. I *do* know she never sent me back to that place.

And that's where things have been ever since. A tentative and dishonest peace I have to keep long enough to survive graduation — until then, my parents can put me on lockdown for my "own best interests" and take away my college fund for the same. I need to keep them believing just a little longer.

I start toward the front doors again, the sun just beginning to burst through the clouds.

I don't want to think about any of this, much less talk about it. "Anyway, they were so preoccupied with the fire, I was able to escape."

Twice, actually. Not that I got far the first time — the fence surrounding the camp put a major crimp in my escape plan. And that's where I met Detective Harper, who put me in his car and listened to my story like he cared. Like he was as furious and horrified as I was.

And then he called my parents to tell them he was bringing me home.

I jumped out of his car at the first stoplight.

I skip that part in the version for Jake. "And then one thing led to another, and the guy that owns this bar found me on the side of the road. He could've left me there like a hundred other cars did, but he didn't. I'm not too good for a place like this."

"Jesus, Caroline."

The gravel slips beneath my shoes, uneven and shifting. "Jesus. Yeah, the 'counselors' talked about him a lot too."

He nudges my shoulder so I'll stop to face him. "I didn't know. Honest. About any of it."

"Well, now you're one of the few people who do, and I sort of wish you didn't."

My hand closes over the door handle and it's solid and cool against my skin. I take a deep breath and do my best to forget I told Jake Monaghan anything at all.

Jake blurts, "I fu— Madison and I, a few times." His fingers cut new paths through his hair. "I had sex with Madison."

"Ah."

That's the only response I can muster. Two of my friends. And I had no idea.

I know his confession isn't meant to hit me like a punch to the chest, but it does. But I also know how sometimes you just need someone else to shoulder the weight of your secrets.

Jake's insistence on joining me today makes far more sense now. But what I *don't* know is if he thinks he can truly find Madison or if he just wants to avoid having the cops show up at *his* locker. Or if he's just like me, questioning all the decisions that led him here.

I hate that I'm suspicious of his motivations, but he's guaranteed to catch hell from his parents and his coach for skipping school and practice, and Jake Monaghan does nothing without careful analysis and reason. Whatever he thinks he's gaining here is worth whatever he's giving up, and I can't imagine how.

He clears his throat. "She wanted to come over after the study session she was supposed to have with you the night she disappeared. But she's never been the one who I —" He pauses. "I never texted her back."

"Double ah."

He steps into the wedge the building has cut from the sunlight, then he yanks open the door. "Now we both know things the other wishes we didn't."

IN THE BEGINNING

I cried when Larry told me how chefs kill frogs.

In my defense, I was only eight, and Larry had no idea how to talk to kids.

I don't even remember if his name was Larry. Mom had two consecutive boyfriends named Larry, and after the second one left it was just easier to call all the ones that came after by the same name. Most of them never bothered to correct me. Plenty never noticed.

But I remember the frogs. I remember if you put a frog in boiling water, it would jump right out, but if you start slow, let it get comfortable, then gradually turn up the heat, that poor little bastard would find himself cooked.

"Before he knows what hit 'em!" That's what Larry said a second before his meaty palm slapped onto the fold-out kitchen table, rattling the cigarette ashes in the tray and toppling over his can of beer, all before my tears hit my cheeks.

He scowled at my wet face, the rim of red around his blood-shot eyes narrowing. But his voice dropped into a slightly less growly growl as he said, "It ain't the worst way to die, sweet-heart."

Livie slipped me into her life like that frog in a pot of slowly boiling water.

If she'd come in too hot, I would've run. I think she knew that somehow. So she let me ease in. Let me get so comfortable I didn't realize how my muscles started to relax in the heat of her presence. How protected I felt in that high-walled pot that only fit the two of us.

I found her in the diner's parking lot as I left my shift, my apron wound tight around my ticket book and my wad of tips tucked into the heels of my shoes just in case someone decided a seventeen-year-old girl with no one waiting up for her might be a good target. Livie's sobs cut through the silence before wind rushed through the lot.

I told myself to keep walking. *A crying girl ain't nothin' but trouble.* Another gem of advice from one of the Larrys.

But I'd shed enough tears no one was around to listen to and, trouble or not, my footsteps stuttered to a stop.

I strained to pinpoint the crying in the smattering of cars. There weren't many since the flower shop in our little plaza was long-since closed. Same for the attorney's office that never seemed to house an actual attorney.

I headed around a Chevy's back bumper and to the left, grinding every footstep into the gravel. Several of the Larrys, in several different ways, taught me about what happens when you sneak up on people.

Three bumpers later, I found her huddled on the edge of the diner's walkway, her long legs tucked to her chest.

I stepped forward, until only a car door's length separated us. "Hi."

She hiccupped on her inhale and looked at me with a mascara-streaked face. "What?"

"Umm … hi?"

"Oh." She blinked at me, twice. "Is this your car?"

"Don't have one."

"Oh." Her legs tumbled out in front of her, ripped jeans revealing slices of skin. "Guess I can't ask you for a ride then."

52

A million thoughts warred in my brain, just like always. A constant battle between my heart and everything the world had taught me. "How'd you get here?"

Her face changed in a blink of time, sadness flipping to anger with no transition between the two. "I was driving with my boyfriend. We got in a fight and I told him just to let me out here and he did."

She wasn't the first girl to end up on the side of the road for the same reason. "Any chance he's coming back?"

"He *left* me, with no money, in a parking lot. I'd set fire to his truck before I'd get back in it."

My mom would've gotten back in. I probably would've too. I scanned the lot, the way the moonlight glanced over the sleek metal.

Everyone inside was scheduled to work until close, so there'd be no way to set her up with a ride, and I couldn't just leave her here. "Where are you headed?"

"Not far. Like a fifteen-minute drive."

The trilling chirp of cicadas filled the silence while I calculated how much it would cost me in cab fare for that kind of drive. Even if it was a dollar, I couldn't spare it. The water was days from shutoff and my school-clothes fund kept drifting back to a pile of change.

Sometimes though, when I begged and cried in his office enough, Davey would let me pick up extra shifts.

The breeze twisted between the cars and sent my hair tumbling against my face as I bent to pull some of my tips from my shoes.

"Are you going for some kind of weapon? Should I run?"

The smile that lit her face transformed her. But it wasn't just the change it made in *her* that was so striking, it was the way it made *me* feel. Like I'd lit a torch in the darkness. Like I'd been let in on this delicate secret, something to be cherished and revered.

Later, I'd learn my reaction wasn't unique. I'd watch the same emotion play over other faces when she invited them into her world.

But by then, it didn't matter.

I'd planned to walk home from work that night, but it would've meant leaving her behind.

Some people you don't walk away from.

We took the bus to her house. When she invited me in, I said yes.

And even now, even knowing how it ends, I'd do everything the same.

CHAPTER FOUR

I step into The Wayside and sunlight filters in from the handful of small windows, bits of dust dancing in the rays. I blink away the spots in my vision, and when the darkness evaporates, I'm standing in the last place I saw Willa smile.

I unclench my fists as the door behind Jake thumps shut and Madison's missing person poster falls limply against the bulletin board. It's different than the one tacked all over St. Francis, but it's even weirder that someone would post it here at all. I need to find even a single reason Madison would venture here. Or a single reason that doesn't include me.

I weave through tables and toward the bar, Jake trailing behind me.

The curves of the bottles behind the bar draw me closer, promising a way to bury all those thoughts that keep bobbing to the surface.

The barstool scrapes against the floor as I pull it back and slap my ID onto the shiny bar, avoiding my reflection in the gloss.

The Wayside may look sketchy as hell, but the inside is clean, despite the stains and gouges in the floor, the cracks and tears in the vinyl booths. The bar's varnish may have worn thin, but the food is better than decent — even on packed weekend nights. And the drinks are outstanding — depending on who's doing the ordering. The Wayside doesn't exactly cater to outsiders.

I don't know the guy tending bar, so I do my best to look like I'm not seventeen and holding a fake ID.

His stubby fingers peel it from the bar and a sheen of sweat breaks out over my skin as he tilts it back and forth in the muted light. He gives a slight nod and my heart lifts.

Then his gaze travels to Jake and his mouth pulls into a frown.

A chameleon, Jake is not.

He's undergone years of conditioning. A lifetime of respect that's as much given as earned. A confident expectation that the world will bend to him, because it always has. And it's never more apparent than when he's surrounded by people who've had to bend themselves to the world.

I give the bartender a defeated shrug and hold out my hand, and he graciously lets me keep the ID he should be confiscating.

A half second later, a large frame flirts at the corner of my vision.

Very large. Marcel is as tall as he is broad. He also has cameras all over the parking lot and has undoubtedly been waiting for me to come inside and explain why I'm here.

Getting into a car with a man like him, even if I *was* fleeing camp and an inept cop, was probably not my smartest move. He lectured me about it nearly the whole ride, and that was when I realized getting into a car with a man like him was one of my *best* moves.

Marcel jerks his head toward his office in the back but his gaze zeroes in on Jake. With a single slow shake of his head, Marcel freezes Jake in place.

"He stays out here." It's meant to be a whisper, but instead it's a low rumble, his voice too heavy for anything less.

I don't know why, but I say it's okay for Jake to come with us. That he's cool and I vouch for him. Maybe it's because of what he said in the parking lot. Or just because I don't want sole responsibility for making sure Madison makes it home alive.

Marcel nods and his heavy boots thud against the floor as he leads us toward his office, where the lights are bright and the air tastes like warm cinnamon. He shuts the door most of the way but not fully — that's one of the rules: we're never in here together with the door shut.

When he first laid down the rule, I laughed, told him it was obvious he was my second, better dad. The comment pulled one of those trademark belly laughs from him as he laid his arm next to mine, his skin a midnight black and mine so pale it's nearly translucent, and said, "Don't think anyone's buying that."

Marcel leans against his desk, his gentle tone at odds with his words. "You can't be here, baby girl."

I stammer through several breaths and finally manage a "What?"

There were times I had to stow away in his office or the back break room so it wasn't obvious an underage girl was hanging out in a bar. But never, not once, has Marcel turned me away.

He blinks twice, and I don't miss the glossiness in his eyes, or the way they dart to Jake. "I'm not saying never again, but right now, you and me, we need to keep a low profile."

I look anywhere but at him. The couch where I've slept more than once. The big recliner in the corner where he lets me read. The tiny, scratched-up desk he found on Craigslist so I could do my homework "the way homework is supposed to be done and not all slumped up on the damn couch." My tiny corner of refuge when I couldn't stand to be at home.

He asked me once if my parents questioned my absence. I defended them, and how easily they accepted my lies. I acted like any parent would've believed me. It was because I had so many extracurriculars. Sports and clubs and friends and things that kept me out late.

It wasn't that they didn't care, I told him. It was that I had a best friend who knew to automatically lie for me, and me for her.

None of that stopped the pity that crept into his eyes.

Willa never pitied me. Willa understood — the way only another person who knows they're on their own can.

"Marcel." I stumble back because my anchor is gone and the floor feels uneven. "I won't cause trouble. I'll be quiet and no one will see me. I'll be good."

I hate the pleading in my voice. I hate that Jake is witnessing me fall apart. And I hate that I'm begging, just like I did with Willa.

But it didn't work then, and it won't work now.

My vision tunnels and I still can't fucking cry.

The door swings open and I have to jump so it doesn't slam into me.

A woman enters, bleached hair piled high on her head, and her greeting fades the second she sees me.

But when she sees Jake, everything in her face closes down.

There's a weighted pause, a silence so heavy it thickens the air, and when her expression changes, it's filled with an illogical level of hatred for a complete stranger.

I place that she's one of the day waitresses right before she says, "Is this your boyfriend?"

"What? No."

"But you came here to ask questions about your friend, didn't you? *She's* the missing girl everyone cares about. Crooked cops and PIs and television crews aren't enough for you? Pretty rich white girl goes missing and everybody's interested. Not like she's white *trash* or Black or Brown, 'cause then she's —"

"Chrystal."

If she notices the threat in Marcel's voice, she doesn't cower under its force. "You know I'm right. They're not looking for anyone else. Not for any other girl —"

"Chrystal." Marcel's baritone booms in the open space.

They have an unspoken conversation in some eye-language I can't begin to understand.

I shouldn't have brought Jake here — Chrystal barely had time to take a breath before she connected Jake to Madison.

Chrystal wraps her arms around her middle, fingers twisted in the fabric of her shirt. "I just came to grab my check."

Marcel unlocks the check drawer and *not for any other girl* rings in my head as he says, "I'll walk you out."

I don't know which one of us he's talking to. But then his broad hand strokes over the back of my head, just like I've seen him do to his daughters when they come to visit. It's meant to be comforting and it is, until reality snaps into focus.

I'm not wanted here anymore. All the places I'm free to be my true self are gone. All the people I love are too.

I duck from Marcel's outstretched arm and maneuver around Chrystal, stomping my way toward the back exit.

I'm barely past the men's bathroom when someone barrels out of it.

I bounce off the wall of muscle and crash into a row of liquor boxes someone neglected to put away, and I suck in a breath, my ribs throbbing, my tattooed skin screaming. Maybe I should sue Marcel for however much The Wayside is worth, and then I can buy it so he *can't* kick me out.

I shrug off the apology and ten seconds later I'm bursting into the lot, where the sun's gone into hiding again, giving way to drizzling rain and the gray haze of clouds. My lungs heave like I haven't taken a breath in hours.

The heavy door whooshes open, then thumps shut, gravel crunching beneath Jake's tentative footsteps. "Are you okay?"

Nope.

I nod a yes anyway. I take in a breath so big my lungs burn, then let it out slowly, my best Ujjayi Pranayama, even though I'm sure Jake's wondering why I've transformed into Darth Vader.

I can't stay here. I can't think about what just happened.

I force myself upright, pin my shoulders back. St. Francis Prep posture. "Let's go."

I'm two steps closer to my car when the rain slants sideways, rippling the puddles, dredging one of Madison's posters from its depths. Even from ten feet away, it's obvious it's *not* the same as the ones from school. The picture is all wrong. The smile not bright enough, the hair too dark, the lighting all wrong.

Madison would never let a picture like that past the delete key. Head yearbook photographer. Selfie queen. She knew everyone's best angle, but none better than her own.

I ignore whatever Jake's saying and grab the limp poster before the wind steals it.

Beads of water leak from the paper's edges, trickling down my forearm as Jake reads over my shoulder. "Who's Sydney Hatton?"

I'm about to say I don't know when my thoughts snap into place.

Sydney Hatton is the girl no one cares about. That's what Chrystal said.

Everyone cares about Madison. Not Sydney.

Sydney. The *other* missing girl.

Other.

Two girls have disappeared, and both their posters hang in the bar I call my second home. The bar Madison went to visit. Where she got someone's number.

I grasp tight to the matchbook in my pocket, let the hard edge press into the pad of my finger.

I'm missing something, and if Marcel won't talk to me, then I'll figure it out on my own.

Jake matches his pace to mine, heading toward my car. "Why do you have a fake ID?"

"Why *don't* you have a fake ID?"

"I'm serious, Caroline."

"So am I." I hit the button on my key fob and my trunk pops. My fingers slip off the edge the first time I try to shove it all the way open. Because it's wet, not because my hands are shaking.

I get it right the second time and shove a tendril of drippy hair out of my eyes.

Jackets, hoodies, skirts, shoes and bags get tossed around

before I find the backpack I'm looking for. I rip open the zipper and pull out my flask.

The warm shot of shitty vodka hits my stomach, and Jake throws his arms in the air in what I can only assume is a moment of deep regret for asking to come along today.

I slam the trunk shut and head for the door but Jake beats me there. "Give me the keys."

"My dad says I'm the only one who's allowed to drive my car."

"Does your dad say it's okay to smoke and hang out in low-rent bars and keep a flask in your trunk?"

I stare at the sharp lines of The Wayside and wait, a theory forming in my brain.

Jake shoves his hand out again, even though he doesn't actually need the keys to start the engine — I think he's just afraid if he gets in the car, I won't follow.

He says, "Can we get in the car?"

"No. I need clear vision."

"What?"

"For when Chrystal comes out. I need clear vision."

"No offense, but she seems a little nuts."

I shake my head, rivulets of water dancing across my skin. "I found a body once."

His eyes flare wide, lips parting while he attempts words. "A dead body?"

I nod and he says, "Where?" like *that's* the important part of the story.

But actually, maybe it is.

I flip my hood over my head to block the rain, and maybe

a bit of the memory too. "Somewhere around here. I think. I wasn't exactly paying attention."

Truth is, I wasn't paying attention to where my dad was driving that day, nor any of the mind-body connection or real estate knowledge he attempted to throw down during the ride.

It didn't matter where we were headed, because I didn't plan on coming back.

I spent the ride with my hand around a bottle of pills he'd never allow me to fill the prescription for. When he met with his associate and told me I could go enjoy the sunshine, replenish my vitamin D, I didn't argue.

But I don't say any of that to Jake. "My dad was looking into a big chunk of real estate. Crappy houses on land he thought he could build up. He sent me to go explore and I found her."

"Holy fuck."

"Pretty much. But here's why Chrystal isn't crazy. I called the cops, Jake. Sure, I gave them shitty directions because I didn't know where I was, but do you know what the *cop* who answered the phone and listened to me talk about a dead girl just ... lying in the middle of nowhere ... said to me? He took my name and number, and then we got to my address. He paused, and then he asked me where I went to school. When I told him, he said, 'St. Francis, huh? Listen, sweetheart, that girl you found is probably a junkie who got herself into trouble. We'll take care of it, but you go on home.'"

My hand curls into a fist, just like it did then, nails biting into the flesh of my palm while the other holds tight to the poster of a girl who is not Madison. "He didn't care. He basically patted me on the head and sent me back to my little rich girl life, and you know what? I went. I called the station for a few months to ask for updates. I googled. But eventually, I forgot about her too."

"You're not a cop, Caroline. It wasn't your job —"

"Not the point."

"Well, what did your dad do about it?"

"Nothing. Because I didn't tell him."

His face goes slack with shock and I know I won't be able to explain this to him.

I mumble, "I don't really *tell* my parents things," because it's close to the truth — I don't tell them anything that matters. I don't trust them to hold the things that count, because I've learned how much damage those can do.

But Jake will never understand what it's like to have parents that make things worse instead of better, so I say, "It wouldn't have helped anything, okay? I told the people whose *job* it was to care. That should've been enough."

I hold the poster where he can see it. "You think Chrystal's crazy? Have *you* heard of Sydney Hatton?"

"No."

"Me neither. No news reports. No … flameless-candle vigils. No journalists around here, right?" I slam the soggy poster into his chest. "Google her, Jake. Tell me what you find."

Chrystal bursts from the building, a plastic bag slung over her head in a terrible attempt to keep her teased hair from wilting under the rain. Her mouth is still stuck in the scowl that appeared the moment she saw Jake. Right before she talked about crooked cops and missing girls.

I don't need Chrystal to like me for her to tell me what she knows.

I whip out my phone and dial the number that's branded into my brain, scripted in Madison's handwriting. It rings once, twice. And then, on the third, Chrystal drags her phone from her purse and all the jumbled pieces start to fall in line.

Chrystal stops, brows pinched in confusion over a number she doesn't recognize, and then she sends me to voice mail.

Jake says, "Jesus Christ. Are you bleeding?"

"Highly probable." My ribs hurt like hell.

"What happened?"

I could lie. Say I fell or something equally unlikely. But then Chrystal's car sputters to life, a gust of white smoke coughing from the exhaust and dying beneath the force of the rain. "I got a tattoo. It's a flower. Totally cliché."

I ignore his widening eyes and shoo him toward the car. "We have to go."

He holds out his hand, palm up, and the gesture looks a little too mirror-image of me showing him my scars. Rain pools in his palm, droplets clinging to his fingertips only to fall when their weight gets too heavy.

The white glow of Chrystal's reverse lights reflects in the steady drizzle and we're officially out of time.

I slam my keys into his hand as I run to the passenger seat.

Jake already has the car running by the time I shut the door behind me. He cranks the heat and I can't stop the shudder that racks through me.

I point to Chrystal's fading taillights. "Follow her."

CHAPTER FIVE

It's obvious Jake Monaghan has never tailed another car in his life.

We spend the entire drive arguing because Jake has no concept of biding his time. He's so afraid of losing Chrystal he's never more than two car-lengths behind, which is stupid. And clearly Chrystal notices, because she takes us on a twenty-five minute detour before leading us to her home, which sits not more than seven minutes from The Wayside.

We pass sleepy, single-story houses set far back from the road, but not so far back you'd forget you had a view of a two-lane highway. A short wooden sign pokes out from a cluster of spindly shrubs at the corner of the street, declaring this neighborhood the "Hampton Estates," and Chrystal's car eases through the entrance next to it.

Jake's only one car behind now, though in his defense, traffic is light so he doesn't really have a choice. The car rocks as we switch from highway to gravel and enter a maze of mobile homes. Kids' toys sprinkle the yards, their plastic faded into pastel versions of primary colors, and Christmas lights still dangle from more than a few gutters.

Jake's voice lowers like someone might be able to hear us through the walls of my car, his knuckles white on the steering wheel. "How would you even throw a football in this place?"

I try to keep my tone light, but it comes out every bit the

accusation it is. "Not everyone can have a full-sized basketball court in their backyard, Jake."

"I wasn't saying it like that. It's just —"

He pauses, still looking for the end to his sentence. The truth is this, he's standing on the St. Francis tightrope, and he's trying not to look down.

His palm slides over the wheel as we make a sharp left, and Chrystal's car stops in an empty spot. He keeps driving like we're not really following her, even though there's no way my BMW isn't going to stick out in a trailer park.

He slides into an empty spot with a big yellow Visitor spray-painted on the concrete. "It's just that it would be hard to grow up in a place where you couldn't throw a football around." His gaze follows Chrystal as she jumps from her car, holding her purse over her head.

I want to buy her an umbrella. Or give her one of mine.

Jake flips off the wipers and rain beads over the windshield. "Why are we here?"

I planned to think about everything on the way over and decide what I could trust Jake with, but I didn't, and now my brain whirls through a million different arguments so fast I end up staring at him blankly — just long enough for him to figure out what I'm doing.

A flush climbs up his neck and into his cheeks.

It's not like he didn't see the missing poster, and there's not much else to tell, so I sigh and focus on the trails of raindrops on the window behind him. "The matchbook I found in my locker had a phone number on it."

He stares out the windshield, his reflection blurred. "That's the number you called in the parking lot, right? And Chrystal answered."

"Well, didn't answer, but yeah." I rub my palm against my thigh, warming my numb fingers. "Madison is my best friend. I was supposed to be there the night she disappeared. I can't just walk away."

Jake nods, because he may not owe Madison as much as I do, but he was supposed to be there too. "You think Sydney Hatton's disappearance is related to Madison's?"

"Maybe? How many girls have to vanish before it's a pattern?"

"I don't know, Caroline, it feels like the only thing Madison and this Sydney Hatton have in common is that they're both missing."

"And they're both connected to The Wayside."

It's too close to ignore. *Impossible* to ignore when both posters hang on the walls. When Chrystal's phone number is in my locker.

I'm the one thing that straddles both worlds. And I'm terrified I led my best friend into something that got her kidnapped.

"We don't even know what they might've had in common, because I just googled her, Jake, and there *are* no search parties, no vigils, no press conferences. Chrystal was mad at the amount of attention Madison's case is getting, and she's right. If Sydney's really missing, the cops don't seem to care. Just like they didn't care about the girl I found."

He tries to respond, but I'm not done. "And did you see Madison's poster in the entryway? Why is it there? I mean, I haven't been in Mads's French-lace underoos like *some people*, and clearly there are things she kept from me —"

I cough to cover the way my chest caves. She didn't tell me because I didn't want to listen. I set the parameters on our friendship, and now all the secrets I don't know might be the only thing that can save her.

Jake mercifully fills the space where my words should be. "Don't call her Mads. She hated that."

"I know. You're right." I can totally respect that. There's no good way to shorten Caroline either. Care? Line? Ro?

It's like my parents wanted to ensure their precious miracle baby would remain pretentious for her entire life.

I turn toward him, silently begging him to understand. There's only one person left in my life who knows the most important parts of me, and I don't know where she is. She may be suffering because of me, and that possibility threatens to wrench me apart. "Maybe there *is* no connection, but are you willing to sit around and wait for the cops to pull you out of class to tell you how they think you're involved? Do you think *Madison* would want us to wait?"

There's the briefest of pauses before Jake flings open the door and the scents of earth and rain rush into the car. I'm out a second later, jogging to catch up as he heads toward Chrystal's trailer.

The blinds in the front window shift just as my knuckles hit the door, but two knocks later it's obvious she has no plans to answer.

A beam of light shifts in the woods behind the trailer, and we both freeze.

Jake whispers for me to stay, and then he's inching toward the tree line.

I creep toward the door, listening so hard it's almost painful.

A murmur filters through the wall of the trailer, so low I can't make out the words even with my ear pressed to the frigid vinyl.

Twigs snap amidst the crunch of leaves, but it's too dark in the woods to see past the first layer of trees.

Jake rushes from the woods, gripping my arm as he leads me back to my car, but he doesn't speak until we're sheltered inside. "She was at the window. I saw the blinds move and there was a light, like she was on her phone. Someone was in the woods, and the light earlier … I think she was talking to someone out there."

The engine turns over and he jerks the car into drive as I say, "I'm not leaving. I —"

He holds up his hand, cutting me off. "You're right. Madison wouldn't want us to wait. And right now, the only thing we have to go on is Chrystal, and she won't even answer the door."

His jaw flexes, eyes narrow. "If she won't talk to us, maybe there's a reason. So maybe we talk to someone she *will* talk to. Maybe we find our own answers."

Chrystal's trailer shrinks in my mirror until we turn the corner, and his words sink into my gut. The insinuation is that people who won't talk have something to hide. That Marcel has something to hide. "Marcel wouldn't —"

"He didn't throw you out for no reason. And he wouldn't let Chrystal talk about Sydney being missing. And then there was all that 'low-profile' shit."

He sighs when I shake my head. "He seems like a good guy, Caroline, but if Madison went to his bar and he won't talk about it, then you can't guarantee what he would or wouldn't do."

I press my head into the headrest and breathe through my

nose, because even thinking Marcel may be involved is enough to trigger a spasm of anxiety.

Jake tucks the car into the driveway of an old house, so hidden by overgrown grass and weeds I didn't realize it was there.

By the time I make it to my trunk, Jake is stuffing my backpack with whatever he finds useful.

Things Jake finds useful: Band-Aids and individually packaged alcohol swabs from the first aid kit my dad put in the car, my shirt, another shirt, my flask.

Maybe he's not hopeless.

He stuffs a hoodie into my arms and grumbles, "Put that on."

I ditch my jacket in favor of the hoodie, and my battered skin stretches and stings as I pull it over my head, but it's worth it for the way the thick cotton blocks out the chill.

Something smacks into my palm and my fingers curl reflexively around the hilt of a flashlight. "It's the middle of the day."

"Preparation is important." He holds up another hoodie, then checks the size tag. "Whose is this?"

When I shrug, he tugs it over his head, but the little crease between his eyebrows shows he's not at all happy about putting on the sweatshirt of some rando. Jake's sweatshirts are probably stacked in his closet with the precision of a Neiman Marcus display.

I flip the hood over my head even though my skin gets twitchy at the idea of muffling my hearing. "This is sort of dangerously stupid."

He slams the trunk shut and beads of water jump from the metal. "Now? We ditched school in the middle of the day and went to a bar and *now* you want to develop common sense?"

"All I wanted to do was talk to Chrystal!" I drop my voice without losing any of the heat in it. "Not snoop through creepy neighborhoods looking for kidnappers."

"What if she's here, Caroline? What if she's ten fucking feet away and we left?"

His words freeze me in place, cold prickles of anxiety crawling up the back of my throat. He's right.

The cops aren't here, we are. They're too busy walking the halls of St. Francis, acting like they're investigating. If stupid Preston Ashcroft's rumors about Mr. McCormack answering a call from Madison's burner phone are any indication, the cops are convinced he's involved.

It's not that Mr. McCormack doesn't have secrets of his own, but they've got nothing to do with Madison. And if Jake's telling the truth about the night she went missing, then it's *when*, not *if*, they'll assume Jake's involved too.

The cops need someone to blame, and if those are the leads they're following, Madison's odds of being found are zero.

I nod. "Okay."

He holds out the canister of mace I'd forgotten I had and shrugs the backpack straps over his wide shoulders before he walks away, tire iron swinging lazily at his side.

Soggy leaves slip beneath my shoes as I follow, my eyes trailing over the ground, searching for I have no idea what.

It's easily five million footsteps and an hour later and I still don't know.

We've searched the entire grounds of the creepy, abandoned house and found nothing more than a whole bunch of rusted, twisted tool parts and one very angry cat that nearly clawed

Jake's face off. The only thing I've gained is a sharp throb in my right temple and knots in my shoulders.

I can't pretend Madison left on her own anymore.

There's a countdown in my head now, seconds barreling faster toward an end I can't quite fathom — where's she not there to walk with me, hand-in-hand, across the stage to get our diplomas like we've planned since we were thirteen. Where all the inside jokes we've created shrivel and waste because there's no one to share them with.

I close my eyes and we're floating side by side, my skin sticky with sweat against our matching pool floats, the gentle lap of water carrying us beneath the blazing sun. And then her voice — the quiet one she used when her heart lay open — murmurs against the thick air. "Hey, Caroline?"

"Yeah?"

"I love you, bitch."

My smile stretches, slow and lazy like the clouds that float overhead. "I love you too."

I'm not good at those words. They've never come easily. Except with Madison.

And then, with Willa.

My eyes snap open to darkness — memories of sunlight draining from my skin.

The clouds form a fortress around the sun, leaving everything in a haze of drizzle and muted light, and I scramble to catch up to Jake.

Every time I look at Jake's hand around the tire iron, the tendons in it look tighter, popping farther beneath his skin.

The air feels wrong here — the clean that comes with rain

overrun with the sharp scent of decay and smoke. Jake and I have made eye contact exactly once, and it ended in a race to see who could look away faster. I'm afraid to look at anything, terrified of what I might find.

But I'm even more terrified of what I might miss.

I swipe the glaze of rain from my cheeks, then clear my throat and pray it won't sound as rattled as I am. "Maybe we should just move on to the trailer park."

Jake's gaze snaps to mine and skitters away just as quickly, his eyes going wide like he'd forgotten I was even there. He drags the tire iron over a heap of crinkled plastic bags. "Yeah. Okay."

He nods just as my eye catches on a tiny glint of mirrored gold in the dark foliage at the edge of the woods, familiar enough that I know it doesn't belong *here*. "Hey, wh—"

Metal slides against metal. A quick *click, slide, click.*

A gravelly voice says, "Neither of you move and maybe I won't blow your little boyfriend's head off."

I force myself to look, my gaze dragging over Jake without focusing and moving up to the mountain of a man behind him.

Rain trickles from the man's unkempt beard and seeps into the ribbed shirt where it's not protected by his yellow raincoat. But the shotgun that forms a bridge from his hand to Jake's back, he holds that steady.

My brain tries to convince me this isn't happening, but the neurons firing through my body, pumping my muscles with the need to *move move move* are on full alert.

Mountain Man's eyes narrow, and the only thing I can think to say is, "He's not my boyfriend."

It's a stupid comment but it breaks Jake free from his statue impersonation. His lips part in shock. "Is that really the most important thing here?"

He has a point. "No, but —"

Mountain Man shoves Jake into me using the barrel of the gun, and I stumble back before my body remembers how to work right.

Jake gives my arms a little squeeze and whispers, "It'll be okay," at the same time Mountain Man barks out orders to start walking.

A droplet of rain sneaks across my collarbone and trickles down my shirt, but I'm afraid to move. Sticking my hand down my shirt seems like it might give our present company ideas I'd rather he not have, so instead I loop my arm through Jake's and propel us both forward, Mountain Man close behind.

Branches scrape at my face as we trudge through the patch of woods that separates the abandoned house from the trailer park, and my heart ricochets against my ribs.

I stumble over a slick rock embedded in the dirt and Jake keeps me upright, his elbow locking down on mine hard enough to wrench my shoulder. But it's the flare of pain along my forearm that reminds me he never ditched the tire iron.

And I have mace in my pocket.

Mountain Man yells to keep moving so I do, scouring the path for anything that might give Jake even half a second to yank the tire iron from his sweatshirt and get the hell out of shotgun range.

I see it just on the outskirts of the trailer park, where the gravel meets the woods.

A slightly deflated soccer ball tucked against a line of white rocks.

The deflated part doesn't exactly work in my favor. Neither does the shotgun trained on my friend.

The "rainbow flick" is always a favorite with the kids at soccer camp. Roll the ball up your leg and kick it with the opposite heel until it arches overhead.

Except I don't need it over my head today — I need to kick it into Mountain Man's face. I'm just praying years of muscle memory is enough to not get us killed.

I inch my fingers toward my pocket, until the tips brush against the cylinder of mace, the metal warm to the touch. "I'm just waiting for a rainbow."

Mountain Man yells at me to shut the fuck up and Jake's eyes are so wide it's clear he thinks I'm suffering from shock, but then his gaze flicks to the ball and he gives me the subtlest of nods. Almost like he trusts me to not screw this up, which proves Jake doesn't know me as well as he thinks.

Beads of sweat roll down my back, and my mouth is so dry I have to stop myself from sticking out my tongue to catch the rain.

A twig snaps beneath my foot and I swallow a yelp, and then we're five feet from the ball. Then three.

We stumble from the protection of the trees and the rain spikes against my skin, but I barely feel it.

Two feet away and everything goes quiet.

The ball doesn't roll like it's supposed to but my heel still connects, and the world snaps back into existence the moment the blur of black and white leaves the ground.

Momentum carries me forward and my palms slam into the gravel just as Mountain Man shouts a garbled curse. I swear the ground shakes when he plows into it, and I fling myself over in time to see his chin bounce off the grass.

Before he can get up and reclaim the shotgun that's wedged beneath his shoulder, Jake has the tire iron free.

Still, Mountain Man is surprisingly spry, and he's to his knees before Jake swings.

It's a brutal stroke that holds nothing back. The crack of ribs is unmistakable.

Mountain Man lets out a guttural howl and I'm not sure Jake even hears it.

His jaw is locked tight, eyes narrowed viciously, and when he pulls back for another swing, I can't tell what body part he's aiming for next.

Baseball, hockey, lacrosse, golf. Jake's muscle memory puts mine to shame. If he makes use of it again, we're both going to find out what brain tissue looks like.

I scramble forward, screaming Jake's name.

I flick the safety off my mace and get way closer than I need to. The liquid jets out of the canister and blasts Mountain Man's face, splattering back so far I have to jump to avoid it.

A door crashes open behind me and a woman shouts something I can't make out because Jake is yelling at me to run, run, run!

We sprint back through the woods, the sounds of our breaths the only thing grounding me in this overcast tomb of a forest. We pass the spot where Mountain Man found us and the memory of a *click slide click* echoes in my head.

I skid to a stop, the wet leaves beneath me giving way so my ass collides with the ground and the mace tumbles from my hand.

I crawl to the place I'm looking for, that hint of gold that doesn't belong. Jake's hand clamps around my arm to haul me up but I yank myself free.

I shove aside the pile of plastic bags and reach for the tube of lipstick I saw earlier. I want to search more, to see if there's anything else, but Jake has me off the ground before I can.

He doesn't put me down until we're ten feet past the spot — too far to go back.

We fling open our doors in unison and the engine turns over before we're fully seated. The car lurches backward as Jake pins the gas pedal to the floor, and then we're moving forward, flying past those same quiet houses, down the same two-lane road, but in my hand is the one thing that might prove Madison was here the night she disappeared.

CHAPTER SIX

I'd give my left ovary to avoid this meeting.

I've managed to avoid it for weeks, but this morning I was so distracted by the warring thoughts in my head I was completely unprepared when Mr. McCormack appeared out of nowhere. And now I'm stationed in the quad, shivering against wind that's too sharp, waiting for him and actually hoping for the cops to show up again.

If not for the lipstick that sits heavily in my pocket, I would've skipped school completely. Especially since every slam of a locker is a shotgun being loaded. Or the way Mountain Man's ribs cracked beneath the force of Jake's swing. Or the look in Jake's eyes when he decided he was going to do it again, just a little higher next time.

I had to peel myself from the seat last night when we pulled into campus so I could drop Jake off and climb into the driver's seat. He met me at the front bumper, caught in the dark zone between the beams of my headlights. He paused, every movement halting, and then he gathered me into a hug I didn't return, because I'm an emotionally stunted asshole who can't figure out affection, and he whispered, "I'm glad you're okay."

He didn't give me a chance to respond.

And then I drove nowhere, for hours, before eventually going home rumpled and wrinkled, with spots of mud on my knees and blood on my shirt. My mom overlooked all of that when I told her I'd spent the night hanging out with Jake.

And in the walk to the room that doesn't feel like mine, I made more promises than I may be capable of keeping.

I promised I would find Madison. That I wouldn't give up on her like I did the dead girl in the middle of nowhere. That I wouldn't let time dull the memory and erode my sense of responsibility. And I wouldn't let everything fall apart like I did with Willa.

I promised that this time I would do everything right. This time, I'd be enough.

And then I'll leave and not look back. That hasn't changed. It's been my only goal since the moment I set fire to that kitchen and went home to people who can't love every part of me.

In three months, I graduate. Two days after that, I turn eighteen, and then I'm free to be the person I am rather than the person everyone needs me to be.

But I can't do that if Madison is still gone.

If Mr. McCormack tries to stop me, I'll give him every chance to walk away. If not, I have a plan for that too.

I shiver as the sun drops behind an army of gray clouds and Mr. McCormack jogs down the steps of Olivet Hall, scanning the expanse of the quad for me.

He finds me sitting at one of the teak patio tables that are still too damp from this morning's rain.

He smiles and waves, and now we have to drop eye contact and pretend we have something better to look at, or engage in some creepy stare-off while he hurries across the thirty-foot separation.

I choose to maintain. Might as well set the tone early.

Thankfully his long strides get him to my table quickly, and the wind draws a burst of mountain-fresh fabric softener and starch from his shirt as he hoists the other chair and sticks it next to mine. Close, but not too close. Friendly and attentive, but never inappropriate.

This is not a man who kidnaps girls.

He leans back in his seat. "So."

I'd give my other ovary for a fire drill that would send hundreds of kids streaming into the quad. "So."

"Wasn't sure you'd show."

"I said I would."

"You also said you'd attend my class on a regular basis."

I want to grab my phone to remind myself it's still there and I'm not out of options yet, but my hands are shaking and I don't want him to see. *Can't* let him see. I know he'll ask how I'm doing if he does, and I don't trust myself not to answer — to admit I'm not okay, that I haven't been since the day Willa left, and especially not now, when Madison is still gone and it's partly because of me. "I was in class yesterday."

Only because of the vigil, but probably best to leave that out.

"But not the day before and not today. Not last Thursday. And if I count the note with the forged signature from your mom from two weeks ago, you should be on third warning this month alone. You *should* be a step away from probation."

His hazel eyes are hard, and I'm suddenly desperate for them to soften while he feeds me the "I'm worried about you, Caroline" line like the other teachers before him.

I tuck my hands between my knees. "So why aren't I?"

He sighs — exhausted, not irritated — and his voice loses just a hint of the edge. "I don't know why."

We're not being honest with each other. We both know why. It started with the day I showed up to school and he asked about the marks on my palms and I almost told the truth. It's because of what he said to my mom after. It's because for some reason he's never explained, I've always been his favorite student — the one he expects the most from. It's because he's the best teacher I've ever had, and he's never even tried to collect on the debt I owe him.

Preston Ashcroft's rumors are wrong. Mr. McCormack had nothing to do with Madison's disappearance, and I'll prove it when I find her.

I force myself to look at him. "Attendance only counts for 5 percent of the grade in your class."

His eyes widen. "That's your response? I'm supposed to be impressed with your manipulation —"

"It's not manipulation! It's —" I snap my mouth shut.

It's *not* manipulation. It's survival.

I say, "I'm still getting over a four-point —"

"Barely. Four-point-zero-seven. You missed a quiz today."

I wince before I can stop myself, and when I catch his gaze narrowing in on my hand, the one clutching the necklace that matches Willa's, I jump from my seat. "I'll be in class tomorrow."

He has no problem matching my strides down the cobbled path as we pass by the entrance to one of the dorms. "You're well-liked. That's probably the only thing that's kept other students from reporting your absences — and my lack of discipline regarding them — to Headmaster Havens. This school is too competitive for that to last."

That's not the only thing. People with secrets always find

each other. That's how I know Penelope Yi is dating the son of a St. Francis janitor even though her mom thinks she's still with Edward Simmons, son of Wall Street guru Matthew Simmons. Or that Brock Olding sometimes goes to my favorite spot on the roof to smoke weed to manage his anxiety.

And then there are the kids I tutor — the ones I meet in the most remote study room in the library, where they slip me cash like I'm handing out tiny bags of Molly rather than knowledge, at three times the rate they'd normally pay because they can't let anyone — not even their parents — know they're struggling.

But it's better if Mr. McCormack continues to think my classmates are so magnanimous because they like me lots.

The sun is still being a coward, and I hug my arms across my chest to get some feeling back in my numb fingertips. Tendrils of black hair curl into the crooks of my elbows, and the misting rain sticks my white shirt to my skin. I suck in a breath and rip the fabric from my side, igniting sharp flares across my ribs where last night ravaged the parts of my tattoo that had barely begun to heal.

Mr. McCormack steps right into my path and I have to pull up to avoid crashing into him. He ducks his head to meet my eyes. "Are you hurt?"

"Let this go. All of it."

"One of your classmates came to see me this week. She's worried —"

I cut him off with a snort. "Which one? Sarah Ellis? Shondra Marks?" I pause, and get no response. "Aubrey then, right? How many buttons?"

His brows furrow and I roll my eyes before pointing to my shirt. "How many buttons did she have undone when she arranged alone time with you under the guise of being concerned about my well-being?"

"Caroline." The edge is back in his voice. "You *know* I don't think about any of you like that."

"I know." I *do* know. He proved it months ago, when a lesser man wouldn't have chosen to order me and Willa into his car at The Wayside and driven us home. *Our* homes. Not his. Because he wanted to make positively sure we got there safely. Or maybe because he didn't trust me to make it home at all.

I can't meet his eyes when I say, "Did you really talk to Madison the night she disappeared? Did she text you?"

It's a betrayal, that I'm asking this at all. The suggestion I have even a hint of doubt.

"That's not something you need to worry about."

"She's my *best friend*."

"And you know if I had any information that would help the police find her, I would give it." He doesn't give me time to say that I know. That I trust him. That I just want — *need* — to know what she said. If she was crying. If she was scared. How much I just want to hear she was okay.

And if not, what clues she might've given that could bring her home.

Instead he says, "I know Madison's disappearance has been hard on you, but the issues here started well before that." His gaze settles on the sprawling campus, and for a half-breath, it's like he's somewhere else, like he's had this conversation before and is hoping this one ends differently.

His hands reach to grasp mine and I freeze, and then his fingers twitch like he regrets it instantly, but he doesn't let go. "If you're honest with me, I could help."

I want to believe him. I want to unleash the tangle of thoughts and feelings inside me and exorcise them from my head.

But I can't risk falling apart now. Not when I'm so close to graduation. Not when I have to find Madison.

I press my lips together to stop the words from fighting their way free.

His voice releases on a sigh. "I know you're struggling with what happened, but no one is worth throwing away your future for."

My gaze snaps to his, and for a moment, I'm not sure if he's talking about Madison or Willa — and then he tips his chin in the direction of my necklace.

He's never asked about Willa, but he knows she's gone. He has to. His pity is the only reason we didn't have this conversation after my first missed quiz.

The one he gave the day after Willa left.

All my nervous energy calms into a rush of warm certainty. "She's the only reason I have a future." The only reason I lived past fifteen.

He studies me, and when he crosses his arms over his chest my eyes fall shut. "Caroline, as your teacher, it's my job to report any academic or personal concerns."

"Don't do this."

"If I don't see immediate changes in not only your attendance, but your —"

"*Please*, Mr. McCormack."

He sighs, and this time he's both exhausted *and* irritated. "You've left me no choice here. I will have to tell your parents. Everything."

Everything.

Except I'm not going back there. To that place in my life that left me holding a bottle of pills. To that place in my head that made me question who I was. Been there, done that, have the scars to prove it.

And I won't trade that prison for one in my own home while Madison is out there and I have the only leads to find her.

I tell myself I did everything to avoid this, but that does nothing to ease the tightening in my chest as I raise my phone. Two quick swipes of my thumb and I meet his eyes again. "I sent you an email."

He pauses, undoubtedly waiting for the notification to sound on the phone he's got tucked in his pocket. When it doesn't come, he raises an eyebrow.

"Not your school email, the other one."

I used the email he accidentally left open on his computer one day when I jumped on it to google something after my phone died. He did me a favor by letting me stay in his classroom to study so I didn't have to go home, and now I know he's been shtupping the headmaster's much younger wife for six months.

As of twenty seconds ago, he's got my copies of their correspondence in a nice, tidy email to that same account.

To his credit, Mr. McCormack doesn't react, even though it's obvious he understands. "I see."

"Three months. Not even three months. And then you can forget I exist."

He keeps his voice level, but a muscle twitches in his jaw. "Who else knows about this?"

"No one."

Maybe no one. I didn't tell Willa. That part is true. But I wasn't expecting Madison to come looking for me the day I discovered the evidence on Mr. McCormack's computer.

I didn't ask if she saw, and she didn't tell.

He raises an eyebrow and I swallow — then again — because my throat is too thick to breathe quite right.

I say, "Not even her," and stumble through my next words before he can ask me to clarify. "I'm sorry. I know I owe you better than this. But you left me no choice."

I leave him standing there, wet leaves dragging near his feet as the wind kicks up again, but I barely make it ten feet before a familiar form blocks the path ahead.

Headmaster Havens's coat flaps at his thighs, fisted hands barely visible beneath his cuffs, tie strangling his jowly throat.

His gaze shifts from Mr. McCormack to me and back, and it's obvious he's been watching for longer than either of us realized. Probably the entire time Mr. McCormack's hands held tight to mine.

From the way Havens's eyes narrow, he doesn't like what he sees: not a teacher and student discussing grades, or projects or anything remotely appropriate.

We look like what we are — two people with too many secrets.

His voice warbles across the ten-foot span between us. "Ms. Lawson, which class are you supposed to be in?"

If Mr. McCormack is bothered, he doesn't show it. Instead,

he appears by my side, nudging me forward and putting himself directly into Havens's path as we walk toward the building entrance Havens is guarding.

Mr. McCormack's voice is so low I strain to hear it. "Head up, shoulders back, Ms. Lawson. You just blackmailed me — now isn't the time to get timid."

We walk in step, both of us nodding at Headmaster Havens as we pass him, and as we part ways to head to different buildings, I can't stop my rush of gratitude for the man I just blackmailed.

CHAPTER SEVEN

Hell is being forced to sit through French translations when you should be investigating the disappearance of your best friend before it's too late for her and before your favorite teacher ruins your entire life forever.

The brick wall bites into my back while I scan the stream of students rushing to lunch. There's a different energy since Madison went missing. Her posters still line the halls, as do the flyers for the search parties, the yellow and green ribbons.

There's no way to escape the reminder that even here, inside these stone walls of higher learning, we're not safe. Safe is something most of us didn't know you could take for granted.

But there are still shouts of laughter, playful shoving, talk of the various sportsball games I missed last night. Some things haven't changed at all, and that scares me more — how easy it is for life to go on, even with the most important people missing from it.

Aubrey shoves her way upstream, slipping her tiny body between the gaps.

She darts around a gaggle of freshman volleyball players, and I have to spring from the wall to catch her before she makes it into the bathroom.

I loop my arm into hers just as she shoulders open the door, and then I'm choking on the potpourri of twelve different scented lotions while Tabitha Zhao and her entourage fall quiet.

Tabitha makes a grand production of looking us over, pausing dramatically at our linked arms, and raises an eyebrow.

Seriously. Fuck her. I'm sure her friends would love to hear about how I discovered she has a teardrop-shaped beauty mark well below her bikini line.

I wink as I pass her, dragging poor Aubrey into the stall with me.

Tabitha calls out, "If you guys are gonna go down on each other in there, at least give us time to run away."

I flip her off over the top of the stall and shove the lock into place, and for a moment, the *click slide click* of metal is a shotgun being leveled at Jake's head.

I fumble for the lipstick I'm trying to dig out from my bag.

"Are you okay?" Aubrey's voice is nearly a whisper, and guilt slams into me for involving her in this.

I stop searching and meet her eyes. "We can talk somewhere else if you're afraid of what people will say."

She shakes her head, but there's no hiding the blush in her cheeks, even with her brown skin. "No. But I actually do have to pee, you know. Anyway, fuck Tabitha."

I laugh for the first time all day, and the sound bounces off the tiled room. "Can I tell you a secret?" At her nod, I say, "I did."

Her brows knit together, and then her mouth forms the perfect little o. "You didn't."

I shrug, because I don't think Aubrey will tell anyone, and because I have to laugh about something so I don't keep thinking about blinding a man with mace last night, or blackmailing a man with his secrets only a few hours ago. "Form your own conclusions. Listen, can you *keep* a secret?"

"What kind of secret?" Her eyes are narrow and wary.

We're friends, but we're from different circles. I'm sports and academics and she's drama club. That's not to say she's not smart — I happen to know she beat me by four-hundredths of a point on our English lit midterm — it's just that she makes blending in an art form. Until she gets on stage.

I drop my voice. "It's about Madison."

"*Oh*-kay." Eyes narrower and warier. "Is that a *vape*?"

I shush her because the last thing I need is Tabitha marching her perfect spiral curls down to the headmaster to report on my contraband.

Aubrey's having none of it. "You know vapes still contain nicotine, right? Did you know nicotine causes cardiovascular damage such as hypertension and heart disease?"

"I'll be sure to look out for signs of hypertension."

She glares at me. "You shouldn't joke about your health. We're young, not invincible, Caroline. And there have been no protracted studies on long-term usage *or* the impacts on the body in juveniles so —"

"Okay!" I drop my voice to a whisper. "You're right."

Of course she's right. Her mom has probably supplied her with talking points.

"Sorry," she mumbles. "Sometimes I swear the Great Doctor Patel takes over my brain and I become my mother."

"It's fine."

"I don't take it back, but —" She stares at the tile, an obvious attempt to avoid looking at me, because … it's the bathroom floor. "I've seen people get sick, you know? I don't want to see —"

She coughs to cover her quavering voice. "It's smart to take care of yourself."

The stall is suddenly much too small, like Aubrey's genuine concern is crowding all the space.

I'm probably supposed to hug her or say thanks but I can't force myself to do either when all my emotions feel poised on the brink.

"What can you tell me about this?" I shove my vape to the bottom of my bag and pull out the lipstick, one end of the matte pink tube tapered to a point and the other blooming into a shiny gold rose.

She slaps her hand over her mouth to stop from squealing, all concerns about my hypertension risk swept away. "How did you get that?"

"You don't want to know. It's expensive, though, right?"

"Yes, it's expensive. Can I hold it?"

"No." I tuck it against my chest and away from her reaching hands. She'll thank me when she finds out where it's from and what it might mean.

Her face falls, along with her shoulders. "Oh, well. Yes, it's expensive. But not just expensive, it's not available. Anywhere. It won't hit stores until June. They all have the rose on top, but see that little iris on the side? Each color has a different flower."

I don't have to look at it — I remember exactly what it looks like. I've got a replica of it etched into my skin.

It has to be a coincidence. I didn't even have my tattoo when Madison bought that lipstick.

But it doesn't feel like it.

It feels like coincidences don't exist anymore. "So there's not a huge chance lots of people have this."

She rocks onto her heels and her arms fold across her chest like armor. "You said this was about Madison."

Like I said, not stupid. The heavy bathroom door bangs open and footsteps echo until they stop — at the stall right next to ours. Because of course.

I rub my palm against the scratchy wool of my skirt to buy time until I can unglue my tongue from the roof of my mouth. "Right. See —"

"Is that —" she mouths "— Madison's?"

"Probably?"

She snatches the lipstick from my hand and flings open the door before I have the chance to blink, and then she's storming out of the bathroom and down the hall.

She's ridiculously fast. Practically a blur of movement past a stream of open classroom doors where anyone can overhear.

I keep my voice down while speed-walking toward wherever she's headed. "I need that back."

"It's evidence."

"Of nothing. What are the cops gonna do with it? There's no way to even prove it's hers." Except I remember her putting it on after practice last week, her reflection staring at me in the mirror as deep red stained her lips with every stroke. And then she reminded me about our plans to work on our chem project — the plans that would've kept her far from the reach of whoever took her. She wouldn't have left on her own. Her early acceptance letter to Yale's art school has been tacked onto her board since the day she got it.

Not that any of that matters. The cops aren't in the habit of believing anything I say. And I'm not in the habit of trusting them with anything — that may be the first and only thing Chrystal and I agree on.

Plus I'd have to say how and where I found the lipstick, and I'm not sure I'm ready to give them Chrystal before I have the chance to question her myself.

And it's not just me on the line. Jake was there too.

Aubrey says, "They could test it for fingerprints."

So that's actually a valid point. "They're probably all rubbed off by now."

"Why didn't you just call the cops when you found it?"

"Sort of a long story. I don't really have a great history with cops."

We turn a corner and both stop dead.

Tucked deep into the end of the hall, in the shadows next to the stream of light filtering through the stained-glass doorway, stand Mr. McCormack and Headmaster Havens.

I can't hear their words, but I don't need them to prove what I'm seeing.

Mr. McCormack stands easily a foot taller, muscled where Havens is flabby, and every fiber in his body screams aggressive intimidation.

Aubrey sighs, almost like a whimper. She's far from the only girl with an inappropriate infatuation with Mr. McCormack; she just happens to be really bad at pretending she doesn't.

Eavesdropping on your teacher and the headmaster probably fits under some "inappropriate conduct" umbrella in the St. Francis handbook, but I can't leave now. Especially when I swear Madison's name floats on the air.

I could never forgive myself if our conversation in the quad — or any of the things that led to it — gets Mr. McCormack fired.

And I don't want the cops wasting time framing him instead of looking for the real reason Madison is gone.

I don't want to be the only hope she has.

A door midway down the hall swings open, and both men turn toward the sound.

I jump around the corner and out of sight, and Aubrey knocks me over in her attempt to do the same.

We both go down in a tangle of body parts and my teeth clack together as my chin bounces off the floor. The weight of Aubrey's body slams onto mine, shoving my stomach up my throat.

Her tiny hands wrap around my bicep and pull. "Get up. Get up. Get up!"

She yanks us both into the next open classroom, and I shove her toward the closest hiding spot — beneath the teacher's desk — because neither of us want to be in sight if Havens and McCormack decide to investigate.

We scramble into the tiny space, our legs bent and twisted around each other's in a square of wood- and Pine-Sol–scented air, and voices drift from beyond the doorway.

I stop breathing.

The heat of our bodies pressed into the small space draws a sheen of sweat on my skin, and my pulse jumps against the tendon in my wrist.

Fabric rustles as Aubrey shifts forward, and then something soft presses against the spot where my chin collided with the floor.

I startle and my head clunks against the desk, but it must be too quiet to hear because the voices outside the door fade into silence.

Aubrey whispers, "Sorry," and offers the Kleenex in her hand that's stained with blood. "I just didn't want it to drip."

She ducks her head, her shoulders curling inward, and my heart pangs. I knock my knee into hers. "Hey. Thanks. I'm just ... I'm not always great with touching people. Or people touching me."

"That's not what Tabitha said."

My attempt to stifle my laugh turns it into a snort, which sets off a fit of giggles in Aubrey, and soon we're both laughing so hard Aubrey's crying and I would be if I could.

When I finally catch my breath, I say, "McCormack looked pissed."

"He looked hot as hell."

"Eww."

Her mouth opens and closes, and then she wiggles her phone free, eyes narrowed in concentration as she flips through screens. "Last summer, I'm lying out by the pool, right? Practicing my lines. And I see something out of the corner of my eye. So I look up. You want to know what I see?"

"Mr. McCormack."

"I see the most perfect specimen of man ever. If I hadn't been so distracted by how he looked pulling himself out of the water, I would've gotten video." She emphasizes every syllable and thrusts her phone a half inch from my face. "Look at him, Caroline."

I inch her wrist back while my vision unblurs, and okay, I can see her point. Except, he's still Mr. McCormack. "Why did you tell him you were worried about me?"

"He didn't tell you that."

"No, he didn't."

"Then who says I did?" She slips out of our hiding spot, but her saddle shoes root to the floor instead of running away.

I duck out too, and say, "I need the lipstick back."

When I hold out my hand, she drops the tube without a word, her gaze focused on my gashed chin.

I pin the Kleenex against it and head for the door before pausing. "Thanks. For, you know …"

She nods, and I'm almost turned around when she calls my name. "Should I be? Worried?"

I'd feel a lot better about my plans for the evening if someone knew what they were, just in case I don't make it back. But I don't need another person to add to the list of lives I'm ruining.

I give her my "family picture day" smile — the one my mom made me practice in a mirror until I'd perfected it, just so she'd have a photo to prove we aren't the mess she knows we are.

I shake my head. "What's there to worry about?"

THE KINDNESS OF STRANGERS

Maslow made it all seem so simple.

A tidy stack of wants and needs, divided into a perfectly segregated pyramid.

The angles sharp, the lines straight and exact.

Like people aren't messy and muddled. As if survival is dependent only on basic needs. Like love and belonging can't become as basic as food and shelter if you're denied them long enough.

I'd never seen love — not up close. The Larrys were about needs. Each serving their purpose. I met each of them wordlessly, my mom's voice hard against my ear. *Be nice. We need ...*

We need the car fixed. The fridge replaced. Half the rent for the next month.

Maslow didn't count on love becoming so entangled with needs it ceased to exist.

But there were moments, and men, when I'd see the spark of wanting in her eyes. When the loneliness left her head in her hands, tears soaking the cuffs at her wrists.

I didn't comfort her. I'd forgotten how to touch another person, my skin having long since given up hope of nourishment. All my wants and needs had curled themselves deep inside, buried beneath my protective layers.

Wanting love was a betrayal of needs. The sacrifice too great. The level beyond my reach.

Those kinds of wants were reserved for the people who

never questioned the bottom of that pyramid. The kind who climbed Maslow's levels until they reached the apex.

Those were the people who ordered food they'd never eat and signed their credit card receipts without glancing at the totals. They were the strangers who stumbled into the diner where I worked on their way through a town they'd never live in.

It was only a few weeks after I met Livie when one of those strangers slipped through the double doors and into my section, without even a glance at the sign that asked her to wait to be seated. She dropped her backpack in first, then her camera bag after, the contents tumbling onto the table as the bag unlatched.

Her hands stumbled over the camera that *had* to cost more than most of the cars in the lot. The strap alone, with its supple leather and monogrammed cursive *M* pressed deep into the hide, probably did too.

She slid into the booth and smoothed the plaid of her skirt, tugging the hem to meet her knees.

She stammered through her drink order. Coke. *Diet* Coke. No — lemonade. Her blond hair tumbled over her shoulders as she shook her head, her lips drawn tight as she gave her final choice. Water. With lemon.

The food came easier — she chose the first item her gaze landed on when she flipped open the plastic menu, her manicured nails glossy and pink.

I hurried back with the water, convinced if I left her alone too long she might run.

She sucked in a breath, not daring to meet my eyes, her voice skimming a whisper. "Do you —"

I waited. I wish I could say I did it to give her the space she needed, the time to unburden whatever made her eyes shine with stifled tears. I wish it wasn't because I needed to see this stranger — this girl with the prep-school emblem stitched to her sweater and the Rolex around her wrist — prove she wanted things. Just like me. At least for a moment.

She stirred her water, ice clinking against the glass, lemon caught in the swirling tide. "There's this guy."

I tucked my pen inside my order book and angled myself to cut her from the view of the men at the counter. "There usually is."

She smiled. "Yeah. It's just —" She pinned an ice cube to the bottom of her sweating glass, stabbing with her straw. "Do you ever feel invisible?"

I couldn't stop the laugh that burst from me. "All the time."

"Really?"

It should've been an easy answer, because *yes, really*. Every time I came home to empty rooms — or full rooms with empty stares. Every time my voice got met with silence. Every time I waited for someone to ask where I'd been, where I was going, whether I was okay.

Yes, really. All the time.

Until Livie.

Until every time she looked at me and I felt seen. Until she took in my every word, attention never wavering, her arms always — *always* — waiting to draw me in.

And not once, in all the times Livie reached for me, had I flinched. That protected place deep inside had never recoiled, not even the first time her palm cradled my cheek. Not the first time her lips brushed mine.

She acted like I mattered.

She took all my doubts and proved them wrong. I recognized all my fears in her eyes, saw hers reflected back, and together, we burned them to ashes.

That place I'd kept hidden hadn't drawn tighter — it had bloomed.

Never, not once, had I felt invisible in her eyes.

The girl smiled, until sadness pulled at her mouth. "Maybe not *all* the time, huh?"

I cleared my throat, my own smile too big to cage. "Not all the time."

She traced circles in the swirls of the table. "If you knew something — or if you thought *maybe* you knew something — that would ruin what you had, would you tell?"

The kitchen bell dinged twice, a sure sign I was about to be in trouble for letting food sit too long. "I guess it depends."

But even as I said the words, they rang false. I wouldn't risk what Livie and I had over anything, except something that would hurt her.

The bell dinged again and I mumbled, "One sec," before running to grab her food.

The plate had barely hit the table before she said, "That wasn't a fair question. Sorry for vomiting all my feels on you."

"I wouldn't tell. Barring mortal danger. But if not, I wouldn't tell."

Her head dropped, and I barely heard her thank-you. And when she walked toward the door ten minutes later — her french fries barely nibbled and the rest untouched, a twenty-five-dollar tip on the ten-dollar tab I'd used my earnings to pay for — I grabbed her into a hug.

I gave her the chance to live in a world like mine — just for a moment.

Her body went rigid, then melted into me for a half-breath, before she headed out into the night, to a place where she belonged.

When Livie walked through those same doors less than an hour later, I hugged her too. Unrestrained and without hesitation. And then I pulled her into the cramped closet that overflowed with cleaning supplies and paper goods, and the staff's coats and purses, even though it wasn't close to my break time.

She smiled at me, that smile she reserved for the best moments between us. "Why are we locked in a closet? Is this some kind of a metaphor?"

She was so much of what I would never be — confident, self-assured, magnetic. The type of person everyone flocked to the moment she walked into a room. Part of me would never understand how she could look at me like she was the one who'd gotten lucky.

And it had only been a few weeks. How many times had I watched my mom give every part of herself only to have it thrown back? How many times had I told myself I'd never *be her*, never follow her path?

Livie brushed the tear from my cheek, her smile washed away by concern. "Hey, what's wrong? Did someone —"

"I love you." The words burst into the air between us, too late to take back, too late to form any defenses, and Livie blinked.

Once. Twice.

Her arms banded around me, momentum crashing us both

into the closed door, our laughter filling all the dark corners and muffling the response she whispered against my ear.

And then her mouth met mine. Not soft. Not gentle. Her hands buried in my hair and mine in hers.

I'd give days of hunger for every kiss like that. Months of shelter for every moment in her arms.

I'd give everything to hear her whisper she loved me again.

If I ever meet Maslow in the afterlife, I'll tell him he got it all wrong.

CHAPTER EIGHT

I'm a coward.

That's the only explanation for why I have not:

> 1. Asked Mr. McCormack if our conversation got him in trouble.
>
> 2. Read any of the numerous texts Jake has sent me today.
>
> 3. Walked into The Wayside and demanded Marcel tell me why he completely abandoned me. Why, after years of being my sanctuary, he ushered me out like he regretted he ever plucked me from the side of that road.

Right now, that last one is the hardest to ignore. I've done an excellent job of ignoring the first two all day. I even crawled out the window after American history rather than face Jake in the hallway.

It's not like I can avoid everyone forever, but after the showdown with Havens and Mr. McCormack in the hallway, I can't stop the reel of worst-case scenarios in my head: That Mr. McCormack will tell me he's been fired and it's all my fault. That Jake's text is going to say Mountain Man went to the cops and there's an assault charge with my name listed. That Detectives Brisbane and Harper are going to call us into the auditorium and tell us all my worst fears about what happened to Madison are real.

I don't know how to deal with any of those possibilities.

So I choose to ignore, and focus on the goals. Find Madison. Graduate. Leave.

And I'm not waiting around until the end of the school day when I could be finding Madison *now*.

Sunshine barrels though the etched glass door of Olivet Hall, and I'm steps from freedom when Aubrey appears in front of me.

I pull up short, losing my chance for escape while I attempt to figure out where she came from.

Before I can ask, she has me spun around and walking back toward the classrooms.

I stop and say, "I was leaving."

Her whole body sighs. "Please?"

My resolve fractures but I manage to hold firm, until the lights reflect off the shimmer of tears in her eyes.

This is the girl who nearly cried because she doesn't want me to develop hypertension. I can't just leave her standing in the hallway looking all sad. "Please what?"

"Come see someone with me." From the way she's death-gripping the straps of her backpack, I'm not going to like the someone.

"Aubrey —"

"You can't keep evidence, Caroline. It's illegal and immoral, and if it keeps Madison from being found, you'll never forgive yourself and I'll never forgive you for showing me, and we'll all hate ourselves *and* each other and I can't —" She takes a heaving breath and I hate how right she is about everything — so much that I want to turn and storm out the door on some kind of weird reverse principle.

But then she stomps her foot and says, "No. I *won't* allow it."

I duck my head so she won't see the smile I'm smothering, and so I don't have to admit I'm laughing when Madison is missing and Willa is gone.

"Are you laughing at me?"

I can't see her arms but I guarantee she's crossed them over her chest.

She steps closer, ducking to meet my eyes, and there's something in the closeness of her, the lack of reservation in her expression, that makes me ache to draw her in. To let her hug me back. To let her be the first person to really touch me since Willa left.

She whispers, "Please. I know you said you don't like cops, so I — *we* — came up with an idea."

I step back, the tension snapping taut again. "*We* who? How much am I going to hate this?"

She cringes, and as I discover four minutes later, I hate it a lot.

Aubrey delivers me to a room with Jake and his dad — his dad who is a judge and would probably have *opinions* on the things I've dragged his son into — and the comfort of knowing there's a Xanax in my backpack is the only thing stopping me from bolting for the door.

They're perched on a long table, cell phones tucked into their hands.

A mirror image. The present and past of St. Francis paving the way for the future.

Both their heads snap to attention the moment I enter the room.

Mr. Monaghan's smile stretches wide as his strides carry

him toward me. He extends a hand I shake on instinct, and then he clasps his other over them both, warm and steady. "Great game against St. Matthew's last week."

I mumble a thank-you, socialite instincts bred too deeply to fail even when all my attention is focused on Jake, who's giving me an apologetic shrug.

Mr. Monaghan releases me and motions toward a chair before pulling another to face it. He lowers into the seat, all athletic grace and practiced poise, while I stumble into mine, shoving it back a few inches to put more space between us.

This is why they sent Aubrey — to lure me in.

Mr. Monaghan's eyes go soft as he says, "How are you holding up? I know you and Madison were close."

"Um … yeah. And I'm okay."

He doesn't look convinced.

He leans forward, elbows on knees, voice low. "I know this is uncomfortable, Caroline, but Jake and Aubrey are your friends and they're trying to help."

He scans the doorway without pausing, and I'd guarantee it's because Aubrey abandoned me at the first possible moment. When he turns back to me, all the softness has bled from his eyes. I know this face — it's the one my mom gives me right before she tells me all the things I don't want to hear.

He says, "I, however, am not your friend. I'm an adult — one that's concerned about his son's safety, and yours too. And as an adult, it's my responsibility to point out when your decisions compromise your safety. Like they did last night."

I don't respond because my mind is spinning from all the déjà vu in this conversation, except I don't have anything to blackmail Jake's dad with.

Jake finally speaks, but he doesn't look the least bit motivated to join our little chair circle. "I told him about what we found last night. The lipstick."

His gives a look that tells me he didn't get monumentally stupid and tell the whole story, so I force my fingers to unlock from the edges of my seat.

Mr. Monaghan's voice ticks up a notch and his words sharpen. It's not difficult to picture him with a courtroom at his mercy, shouldering all his power and authority with practiced ease. "First, I want to make it clear I am not your attorney, and I have no knowledge of Madison's case. But Jake tells me you're not comfortable with the police, and truth be told, I don't always like them so much either."

He gives me a smile so genuine I almost manage to return it, and just like that, he manages to marry the stern father with the approachable confidant. "But I know all of you want to do everything in your power to make sure Madison comes home safely, so I'm here to advise you as best I can."

I will kill Jake and Aubrey for this ambush.

My body is frozen, but my brain won't stop calculating all my very limited options. There's no way out of this. The fastest, safest end to this conversation is to hand the lipstick over.

I reach for my backpack and pull it free, but my fingers clench around it.

This could be the last thing Madison touched. Letting go feels like letting go of *her*.

I force my arm to move and the lipstick tumbles from my palm into the wide span of Mr. Monaghan's.

He tests its weight, delicate gold petals of the iris on the side catching the light. "What is this?"

"Lipstick? *Madison's* lipstick."

He tips the tube end over end like he's looking for her name to be Sharpied on it like we're in second grade. "This could belong to anyone."

"No. I saw her with it, before she disappeared, and it's limited edition or not available or something. You should ask Aubrey."

I feel only nominally guilty about siccing him on her.

Mr. Monaghan's hand closes over the metal rose on top. "Where did you find this again?"

Jake fidgets but I can't look at him. Clearly this is a test to see if we tell the same story.

It's an easy test, because there's no way Jake lied to his dad. He's not like me.

Mr. Monaghan leans closer. "Caroline." He waits until I meet his eyes. "Everything is going to be okay."

I nod, but he has to see how little faith I have in his sentiments, how "okay" will never be a path for me. Not as long as my parents have control over who I am.

He holds the lipstick between us like a sacred offering. "Thank you for giving me this. I'm afraid it's a bit too late, not to mention outside the proper chain of custody, to be considered official evidence, but you never know what clue might be the thing that brings Madison home."

His eyes are so concerned, his tone so comforting, I have to choke down the confession forcing itself up my throat.

It would be so easy to hand him the whole messy story. But I've learned what happens when you trust people without knowing their full motives. Last time, it ended with my mom's signature on camp intake papers.

I swallow. "I found a matchbook for this bar in my locker, so we went there to ask about Madison and there was this waitress. Anyway, we went to talk to her and we found the lipstick in the woods near her trailer."

I hold my breath while he assesses me, and at least some of that hyper-streamlined version must've matched Jake's, because Mr. Monaghan nods.

He holds out a hand and pulls me to stand, and then Jake is there and Mr. Monaghan's arm is slung around his broad shoulders.

I can't remember the last time I didn't flinch when my parents touched me.

Mr. Monaghan gives my shoulder a tiny rub. "Thank you both for coming to me with this, and I want you to know I don't take that trust lightly. This is hard on everyone, and it can be tough to go about your normal life in a situation like this. But as a parent, this is the kind of thing you hope to protect your kids from, so I know I speak for your parents, as well as myself, when I say your safety isn't worth the risks you took last night."

He puts on his judge face to say, "Madison's best chance relies on letting the professionals do their jobs. Got it?"

Jake and I nod, neither of us daring to look to see if the other means it, before Mr. Monaghan asks if he can steal Jake for a chat in the hallway.

I'm tempted to hover near the doorway to see what advice he gives to Jake that he couldn't give me — but I'm too busy crawling out the window to do exactly what he asked me not to.

CHAPTER NINE

It's quiet in the back lot of The Wayside. Only the employees —
and me — park here.

I *could* go in. I still have my key.

But I can't risk the fallout from a conversation with Marcel
right now, not when I have to get answers from Chrystal before
she locks herself inside her house again.

That means I'm standing in the darkened lot, covered in
goose bumps I can't feel because my skin went numb an hour
ago.

According to Tammy, the night-shift bartender who sneaks
me energy drinks on major study nights, Chrystal's shift was
supposed to end forty-five minutes ago. Her car is still in the lot.

I'm standing less than three feet from it.

Yesterday I left without answers. Today I won't.

Light seeps from the edges of the back door as it swings open,
and for a second, there's only Chrystal's thin frame outlined in
soft yellow.

The floodlights kick on and I blink three times before my
eyes adjust.

Chrystal scans the lot, her key fisted between her fingers.

The door clips shut behind her, and when I step out of the
shadows, her expression swings from terror to fury.

She clutches a stack of books to her chest. "Are you alone?"

"Yes."

"What the hell do you want? Gonna follow me home again?"

I didn't expect to get this far with her, and now I have no idea what to say. "I just want to ask you some questions."

"Questions." She snorts. "What does the spoiled little rich girl want to ask me about?"

Heat blossoms in my cheeks. "I want to ask you about Sydney."

"Get the fuck away from my car before I call the cops." She charges forward, her mouth pulled into a straight line, and I press myself against the side of her trunk.

"Name your price."

She stops not six inches from me, shadows sinking into the deep lines on her face. "My price?" The corner of her mouth tilts. "Okay, get in the car."

I should've told someone my plans. I should've texted Jake back, or confessed to Aubrey, and I definitely should *not* have altered my phone's location to make it seem like I'm on campus in the event my parents — or maybe the police, eventually — decide to check.

Chrystal barks out a laugh. "Didn't think so. Rich girl likes to pretend she's slumming, but when it comes to —"

"I'm getting in."

I am fully aware this could be a decision that leads to my death — especially when the first thing she says to me when I sink into her torn bucket seat is, "Figured you and your pretty-boy boyfriend learned your lesson yesterday."

She cranks the engine and it coughs before acrid gray smoke fills the interior. "*Goddamn* are you stupid."

⊰━⊱

She's not wrong.

I spend the whole ride thinking how furious Marcel would be with me if he knew I got into a car with another stranger after his epic lecture the night I got into the car with *him*.

Then I remind myself that yesterday he threw me out and told me not to come back.

I ask Chrystal for one of the cigarettes she's smoking, and she shakes one from her soft pack and into my hand, watching me from the corner of her eye. It's the only words we speak the entire ride.

By the time we step into the cold night air, my head is soft and fuzzy, my fingers tingly. The spot where Jake nearly decapitated a man lies in darkness, just beyond the dim glow of trailer lights. When Chrystal offers another cigarette, I don't hesitate.

Smoke curls in a thin stream above her head as she pushes inside the trailer, and when she thumbs on the lights and locks the door behind me, I'm not sure if I'm relieved or terrified.

It's a single wide with a living room and kitchen that's bisected only by a row of lower cabinets, a narrow hallway disappearing into a tomb of black. A faint water stain runs the length of the kitchen wall where Chrystal drops her stack of papers onto the counter.

The faux-wood cabinet creaks when she pries it open and motions for me to sit.

I nearly drown in the sofa that's deeper and softer than any sofa has a right to be, and I try not to think how hard it would be to get out if I have to run. Except seeing her here, moving methodically through her kitchen, Chrystal doesn't seem dangerous. She seems sad. The kind of sad that weighs a person down until they struggle to stay upright.

But I can't rule out Mountain Man's involvement either, or that Chrystal really might have something to hide.

Glasses clunk against the counter and Chrystal pulls a bottle of vodka from the cream-colored fridge, along with a tray of ice cubes. "Thirsty?"

I nod because I can't say no, and I'm too busy staring at the ice cube tray. I'm not sure I've ever used an ice cube tray, which I guess makes me every bit the privileged bitch Chrystal thinks I am.

Vodka splashes against the glass and cracks the ice cubes when she tosses in a dash of soda. She crosses the worn carpet and holds out the drink, and fizzy bubbles tickle my palm when I reach for it.

I take a sip, then a full drink, as she watches me above the rim of her own glass, vodka exploding on my tongue and oozing into my belly, all warmth and quiet.

Her arms lock over her chest and there's nothing but the *tick tick tick* of her manicured nail striking the side of her glass while she searches my face for something I'm certain I don't have. "So ask."

"Why were you such a bitch to me in Marcel's office?"

She laughs, and for the briefest moment, I see the person she must've been before she realized life wouldn't turn out the way she hoped.

The chair groans as she drops into it, the flame from her lighter flaring high before the paper in her cigarette crackles. A plume of smoke snakes from her open lips. "Honey, you don't have time for that answer."

"You don't even know me."

She points the scarlet tip of her cigarette at me. "I've seen you around. Pretending you belong. Almost had me fooled — until you brought that boy around yesterday. I know your type and I know his. I know the difference between you and everyone who has to work for what they get."

I slam my drink onto the scratched coffee table. "You know my type? I'm here, okay? I came here to ask about my friend, yes, but about Sydney too. A girl I don't even know."

"And what are you gonna do if I don't answer? Send the cops to come searching around the woods again?"

I have no mace. No Jake with a tire iron. Her questions feel as much a threat as an inquiry. "The cops were here?"

Jake's dad had to have told the cops about the lipstick, but I can tell from the smug look on Chrystal's face it didn't exactly spark a county-wide search.

She shrugs. "Didn't find nothing. Not where they're looking."

There's only one way she'd know: she's got Mountain Man to watch for her. Then, and probably now too.

Outside, tires crunch over gravel, and twin beams of light pierce Chrystal's thin mini-blinds, tossing the room into a whirl of light and shadows. My thoughts feel foggy, my movements sluggish. "Why did you get so mad when I asked about Sydney? I'm trying to *help*."

My voice nearly cracks and I hate that I let her hear it. But there's something so goddamn familiar in the feel of this place. A sadness that coats the walls and bleeds into the fabrics.

I haven't been able to stop feeling it since Willa left.

I miss her like the world stopped being the same place the moment she walked away. There's a void where her smile used to be. Emptiness where my laughter used to be, when she'd pull from her endless catalogue of terrible jokes when I needed them, giggling before she'd barely started. *How does a penguin build his house? Igloos it together.*

She let me be the version of myself that was truer than any other.

And I was there for her too. The days her life got too heavy and she'd let me hold her, whisper into her hair. The days she'd smile and I'd realize I told her something I barely admitted to myself. Things only my therapist knows.

I told her about camp, about the day I walked away from my dad with a bottle of pills and what I planned to do with them. She cried the tears I couldn't, and then, her voice quiet and her eyes locked on mine, she said, "It was wrong, what your parents did to you."

I laid my head on her shoulder. "I know."

Her silence stretched. "Do you?"

That was the day Willa taught me knowing something is different than believing it. I believe it now. Willa gave me that. And as the world before me blurs, I can almost feel her hand in mine.

Chrystal's cigarette flares violent red on her inhale, and her answer comes in a haze of smoke. "Sydney is my niece. The cops say she ran away with her boyfriend."

"Why?"

"Because that's what they always say when they don't think someone's important enough to look for."

Not important enough to look for.

They're not looking for Sydney, not even trying to help her. Just like Detective Harper didn't try to help me.

She heads to her stack of papers and yanks one free. "You want to find your friend?"

I move toward her on shaking legs, my brain too wobbly to control, carrying warnings I'm too fuzzy to understand. "Yes."

Footsteps rattle the stairs outside the trailer, and I know I should be scared, but the knock at the door seems far away, my body too light to stay fixed to the ground.

"Well then, rich girl, find Sydney. Then I'll tell you what I know about your friend."

CHAPTER TEN

My brain slices in half with even the smallest movement, and a cocoon of blankets drags me back toward sleep. I roll to my side, bundling the covers until I'm surrounded by sandalwood-and-spice-infused cotton.

This is not my bed.

I rocket from my once-cozy place and my legs tangle in the sheets. My scream starts but doesn't finish as strong fingers wrap around my biceps.

My shoulder wrenches when I rip my arm free, and then that same hand is cradling my jaw, gentle now, and someone whispers my name in the darkness.

"Take a breath for me." Jake's voice is soft, concerned. "I'm sorry. I didn't mean to grab you. I just … I was afraid you were going to fall off and —"

I employ all the deep breathing exercises I learned in the yoga classes Dad insisted I take.

Voices murmur in the hall — normal students starting a normal day — and Jake's steady arms remind me that, for now, I'm safe.

I want to be mad at him for blindsiding me with his dad yesterday, but since I'm in his bed with zero recollection of what happened last night, it's safe to assume I owe him for something.

I clear my throat and slip out of his hands. "It's not your fault. I just didn't expect …"

Any of this? To wake up in Jake's bed when the only thing I

123

remember is thoroughly avoiding him yesterday. He's shirtless, his skin sticky and his hair wet like he just got out of the shower.

Stupidly, my first thought is that Aubrey would kill me for not taking a picture, but I think that's a defense mechanism because what I'm really doing is delaying the moment I have to look down and see what I am — or am not — wearing.

"Caroline." His smile starts slow, then twitches like he's holding it back. "I prefer my sexual partners to be conscious."

"Oh, well, aren't you just a fucking prince."

His smile evaporates and his brows draw down.

I'm being a dick, even if maybe waking up in a bed you don't remember climbing into is a pretty valid reason in my book. "Listen, I didn't mean — I wasn't trying —"

"Wow. Watching you attempt an apology is almost worth being late for practice."

I almost laugh, but then I remember. "What happened last night?"

The mattress shifts as he leans back. "You really don't remember anything?"

I shake my head, and missing Willa hits me all over again. I remember everything about my nights with her. I miss how her body fit perfectly against mine, the softness of her skin, the way my fingers threaded through her thick hair and the way her lips used to whisper against the hollow of my throat when we'd lie together and everything awful would fade away.

It's been over a week since her last letter — handwritten, untraceable slips of paper so I don't "ruin my life by following her to Cali" — and with each new envelope, I wait to hear she's found everything we had with someone else.

She's starting to feel *truly* gone — just like Madison.

I smooth the wrinkles from Jake's comforter. "The other missing girl — Sydney Hatton — she's Chrystal's niece."

"Yeah." He climbs from the bed in a fluid stretch of muscle and pops open his mini fridge. "That's what Chrystal said after I almost busted in her door last night. I knocked for five fucking minutes before she answered."

He yanks out a bottled water and slams the door shut so hard the fridge shakes. "You were barely standing when she finally let me in, and I had to carry you to the car."

He hands me the water and two ibuprofen and I turn them over, letting them roll into the lines of my hand. It's shaking, like my body has figured out something before my brain has, because the reason tumbles from my mouth a second later. "Why were you there?"

He stills, so quick a blink would've missed it. "You were avoiding me yesterday."

"So you *followed* me?"

"No. If I followed you, I'd have stopped you from ever stepping into her house in the first place."

"Jake —"

"Be mad, Caroline, if you need to." He rips a T-shirt over his head. "I knew you were going to do something stupid. And then you weren't answering your phone. I waited. And then I took my best guess, and it's lucky for us both I was right, or you might be a body in those fucking woods right now."

I hate — no, I *loathe* — that he's right. Even more, that I can't find the words to explain why, despite the end, the means still leave me cold with unease. "Well, my *stupidity* got me answers."

"It got you comatose."

"You think she drugged me?"

"You tell me."

"I had one sip."

"You sure?"

"Yes. I'm sure." I pop the pills in my mouth, tiny pinpoints of sweetness on my tongue, and wash them down. "She had no reason to drug me, Jake. I was going to help her."

"Maybe she didn't expect you to. Maybe it's not even her niece. Maybe she was gonna sell you to that fucking piece of shit that nearly blew my head off two nights ago."

"Hey." Chrystal's far from my BFF, and I'm vaguely remembering her threatening to call the cops and tell them about my "relationship" with Marcel if she found out I wasn't really trying to help find her niece, but now Jake's being a dick and it feels good to not be the only one.

"I almost took you to the hospital. If you weren't conscious enough to beg me not to, I would've. So if you're telling me you only had one sip, then she drugged you. Let the cops find her niece. *And* Madison. Like my dad said."

"The cops aren't looking for her niece. They think she ran away."

That's why she's so mad. Everyone is falling all over themselves to find Madison, and she can't convince anyone her niece didn't just leave town with her boyfriend.

Chrystal's voice pierces through the fog in my memories, the glaze over her eyes when she ground her cigarette onto the kitchen counter. *My niece is a good student, got good grades. She's going to community college in the fall. Already paid off her first semester's tuition. No one's running away after putting down that kind of cash. My sister — she's never been the best mom, but*

*she did what she could for Sydney. Now some maniac has my
niece and nobody gives a shit.*

I rub my forehead, straining to remember. "She said, 'Find
Sydney first. Then I'll tell you what I know about your friend.'"

"What the fuck does that mean?"

"I don't know. Maybe she doesn't know anything. Maybe
she's just trying to get me to find her niece. But maybe not."

If the cops aren't willing to explore the evidence Chrystal
has, Sydney's never getting found.

And now that it's clear Madison was involved with Chrystal
in *some* way, it's impossible to ignore that her story might end
the same way. And, at least partly, that will be because of me.

I blink to clear my cloudy vision. "The minute we met
Chrystal, she called the cops crooked. Maybe she was right. Not
just about Sydney's case, but Madison's too. Either they're trying
to cover it up or they're just too stupid to put it all together, but
Madison's case is too well-known. Eventually, they're going to
pin it on someone ..."

I don't fill in the rest — the texts from Madison that Jake left
unanswered the night she vanished do the job for me. Madison
was his girlfriend, sort of, and he was supposed to be there the
night she went missing. They always look to the husbands and
boyfriends first.

But even if Jake never comes close to facing a trial, even if
he never gets beyond questioning before his dad uses his judge
status to shut the whole thing down, Jake has *plans* after graduation. Going into college with rumors you offed your girlfriend — even unsubstantiated ones — is not the way to earn
the starting job on any sports team.

All Jake has to worry about is himself though. I'm the one responsible for unraveling this entire disaster. And if she's lucky, Madison is out there somewhere, waiting for me to do it.

"Chrystal said Sydney's mom wasn't really involved in her life, but she must have friends. And there was a boyfriend too. Someone might be willing to talk. But, Jake —"

I rub my throbbing temple until my thoughts become coherent, because there's something there, just out of reach, that doesn't fit with Jake's assumptions.

I close my eyes and Chrystal watches me from over the top of her glass.

"She poured drinks for us both."

"What?"

"She made drinks for both of us. I watched her do it." *I stared at her ice cube tray.* "And she didn't even know I was coming. If she poisoned me, she poisoned herself too."

It hits me then, what I'm really trying to say. "What if Chrystal didn't drug me? What if someone was trying to drug *her*?"

"You want to check on her?"

"And maybe get her to talk about Madison when my brain isn't suffocating. I also need to get my car from The Wayside."

"Yeah. Okay." He rubs the back of his neck. "I'm late. I texted your mom and said I was with you last night — said you were staying on campus. My car keys are on the desk if you need to run home to change, which you should. You smell like cigarettes. See you in AP gov."

He slips out the door soundlessly. It's sweet of him, but if he's trying to protect the massive cleaving through my temporal lobe, it's too late.

Sometime between now and first period, I have to gather the courage to face Mr. McCormack and ask him about his fight with Headmaster Havens — to face whether he's in trouble because of me.

Except it turns out that's the least of my worries.

I rush into class with thirty seconds before the bell and pull up short when I notice that my normally talkative classmates all sit silently, unmoving, their gazes directed at the man at the front of the room.

Headmaster Havens wastes no time telling us Mr. McCormack is on leave. Until further notice.

CHAPTER ELEVEN

I've lost track of the number of times I've checked my phone today.

I sent Mr. McCormack an email. To *that* account, just in case the cops are reading his St. Francis one and they decide to take my concern as extra evidence of him being a violent kidnapper.

He still hasn't responded.

There isn't a single St. Francis teacher, administrator or janitor who's giving the slightest hint about why he's on leave, but all the rumors — championed by Preston Ashcroft, of course — say the cops spent a solid hour in the headmaster's office before they sent Mr. McCormack home this morning.

Jake even called his dad for intel and got shut down before Mr. McCormack's name left his lips.

Here's what I *do* know: this is my fault.

I've replayed the detectives' expressions from that morning with Jake and Mr. McCormack at my locker so many times there's no way to deny the truth. They started out suspicious, and then Havens saw me with Mr. McCormack. *Holding hands.*

That was all they needed to confirm their theories.

If someone told them about that night at The Wayside when he drove me and Willa home, their case would be made for them. Teacher takes interest in young student and leaves a bar with her. Two girls — one a student at the very school the teacher works at — go missing.

And now they're spinning his text and call with Madison the

night she disappeared as some kind of pattern of behavior. But Madison's connection to The Wayside, to Chrystal, maybe even to Sydney, is too strong to ignore. Except I can't tell the detectives about it. Chrystal will barely talk to *me*, and she hates cops even more than I do. Sending them to her house to ask about Madison when they won't look for Sydney would be a betrayal.

It should be mine to investigate anyway. There's a link missing between Madison and this other world in West Virginia. And I don't know what else it could be besides me.

If she were here, she'd nudge my shoulder and say, "You're doing it again." And then, not waiting for me to ask what because we both know, she'd add, "Assuming everything is your fault."

And then I'd flip her off and we'd both end up lighter than before.

But she's *not* here now, and this time, my assumptions are right.

I don't say any of that while Jake drives to Chrystal's house for our make-sure-she's-not-as-drugged-as-me mission. Sometimes it feels like the things we don't say are more important than the ones we do.

Jake's palm shushes over the steering wheel as he turns into the mobile home park. He sidles up to a small playground, dotted with plastic climbers and a skeletal swing set, and cuts the engine. "If anything feels wrong, even a little, we're leaving."

"Okay."

"I mean it."

"I'm not stupid, Jake."

He mutters a curse. "You could've died the past two nights. Sorry for trying to break your streak."

The truck's interior lights blind me and Jake's out the door before I can respond, leaving me to catch up.

"I appreciate what you're doing. I really do. I'm just in a hurry to find some answers, especially with Mr. McCormack —"

"What's the deal with you two?"

We creep through someone's front yard where a cheery Easter wreath hangs above an eviction notice. "The deal? He's my teacher."

"Who you email."

"Exactly. Who I email. Not who I fuck, which is what you were asking, right?"

His jaw twitches. "Sometimes I don't know how to talk to you, Caroline."

"Why? Because I called you out on calling me a slut?"

"I didn't call you a slut."

"Sure you did. You just didn't use those words."

"That's not how words work."

"That is exactly how words work."

"I'm just saying maybe it's time you look at the facts. I know you don't want him to be responsible, but —"

"He's not responsible."

He kicks a rock and it tumbles end over end in a dizzying spin, until it comes to rest in a dark puddle. "Believing something doesn't make it true."

I shudder, because I've lost track of the times I wished it would. "Neither does assuming it is."

"I'm not —" He huffs out a hard breath. "Maybe you're just not the greatest judge of character."

It hits as hard as he meant it to, reminding me of all the things I don't know about Madison, how he followed me here last night, how I thought Willa would never leave me — that once, I believed my parents would never hurt me.

I whisper, "Shut up, Jake."

His mouth opens and closes. "I'm sorry. I shouldn't have —"

I cut him off because I can't have this conversation right now, and because I can't stop staring at Chrystal's car.

"There's frost on her car."

He scans the grass at our feet and the dusting of white on the blades that have just begun to spring back to life. "It's cold outside."

"She was supposed to go work earlier. I called to ask about her schedule." And hoped they'd say she was there — walking, talking, and not comatose. "If she went, there wouldn't have been enough time for frost to form."

It takes every bit of my willpower not to turn and run back to Jake's truck. And I'm sure he hasn't forgotten Mountain Man any more than I have.

We stick to the darkness between the floodlights, keeping our footsteps light, and though we never discuss it, we both head to the back of the trailer rather than the front door.

The living room and kitchen lights still glow from behind the blinds, creating a striped picture window against the darkness. Chrystal sits slumped in her recliner, her jaw slack, her glass centered in a dark pool of vodka.

Dead.

I squeeze my eyes shut, but it does nothing to block out the image of Chrystal in that chair. It just makes it easier for me to envision my body lying across from hers.

A screech of plastic pulls me back to reality and sets dogs

barking in the nearby yards — and Jake points to Chrystal's now-open window.

Her blinds sway, and I find my voice. "What are you doing?"

He pauses. "The glass you used is still sitting on the table."

We stare, neither of us willing to vocalize what we're deciding in this moment. If I crawl through Chrystal's window and destroy any evidence I was there, it's stepping over a line we can't cross back. It means leaving her body until someone else reports her missing. But maybe there's mercy in that, because justice for Chrystal probably won't come any faster than it has for her niece.

I press myself against the trailer, letting the cold burrow through my clothes and into my skin. "I'll go."

"No."

"I wasn't asking your permission. I've already been in there. If anyone bothers to look, my DNA is probably everywhere, not just on that glass." I poke him in the chest. "It makes no sense for you to risk it. Now help me up."

He grabs my hips and shoves me upward. My face collides with the blinds, and the ridges of the window bite into my palm when I lock my elbow in place and swing my legs up after me. I slither to the floor, blinds trailing over my skin.

A light flicks on outside and I freeze.

Someone in the trailer next to Chrystal's moves from behind their newly illuminated window, and I try not to breathe. Not that I want to anyway — there's something vaguely sweet and cloying that clings to the back of my throat, mixed with the hint of rot and decay.

From Chrystal's body.

If whoever's out there sees the open window, they'll ask questions — unless maybe the stars are aligned and Mercury is in retrograde or whatever the fuck means good things and Chrystal likes to open her window when it's four degrees above freezing.

Moving so slowly my muscles creak, I stretch and press my palms to the bottom of the blinds, pulling them taut, making sure my body stays out of the window.

My hearing numbs, waiting for anything to break the silence — a door opening, a window rising, a shout. The presence of Chrystal's lifeless body grows stronger until I'm afraid if I don't move or breathe soon, I'm going to scream.

The light in the other trailer flicks off and I let out a shuddering breath.

Clinging to the walls as much as possible, I slide, one panel at a time, until I could look at Chrystal full-on if I wanted to.

I don't.

I drop to my knees and shuffle toward the coffee table, the stale scent of cigarettes coating my tongue. The glass sits quietly, a watermark stretching from its base, ice cubes long-since melted.

My death is in that glass.

If I'd taken even one more sip, or if Jake hadn't come …

My breath catches, that vision of Chrystal staring at me over her glass, but I can't see her *drinking* it. And I can't figure out why, if she did, she didn't pass out.

A knock rattles through the room — not loud enough for a neighbor — more like Jake reminding me to get my ass moving.

I keep the glass steady as I grab the kitchen towel draped limply over the oven door so I can open the drawers without leaving fingerprints.

The drawers scrape open, one of them slipping from its tracks and tilting dangerously. I'm on the sixth one before I find the Ziplocs.

It's not like I know people who can run forensics tests for drugs, but that doesn't mean I can't find them.

I yank open the first bag and the seam rips straight down the side. Same with the second. I'm seconds from vowing to buy her name-brand Ziplocs to replace her shitty dollar store ones and tucking them inside an umbrella, and then I remember she's dead.

I drop the glass into the bag I haven't ruined.

Four steps into the living room, the bag busts open.

I can't control the curse that jumps from my lips.

If it's a poison that gets absorbed through the skin, I could be dead before Jake knows to find me.

My footsteps echo through the hollow floor, and I jam on the faucet and scrub my hands clean before covering them with two more bags.

They fog and crinkle as I press a rag into the matted carpet. There's no cleaning it. The best I can hope for is that the stain won't be completely obvious.

Crisp air gusts into the room and the blinds rattle, and Jake's hand appears through the open window, long fingers beckoning frantically.

I clutch everything to my chest — the not-Ziplocs, the rag, and the sip of alcohol and poison still trapped in the glass. Then

I grab a thick stack of the missing person flyers Chrystal made for her niece.

I shoulder the blinds aside and shove everything but the glass into his hands. That, I hold right side up, showing him how to handle it so we don't lose what little evidence I've managed to save.

His mouth drops open and his hands twitch like he wants to drop it all at his feet. He mumbles, "We're going to jail."

I jump free, soggy grass squishing beneath my shoes, and take the evidence back from Jake. "Wipe the window."

He tugs his sleeve over the heel of his hand and wipes down the window frame, then glances down at me. "Run on three."

The screech of the window isn't as loud coming down, but it still sets the light in the trailer behind us flaring to life again.

Jake's arm presses into mine, hot and tense, as we plaster ourselves against the side of the trailer. My muscles twitch with the need to run, but we've got nothing but wide-open space yawning in front of us.

A door crashes open and I'm shaking so hard my teeth chatter.

A beam of light sweeps over the rocky ground and circles up to join the stars before settling back, and then it clicks off and there's only the shush of wind through the trees.

I slide sideways, Jake following my every step, and a deep voice from around the corner calls out Chrystal's name.

Not a voice I recognize. Not a voice that reminds me of shot-guns pressed into Jake's temple.

Jake flinches anyway and grabs my arm.

There's a quiet ratchet and strike of metal, and Jake whispers, "Revolver," like that's supposed to mean something to me.

Like it'll only take off my arm instead of blowing a hole through my torso?

I pull the bag tight over the lip of the glass and crouch low, streaking across the front of Chrystal's trailer and into the woods beyond.

For once, I'm grateful for the wet leaves tickling my bare ankles, because at least they muffle our footsteps.

I throw myself against a tree trunk, and the bark gouges skin that's already cut and broken from a tattoo artist's needle.

The flashlight beam cuts the darkness again, but it's slow and lazy this time, and the man lumbers up Chrystal's front steps.

I refuse to watch, even though I should. If he finds Chrystal and calls the cops, they could trace every connection back to me.

I nudge Jake forward, through the woods that remind us both of things we'd rather not remember. Because even the memories that haunt my dreams are better than what's waiting for me here.

CHAPTER TWELVE

One of us is going to have to speak.

We left the trailer park and headed nowhere, the car silent.
Then Jake killed the lights when he parked along the road, his
truck lilting where the ground slopes toward a drainage ditch.

Heat blasts from the vents and his phone is a beacon in the
dark, flaring bright every time he checks it — for what, I'm not
sure.

If there's a reason we're sitting here, he's not sharing.

My thighs stick to the leather seat as I fidget and flip open
my bag. I changed out the flavor of my e-cig so Jake wouldn't
have to smoke any more cupcakes.

But then, I made my promise to Aubrey.

The vape lies against my palm, like Madison's lipstick did
yesterday, back when Chrystal was still alive.

The first hit drops into my throat and floats through me,
kicking up my heart rate only to calm it. It's the only way I
find the courage to form words. "I need to tell Marcel about
Chrystal."

He holds out his hand until I drop the vape into it. He takes
a long drag and says, "Mint?"

When I don't respond because what we *need* to discuss is
what we just saw — what we just *did* — he says, "It's good."

"Jake."

"Yeah?"

"I said I need —"

"I heard." He says it like an answer. Like he's giving a verdict.

"You can drop me off if —"

"I didn't kill Madison." His jaw locks, shoulders bunched beneath his jacket. "I need you to know that."

"I do know." I say the words, and they sound so sure. *He followed me yesterday.*

"I didn't kidnap her either, and I don't know who did."

I don't think Jake kidnapped Madison. I *don't*. But protesting your innocence when no one's accused you feels like the defense of the guilty.

"I was a dick for blowing her off and maybe —" He tries twice before he can finish his sentence. "Maybe it got her killed. But I don't have anything to hide."

I get it now, what he's trying to say. I *understand* it too. The guilt over the things you should've done. The things you should've said. And how all those failures make you just as responsible as the real culprit.

And it makes me think he understood, even better than I realized, exactly why I cried myself to sleep in his arms that night on the St. Francis rooftop. Why it was always his voice I heard from the stands at all my games — and Madison's right behind.

It's *that* Jake I need right now — the one who was there when I needed him, without expectations.

He stabs the start button and the engine fires to life. The tires spin in the wet grass until we lurch forward, plunging into the stretch of quiet that swallows us whole.

We park in The Wayside's back lot, and when I use my key in the heavy steel door, a wave of unease worms beneath my skin.

All my movements feel shaky as I drift down the hallway.

People pass but I look without seeing.

Jake's presence looms behind me, his shadow draping over my skin.

When I raise my arm to knock on the worn wood of Marcel's door, I can't stop the tremble in my hand.

His deep voice bellows a "Come in," but I can't.

Last time he threw me out.

Willa's gone and her next letter is overdue. Madison is missing. Chrystal is dead and she took whatever she knew about Madison with her. Marcel is all that's left.

Every part of this version of me is disappearing, bit by bit, and the pieces that'll be left aren't any of the ones I want.

The door swings open and Marcel looks to me, then Jake, and wordlessly motions us inside.

I lean against his desk, the wood familiar and solid beneath my palms. I stare at my couch and let it tell me he hasn't forgotten me yet. "I need to talk to you."

"Caroline." His voice fills the small room, but I'm not listening.

He called me Caroline.

He never calls me by my real name, and somehow, it feels like all my fears come alive in those three syllables.

I speak, because if I do, he can't. "Chrystal's dead."

The room goes still, the door clicks shut, locking the voices outside in a different world.

"How?"

"I think someone drugged her."

He says nothing, but I know the look he's giving me. He won't settle for half an explanation.

"I went to ask her about her niece going missing, and I got drugged too."

Jake says, "I came to get her. I took care of her." He looks ready to say something else, but Marcel's glare cuts him off.

Jake's cheeks turn the kind of red that shows there's no precedent for adults feeling anything less than adoration for him, and I continue before I have to think about my monumentally bad decision to let him come in here with me. Again.

"We went back to see if she was okay, to ask her what she knew about Madison, and we found her. None of this makes sense, Marcel. Why would someone kill her? Why did someone kidnap her niece? She knew something about Madison. How? She couldn't have, unless this is all tied together. This can't be coincidence, can it?"

Mr. McCormack's hypothetical disappointment over my delivery hangs above me. *No one will believe your argument if you don't believe it yourself, Ms. Lawson. Are you defending your opinion or asking for your opponent's approval?*

"It's *not* a coincidence. I'm the only thing —"

"You need to leave."

I flinch, dizzy as all the blood drains from me. "I'm asking you for help. I came to you because —"

"I know why you came here, baby girl." He's in front of me, hands cradling my jaw, so big they block everything but his soft brown eyes. "I know why, but now you have to go. And you have to not come back, you understand? You need to leave this alone. Pretend you don't know what you know."

Maybe I'm just not a very good judge of character. "Pretend I don't *know*?"

His response barrels through the room, shrinking it. "You don't know a bit of what you've got yourself into. You want your face on those posters too?"

Jake launches forward. "I won't let that happen to her."

Marcel turns so slowly I brace for what he's about to say. "You won't let it?"

Jake says, "No, sir," and it's the wrong answer.

"She found a dead woman earlier, didn't she? How you doin' on protecting her so far, son?"

My voice comes out strained. "Please, Marcel. Please don't —"

His hand unfurls and he nods toward mine.

Because I'm holding my keys.

And my key ring holds one of his.

I'm too empty to move, the last vestiges of the person I was inside this room twirling away like the smoke from an extinguished flame.

His hand closes over mine, and the key falls from my fingers.

He says, "Go back to your real life. You don't belong here, Caroline."

THE WAYS TO LIVE

Hunger is a kind of homecoming.

An old friend. A worn-in pair of jeans.

Starvation isn't supposed to feel good.

But beyond the pangs that claw at your insides, beyond that place where your vision goes light, there's quiet. An empty, hollowed-out hush that grasps hands with the flush of victory. The thrill of survival. The knowledge that you've waged war against your own body and silenced its screams.

Sometimes there would be a Larry who'd make it his personal mission to fill the cupboards and the spaces between my ribs. I hated them the most.

I didn't understand it at the time. None of them did, either.

They'd come with crinkling bags lining their arms, smiling as they littered the peeling linoleum with an avalanche of food. Some would give their offerings silently, sliding boxes of crackers and cereal into empty cupboards, filling the fridge and freezer with milk, butter, sometimes ice cream. All while their gaze followed me from the corners of their eyes, like I was an animal, spooked and rabid.

In truth, I was.

But I reserved a special level of hate for the other Larrys, the ones who would make me acknowledge every box as they presented it to me.

They'd start small. Eggs. Bread. Noodles. Milk. Things they thought no kid would appreciate. Then they'd graduate to the cookies. *The ones all them kids seem to like so much.* Ice cream. Chips.

They didn't know what I knew. That bread transformed into an entirely different food when pressed into a ball to be nibbled on. That a noodle could take an hour to dissolve on your tongue if left untouched.

Ice cream couldn't be hidden anywhere in your room.

But all of that food, any of it — even the crinkle of plastic bag — would bring those gut-twisting hunger pains back, climbing from my stomach until I had to squeeze my arms over my middle just to stay standing.

But the hunger wouldn't last and neither would they, and once they were gone, the fridge would be just as blank as it was before they appeared in our kitchen, presenting their gifts like they weren't a call to battle against my own body and mind.

It wasn't their fault they didn't understand, that they got angry and yelled, called me an ungrateful little shit. I didn't even blame the Larry that packed everything back up when I refused to move from my station on the floor.

There was one Larry, though, who wasn't a Larry at all. He was a Gerald. The only Gerald.

I'd wake to crackers secreted beneath my blankets, warm cheeses tucked into far corners of my drawers and nestled against my stolen ketchup packets. Then one morning, the creamy, soft scent of scrambling eggs slithered beneath my doorway, and the sweetness of syrup sprang water to my mouth.

It took me forty-five minutes to open my door. Another

fifteen to travel the length of the hallway, linoleum cold against my bare feet.

He never mentioned the food. Just left it there on the table, plumes of steam swirling above the plate. It only occurred to me later, much later, how many batches of eggs and pancakes he must've cooked that morning.

He stayed longer than any of the Larrys, stuffing the trailer with memories of a different kind of quiet. The kind that comes with long nights of contented and sated sleep, the calmness of continuity.

He stayed longer than he should have: Through one of Mom's downturns as she took advantage of the freedom from the burden of my care. Through the yelling that barreled past the barrier of my thin pillow. Through the broken plates that gouged walls and then the floors where they came to rest.

Even after Mom had taken in another Larry, I came home to a letter from school and a district account filled with enough money for breakfast and lunch for the year. I buried the letter and its tear-smeared ink alongside the expired ketchup packets in my drawer.

We moved that summer. There was never another Gerald. But there was a stronger me. A more resistant one. There were times I slipped back into the comfort of hunger, but not like before. Never like before.

I remember every minute I spent in my room that morning when he first cooked me breakfast, the rage of needs that conflicted with emotion. More than anything, there was fear, a soul-deep terror that when he left, I'd never find my way back to loving that empty place again, even when it was all I had.

That's what loving Livie feels like — like when I finally

stopped being too scared to open the door and walk those cold, lonely steps toward happiness.

Once she entered my life there was no returning to the weaker version of me, even if she left.

She'd show up at the restaurant and request my section when it was slow, or sit at the carry-out counter stools when it wasn't so she wouldn't tie up one of my tables and cost me tips.

I never told her how she cost me tips anyway, when I'd catch myself watching her. She'd sit in her booth, an anchor in a rainbow sea of textbooks and highlighters, and she'd go to another place. The smallest crease would form between her eyebrows, her teeth puncturing the soft cushion of her bottom lip, her hair deep black now that the auburn had faded.

She transformed me into a study in awe and envy. I'd spent so many years surviving, I'd forgotten to dream.

Livie hadn't forgotten. She planned to be the first person in her family to go to college. She planned to *live*.

After three weeks of visits, three weeks when the crux of my night rested on the thirty-minute window when she'd either bound through the door or leave me with the pangs of hunger, we ended one night on her front porch with the moon draped low in the starry sky.

She brushed away a mosquito that flitted near her calf. "So what schools are you considering?"

I paused, plastic cup halfway to my lips, the tartness and heat of vodka and cranberries flavoring the air, and blinked away the tears that rushed to my eyes. "I'm just trying to make it through high school."

"Hmm." Livie stretched out her legs and leaned back on her

elbows, chin tipped toward the open sky where she saw each of the stars like a new possibility. "Not good enough."

A violent heat rushed over my skin. "Excuse me?"

Her eyes met mine, not the least bit sorry. "You're smart. And don't say you're not, because I've seen your tests when we do homework and I read that paper you wrote about modern slavery — don't get mad, you left it out where I could see it. Anyway, it was good. And you didn't leave me alone in that parking lot. Do you know how many people did?"

I shook my head because speech was still beyond my reach. My soul was tangled in her expectations of me. Save for a few teachers who I assumed were paid to say nice things, no one had ever given me a standard to rise over.

No one had ever let me believe in the version of me I hoped to be. Livie didn't believe I *could be* that person — she believed I already was.

My sobs broke through, settling only when Livie's arms and legs wrapped around me, her cheek pressed to the top of my head.

Her fingers stroked my bare arms, long, calming brushes followed by the faintest skims of her fingertips. "You don't want to go to college?"

I fumbled through a response that ended with the root of all my evils — money.

I felt her nod against my hair. "What you need is a plan."

And then she was gone, the front door slamming shut behind her, until she bounded back through it, laptop held high.

We spent the night with grants and government loans, financial aid forms and student housing. We researched schools on her shitty laptop that kept dropping the stolen Wi-Fi connection.

We ended the night with promises of another session tomorrow, armed with the research Livie had already done for herself, and my confidence still unshaken.

We ended the night with a plan, and I went to bed with hope.

One of my mosquito bites from that night scarred, leaving behind those memories in a perfect, faint circle just below my ankle. I prayed it would never fade.

But hunger and fullness, love and loss, like all things, like everything, they come to an end.

CHAPTER THIRTEEN

It's late when I get home. So late I refuse to look at the clock as I ease my car into the garage.

I'm not sure I care anyway. I walked away from the last thing that matters when I set foot onto gravel in The Wayside parking lot.

You don't belong here, Caroline.

I don't belong anywhere. The person I really am is buried beneath layers of pretense, and the only person who's ever known the truest parts of me — the only parts that matter — decided they weren't enough to stay for.

I'm a fraud and a stranger in this home that doesn't feel like mine and the parents who need me to be something I'm not.

I considered bringing Jake home with me just so my mom could watch him wave goodbye from the driveway. I could practically *see* how she'd sigh in relief, the tension at the corners of her eyes drifting away. She's never brought up the conversion therapy she sent me to. Not once. It could be she feels guilty, that she wishes it hadn't come to that.

I'm trying to help you, Caroline. That's the explanation that rings in my head every time I try to understand what she did. *You're making your life so much harder. Not everyone will understand. You'll be ostracized. You'll never know what it's like to be a mother.*

I didn't state the obvious counterarguments to that last one, because all her words blurred together in a mess that felt like a door slamming closed.

She's never settled for anything less than perfect: the drapes that had to be remade when they were a sixteenth of an inch too long, the custom-made chair that felt too firm, the smudge in the lacquer of her special-order dining table. And every time, Dad would tell her it was fine, to just let it go. *Free your mind, Violet.* And then her face would shade to crimson as she said, "We *paid* for this, Kyle."

She paid for me too. Her miracle baby. The one all the doctors told her she'd never have. And I swear all that time she spent waiting and hoping only elevated her expectations. Now there's this part of me that's smudged, and she can't send me back to be remade.

Maybe some part of her does feel guilty, but it rings empty against the truth — that she's happy it "worked." At least as she sees it. She gets to keep her social standing at St. Francis without worrying if people "understand." She won't have to *explain* me to her mother — not that you can explain anything to Grandma Caldecott. She's too rich and too old to give a shit about changing any of her ways — she still hasn't forgiven Mom for marrying Dad. That, however, works in my favor, because Grandma C has a regular habit of writing me checks without Mom's knowledge, just because *that father of yours is certainly not going to provide for you.*

Grandma wouldn't be any happier than Mom if she knew her cash gave me enough freedom to make my relationship with Willa a reality. But until I can get out of here, until I don't need any of them, I'll work with whatever resources I've got.

Denying Mom that moment of reprieve tonight — that flash

of relief at seeing me with Jake — almost makes up for the excuses I'm going to have to invent to explain where I've been.

He hinted I could stay with him again tonight, which I pretended not to understand, because my short answer is no and I don't feel like giving him my reasons. I don't feel like navigating the unspoken questions that come with spending two straight nights in someone else's bed.

Anyway, two nights away from home would just mean twice the questions and twice the number of lies to keep straight. And I don't know whether it's drugs lingering in my system, Marcel's voice like a constant presence in my head or the gaping absence of Madison, but my brain is still too fuzzy.

The garage door rumbles open, shadows swallowing my car as I ease it into the bay. I cut the engine and wait, conjuring the right mood and expression that I don't check the mirror to see if I've managed.

I tiptoe through the other bays with my palm hovering inches above the car hoods, but they're all cold and unresponsive, keeping their secrets about whether Mom or Dad might be just coming home and awake, or if they're both in bed, pretending to sleep.

I don't bother with quiet once I'm in the house, toeing off my shoes in the mudroom and slipping my coat into the closet. I hoist my backpack higher, and smother the panic that comes with the thought of how far behind I am on classwork. How close I am to getting expelled. How close I am to losing everything and spending my life imprisoned behind these walls.

I'm past the formal living room before the light spilling from the kitchen brings hushed voices, and my steps slow until they stop.

Someone says my name and I don't need to turn to know who it is. I know I'll see Detective Brisbane's lumpy body marring the view of Dad's baby grand piano in the bay window. And where Brisbane is, Harper is sure to be too.

Before I can charge back to my car and beg Jake to let me stay the night, both my parents appear in the kitchen entryway.

People always talk about a fight-or-flight response in a way that shames the person who chooses to flee. Sometimes, they're the smartest one of the bunch.

"Caroline, don't." Mom pins me in place and both our jaws set, because we're a mirror image.

"Don't what?" We both know what. I also know she won't say it because it leaves me the opportunity to deny I was ever thinking it. I leave my tone light, though. Mom won't do with being embarrassed, especially not in front of detectives. Or Dad.

Detective Brisbane says, "Caroline, I'm not sure if you remember me."

I turn slowly because I need the extra seconds to gather the shards of my temper and dull the edges.

He is going to ruin everything for me. I have worked for years to build this house of cards I'm standing in — creating the perfect persona for each parent so I can make it to graduation, and then college, before they have a chance to decide I can't be trusted. With everything else gone, this is my only path to freedom, and this asshole just busted into the middle of it.

My jaw aches when I unclench it enough to speak. "I don't

get interrogated by the police without parental supervision or legal counsel often, Detective, so yes, I remember you."

Mom's shoulders are probably to her ears, a vein bulging from the left side of her forehead. Dad is probably covering his mouth with his hand, eyes teeming with parental concern.

He's my best bet, I think. The best ally I'm going to get, even though I'd give him up if it meant doing this with only one parent present. So as much as I want to be the defensive and uncooperative Caroline the detectives met yesterday, I can't let her fully loose. If I could make myself cry I'd have Dad throwing them out before I could get past my second sniffle, but that's a solid no-go.

Brisbane's arm stretches toward the living room. "We'd just like to talk to you for a minute."

I follow, hugging my backpack straps across my chest like armor. Mentioning we talked already was stupid. I didn't tell Mom or Dad, and now they're wondering what else I haven't told them, which is everything.

Brisbane tugs at his pant legs and lowers into the couch, his outstretched arm telling me I should do the same.

I shake my head and dig my heels into the plush carpet. Beads of sweat form along my spine as fury snakes its way through my system. He's in *my* house, ruining *my* life, and I'm in fucking socks while he gets to keep his scuffed shoes on.

The grandfather clock breaks into its song, each note an extra second for me to decide how I'm going to play to a crowd where everyone expects me to be someone different.

I wince as it hits its eleventh bong.

Brisbane nods toward Detective Harper, who refuses to sit and who is also wearing shoes. Harper is the "good cop" so he smiles politely, and I want to punch the expression from his face.

Since Dad is watching and I'm Vulnerable Caroline right now, I do my best to return a scared and overwhelmed smile. After what happened with Marcel, after what I saw at Chrystal's, it doesn't take much acting.

Brisbane fidgets on the couch and my spirits float just a little because I know he's regretting that he's the only one sitting, but he can't take it back now. He says, "I don't want to take much of your time, Caroline, especially when it's so late and you've got school in the morning."

Score one for Brisbane. A shot at my parents for their lax supervision, cloaked in the lie of concern.

When no one answers his nonexistent question, he continues, "Was there a problem that kept you out so late?"

"I was with a friend." The tremble in my voice is just enough to draw Dad a step closer. "I've been — it's scary, what happened to Madison. Anyway, I've been struggling with it."

I make sure to meet Mom's eyes with that last part. It's a dangerous game I'm playing here. A delicate navigation between parents and their secrets.

Mom's depression and her hidden stash of medication. The prescriptions she fills for me without Dad knowing.

For that, I need her.

Because the man who doesn't suffer any mental illnesses prescribing sunshine and enough kale to bury the house in is not actually a substitute for a medical professional.

But we've all given up on arguing. A family built on secrets and half-truths.

Good Cop Harper steps in. "I can assure you everyone is struggling with this case. Madison is a bright young woman and we are working very hard to make sure we bring her home safe."

Right. Everything except looking into the other bright young woman who isn't home safe, the one who may have been taken by the same person as Madison. I don't know which possibility is worse: that they haven't figured that out, or that they have and just don't care.

"Anyway, I'm really tired so —"

"Just a few questions." Brisbane again, and the house waits in hushed silence marred only by the grumble of the furnace beneath us. He's watching me, studying, drawing this out to see the level of damage his next words will cause.

I expect to hear that someone overheard my conversation with Aubrey, or they know what really happened with Mountain Man the night I found the lipstick. Or that someone tipped them off to my investigation. I brace myself to hear they know Chrystal is dead and they think I'm involved. I brace harder at the possibility they've found Madison's body.

The last thing I expect to hear is, "Can you tell me about your relationship with Landon McCormack?"

CHAPTER FOURTEEN

The unexpectedness of the question is enough to finish what my albatross of a backpack started and my knee buckles, tipping me backward.

Dad is there before I smack my skull against the end table, and when he slips the backpack past my fingertips, my shoulders weep with relief. But my little tumble has sent the wrong message to the entire room, and this time it's Mom's turn to blanket her mouth with her hand.

Her concern looks genuine for once, not a performance meant to show the version of us she wants strangers to believe in, and the part of me I thought I'd buried wants to run to her. Like I used to do. Before.

But tomorrow will still come and nothing will have changed, and I'll have to gather all my broken pieces and pretend their edges aren't capable of slicing me clean through.

I massage my shoulder. "Mr. McCormack is my teacher."

I can't call him Landon. It's too weird. Is that what his friends call him? Landon? Lan?

Brisbane's elbows spike into his knees. "Seems like you guys are close."

It's not a question, so I don't answer, even though words shove themselves up my throat. Ironically, it's a debate technique Mr. McCormack taught me.

When I stare mutely, Brisbane says, "What were you two talking about in the hallway after the vigil?"

"Nothing. You can ask Jake Monaghan if you don't believe *me*." Not that I want them to talk to Jake about Mr. McCormack, since he seems so willing to buy into all the rumors, but the suggestion feels like it strengthens my argument.

"What about in the quad?"

Goddamn Headmaster Havens. "My grade in his class." True enough.

"Is that so?"

"It's over a four-point." I say it because it's absolutely true, and with Headmaster Havens teaching the class now, it won't be for long.

Harper's voice is soft, soothing, meant for lullabies. "I want you to know, Caroline, that we're here to help you. If you tell me something, I *will* believe it."

My muscles tense to grab my laptop, first to use St. Francis's servers to prove my grades are legit, and then to hit Harper with it if he uses my name one more time. "You think I'm lying about my grades? Because I can —"

"No, no. Nothing like that, Caroline. We know you're an excellent student, and that's why it wouldn't be surprising if Mr. McCormack took a special interest in you. If he cultivated a relationship with you that might leave you vulnerable to his influence."

The air around Dad charges, his entire body bristling. "What the hell are you trying to say?"

Dad doesn't swear. He's all peace and love and vegan diet because animals are people too. My gaze bounces between him and Mom, whose eyes are glazed with tears.

I get it then, what the detectives are really saying: Not just that my scores in Mr. McCormack's class are biased because he calls on me all the time. That I'm his favorite. I've been fielding those complaints from other students for years.

He's not even saying that Mr. McCormack seduced me and I'm willingly screwing my teacher for my grade or some other reason.

What he *is* suggesting is ludicrous: that Mr. McCormack is *forcing* me, and I'm too stupid to realize it.

Instead of being indignant like a normal person, I laugh.

Mom looks horrified. Dad rubs my back in stuttering strokes, like he doesn't know if he should be comforting me or holding my wrists for the cops to bind for my own protection.

I step forward so everyone can see I'm capable of standing all on my own, even in my socks. "Mr. McCormack is not molesting me. He's never forced me to do anything against my will. And I have one, you know. Also, a brain."

Harper alternates between Mom and Dad, concerned puppy-dog eyes driving home every word. The Nice Guy who will say all the right things and do all the wrong ones. "Landon McCormack is a bit of a legend with the girls at Caroline's school. There's a fair bit of hero worship and vying for his attention. Meetings, emails, texts. It's likely they'd consider themselves consenting participants —"

"No." I bite out the word so hard spit springs from my mouth.

They're not hearing me, not even seeing me. I'm standing right here, telling them they're wrong, and my words mean nothing.

If Mom weren't here I'd point out that if I were going to bang one of my teachers, I'd be about 70 percent more likely to go with Mrs. Carter. "Mr. McCormack has never —"

"He's never said anything of a sexual nature to you?" Brisbane takes over the questioning, not trying for concerned or gentle.

"No."

"He's never looked at you sexually?"

"No." That's a half-lie. Half, because he didn't know it was me dancing with Willa that night. Until the moment, still breathless from the feel of Willa's hands, the taste of her tongue, that I turned to see who we'd been entertaining.

"Have you ever met with him outside of school?"

"No."

"Ever been in his car?"

"Jesus! No."

"Caroline!" Both parents stare at me, their eyes wide. Like they know it's a full lie.

I don't know how to interpret any of it. Not the look of horror on their faces or the way it feels like I'm hydroplaning through this interrogation and I want — *need* — something to grab on to.

But there *is* nothing. Just me, free-falling off this ledge, too late to notice the jagged rocks at the bottom.

Sometimes, flight really is the best response.

I wheel on Brisbane. "Madison is *missing*. And you're here asking pointless questions. And she's not even —"

I suck in a breath and stare at the puzzle of light the chandelier blasts onto the ceiling, pretending to blink away tears that aren't there to cover that I almost revealed I know there's another missing girl.

Another girl that *someone* should be looking for, and now that Chrystal's gone, there *is* no one. No one but me.

There's no way to admit I know about Sydney that doesn't end with me locked in my room and my parents researching homeschool teachers. Maybe they'll find a camp that'll promise to reconfigure my brain so I never want to leave.

There's no way of explaining how I know about Sydney without explaining the matchbook in my locker, The Wayside, or Chrystal.

Chrystal, who's lying dead in her recliner right now. The people in this room are the last ones to whom I should be admitting a connection to Chrystal.

I drag my gaze back to Brisbane's. "Mr. McCormack has never done anything to me. He is my teacher. One of the best I've ever had. That's it."

He rises from the couch, slow and steady like he's pulling himself from some shitty lawn chair on the way to the cooler for another beer. The carpet muffles his footsteps and the world shifts to slow-motion as his hand slips into the inside pocket of his sports coat.

He stops in front of me, and his voice dips low enough it feels conspiratorial even though everyone can hear. "You're just a kid, so there's a lot of things going on that you don't understand. But if you're telling me Landon McCormack has never made any passes at you, never taken you anywhere, never done anything but normal student-teacher stuff, then I have to say, I don't believe you, Caroline."

I wait. For the next tick of the clock, the next muffled sob from behind Brisbane's back. I wait for whatever's on the folded square of paper Brisbane pulled from his pocket.

He flips it over, calloused fingers grazing the sharp edge of the paper. "If what you say is true, then I can't for the life of me figure out how he would've come to have this."

And then I'm staring at a color photocopy of the fake license Mr. McCormack took from me that night at The Wayside.

CHAPTER FIFTEEN

I'm stupidly convinced if I keep moving, everything that just happened can't catch up with me.

Except it's not *me* my words are going to convict, it's Mr. McCormack.

I should've seen Brisbane coming. Harper too. Should've known they weren't sitting in my living room at eleven o'clock at night because they thought Mr. McCormack and I were standing too close that day in the quad.

But then Brisbane hit me with that bullshit with my license. I managed to squeak out an explanation: that Mr. McCormack caught me with it at school, except Brisbane trampled all over that with, "Why would your teacher have your fake license in his apartment, Caroline?"

I should've shrugged. A casual "How the hell should I know?" But I couldn't think past the knowledge that Mr. McCormack took my license home — that once again, he's in trouble because of me — and beyond that, the cops had searched his apartment.

I might've done an awful job of lying, but I don't know that the truth would've helped. I doubt Mr. McCormack would be any better off if I'd marched into the room and told everyone he watched my girlfriend fondle me in a bar we weren't legally allowed to be in.

Plus, Marcel would be in more trouble than he's already in,

and I would destroy the careful construction I need Mom to believe in until three days after graduation.

But the most terrifying part of all of this is that I was right. The cops think Mr. McCormack took Madison. And they're so busy building that case they're not looking at other possibilities. They're not looking for Madison's real kidnapper.

And that means if Madison is going to come home alive, I'm the one who has to find her.

I don't expect to find her here — outside Aubrey's dorm room — but I need to sleep. Preferably someplace other than my car.

Crickets chirp from their hiding spots, nestled deep into grass that's only begun to emerge from the frost. The Xanax I took when I was far enough from home to pull over and rummage through the corners of my bag is still bitter on my tongue.

The crew of news vans barely registered as I passed them, throwing an extra twenty bucks to my favorite security guard, who sometimes "doesn't notice" when I come and go at the wrong hours.

My body is liquid silk as I conquer the sidewalk to the safety of Aubrey's dorm, where maybe she'll let me crash.

I scan the Administrator ID I swiped from Headmaster Havens's desk when Mrs. Elvan used his office for her "I'm worried about you, Caroline" meeting. My heart rate barely accelerates even though it's possible — but not likely given the chaos of Havens's office — he discovered it was missing and disabled it.

The light turns green and the lock thunks over, buzzing until I yank open the door and slip through. The dorms are quiet. No one's allowed to be up this late. Not even the students with late light permissions.

I hug the wall, scanning for movement or a flash of light. If I run into a dorm head or dorm parent, there is no way to talk my way out of suspension. The number of demerits I'm earning right now might fast-track me to expulsion.

No student shall enter housing in which they do not reside without permission from a resident faculty member or Dean of Students.

No student may cross campus alone after dark.

No student shall leave their room after lights out.

No student shall "borrow" Admin ID badges that grant them access to campus buildings for the purposes of hiding from police and parents after wordlessly storming from their home despite four separate voices yelling said student's name.

I console myself with the knowledge that at least tonight I'm not breaking the *Students may not enter dormitory halls of the opposite sex* rule.

I have done one hell of a job of bookending this day.

My skin prickles the entire stretch of the common room, where the furniture sits cloaked in shadows, and triangles of light from the wall of windows dissect the empty space.

It's the type of silence that feels like a sound. The communal breathing of a hundred students snuggled beneath warm blankets and the gentle glow of night-lights.

I don't dare use the elevator, so I slink up each step, and at the third floor I have to pause to rest my head against the cool metal railing. It's not just the Xanax. It's *everything.*

This isn't fair to Aubrey — showing up on her doorstep. But she and Jake are the only ones who know even a hint of what's going on, and everyone will be ravenous for rumors about Mr. McCormack. The least I can do is limit the people I infect with my knowledge.

I ease down the hallway on the fourth floor and smother a yawn with my hand while the gentle swirls of jewel-toned wallpaper float by.

My phone buzzes in my pocket, and when I steal a glance, my dad's name lights the screen. I decline it.

Aubrey's room is tucked into a corner — no neighbors on the left side. It's a prime spot her highly respected surgeon of a mom secured for her two years before she was even eligible to live on this floor. Right now I wouldn't care if Aubrey's mom had to kick a penguin to get her this room. I'm just grateful there's one fewer potential witness for when I try to wake Aubrey up.

I puddle onto the floor and press my cheek to the musty carpet that tickles my nose. My lips brush over the base of the door when I whisper her name.

I'm risking lip splinters, but options are limited.

I try again and fabric rustles, then a creak of mattress.

Another whisper brings her to the door, then blue-painted toes press into the tile that peeks through the crack at the floor.

I whisper, "Down here!"

Warm breath snakes beneath the door as she says, "What are you doing?" in a way that makes each word seem like its own sentence.

"Waiting for you to open the door."

"Oh." The lock clicks over and a rush of vanilla air blasts over me. Aubrey grabs the handle on my backpack and hauls me upright before shoving me into the room.

She taps one tiny foot against the floor. "I know you're 'too cool for the dorms' and all, but do you know how much trouble I could get in for this?"

"Yes, and I'm sorry." I'm not too cool for the dorms. I got yanked out of them the second I told my mom I was bi. No Special Senior privileges for me.

I let my backpack sink into her pink shag rug and kick off my tennis shoes. I can't wear tennis shoes to school and I can't wear my ripped-up jeans either, and all my clean uniforms are at home where I can't return. Not that it matters — I can't go to school either. Brisbane and Harper will probably be waiting at every one of my classes, and climbing out the windows only works if you're on the ground floor.

My phone vibrates again — voice mail this time — and I scan the transcription for key words. Dad is "concerned for my well-being" and hopes that "some time away will help me re-center and find my balance." There's mention of the importance of eating and sleeping well, but I have all the info I need: They're not calling out the search parties for me. For now.

Really, they're just pretending it's unusual for me to be gone. That I haven't been telling them I'm sleeping over at friends' houses for years. Because we're studying late. Because the commute is just too long some days. Because of any reason they'll accept, honestly. But at least this way, if the cops look into it, it'll look like they care.

I drop into Aubrey's couch and my body goes limp. "How much do you want to know?"

Her messy bun flops to the side and she lowers onto the couch next to me, legs twisting crisscross applesauce. "Will I go to jail if I know?"

"What? No. I don't think so." I'm too tired to think right. "I've done some stuff that may be illegal. You know what? Never mind."

Aubrey's eyes go so wide the deep brown is completely rimmed in white, and then she smacks her hands on her knees before jumping back up. "Not okay, Caroline."

She's wearing a T-shirt — and no bra, which I force my gaze to skim past — with a fuzzy alpaca that says, "Save the drama for your llama," and pink gingham pants that gather in rumpled layers where another several inches of height should be. Her lips are pursed, hands on her hips, totally pissed off and yet utterly adorable.

She points her finger at me, but her lips are already twitching into a curve. "Don't you smile at me. I am *mad*."

I raise my brows because if I try to talk, I'm going to laugh, and she lets out an exasperated sigh. "You look like hell. I'm guessing you need a place to sleep, so you can stay here, but dorm check is early. Like, seven thirty, so we have to sneak you out before then."

"Thanks, Aubrey." I'm not smiling anymore because I'm too busy rubbing my eyes against the tears that won't fall.

"Caroline?" Her voice breaks and trembles. "Did something happen? With Madison?"

I meet her eyes and they tell me what she's really asking. *Is Madison dead? Did they find her body?* "Nothing like that. But she's still missing, and I'm the only one who can find her."

"That's ridiculous. It's not healthy to put that kind of pressure —"

"It's not ridiculous. It's the truth." I want to tell her why. Lay out my arguments so she'll understand. Or maybe, so she'll tell me I'm wrong. But this isn't Aubrey's burden to carry. "Let me think about it while you're at school tomorrow, and I'll figure out what's okay for you to know."

"While *I'm* at school tomorrow?"

I wish I had stupider people surrounding me. "The cops were at my house tonight and I left without answering their questions."

Her jaw unhinges in a display of shock I suspect she normally reserves for the stage.

She sucks in a breath to unleash a barrage of questions but I hold up my hand. "Tomorrow."

I've got one shoulder sunk into her couch, my head inches from glorious sleep, when a jasmine-scented pillow smacks my face.

She peels it back and tosses it onto the bed. "Don't be stupid. You're too tall to sleep on a love seat, and it's a full-size bed, so you don't even have to touch me. But I don't know where those clothes have been so take them off."

She giggles at the way my jaw drops and yanks a pair of pajamas from her drawer. "They'll probably fit you better than me anyway."

I barely manage another thank-you and she climbs into bed and turns toward the wall so I can change where I'm standing.

When I slip in next to her, the hollow between the mattress and comforter is still warm from her sleeping body, and softness snuggles around me and fills all the empty places.

The bed shifts as she turns, her eyes dark in the barely there light. "Where'd you go this year, Caroline?"

"I've been here." It's a weak protest, because she's more right than I am.

"I know, but … you were gone a lot too. You'd come to practice and games but never anything after and — you didn't see our fall show."

The way her voice thickens is all the proof I need that me missing her show is what she's really talking about, and the weight of it crushes against my chest. I can't even puzzle out how she remembers I wasn't there. "I was dating someone."

"Oh."

It's not an understanding "Oh," it's a judgmental one. "I just didn't take you for the type that ditches her friends when she gets a … girlfriend? Boyfriend?"

I roll my eyes. "Girlfriend. And I didn't just *ditch my friends*. And she wasn't just some random girl."

"Was it …" she whispers, "Tabitha?"

"Seriously? No."

"Well, you said earlier —"

"That I randomly hooked up with her, not that we were *dating*. Have you ever known Tabitha to date *anyone*?"

"You mean aside from the yearbook?"

My snicker morphs into a snort, and then Aubrey's laughing so hard the bed shakes. "See? Tabitha doesn't need me. She's already found true love."

"So, not Tabitha."

"Definitely not Tabitha."

"So this mystery girl … the love of your life at seventeen?" Her voice barely drifts across the chasm between our pillows.

My laughter fades and my legs draw closer to my chest at the dismissiveness in her tone. In spite of the Xanax, my voice is sharper than she deserves. "She's the only reason I'm alive. Is that good enough for you?"

She's the only thing that proved there was goodness even in the face of everything ugly. She taught me how to survive without losing the best parts of myself.

Ironic that those lessons were the thing I clung to most when she walked away.

It takes a second, while Aubrey raises and dismisses my possible meanings, finally settling on the right one. With Aubrey, every thought telegraphs. "Oh, Caroline."

"Don't. Oh Jesus, don't cry." When she smooshes her face into the pillow to wipe away her tears, I say, "It was a bad time in my life, but I'm good now, or at least much better. Really."

She plucks at the end of a rogue thread in the comforter, twirling it around fingernails she's somehow painted with little tragedy and comedy faces. "You guys broke up? That's why you've been sad?"

I roll onto my back and hug the covers to my chin, my eyes skipping across the glow-in-the-dark solar system on the ceiling. "She left me."

I add, "She said she wished I could come with her," a little too fast and a little too defensively, because actually what she said was that she wished I could come with her, if things were different. "But it's not like I could've left *high school*."

My reasoning was sound. It's still sound. Even if my instincts said what we had was worth it all.

But then she was gone and I was wrong about everything, and every letter from Willa puts her voice back in my head, draws out memories I thought I'd buried. Every private joke and shared secret I'm forced to see in her looped handwriting is an argument for why I chose wrong.

But then, she chose too.

"Caroline?" Even once I've turned to look at her, Aubrey hesitates. "I'm the one who told Mr. McCormack I was worried about you."

"I know."

"I'm glad you stayed. Not just in school, but … you know, *around*."

"Me too." I smile at her and she smiles back, twice as big, but as both our eyes fall shut and sleep drifts in like a slow fog, I'm not sure I'm glad at all.

CHAPTER SIXTEEN

I roll onto my back, cushioned by Aubrey's shag rug, and tap her glitter pen against my chin. Sunlight streams through her floral curtain, so glaring I have to squint while I scrounge my head for any facts I might be missing. The current list is already so terrible I'm not sure I can add any more. That it's scribbled in my notebook in purple glitter makes it worse, like I'm celebrating when there's not a damn thing on the page to celebrate.

The absolute clusterfuck I've gotten myself into is broken down in facts and sub-facts, plans and conclusions. Except all my plans are terrible and my conclusions are even worse.

The cops will be waiting for me at school, so I can't go back until Madison is found, which means I have four days until expulsion.

I need to talk to Mr. McCormack, but I have no idea how, and my plan to use Headmaster Havens's wife as messenger is likely to go horribly wrong.

At least two girls are missing, and if I'm going to find out the connection between them, I'm going to have to research them both. The plan for that is especially awful, and Aubrey will hate it even more than me.

Mountain Man is still out there, and I have questions for both him and Marcel, but I don't want to see either of them right now, for very different reasons.

All of this sums up to one very short conclusion: I'm screwed.

Voices rise and drop beyond the door. Laughter. Plans to meet later to go to the library to study, not to research missing girls. It's like there's another world on the other side of that door. I'm so desperate to belong to it my heart aches.

Three months. I am *three months* from being able to take what I've worked for and make it mine.

But even that barely registers, because even though I'm almost there, the finish line hasn't just moved, it's been lined with landmines that could destroy Mr. McCormack's career and cost at least two girls their lives.

If they still have them.

One of them is my best friend.

And I'm lying facedown on the fucking floor.

The pen launches from my hand and cracks against the door just as it swings open and a wide-eyed Aubrey fills the frame. She stares at me long enough for me to feel like a complete douchebag for throwing her pen and slumping around on her rug.

She slowly eases the door shut behind her, then lowers herself to my level. "Did we have a bad day?"

"Not funny."

"You're kind of throwing a temper tantrum."

So she's right, but that doesn't mean it's not justified. I rock back onto my butt and flip my notebook around so she can see it.

Her face goes dark before she finishes the first sentence. "You *cannot* let yourself get kicked out of school because you think you're the only one who can find Madison."

I shrug and snatch the notebook back before she can read the rest, giving her a stern glare when she nearly rips my page trying to grab it. "I have a favor to ask. *Two* favors."

"I don't like either of them."

"Very astute of you. I need to borrow your car. You can use mine if you need one but just know it comes with a possible police escort along with Roadside Assistance. Actually, I'm only assuming we have Roadside Assistance so don't count on that. Two, can —"

"What if I say no?"

"Then I'll ask Jake."

"Hmph." Her mouth twists into a frown. "Fine. You can take my car."

"You're a queen." I hold out my hand for her keys because now that she's agreed, I want to have them in hand before I move on to the next request.

I gather my gear as her silence grows.

My life fits into one bag. It holds my computer, my notebooks, meds, clothes, shoes and the money I withdrew from my bank account today — which is hopefully enough to do what I need to do. As of this morning, credit cards are not an option.

I woke up a different version of myself. A new Caroline that started like a fog, a formless impression of a thing, barely held together. But each item I chose from my bedroom today solidified me, gave me structure. And even though I fled my house through the back — just the same as I went in — I've never felt more like myself.

"Caroline?"

I wince at the tenderness in her voice because I am definitely not capable of fielding high-level emotions right now. "Yeah?"

"Did you, like, break into your house this morning?"

"Yep." Parked a half-mile away, snuck through the neighbor's yard, climbed the back trellis and everything.

"Oh. Well. Are you planning on staying here —"

"I have a place I can go." I heave my duffel onto my shoulder and wince when it slams into my ribs.

"What do you mean you 'have a place' —"

"I need you to skip drama practice tonight."

She stumbles back two steps. Like I kicked her in the stomach rather than spoke words. "Skipping could cost me the lead."

I can't meet her eyes for more than a half-second, not when they're glazed over and her lip trembles beneath them. "You know what? Forget it."

"No. I —"

"Don't blow your senior year on this, Aubrey. It doesn't make sense for both of us to get kicked out." I squeeze by her before I'm tempted to ask for something else she can't give.

She says something my ears refuse to hear, but I'm halfway out the door, so I won't have to answer her. Instead I turn and give her my real smile before I run like hell toward the exit.

Not having Aubrey tonight will make things harder, but not impossible. And even the odds on impossible feel good when you've got nothing to lose.

FROM THE INSIDE

It's easy to forget there's a world beyond what you grew up in.

Maybe it's because of the slowness of youth. How days last weeks, summers an eternity of scabbed knees and dirt-covered feet, powered by the sun that becomes a dictator of the sky. But every year the world spins a little faster and seconds shave off each minute until eternities are mere moments we forgot to enjoy.

Those early years though, maybe they pass slower so we can build our view of the world. We creep through the passage of time so we can take in the details, constructing the size of our stage, our main characters, our antagonist. By the time we assume our role, the lights are down, the curtain set to be drawn. Once we're in the play, it's too late to change the stage.

So we don't.

My stage was any number of trailers in any number of West Virginia towns where the actors may have changed but the lines didn't.

I should've recognized it for what it was when the new character came into frame. But there's comfort in playing your part. In relying on the script life hands you.

I'd gone off script with Livie, from the moment we met and every one that came after.

Loving her meant rewriting the plot and destroying the stage. Fear cloaked in excitement and bathed in the hope for what came next, for the anticipation of a life lived rather than followed.

But it's a tenuous thing, burning the house to the ground

when you haven't made it out the doors. So the night John appeared in the restaurant parking lot after my shift, his gun bulging beneath his cheap suit coat, I clung to my role.

A layer of snow rested on the parking lot, making the ground slick and the glow of the restaurant lighting quiet. Cold nipped through my too-thin coat and snaked between the gaps at my wrists, but John stood solid in his long wool trench, even if the edges were worn and the top button chipped.

He smiled. The easy sort of smile born of practice in masking bad words behind a friendly face. "Hi there."

He may have introduced himself then, but no matter how hard I try to recapture those moments, I can't remember if he referred to himself as an officer, or just let me fill in the gaps. Instead, I leaned back on my heels, letting the bundles of cash in my shoes reassure me I hadn't forgotten to hide my tips. "Can I help you?"

"I'm more interested in helping you."

Any man offering help ain't doing it for nothin'. And you only got a couple things to offer. If there is anything the collective Larrys taught me, it's that altruism is a trap laid for the unsuspecting.

I stepped back, wobbling on the chunky rock salt, and out of the streetlamp's ring of light, but an inch closer to the diner door. "I don't need anything."

"That mom of yours does."

My exhale formed a billowing cloud of white against the clear night sky. My brain flipped to the list that never left my mind — I'd paid the water bill, and the rent, and the electric. I was a little late on the heat because the current Larry always cranked the thermostat when I wasn't there to monitor.

But utilities companies don't send bill collectors who wear wool coats and guns tucked beneath their suits.

I stared at the ground. "What are the charges?"

"None as of yet." He shoved back the sides of his coat as he tucked his hands into his pockets, seemingly impervious to the cold that left me shivering. "You know she got busted for possession a few weeks back?"

Tears burned in my eyes. I'd been holding my breath, so close to the final curtain call for this part of my life, and now there was this. "I didn't know."

"Yeah. The guy she was with — what's his name?"

"Larry?"

"Don't think so. Anyway, he took the rap for her weed since he was going down for the Vikes and Pins already." He paused. "Vicodin and Klonopin. You don't seem like the kind of girl who'd know those things."

I kept my face blank. Willed every muscle into relaxed indifference.

I was the kind of girl who helped count and seal those kinds of things in tiny baggies when I was too young to know better. I was the kind of girl who watched every drug imaginable cross my living room coffee table at some point or another. If I looked closely, I could still make out the worn spots in the wood where one of the Larrys kept his scale.

And I was the kind of girl who cried the first time I lied to the cops who came to the front door asking questions about what sorts of things happened on that coffee table. The first time, and every one that came after.

I gripped my coat tighter and hugged myself against the razor-sharp chill. "If the Larry took the charges, I don't see what you can do for me, or my mom."

He held up a finger and slipped something from his inside pocket with his free hand.

That's the other thing people on the outside can't see. Finding a new stage means leaving your cast members behind. They may not be much, but they were there for you, weren't they? They understood when others couldn't. With them, you aren't a fraud trying to fit into a world that will always be foreign. And those people on the outside, the ones who shake their heads and wonder why we all just don't leave the theater — they don't understand the doors are locked. Not just from the outside. From the inside too.

Snow whispered against my skin, soft and light, as my footsteps propelled me forward, until my fingers closed on the sleeve of chilled paper.

The envelope wasn't sealed. He wasn't trying to keep anyone out. He was trying to pull me in.

Though grainy and distant, the pictures were unquestionably of my mom. I've spent most of my life studying her in one form or another, trying to understand. It wasn't hard to recognize her.

I paged through the stack of pictures, their glossy faces sticking to the pads of my finger as the snow transformed on their surfaces.

John said, "That's just the beginning. Those are the small-time deals. You know Max Edwards?"

I shook my head, wondering if I'd been home the night the

picture in my hand was taken, my mom silhouetted by the kitchen light as she loaded bricks into her arms.

"She's running for him. Not petty shi — uh, stuff, either."

My vision blurred. From rage, not tears, because I was tired of being in that fucking place. I couldn't take another day of held breaths and burying my screams beneath pain so I could feel *something* that wasn't impotent fury.

I did everything right. Every fucking thing. And I was still shivering in a pitted parking lot with a man with a gun on his hip.

I flung my arm in his direction, holding on to the photos only by willpower and desperation, when I wanted to let them sink to the ground to be trampled by heavy boots and rolling tires. "What is it you want?"

"Information."

My snicker grew into a full-body laugh, until I had to wipe away tears. "Sorry. Sometimes I have fits of inappropriate laughter."

"You think this is a joke?"

"No. I don't. That's why I said inappropriate. But I'm guessing you haven't met my mother. I guarantee she hasn't paid enough attention to tell you anything useful, and asking her to go undercover is a death sentence. She'd be better off fighting the charges. Thanks for the offer."

I turned and headed back toward the restaurant door, tracking over the footprints I'd pressed into the snow. Calling a cab would mean the heat might get shut off, but I could wear a coat and a few extra blankets. What I couldn't do was walk to the bus stop without him following me.

I sucked in a ragged breath, thin air scratching against my throat.

She wouldn't survive in prison, and she couldn't afford a decent lawyer. I could warn her the cops were onto her but I knew my mom — she'd think she could outsmart them. And what was he doing coming to me anyway? I wasn't the one breaking the law, I wasn't the one in jeopardy. I wasn't my mother's keeper — I was barely my own.

"You're graduating soon, right?"

I spun, a wall of fat snowflakes falling between us. His voice carried across the distance, too clear and too confident. "Who will pay all those bills with you at college? Will you be able to study and go to parties, knowing your mom is on the streets? Will you be able to leave if she's locked up somewhere too far for you to visit? We've got connections to local halfway houses if she helps us."

John was one of the others — most cops are. The ones that look at us with disdain and preach about staying clean, staying out of trouble, like those minimums are enough to propel you from your spot on that stage.

But they're different too, because they've seen the theater from the inside. They may not live there, but they've memorized every actor and seat too. They *know* the doors are locked from the inside. And every word he'd just spoken was the clear sound of him flipping that lock into place.

CHAPTER SEVENTEEN

Bianca Havens is gorgeous. Thick honey-blond hair, tanned skin and cheekbones that belong in the movies.

I've never seen her in person, but Havens has a picture of the two of them on his desk — some black-tie shindig where they're both holding champagne flutes and smiling politely.

I'm as impressed with Mr. McCormack's taste as I am baffled that someone like Bianca would ever touch Headmaster Havens.

I don't pretend to have the slightest understanding of marriage, or the concept of an entire life with a single person. With Willa, I never wanted to envision a life without her, but I never considered forever either. Maybe I should've.

Bianca struts through the parking lot, no hint of uncertainty in her stride. She's the type of woman who has definitely considered forever — every potential version.

I brush the crumbs from my shirt, because I am definitely not the same type of woman as Bianca Havens. We don't have to be though. We just have to agree on one thing, and that's saving Mr. McCormack. I can only hope he didn't throw his career away over a woman who won't make a single sacrifice to ensure his freedom — and that maybe she can get me access to the last person who spoke to Madison before she disappeared.

It's Thursday. She's been gone five days now, and every minute that passes feels like time is moving faster, rushing toward an end I can't face.

I step from between two cars and she stops so fast her heels scrape the concrete. There's a pause weighted by recognition and indecision, then her hand darts out to clutch the sleeve of my coat.

That she recognizes me at all is probably not a good sign.

She yanks me forward, her stilettos attacking the parking lot with each step toward her car. By some miracle, I manage to follow without tripping since she still hasn't let go of my coat.

She releases me with a kind of violence that feels like a slap, even as she's motioning me into her car. The locks click a second before she slides into her seat, and the keys are in the ignition before I can finish tucking my bag between my legs.

The air holds a hint of peppermint infused with cherry blossoms — harsh and feminine all at once.

My head spins as the car lurches backward, and we don't speak the rest of the drive. All nine horrible minutes of it while I wonder where she's taking me but am too afraid to ask because it might make her throw me onto the curb. I keep reminding myself she cheated on her husband, because I need some form of superiority, but not even that stops me from feeling outmatched.

It gets worse when I have to follow her through the back doors of her apartment building and into the elevator, where I focus on the marble floor rather than return her stare.

Her apartment is like nothing I expected Headmaster Havens to live in. Sleek lines and open spaces patterned with warm leather and suede. It's modern with a marriage of cherry-wood and cigar lounge. Breathing the air calms my rapid heart rate, and I don't know if it's the subtle taste of coffee and cedar or the quiet order that makes every object feel like it was designed to be in exactly that spot.

I've been in Havens's office — there is nothing of him here. I'm so stuck on trying to envision him in this space that I don't notice the way Bianca's studying me — the way she's clearly *been* studying me — since the moment we stepped inside.

It hits me then, in a domino-fall of understanding. Bianca Havens is way smarter than I assumed. In my defense, her marriage to Headmaster Havens was ample reason to doubt her intelligence. But it turns out everything she does is a show of Machiavellian grace, every movement precise and exacting.

She brought me here because this isn't Headmaster Havens and Bianca's shared home.

This apartment belongs to Mr. McCormack. And she wanted to see if I've been here before.

I say, "He's my teacher. He has *never* done anything to me. Never tried to. Not ever. And not to anyone I know."

"The text messages?"

"School stuff. Always. For every person I know. He wanted people to 'have an outlet'" — I air quote his exact words — "because he knows how much pressure there is at St. Francis, and how tough it is to be away from home and family in high school."

I had to stifle my scoff when he said that — there isn't much I wouldn't give to be away from my home and family. In high school and beyond.

Bianca's voice strains. "And the license?"

"He found me and my girlfriend — *girlfriend*." I emphasize the word because even though having a girlfriend doesn't mean I've never had a boyfriend, I need her to believe me. "He saw us in a bar and he obviously knew I was underage, so he made us both leave and drove us home."

The relief that washes over her is a physical thing, a softening of every hard line. I know that look. It's what happens when you discover the thing you're most afraid of isn't a thing at all. It's a pardoning of your soul.

Terrified as she must've been, she asked anyway, and that alone makes me think maybe I can trust her. Her keys clink together when she hangs them on an empty hook. "Why did he only have your ID and not hers?"

"He took them both at first, but then Willa started to cry because there's this super shitty bar" — even worse than The Wayside shitty — "on the outskirts of town that's not exactly strict on employment law. As long as she's got an ID that says she's old enough to serve alcohol, the owner lets her work under the table."

"He's worried about her having ID while letting her work illegally? That's stupid."

I shrug, because it *is* stupid.

Bianca waves me off and heads toward the kitchen, where the fridge makes a sucking sound when she pries it open, then she holds the water she's offering me as far from her body as possible. I don't want it but she's already shut the door and this seems more of a directive than a question.

The cold hits my palm and I can't help but remember the last time someone offered me a drink while I visited their home.

The plastic cracks as she cranks off the cap. "So he got sappy and gave her back the license."

It's not a question, not really. She stares at an empty space near the ceiling and whispers his name. It sounds weird coming from her mouth. Too private somehow. Too personal a detail for a man I only know from behind the wall of his position.

I clear my throat and say, "Anyway, he kept my license and made me promise not to get a new one."

"And did you?"

We both know the answer so I don't bother to respond. "I need to talk to Mr. McCormack."

"You need to talk to the cops."

"I can't do that. And what am I supposed to say to them anyway?" The words are barely out of my mouth before I realize how badly I want her to answer. How badly I want someone to just tell me what to do.

"Tell them the truth so they don't think Landon is a child molester?"

"I *did*. Literally, I said: Mr. McCormack is not molesting me. *Literally*, I laughed at the suggestion."

I need to know if that's all they think. If this whole thing is about whether Mr. McCormack molested his students or whether he killed them. But if I throw out the concepts of kidnapping and murder and they're not already on the table, Bianca may lose her shit.

The water bottle crinkles in my hand, condensation pooling against my fingers. "They think he's made me believe he's not abusing me even though he really is. Want to tell me how I'm supposed to argue with that?"

She rubs her temples. "Did you tell them the truth about the license?"

"Did *he* tell them the truth about the license? It won't help if we have different stories."

She swallows so hard it pulses in her neck, and that's checkmate, boys and girls, because she doesn't know what Mr. McCormack said either.

"And what about you? Did you give him an alibi for the night of Madison's disappearance, or were you too busy trying to save your reputation and your shit marriage?"

A flush creeps into her cheeks. "Why did you come to see me?"

"Do you have a pen?"

She moves through his kitchen like it's her own, grabbing a pen and paper before tossing them toward me.

They slap against the marble before sliding within my reach, and she says, "Why aren't you in class, anyway?"

I rip the top sheet of paper free so the indent doesn't show on the ones beneath it — just in case — and the pen glides across it, countertop cold beneath my palm. "I can't go back to school."

"You'll get expelled."

"Eventually."

"And Landon said you were smart."

"I'm trying to help us both."

I'm trying to salvage something of this life before I can move on to my next. I'm trying to find my friend.

She sighs and plants her elbows on the counter, stiletto heel tapping against the floor. "Honey, I'm not sure you know *what* you're trying to do."

My skin flashes hot, a million words poised on my tongue. How I need Mr. McCormack to be here so he can pull apart my arguments, counter them, tell me my logic is flawed and filled with false equivalences. I need him to tell me this isn't all on me.

That I'm not the only hope for his future and for Madison's life. I need him to say this isn't my fault, just so I can believe it, even if only for a second.

I ask the question I should've demanded the answer to that day in the quad. "Someone said Madison texted Mr. McCormack right before she went missing. That he called her back."

I wait, because I can't seem to ask what I want to know.

For the first time, Bianca can't look at me. "He said he didn't recognize the number, and the text just asked for him to call, so he did. He didn't talk to anyone. Just left a voice mail."

"Do you believe him?"

She says yes, but her eyes betray her.

I slam the pen onto the paper, then grope through my bag for the cell phone. When I toss it, it hits the counter and tumbles to the other side. "That cell phone is for Mr. McCormack. The only number programmed into it is for a cell exactly like it — it's mine. On this paper is an email address and password. The one below it is mine. I need you to give these to him."

Her perfectly contoured eyebrow arches, and for the first time in this conversation, I feel something more than totally inadequate. Her hand closes around the cell phone and she weighs it in her palm. "Do you know how much worse this will look for him if he's caught secret messaging you on a cell phone you bought?"

"As opposed to us telling different stories to the cops? They already think he's brainwashed me — they'll think I'm lying to cover for him. I just need to talk to him. To have him —"

I clamp my mouth shut so hard I draw blood on my tongue, because I was about to say *to have him tell me what to do*, and

I don't need Bianca thinking he really *has* brainwashed me.

I hoist my bag onto my shoulder, the weight heavy and reassuring. "Just tell him not to get caught."

"Or I could pretend you were never here."

My fingers grip the counter so hard my knuckles blanch. "Are you in love with him?"

A quick double blink is the only indication I caught her off guard. "I'm not discussing my relationship with you."

"There are three people who know what happened the night he took that license, and if I can't find the third one, no one can. That leaves me as the only person who can clear his name. Think about whether you want to make me an enemy." I'm choking on every word, betrayal to Mr. McCormack burning me from the inside out.

Lately it feels like where before there were endless possibilities, now there are only last chances.

I float toward the front door on legs that don't feel like my own, and the second my hand wraps around the handle, I remember I didn't drive myself here. I spin to face her. "If he finds out you hid this from him, he'll never forgive you."

It takes until I'm three doors down for the lock to click into place behind me, and it's not until then that I let out my first wheezing breath, because no matter how hard I try to convince myself otherwise, Bianca is right.

I don't know what I'm trying to do.

CHAPTER EIGHTEEN

A dollop of milkshake drips from the tip of Aubrey's silver spoon and splats onto my open notebook. She gasps and grabs a napkin from the dispenser, apologies spilling from her mouth in a well-rehearsed chorus.

The drip is barely wiped clean when she wads the napkin and throws it at me, then scowls when it tumbles to the table in a flutter of limp edges. "You know what? I'm not sorry, Caroline. Do you want to know why?"

"Because you've reached the last conclusion of Fact Three?" Otherwise known as: *Find out details of Madison's disappearance. (Note: I have a plan for this. I don't like it. Aubrey won't either. Subject to change.)*

She leans across the table and hisses out a yes.

It's not the actual conclusion she's upset about, it's the plan I scribbled in the margin because I was too chickenshit to ask her. She's already done so much for me, been a much better friend to me than I have to her. But Aubrey's always been the person who has a compliment for every occasion, remembers everyone's birthday and genuinely wants an answer when she asks how someone's doing. She's always there for everyone, when I've barely managed to be there for myself.

I certainly wasn't there for Madison.

But I still lured Aubrey with the promise of free dinner and a milkshake at Mamma Lou's, where they have the best damn burger in town. It also has a corner booth where I can hide, and enough business to drown out both our conversation and Aubrey's rage, which I think I'm about to experience.

She cut practice short for me, then took advantage of her Special Senior privileges and raced to meet me. I can carry out my plan to visit Madison's house alone — but it'll be much easier with her help. If she chooses not to follow it with me, I won't blame her.

Aubrey's long black hair was still wet when I climbed into her car earlier, and now it's dried into shiny loose curls that brush the soft curve of her cheekbones before winding to rest on her slim shoulders.

She's mad at me and my world is falling apart, but the only thought in my head is a vision of her hair, tangled with mine, fanned out over my sheets, my mouth closing over hers.

She snaps her fingers and I'm back to fluorescent lighting and red vinyl booths. "Focus, Lawson. This won't work."

"Yes, it will." That's it. That's the sum total of my argument, because all my thoughts are focused on how, for the first time since Willa left, I considered that someone else could take her place.

The quarter pound of meat in my stomach turns to sludge.

Aubrey's spoon clinks against the fluted glass and she shoves the notebook back to my side of the table. "I'm not that good of an actress."

"You're absolutely that good of an actress." I drop two twenties onto the table, even though it's way more than necessary and the money I withdrew has to last me until I can go home again. But our waitress deserted us and I can't give Aubrey any more time to think this over. I scoot from the booth and gather my things.

Aubrey follows but she's also twirling her hair in that way I've come to recognize as DEFCON-level uncomfortable. Then she's charging through the diner at warp speed, her voice low and vicious. "My mother is Hindu. Did you know that? Now you do."

Her fingers dig into my bicep as she steers me around a corner, then she shoves us into the night, where gray clouds line the sky and hold up the glowing moon.

We're alone in the lot but she doesn't give her voice any more power than a whisper. "Karma, Caroline. I believe in karma, and I'd prefer not to be reincarnated as an ant or a slug or something."

She waits, staring expectantly.

If she's looking for answers or explanations, she's come to the wrong girl. I don't know the truth anymore. It used to feel like such a solid thing. Impenetrable and unbreakable.

Now it feels like more people are trying to bury it than find it.

To find the truth about Madison, we're going to have to talk to the one person who might know more than anyone else — her mom.

I stare past Aubrey to the empty road where a lone streetlight glares off the wet concrete, because if I look her in the eye, she'll know exactly how much I want her to come. "You don't have to come, Aubrey. I mean that. You can just drop me off."

It takes her so long to respond I start reformulating my plan.

But when she finally speaks, it's to say, "Tell me what you need me to do."

Textured brick pricks my forehead and I press the pads of my fingers into all the sharp edges. The night air is cold against my lips, carrying flavors of crisp leaves and crackling fireplaces.

It's quiet outside the Bentleys' house. All the reporters and news vans are stuck behind the vast iron gate of Madison's community. And even if they made it through that, they'd be stuck behind the vast iron gate that belongs solely to the Bentleys.

Any moment now, Aubrey will hurry up their front steps and ring their doorbell, and when Madison's mom answers, that will be my cue.

That is, if I can move from this spot when I'm stuck on a loop of the role-play Aubrey made me do on the way over. I had to play Madison's mom so Aubrey had a chance to practice before she had to perform.

It's a simple plan, really. Aubrey just has to go in, be *Aubrey* and ask genuine questions and say genuinely good things designed to comfort the other person. Talk to Madison's mom about her daughter, share a few good memories and remind her how much people care. And maybe gather some intel about what sorts of things Madison might've been doing prior to her disappearance. Like hanging out in bars in West Virginia.

Aubrey made it two questions into our mock conversation before she started crying. Three before she asked me why I never do.

She didn't pry when I didn't answer.

A light blinks on near the front of the house, its soft yellow glow spilling through the window panes onto the bed of frost-laden flowers sleeping in the dirt.

It's guilt that compels me forward, my fingers wrapped around the tree next to Madison's bedroom window as I hoist myself onto the lowest branch. It bends beneath my weight, branches scraping against the window like a warning of all the ways this could go wrong.

There are more than a few. Like how I might not even be able to get into Madison's bedroom if she suddenly stopped leaving her sliding balcony door unlocked — or if her mom has locked it since.

I reach for the next branch, and the bite of cold air leaches the warmth from my skin where my shirt rides up. I fight a shiver and heave my legs up after me.

My ankles wrap around the branch, locking together until I can twist the rest of me to the top. The balcony sits so close I don't have to reach to touch it.

I force my hands to the railing and hoist myself up, locking my elbows above the railing. The metal's so cold it burns, and for a moment, I'm back at camp, door handle searing my flesh on my way to freedom.

My arms unlock and my ribs slam into the balcony, my legs dangling in the open air. My muscles burn as I pull myself upward until the tip of my shoe grips the balcony's edge. I tip over the railing and before I can think too hard about it, my feet touch the wood-plank floor and I'm marching toward the door.

My fingers grip the handle and I raise up on my tiptoes, hoisting the door upward in the frame so the lock doesn't catch when I slide it open, just like Madison used to do. It swooshes in the track, slipping aside so I can walk into a place I've got no right to be.

I snap on a pair of gloves and the tang of latex smothers the faint brush of peony lotion Madison wore every day.

It would be helpful if I knew where I was starting.

The cops must've gone through her room, but maybe there's something they missed. Something they wouldn't know to look for or wouldn't recognize if they found. A note from the wrong person, evidence from the wrong place. Something that shows what she learned from Chrystal, or why she had her number in the first place.

Something only I could see.

I close my eyes and utter a silent plea: *I'm trying. I'm trying to find you. Please don't give up.*

And then, selfishly: *Please don't leave me too.*

I search through drawers, through closets, Madison's desk, all while waiting for the warning buzz that tells me Aubrey's leaving and I need to too.

This is the second flaw in my plan: all the secrets Madison didn't trust me enough to share are the ones I need to know now.

That's my fault too, the distance between us.

My heart jumps with an idea I should've had hours ago, and I wrestle my phone from my pocket, then waste precious seconds working my fingers free of the gloves.

Texting Jake doesn't take long, and the string of moving dots that tells me he's typing takes even less.

His answer is useless. So is his immediate follow-up phone call that I decline with all the strength in my pointer finger.

I respond: *Details later. Just tell me if M had a hiding spot.*

Truth: I know she has a hiding spot. It's where she keeps all the stuff she doesn't want her mom to see. When we were younger, she'd stash our stolen cigarettes or ill-gotten liquor in the sweatshirt cubby in her closet, until her mom went on a cleaning binge and found it. That was when we were fourteen.

I already checked the heating vents and the zippered access panel beneath the chaise in the corner of her room.

I know she has to have another spot, I just don't know *where*. But I'm betting Jake does. If he lies, I'm in much bigger trouble than I thought.

His message flashes onto the screen and I stuff the phone back into my pocket and heel-toe across the floor, keeping my footsteps light, until I can duck beneath the rows of clothes hanging in the closet.

Silks and wools brush over my skin, whisper-light, and my fingertips search out the edges of the plumbing access panel. Splinters threaten my skin, but they're too worn from use to do much damage, and the panel pops off, the holes wide and gaping. I set it aside and reach into the blackness.

Smooth metal, the scrape of sawed drywall, the gritty sandpaper of the underside of the tub and the warm wood of support beams. Then, finally, my hand lands on a sharp edge.

I walk my fingers across the expanse of it until I get to a handle that clinks as I take hold, dragging it from its hiding spot and into the pale glow of moonlight.

The size of the safe doesn't match its weight — it's the length and width of a piece of paper but at least ten pounds, and I can't fit my wrist through the handle.

I rock it to its side, and whatever secrets it holds tumble against the walls. Before I can text Jake to ask him if he knows the password, my phone buzzes — once, twice, and a third — and that means it's time to go.

I yank a belt from a cubby and feed it through the handle, fastening it so I can loop it over my shoulder when it's time to climb. Not perfect, but better than dropping it from the second story.

I shove the panel back into place and wince as the ridges of the screws zip against the edges of the holes, but the time for careful was twenty seconds ago, before Aubrey walked out the front door.

There's no guarantee Madison's mom is headed up here, but there's no guarantee she's not.

I make it out the door and down the tree while the safe slams into my back so hard I'll have several bruises to show for it.

It may have answers, or at least clues, and I can't help but feel a bit lighter than when I stood in this spot just minutes ago.

But when the light flares bright in Madison's bedroom before I can even turn to leave, spilling from the second floor to shout into the darkness above me, I still find myself whispering an apology she'll never hear.

CHAPTER NINETEEN

It's morning, and Mr. McCormack still hasn't called me. Or texted. Or emailed.

Bianca didn't mention him being in jail, so I have to assume he went home last night. And now he's had part of an after-noon and an entire morning to respond, but both my phones sit silent. No amount of willing them to ring has made a difference.

The only adult I *have* heard from is my dad. *Just checking in, Caroline. Your mother and I are giving you emotional space.* (Translation: *I* am giving you emotional space because I know what it's like to be the focus of your mother's displeasure and I hate it as much as you do.)

Then he followed it with a phone call, where I convinced him I was fine and safe and coming home soon. I used all his favorite buzzwords, and if there's one thing I know about my dad, it's that he'll avoid confrontations at nearly any cost. I haven't bought myself forever, but at least another day or two.

I've been targeting my rage at Madison's safe, and while the slick metal trim on the edges and corners is dented and chipped, it's still not giving up its secrets.

I'd set the goddamn thing on fire if I wasn't so afraid I'd ruin whatever's inside.

That's not a risk I can take, not when it's my only lead. Not when Madison's been gone six days.

The number shocks the air from my body. Six days. How much damage can a person do in six days?

I shove the thought from my head, tell myself there's still time and, mostly, that if I'm going to save her, I need to focus.

The safe has two combination locks — one for each latch — and I've tried every combination of numbers that might be important to Madison. My screwdriver managed to warp the metal surrounding them, but even slamming the end with a hammer didn't work.

Last night I made Aubrey go to the hardware store with me to rent something with a sharp blade and a vicious motor, but it turns out there are rules about who they'll give those things to and I don't fit into any of them.

I rub the grit from my eyes. It took twenty minutes of convincing before Aubrey agreed to leave me at the motel last night, and another fifteen before she finally pulled out of the lot. I know because that's how long I had to wait — wedged against the ice machine — before I could stop pretending I rented a room.

If she finds out I walked to my dad's vacant rental property three miles away, she might kill me, especially after I made her talk to Madison's mom last night.

I made Aubrey recite the conversation, even if watching her relive it sunk my heart lower with every word, especially when she got to Madison's mom saying how much it meant to her to have visits from "the people Madison was closest to." I don't know if it was a reproach because I haven't, or if she no longer considers me part of that group.

But amidst the rest, through all the reassurances by Mrs.

Bentley that Madison had been acting normally, there was a question, dropped casually into a statement: *I told the police how helpful Madison always is. How she took that new student — Tammy? — under her wing when she was having trouble fitting in.*

Here's what Aubrey knew last night, and I know this morning, and I'm pretty damned sure Mrs. Bentley has known for at least a few days now: there *is* no new student named Tammy at St. Francis.

We got three new students this year. One is now the co-captain of the hockey team so I doubt he needs Madison's help fitting into anything. The other two are girls, but their names are Olivia and Sarah. I've never seen her with either.

But even more important was the way Aubrey looked while telling me about it, the way her gaze fixed on the vacancy sign as its neon letters twitched between blinding and absent. "She just stared at me, Caroline, like she was waiting for me to confirm or deny it, but I was so scared to say the wrong thing. Like if I said no when she needed to hear yes, it might just tip her in the wrong direction."

Whatever Madison was doing, she couldn't tell her mom about it, and she obviously couldn't tell me either.

My stomach growls and I nibble another cracker while I gather all the shit I have to bring with me on my three-mile hike back to the motel so Jake can pick me up. He promised to bring power tools. And food. I'd walk seven miles if he'd bring me a bacon cheeseburger.

But at least walking is action. It's not sitting in an empty house, waiting while your friends live their lives, doing all the normal things I should be doing. Like showing up to soccer practice. That's two more demerits. It might be stupid to care when everything else is so shitty, but there's no way to stop the tally that feels like a bomb countdown in my head.

Three miles later I'm waiting at a rotten picnic table, my heels digging into the weathered length of the seat and my knees drawn tight, so I can wrap my arms around them to salvage what little warmth I have left. The tiny courtyard behind the motel faces a dense forest, its trees just beginning to discard winter and rebirth spring. Air gusts into a plastic bag and gives it life, sending it tumbling across a battlefield of broken liquor bottles and crushed cigarette cartons.

The sun tears through the smoky gray sky, sinking warmth into my exposed skin.

I don't open my eyes when footsteps crunch behind me.

The whole table shudders when something heavy thumps onto its surface, and Jake says, "Caroline."

I spin my vape on the warped table. "Don't say it."

The wood bench groans as he straddles it and lowers down. He mumbles, "Jesus," and shifts himself a little closer until his legs cage mine. "If I get splinters in my ass you have to promise to take them out. I can't go to the ER for that. It'll ruin my reputation."

"What reputation?"

"The one for not getting splinters in my ass."

It's so ridiculously stupid I can't stop myself from laughing, and he beams back at me, ducking his head to rest his chin on my knee. "You can't stay here again tonight."

I slide out from his reach and point to the battered safe. "I can't open it."

He pauses, then sighs. "Did you try dropping it?"

"Everything but."

He lifts his chin and motions for me to hand the safe over, which I do begrudgingly because while I really want it open, I'm gonna be insanely pissed if he drops the thing on the ground and it pops open like he's Thor and it's some magical fucking hammer.

That's exactly what happens.

He angles the corner toward the ground and the bang chops through the courtyard, the hinges twerking just enough to spring the locks mostly free. The left one is still engaged but the arm is so bent it's useless, and he gives me a smug grin. "I watch that show where people buy the abandoned storage lockers. That's how they open a lot of the safes."

"And you couldn't have mentioned that last night when I asked?"

He laces his fingers and stretches them out. "Yeah, I figured you wouldn't have the right touch anyway."

If there was ever a moment I could hate someone while being intensely grateful for their existence, it's right now.

I drop to my knees and pry off the rest of the lid. The first thing I pull out is a box of condoms. "Guess I know why you knew where to look."

Even the tip of his nose turns red. "Just see what else is in there."

There's a pack of cigarettes, which I pocket before he can stop me, then another he's too quick for, and then there are flash drives. So many I have to pour them out in a waterfall of plastic that smacks against the pitted concrete.

Jake grabs a handful of them. "Wow."

"You don't know what's on them?"

"I'd guess photography stuff?"

"All of it?"

Madison has always been into photography, headed for college to study it in the fall, and she *is* the head photographer for the yearbook, but there must be at least thirty drives in the pile.

He shrugs and cups his hands around the drives before pouring them back into the safe. "Only one way to find out. You want to go to your room and go through them?"

Since I don't *have* a room, that would be difficult. "I already checked out, just in case, and then tonight I'll check back in."

I train my eyes on the flash drives so I don't have to look at him while I lie, and I toss the last one in the safe.

He's still staring at me when I pop up from the ground.

He grabs the safe and heads down the path to his car. "Food first?"

"Food first. We'll go through the flash drives later, when we have time."

"We don't have time now?"

"Nope. Because now it's time to find Sydney and her missing boyfriend."

BETWEEN THE FAULT LINES

Things weren't always bad.

I remember those days like a fever dream, bits of memories that fade in and out of my consciousness, daring me to trust in their realness, making me question if I was — if I *still am* — too desperate to remember the truth.

She told me there were no monsters beneath the bed as she pulled my covers tight, blanketing me with rose-scented cotton and blissful ignorance.

There are no monsters under the bed. In the closet. Outside the door.

Sleep tight, little one. I'll protect you. I'll always love you.

She told me the good guys win in the end and people are decent.

She told me lies.

I clung to them, held them tight in that place I only viewed from a distance. Close up, I might have seen where all the fault lines lie.

But as Leonard Cohen said, the cracks are where the light gets in.

What Leonard didn't tell me was sometimes you have to *be* the light, and you'll be the only one, standing in darkness that feels like forever.

Until something glimmers on the horizon, a faint spark of hope that promises you aren't alone, that there are other lights burning.

There's power in togetherness. Bravery born of common bonds.

I was always braver with Livie's skin only a brush from mine — my kneecaps pressed against my cheek, wet from the slow stream of my tears, and Livie's comforter pooled around my huddled body like the promise of sanctuary.

Her fingers brushed my temple, tugging back the strands of hair cemented to my face. "Tell me."

I closed my eyes because looking into hers was like facing the sun — sometimes Livie's fire was too bright. "It's my problem, you —"

"Hey. Your problems are my problems. Talk to me."

It was the pleading in her voice that cracked me open, made me tell the story I promised to swallow, even though shame bled through every word. "My mom is running drugs."

And once I started, I couldn't stop.

I told her about John. About the pictures. About the deal. And then my breath caught when I started the rest.

"You asked your mom?"

I nodded, tears salty on my tongue. "She said no."

"Why?"

All I could offer was a shrug. "I used to wish she was an addict. Isn't that stupid? But at least that way there'd be a reason for why she does the things she does."

I kicked the covers from my legs, slanted moonlight spilling through the blinds and striping my bare skin.

It wasn't sanctuary I wanted. I wanted to feed this fire in my hand, the one I've always been so careful not to blow out. So afraid I would lose it if I didn't keep feeding it.

But in that room, I wasn't scared. If my candle blew out,

flame giving way to snaking tendrils of smoke, Livie would give me light again.

"If she were an addict, Livie, I wouldn't have to know the truth."

She didn't ask what it was. She gave me space.

"You want to know why she said no? Because she's not going to some halfway house. Because she doesn't trust the cops. Because *this* person or *that* person would find her. Because" — I sucked in a breath — "this is how she ended it: 'Maybe my ungrateful daughter will just have to use some of that money she's been saving up to leave me behind and get me a decent lawyer instead.'"

Livie's eyes flew wide. "She wants you to give up college for her?"

"Yeah, but that's not even the point. It's not the truth."

Her head fell, finger tracing over a swirl in the bedding. "What is the truth?"

"I don't matter."

Her head snapped up. "Don't you dare —"

"No. I don't mean it like that. I mean —" The words I'd always run from now begged to be used. "My whole life I've wished for her to be someone else. For her to be the person I needed her to be. But she's not. She won't ever be. And I can't fix her."

I grabbed Livie's hand, her fingers soft and delicate in mine. "It doesn't matter what I say or what I do or don't do. The only thing that controls her decisions is her. And the truth is I'm not leaving her behind. She was never there at all."

Livie's hands framed my face, threading through my hair,

and then her lips touched mine. We tumbled on the bed, my skin electrified everywhere it touched hers. And there, beneath the weight of her body, in that moment when her tongue found mine and the softness of her lips made me shudder, I mattered.

She pulled back, her cheeks flushed, gorgeous green eyes shining even in the quiet darkness. "Who am I?"

"You're Livie."

"And who are you?"

Who did I *want* to be — that was the real question. Did I want to be the throwaway girl everyone forgot before she even started to live?

I shifted until she lay next to me, that beautiful dark hair fanned in a black pool, and I let my hand settle on her knee.

This was who I wanted to be. Exactly this.

I leaned closer, until the sweetness of cherries scented every breath. "I'm the girl who's not afraid to do this."

I kissed her again, saying all the words I couldn't. But in the second before, just for the briefest moment, she smiled.

She smiled because she was proud of me. Because together, neither of us would ever have to know darkness again.

I carry that light inside me even now, in this dark place where I can no longer search for the fault lines I was once too afraid to see.

CHAPTER TWENTY

There's a party for the students of Walton High School tonight — the school Sydney Hatton is officially enrolled in — and thanks to the shocking number of students who have no concept of online privacy, I know exactly where it is.

Walton and St. Francis may be less than an hour from each other, but the distance is the smallest thing separating them. Their worlds are unrecognizable to each other — haves and have-nots where the former have nearly forgotten the latter exist, unless they need their houses cleaned, their dry cleaning delivered, their plumbing fixed.

First rule of the St. Francis tightrope: don't look down.

But something connected those worlds for Madison.

Jake and I spent dinner crammed in a booth, looking through three full flash drives from Madison's stash and found nothing but smiling classmates and generic yearbook-style photos. That's when we gave up and started quizzing each other on Walton's students. The odds of someone talking to us will be better if they think we go to Walton and, more importantly, that we *don't* go to St. Francis. The odds of us getting our asses kicked is far less too.

Taking the car from my dad's rental property would be much better than Jake's SUV, but I don't know how to explain why I have access to it, so I'll settle for parking way the hell down the street.

As it turns out, we don't have a choice.

Cars line the dirt road on both sides, from the two-lane highway crossroad to the driveway of the party host — Davis Worth, baseball captain, and judging from his Snapchat pictures, an aspiring rapper and Eminem clone. Judging from his YouTube videos, he'd be wise to stick to baseball.

Jake wedges the Rover into the corner of a liquor store parking lot and glances around with the same expression as when I first took him to The Wayside.

Except this time, I understand his concern.

Empty bottles roll through the lot and the store's back wall is a canvas for any number of gang signs — a rainbow of colors in sharp, jagged lines.

My laptop, everything worth taking from my room, and all of Madison's flash drives are in that car.

Jake hits the lock button twice.

We leave the shelter of the flourescent glare and plunge into a blue-black night, grass slick beneath my shoes and the gentle buzz of insects filling my ears. It feels like it should be too cold for insects. Too early. And all at once I'm off-balance, stuck between the need to race toward graduation and pleading with life to take me back to when things were different.

To when Willa was still here. To when I knew Madison was alive.

Jake grabs my hand, warm and steady, and leads me around the sloping ditch that bends toward a placid stream, its surface rippling when the wind tickles it.

A herd of guys jogs around us and one flicks his lit cigarette into the air, a burning beacon that fades just before it meets the ground. One of them turns to give Jake a nod, and he returns it too quickly and with way too much authority.

St. Francis born and bred.

I drop his hand because I'm not really a hand-holding kind of girl. "So listen, you're gonna have to be less like you in there."

He fumbles for a response, so I say, "Everyone is going to know you don't go to Walton if you walk in there acting normal. You need to tone it down. Be less … 'future Senate candidate.' Look down a lot and slump or something. Be a guy that's forgettable."

He stops so fast I'm two steps ahead and have to spin to face him.

He looks at me and bursts into laughter. "Caroline. They're not going to think we go to Walton, and that's not my fault."

"You're saying it's mine?"

He nudges me to walk with him. "Some people are ponds. Or puddles. Fun to splash in but all it takes is a sunny day or two and everything goes dry."

I don't know where he's going with this, but I'm grateful for the mask of darkness and the distraction of movement. "So I'm fun to splash in?"

"Just wait." His footsteps echo as we cross a driveway, his shoes mottled in shades of brown from the wet grass. "Now other people, most people, are lakes. You've got your big lakes and your little lakes" — he tries and fails for a country accent because Jake speaks with lines and corners, not slopes and rolls — "but you can go for a swim in those. Stretch out your muscles, maybe build a dock and a lake house. Really, a lake is the perfect size."

Voices from the party float in the silence and I stifle the urge to sprint toward the promise of diversion.

He knocks me with his elbow. "I'm making you uncomfortable."

"Yes."

"Do you want me to finish?"

"Well, you have to now or I'll spend my whole life wondering if I'm a puddle, or a lake, or the fucking boat dock."

His mouth quirks at the corner but drops before it can transform into a full smile. "You're not a puddle. Or a pond or a lake, Caroline. You're the goddamn ocean."

I can't help it. I am utterly powerless to stop the way my legs snap into action, driving me across another driveway. "Great, so I'm full of terrifying creatures and cause massive amounts of destruction?"

He smothers me into a side hug, pressing me into the warmth of his body, and he slows me down but doesn't stop me. "Relax, Caroline. I'm not asking you to have my babies, I'm just saying you're ... complicated."

"Seriously, Jake, I can't even tell if you're insulting or complimenting me right now."

Shadowy figures gain definition and whispers rise to murmurs as we get closer to the party.

"I'm just saying you don't exactly blend in either. I've known you for years and I feel like there are four other sides of you that I've barely gotten a glimpse of."

He's not supposed to see that far. No one is.

If he can see, others can too, and everything I've been waiting for — everything my entire life's been constructed around — seems like a fairy tale ending I should've known was a lie.

My feet leave the ground, and it's not until I hear Jake's warning that I realize there are strange arms caged around my ribs. My elbows are pinned but my legs aren't, and I slam my heel into the shin of whatever asshole is holding me. He yelps and his arms spring free, but before I can take my first full breath, Jake has me shielded against him, looking not at all forgettable.

The three guys in front of him back away, their hands raised, palms out. They look familiar — not from Walton social media, but not St. Francis either.

The middle one says, "Chill, dude, we were just having fun."

It's followed by a string of mumbles I can't hear as they walk away, and Jake's expression matches mine.

I sigh. "We're not gonna blend in."

"Nope."

Then I guess it's time to go be the ocean and destroy some shit.

CHAPTER TWENTY-ONE

A plastic cup gets shoved into my hand the moment I spring free from the mass of bodies at the front door. Jake and I may not blend, but maybe everyone is too drunk to care.

The steady thump of bass vibrates through my legs and rattles the pictures on the walls, and my eyes water from the sticky beer-and-weed-laden heat.

Jake grabs the cup from my hand and passes it off to some guy splayed on the couch. The guy's pupils are bigger than my head and the blunt in his hand lets off a smoke screen that twists to join the haze at the ceiling.

Jake's voice rumbles in my ear. "Don't drink anything."

It's the perfect opening to ask him about whether his dad might be able to help with the glass from Chrystal's trailer, a subject I've been avoiding all night.

But it's way too loud in here. I grab hold of his coat and weave through the crowd, past a girl I recognize from Snapchat. I put on my picture-day smile and yell, "Hey, Melissa!"

Her wave halts when she sees me, probably because she has no idea who I am. But when I smile at the girl next to her, I get a genuine one in response. I don't have the slightest idea why, but I make a mental note to track her down once she separates from Melissa.

The kitchen is as overloaded as the living room, but a wall blocks the speakers so I don't have to shout.

I grab two beers and crack them open. "So I've been thinking … about the glass?"

Jake finishes his swallow. "*That* glass?"

"One and only. So …" The sides of the can bow inward from the force of my fingers. "I was thinking since your dad's a judge, maybe he knows someone who could test it?"

He rocks backward, eyes wide, and I have to chug a swallow of lukewarm, watery beer so I don't back down.

"Yeah, maybe. I don't —" His gaze snags on a group of girls who are clearly ogling him, but he's so distracted he doesn't even smile back. "I can't tell him the truth."

I snort beer up my nose and my nasal passages are on fire. I try to deflect Jake's apologies, but I'm too busy wheezing, and then a girl hands me a scratchy brown napkin so at least I can wipe the snot from my face. "No. You absolutely cannot tell him the truth."

He frowns and pulls me into the corner next to a couple practically dry-humping on a kitchen chair. "I wasn't saying I was going to. I just have to think of a story for why I'm asking my dad to" — his voice drops to a whisper — "run a drug test on a random glass."

"Fair point. Okay, so …"

We stare at each other until inspiration strikes. "Tell him a girl you know thinks a guy might have been trying to drug her at a party!"

"And she doesn't go to the cops why?"

"You're such a guy. She doesn't go to the cops because they suck and because rape culture, Jake. They won't believe her, or won't care, or they'll tell her no crime has been committed and there's no way to prove it was him, and run along now, little girl, and don't wear such tight shirts and you'll have less to worry about."

"That's kinda harsh."

"Yeah, it is, but not for the reasons you're thinking. Your dad will do anything for you, you know that. It'll work. Do you think it'll work?"

His mouth twists into a frown. "I'll make it work."

I get two seconds to revel in my victory before he says, "Oh, shit." And then, "Hey, Preston."

There is no way Preston Ashcroft is at a Walton party.

Except then a voice says, "Didn't expect to see you here," and it's definitely Preston.

I could leave. He's only seen the back of my head and Jake *did* ambush me with the meeting with his dad.

"Caroline?"

Everyone at St. Francis will know everything about this in less than an hour.

I turn slowly, hoping he'll disappear by the time I make it around.

He looks ridiculous in normal clothes. There are still lines from where the cheap sweatshirt he's wearing was folded in the store, and he forgot to mess the overly gelled swoop out of his hair.

I say, "What are you doing here?" because I might as well ask him before he asks me.

He almost looks offended, but then his true nature takes over and he ignores my question, leaning in close, yeasty-sweet beer coating his words. "So you know my brother is on the task force for Madison's case, right?"

I can *hear* Jake sighing behind me.

"Yeah, so they traced that burner cell she had, the one she used to call Mr. McCormack on the night he kidnapped —"

"Mr. McCormack *did not* kidnap Madison."

My voice is too loud, too sharp, and Preston's head cocks to one side. "You know, I never believed the shit people said about you two, but ..."

I am going to kill him. "Preston, if the cops couldn't get a confession out of me, believe me when I say you won't either. Probably because I am not fucking Mr. McCormack. Is that clear enough for you?"

He leans away, hands raised. "Okay, okay. I'm just saying, her cell pinged to the tower that's a few miles from Higgins Lake."

He seems to think that proves something, but I have no idea what. I don't even know where Higgins Lake *is*.

Jake's voice rumbles over my head. "Which side?"

Preston gives him a look that's as confused as I feel, and Jake rolls his eyes. "Which side of Higgins Lake? It's fucking huge, and there's the high side with the cliffs, that the power company owns, and the low side that's kinda shi—"

He drops his voice to a whisper, despite the thumping bass rattling the walls. "The side that's not great."

Preston starts talking, about how it's not an exact science, about how it can actually take up to a dozen tower pings to get an accurate reading. About how cell towers reroute calls when they're busy and Madison *may* have made the call from hundreds of miles away.

I'm trying to summon the outrage Jake seems to feel when he says, "So what you're saying is it's all bullshit and proves absolutely nothing," but I'm too distracted. The reason Higgins

Lake sounds so familiar is balanced on the tip of my tongue, but I can't get it to fall into place.

And then it does.

A flash of recollection — me, huddled in the passenger seat of my dad's car while driving through West Virginia, my fingers clenched around a bottle of pills, the sign for Higgins Lake flashing by the window.

So much of that day is a blur, and so much is astoundingly clear — like how two years ago, I found a body near there, and now Madison may be missing from the same place.

My beer can thuds to the table and my body goes cold.

Preston says, "It's *not* bullshit though, dude. Because guess what? Turns out Mr. McCormack has spent *a lot* of time in the old West VA. Sorry, Caroline, but things don't look good for your boy."

My name snaps me back to attention, and it's impossible to miss the irritation in Jake's voice as he says, "Yeah, because spending time in a state someone may or may not have made a phone call from is basically an open and shut case, Preston."

Jake's defending Mr. McCormack and nothing makes sense anymore.

Preston says, "Get this, dude. There's talk of the FBI joining the case because it's interstate now. The Bentleys have been pushing for it, but my brother says the higher-ups are arguing about it. Plus, Madison's eighteen, and the FBI can't investigate everything. My brother also …"

I leave before I have to listen to any more.

Almost everyone is congregated in the backyard, and the cold chills the sweat on my skin. I can almost force myself to stop thinking that maybe, if I hadn't forgotten about that girl two years ago, if I hadn't done exactly what the cops told me to and gone about my life like hers didn't matter, Madison might be home right now. And if the FBI aren't getting involved now, they probably never will. The cavalry isn't coming. This is all on me.

But Jake is right. Preston's big reveal is bullshit if Madison could've been hundreds of miles away when she made that call. Plus, there's nothing actually linking Madison to the girl I found — and right now, there's only one I can save.

That goal just got infinitely harder now that people have seen me talking to Preston, and soon everyone will know I was at a party with Jake.

The only upside is that if Mom *does* hear about it, she'll be so focused on Jake she'll ignore the rest.

People clump in circles, laughter and occasional shouts mixing with mentions of class, practice, exams and who's hooking up with who. In many ways, it's the same as a party with kids from St. Francis.

A bonfire rages in the middle of an endless backyard that fades into a dark forest, and the smoke gusts and billows over the shadowed bodies standing nearby. Someone tosses in a plastic cup and the flames jump in a protest, reaching for a guy who leaps away and ends up face-first in the grass.

The friends surrounding him burst into drunken laughter. Those are my people.

I force my breathing to slow and head their way.

My fingers fumble over the pack of Madison's cigarettes as I wrestle them from my jacket pocket. I'm close enough to the fire for the heat to breathe over my skin, and the conversation between the crew dies.

I pat my pockets, cigarette dangling from my mouth and the vague sweetness of tobacco taunting my taste buds. When I look up and pull the cigarette from my lips, they're all staring. "Anybody bring a lighter that's a little less deadly?"

I have to point to the fire before recognition lights their faces. The tallest one digs into his pockets and brandishes a blue Bic.

Of course he has to light my cigarette, cupping his hand around the flame as his palm lights up the color of dawn.

I breathe deep, letting the smoke work its way into my lungs.

Sorry, Aubrey.

He says, "You go to Walton?"

"Transferred this year."

"You don't look familiar."

The whole pack moves a step in and I have to rock into my heels to stop myself from retreating.

Never show fear.

This is a fundamental difference between Walton people and St. Francis people — one of the many reasons why Jake will never fit in and I only barely can after years of exposure to this side of town.

St. Francis people know bullies and mean girls and popularity and social status. They know how to use subtle words and sugar-coated hints of smiles to tell a person when they're not welcome. When they don't belong.

But in this crowd, the suspicion — the wariness — runs deeper. It's born from growing up watching — always watching

— for the signals that something is not what it seems. It's not teachable. It's learned. Hour by hour, day by day, lifetime by lifetime. It's learned by knowing safety is not guaranteed and survival is something you fight for.

It's a lesson the kids at St. Francis don't know they need, until one of their own goes missing and the force of it upends them.

Here's the thing St. Francis *ought* to teach: none of us are safe — some just have better odds.

I hold the guy's gaze because guilty people look away, but I make myself small, shy. "I keep to myself. Hard to make friends senior year."

One of the guys twists his baseball hat around as he takes a stumbling step forward, and I put more distance between us, the fire singeing the back of my legs.

Baseball Hat's words slur. "I would've been your friend."

There is *no* difference between Walton and St. Francis here — drunk guys are asshats at all ends of the class spectrum.

Voices rise behind his back but I can't see why, and since the fire's nearly melting my jeans, it's time to throw out the Hail Mary. "There is this one girl that's nice to me. I was hoping she'd be here. Sydney Hatton?"

Three of them erupt in a chorus of jeers and playful shoves, all fixated on the fourth member of the squad. It's hard to tell from the way the flames dance against his pale skin, but I think he's blushing.

He shrugs off his friends and says, "We hooked up a couple times," without meeting my eyes.

Jake's voice rises from the crowd behind their backs, and the entire party seems to turn toward the same point.

I hold #4's gaze to keep him focused. "Do you still talk to her?"

"Nah."

"Any idea where I could find her?" I'm pushing this too fast. There's nothing natural about the flow of this conversation, but if Sydney *is* missing, this guy doesn't seem to know it. And Jake is starting to draw the crowd.

The guy nods toward my right hand, and I have to glance to it before I feel the sting of the cigarette against my knuckles. I drop what's left on the ground and grind it out with my shoe while he tells me Sydney's got a new boyfriend now — one that doesn't like her going to school.

But then the mob behind him erupts and I shove myself into the herd of people. I know what a fist connecting to someone's face sounds like, and I pray Jake is on the giving end.

I get stuck two rows back, pinned between two massive guys whose combined pressure crushes my ribs and rakes against my tattoo. I wiggle and kick until I pop free to a roar of deafening cheers. The inner row is locked tight, held by the press of connected bodies, so I drop to the grass that soaks through the knees of my jeans and crawl my way in.

When Jake hits the ground at the same instant, I'm in a perfect position to see the surprise on his face.

He expected a fair fight; instead he got a pile-on and a sucker punch from the guy who grabbed me earlier.

His name pops into my head as I scramble forward — Dexter Uttley, second-string defenseman for Hargrove-Phillips. Jake decimated his entire team in their last game — three goals and two assists. And Jake sat the last quarter.

Dexter must be pissed that Jake didn't even recognize him.

I'm too slow to stop the kick Jake takes to the stomach, and his knees jerk up to protect all his vital organs.

I don't make it in time for the second kick either, this one from the guy Jake must have whaled in the face earlier. Blood from his chin is splattered all over his shirt.

Dexter lands a kick to Jake's ribs, and the way Jake's body twitches triggers my scream.

Dexter freezes as his eyes meet mine, like he's just realized actions might have consequences, and then he bails — much like the other person who could actually be of help right now. Preston and his folded sweatshirt are predictably missing.

I lunge for the stomach-kicker and a girl screams, "Davis!" seconds before my arms and legs wrap around his body, latching on and yanking him backward. Baseball captain and rapper extraordinaire Davis Worth's verse about being a "woke bae" autoplays in my head.

We go down hard, rattling my spine, and Davis's legs piston in the air as he tries to stand with me attached to his back.

A female voice yells in my ear to let go as nails gouge my wrists, while the wail of approaching sirens spurs the crowd to run like cockroaches in the sudden flash of light.

I release my grip and Snapchat Melissa is dragging Davis to his feet before I can shove him off me. I'm barely off the ground before Jake's single punch sends Davis tumbling to the grass.

The same voice that told me to let go now tells me to run, and this time I listen without hesitation because a kaleidoscope of red, white and blue twirls against the starlit background of the sky.

She drags me from the stampede headed toward the front of

the house and Jake runs up beside us as she says, "There's a path through the woods that leads out the other side."

The police megaphone kicks on to tell all of us to remain where we are. I'm sure there are some people who listen, but we are not those people.

We plunge into the darkness of the woods, barren branches crisscrossing in a patchwork canopy. Light flares across the path as Jake thumbs on his phone's flashlight, then mutes it to a gentle glow so we'll be harder to spot, but for that brief second, there's something about this girl that's familiar. A flash of memory I can't quite place. And not just because she smiled at me earlier when I said hi to Melissa.

I should be concentrating on not tripping over gnarled roots and fallen branches, but all my focus is on this faint memory. "Do I know you?"

She gives a quick laugh. "Rational functions."

The memory snaps into focus. Sun slanting through the restaurant's windows, Journey crackling through the speakers. Me, waiting for Willa, and the flame to my moth: the sound of soft sobs.

Her name is Clara. Pre-calc is the bane of her existence. And I helped her understand rational functions.

I never thought my mathematical abilities would help keep me from getting arrested, but it's not the strangest thing that's happened this week by far.

The soft shine of the moon gives way to the harsh glare of streetlights as the woods transition into the two-lane highway. There's no way to avoid walking alongside it until we can cut over to Jake's car, and he won't stop checking over his shoulder.

Every minute or so, a new car or truck blows by us, ruffling my hair and whipping my clothes.

Clara is the first to speak, and it's only to ask where we're parked so she can lead us behind a few stores and avoid the exposure.

My entire life feels wrong and I don't know how to fix it. A week ago, I had things figured out. I had a plan. A future. The promise of freedom.

Now I'm hour-to-hour and second-guessing even the smallest decisions because every option feels some shade of wrong.

Jake's car sits untouched beneath the sharp light of the liquor store lot that holds far more empty spaces than when we parked.

His interior lights flare to life and when Clara hesitates, he nods toward his car. "C'mon, I'll drive you home."

Tension melts out of her shoulders and I feel like a dick for not suggesting it earlier.

We climb in and I gasp as the cold leather meets my thighs. Even through my jeans, my skin feels raw and tender. I twist to see Clara in the back seat, and she's studying Jake, his car, and me, trying to figure out how we all fit together.

I want to wish her luck in unraveling that mystery. "How'd you do on that test?"

It's stupid, but I like tutoring, helping people understand something they thought they couldn't, and the light that shines through when they prove to themselves they're capable of more than they'd hoped.

I'd offer it free to everyone, not just the kids on scholarship and the ones whose parents are barely shouldering St. Francis's annual tuition, but I have to supplement Grandma Caldecott's spite fund somehow.

Clara's gaze drops but she has a hint of a smile. "Only 89 percent but everyone did terrible, so he graded on a curve and I got an A."

"That's awesome!" I hold my hand out and she slaps it — not without an eye roll though, so I add, "Don't downplay your achievements. I'm proud of you."

She mumbles a thank-you and tucks her hair behind her ear, eyes cast down, but she's smiling.

She clears her throat and gives Jake directions, probably so I'll stop embarrassing her. Then she says, "So she's really gone? All the way to California?"

There's no small measure of awe in her voice, one that speaks to grand adventures in the City of Angels, but it's a gnawing reminder of how much I need Willa to be here right now, so I can apologize for all the things I didn't say when she left.

I swallow. "Really gone. All the way to California."

"Wow. I'm sorry."

I wave her off because I honestly can't talk about this now and I don't want to give Jake anything else to question me about. "Sorry we ruined your party."

"That wasn't your fault. Cops around here are just looking for a fight most of the time, except when there's something to fight for, you know?"

"Is there? Something happening that needs to be fought for?" It sounds stupid and clunky in my head, and it must be, because I can feel the pinpoints on my scalp where Jake's gaze is fixed.

Clara grabs hold of Jake's headrest to pull herself forward and points a few houses down. "Third one on the left. With the light on."

She waits until we ease into the driveway and a light flicks on in the front window. "Listen, I heard you asking about Sydney Hatton earlier."

"Have you seen her? I heard her mom and aunt think she's missing."

"Where'd you hear that?"

I fight to keep my face blank. "There are missing person posters all over the place. Someone at The Wayside said she skipped town with her boyfriend."

She shrugs. "That guy is old news. I heard they broke up right before he ghosted. I don't want to know why you're looking, but I've heard some people say they've seen her down by The Bricks."

Jake says, "What's The Bricks?" and her hand freezes on the door before she shoves it open.

I blink against the sudden interior light and resist the urge to crawl beneath the seat in case anyone is looking out their window.

A gust of wind tosses her hair over her face and she scrapes it away. "The Bricks is a row of houses that back to a brickyard. Mostly empty but lots of squatters. Lots of drugs. Sydney was cool for a while and then …"

I finish for her. "One of those guys at the party talked about a new boyfriend?"

A tight nod, tighter lips. "Max Edwards. Anyway, thanks for the ride."

The door slams before I can thank her, and Jake's thumb taps against the steering wheel.

I'm guessing he's thinking the same thing I am: if Sydney's alive, we may have this whole thing all wrong.

CHAPTER TWENTY-TWO

The bottle of ibuprofen rattles when I pull it from the shelf and a mom with a screaming kid in her shopping cart hurries past me, two wheels squeaking off tune with a pop song playing in thin, scratchy notes, telling me to be happy.

Jake is off shopping because his clothes are "covered in blood and dirt" from the fight earlier, which is an exaggeration, and I'm not sure if the new outfit is really just an excuse to buy pain meds or if he actually thinks he needs to look presentable to visit a drug house.

Something smacks my shoulder and then clatters to the ground just as the mom yells, "Alexander!"

I pick up the box the little brat just threw at me, and I'm seriously questioning the parenting and general personhood skills of someone who lets their kid play with wart remover. Just as I'm about to hand the box back to the hell spawn, I freeze.

Detective Brisbane blocks the end of the aisle, looking so Hard-Ass Detective the mom shoves her cart fast enough to ruffle the shelves' sales tags.

She makes it past Brisbane but I'm still standing there, with a new appreciation for all the dumb animals that get themselves run over when they freeze in headlights. But I know how this works — I turn and run and Brisbane's partner is waiting to catch me at the other end.

Brisbane slides forward, a slow heel-toe step and an outstretched hand that might as well hold a gun. "Your parents are worried about you, Caroline."

"I left them a note."

"You broke into your own house and disappeared."

"Nope. Still here and visible." The edge of the shelf cuts into my palm while I debate whether to climb the shelves to the next aisle or take my chances that Harper isn't behind me. Maybe he's hunting Jake.

My stomach goes sour, because maybe Jake's the reason they're here. Maybe this little trip to the store was just an excuse to get away from me so he could call the cops, protect me for my own good. Just like my parents.

My head swims with the force of his denials about Madison, how he was supposed to be with her the night she disappeared.

But this is *Jake*. Nothing I know about him makes me think he'd be capable of hurting Madison. It's strange though, how he hasn't been questioned by the cops yet, even though I have and so has Mr. McCormack.

Jake is the only one of us tied to Madison's last night who *hasn't* been treated as some kind of suspect. He's also the only one with a dad who has the power to make the cops consider other alternatives.

Brisbane's other hand comes up and his head tilts, all fake submission and compassion. "Your parents want you home, where it's safe."

His version of safety and mine don't have much in common. "Maybe if you guys started worrying a little less about *my* safety and focused on all the other girls, I wouldn't have to be doing your job for you!"

I can't stop the words from spilling out — for Sydney's sake, and for the girl I found and forgot.

His head rights itself, and for a moment, there's a real Brisbane under that concerned-cop veneer, and he looks confused.

Then a pink and purple Nerf ball blasts him upside the head.

His eyes have barely finished widening before I'm climbing the third row of shelving.

I scan the scene from my new perch and Harper is missing in action, but Brisbane's got his phone to his ear while he tosses aside clothing racks looking for Jake.

That's when the playground ball with a smiley emoji nails him in the face.

His phone pops free and Jake ducks behind the mirror. I am the worst friend for suspecting him. I highly doubt he called the cops just to assault them with playground equipment.

I hit the ground before I can think how much it's going to hurt.

It hurts a lot. Pain radiates up my legs, but Jake's already running toward me faster than physics should allow, even carrying my backpack. We could beat Brisbane and Harper in a race to the parking lot, but if they found us here, they probably know exactly where Jake's car is.

I steer us toward the back of the store, and every customer we pass jumps out of the way or stops to stare. I'm sure we're going to end up on the news within the hour, but when the swinging double doors to the back stockroom come into sight and there are no cops standing in front of them, I couldn't care less if they featured me on the FBI's Most Wanted list.

Jake strong-arms the door and we nearly barrel over some poor bastard with a pallet full of toys, and then we follow the clean scent of light rain to the loading docks.

We run through an open bay and jump to the concrete below, neither of us slowing until we're far from the reach of the parking lot lights.

We stop, waiting, but no one's following.

Jake breaths out, "I think we're free."

But we also have no car, and no one to call, and freedom doesn't feel like much of a victory.

CHAPTER TWENTY-THREE

"What the fuck, Caroline?"

Jake is not pleased with me. He is also quite worried about his car, and a wee bit suspicious about the house we're standing in. He can't stop analyzing every bit of furniture and every picture on the walls like they might provide some clue that would make him feel better about standing here.

I hold out my hand and wait. "Do you want me to dry them or not?"

He pronounces the words slowly this time, apparently hoping the third time will be the elusive charm. "Whose house is this?"

I managed to avoid this topic while standing in the rain, hiding behind the dumpster corral at the gas station until we found our new BFFs, Kurt and Mike. Then I was too busy negotiating the fifty-dollar fee for them to drive us away from Harper and Brisbane. Then I was trying not to breathe the whole ride since my first inhale gave me a contact high.

I also sidestepped this conversation the entire walk here after I had Kurt and Mike drop us off a few blocks over *and* on the other side of the highway just in case the cops found them later — that way they wouldn't give away our hiding spot.

Except now we're here and Jake doesn't appear to be letting it go. In fact, his entire emotional state seems to hinge on knowing. If he's going to the drug house with me later, I need him to have a somewhat stable emotional state.

And it's getting late — Mabel's Swiss-themed cuckoo clock is dangerously close to the little sheep-herder belting out eleven yodels.

I sigh. "Technically speaking, it's my dad's."

"Your dad keeps a shack house in West Virginia?"

"It's not a shack house. It's a house. I'm not saying it's huge but people raise families in houses this size, Jake."

"Jesus. Sorry." He peels off his wet shirt and plops it into my waiting hand. "Why does he have it though?"

"He's in real estate, remember? Pants too if you want them dried."

His abs flex as he pops the button on his pants and I keep my eyes on his face for the rest. His smile makes it obvious he notices. "So he lets you stay here?"

"Not exactly." I grab the pants and take off toward the dryer down the hall, but he's a step behind the whole way.

"Are you squatting in your dad's house?"

"No." The drum bangs against the dryer's shell as I shove the clothes inside.

The draft from beneath the side door snakes around my ankles. I should dry my clothes too but I'm not stripping in front of Jake. "My dad bought it from a nice old lady named Mabel. It was supposed to be a quick buy, fix and flip, make some money, except Mabel's assisted care fell through, and she emailed my dad and begged him to let her rent it back at a monthly payment that still nets my dad almost two hundred dollars each month. My dad's a sucker for a sob story as long as it doesn't involve modern medicine, so voila! Here we are."

"So you're squatting in Mabel's house?"

I turn to face him. "*I'm* Mabel, Jake."

His hand moves toward his hair but makes a detour to scrub against the hint of stubble on his cheeks. "What?"

"Mabel — the real one — is in an old folks' home fifteen miles from here. She has dementia and she thinks I'm her daughter Suzie when I visit her sometimes. We were friends before that though."

He says, "Seems reasonable," in a way that makes it clear it's not.

"Well, it's true. We met when Dad was about to buy the place. I helped her email her daughter one day and then I *used* her email when I pretended to be her and wrote my dad so he thinks he's renting to her when it's actually me. I'm never late on any payments to him or the utilities or taxes, and I've actually really improved Mabel's credit score, which wasn't great, by the way, *and* I feed her soup when I visit, which the real Suzie won't even do, *plus* I read to her."

Silence fills the tiny hallway until the furnace rattles awake — it's the only thing that jostles Jake from stunned silence.

His leans in, his voice so low it's strained. "You stole a grandma's identity so you could live in her house?"

"I did not steal her identity!" Before I realize what my arms are doing, I'm yanking my shirt over my head, then the cami beneath it. "It's not like I'm ordering TVs or opening credit cards with her social security number. I'm just *borrowing* her name for a minute and I asked her about it one time, you know. I told her what I was doing and she said it was okay!"

"She has fucking dementia!" His voice booms and sweat springs out on my entire body, partly because maybe I feel a

239

little guilty about Mabel even though I'm not doing anything to hurt her, and partly because without this house — without Mabel — I never would've had Willa. If I'd taken her to my real home — let her see the gated driveway surrounding massive walls, the gleam of objects that exist for display but not *use*, the echoes in the empty rooms — if I'd let her see the differences between our worlds, she never would've been more than a fleeting presence in mine.

I knew it from the moment I found her again, the day of the disadvantaged youth soccer retreat. I saw the way she looked at my teammates while they rattled off drink orders, her head ducked, her voice small. I saw it in the way so many looked at *her*, like she was invisible.

But because of Mabel, because of everything I did to make standing on these cold, warped floors possible, our worlds merged. Not long enough, but better than not at all.

And now Jake is ruining that. Ruining the only space I have left that's mine, where I can be without judgment or expectation or having to remember which version of myself I'm supposed to be.

For that, I want to shove him onto the sidewalk and lock the door behind him.

"She was lucid at the time, so fuck you *very* much for asking!" I rip my zipper down and stomp the jeans into a pile beneath my feet because I need to do *something* before I do something I'll regret.

Jake's fingers press into the dryer so hard the veins in his forearm bulge, and it's only through the haze of rage that I realize we're both standing in our underwear.

The wind blusters outside and seeps through the gaps in the door, trickling over my skin and drawing out a shudder.

He said I was the ocean.

Jake's breath hitches, and before he can exhale, he's walking back down the hall.

After tossing in my clothes and cranking the dryer on, I creep back into my room and throw him a towel, hoping it's not covered in dust.

He takes longer than he needs to drape it over himself, adjusting and readjusting so I have time to pull on a pair of leggings without feeling like I'm putting on a show.

I've almost got my shirt tugged to my waist when he says, "I thought you were kidding. Didn't figure you for a flower kind of girl."

I'm thrown by how quiet his voice is, how scared he sounds, and the guilt over being the cause makes my insides churn. "Is that your way of saying you don't like it?"

He waves me over and I pull up my shirt to reveal the whole tattoo. His fingers flit over my skin — lightly, like he's afraid to let them land — and he scans the full length of my ribs before his mouth turns down. "It looks great on you, Caroline. It's just —"

"What?"

"Nothing."

"Jake, so help me —"

"Is it supposed to be all … floppy like that?"

I yank down my shirt and smack his arm for good measure. "It's an iris, you asshole. That's how they look."

"I'm the asshole? I didn't know they made sad, mopey flowers like that."

"It's not sad or mopey. It's just not the same as all the other flowers."

"Because you're not the same as other girls?"

The bed creaks when I drop onto it. "Because to me, *she's* not like other girls."

He nods and his elbows drop to his knees, his head bowed. "I assaulted a cop today. Probably on video."

It's not like I didn't know that, but hearing the words turns my muscles to water. "I'm sorry. For —" He shakes his head to cut me off and I talk right over him. "I *am* sorry, and let's fix it, okay? Text your dad and tell him you didn't recognize them."

"Yeah, but you —" His head snaps up with the realization that I *did* recognize them, and his innocence will make me look twice as guilty. "No. I'm not pinning this on you."

"Jake." I grab his hand and it twitches beneath my fingers. "I am royally fucked. You are not. So text your dad and tell him you're trying to help me because you're worried about my safety or whatever, and then you say you saw this creepy dude staring me down in the aisle and you were trying to protect me, and I didn't tell you it was Brisbane until later." It's an explanation mostly rooted in truth, and those are the hardest to destroy. Plus, Jake's dad has fellow judge-people connections. It will work.

He stares into the corner, his gaze unfocused. "I don't know, Caroline."

But it's the "I don't know" of someone who *does* know.

I grab his phone from the bed. "If you want to go to the drug house with me, just tell him you're still trying to talk me into turning myself in. Then turn off your phone."

It only takes a few minutes, and when the screen blinks to black he tosses it onto the bed. "Can I ask you something?"

"I guess you've earned it."

He laughs but it's choked, and a tidal wave of red rushes from his neck to his cheeks. "You don't have to answer, but … what do you like about girls?"

It takes every bit of my emotion-suppression training to keep the laugh in my belly from bubbling up. And then I have to complete a four-count Sama Vritti to keep myself under control. "I'd imagine the same things *you* like about girls."

He scoots back on the bed until his shoulders touch the wall. "No."

"Yes."

"Give me an example."

"Boobs?"

He rolls his eyes and a smile lights his face. "You have your own."

"You have your own tongue and I'm sure you still appreciate other people's."

"Touché. But what else? And don't name other body parts."

"Zero chance of pregnancy?"

"I have no argument for that. What else?"

I jump into the middle of the bed because the ridiculousness of this conversation is exactly what I need to stop thinking about everything else, just for a minute. Because this feels normal, like we're back at school, but with all the layers we've built between us stripped clean. "It's your turn."

"We're not taking turns. You're proving my point for me."

"You have a point? And you expect me to prove it for you?

Mr. McCormack would be very disappointed." Panic lances through me because he *still* hasn't texted or emailed.

Jake balls the towel and tosses it into the hallway with enough speed it thwacks against the wall. "Are you going to be honest about him and —"

"Yes. Yes, I am going to be honest, by speaking the same truth I've been speaking all along. You know what's funny, Jake? Dozens of women can come out and claim some guy assaulted them and millions of people won't believe them, but *my* story has never changed and no one will believe me."

"You're oversimplifying. People are just trying to protect you and —"

"This." I'm off the bed and pacing the floor because otherwise I'll smother him with my pillow. "You want to know why I like girls? Because they might not agree with me but they get it. I wouldn't have to explain this to them. And even if they thought I was oversimplifying, they'd at least start off by saying, 'Yeah, that *is* fucking bullshit.' Everybody likes to act like girls are all oversensitive and needy, but anyone who's ever dated a guy knows exactly how fragile dudes' egos are."

"You know, I'm a guy, and I'm sitting right here."

"And you asked the question."

I don't know if I should apologize or he should. Right and wrong are so twisted together I can't find the threads to follow to the end.

I weave my hands through my hair and press the heels of my palms against my temples. The pressure chases away some of the tension coiling in my head, and I open my mouth to tell Jake he needs to cut his losses and go home, that there's no way he could possibly understand, when he says, "They pay attention. Even when you don't realize you're angry or upset, they do. That's my turn. My non-physical thing I like about girls."

I want to crawl into my bed and pull the covers over my head, let my aching body relax into the softness of sleep and denial.

I keep trying to cast off the versions of myself that don't fit anymore. The ones that chafe and confine. But they're never gone. They find their way back and slip over me like chains, forcing me to break free again.

One day, it will be the last time. One day I'll weaken them until they're in jagged pieces.

But right now those chains are telling me to stay, to spend the night in this silent house with Jake — with the comfort of another quiet creature breathing next to me. They're telling me to hide and pretend, to give up and convince myself it's not my responsibility to find Madison, to burrow into the safety of these walls as the wind ravages the windows and the rain rushes against the roof, where the only things that can hurt me are the two people in this room.

I flounce onto the bed and sit next to him, using the side of his shoulder as a backrest. "They don't make you say the words, and they give you what you need anyway."

I take the shift at my back as agreement, and he adds, "They pick out awesome birthday and Christmas presents."

"Word."

"Shit you didn't even realize you wanted."

"That little spot on the inside of their hip bones."

"That's physical."

I shrug. "The non-physical stuff, guys can do too, you know?

It's personality, not gender. I guess I just never care about what package the person comes in."

"Except for the boobs."

"And hip bones."

"Soft skin."

"That little gasp when your tongue hits that spot on their neck. The way they bite their lip or their breathing goes quick when —"

Jake mumbles, "Jesus, you have to stop," and slides across the bed, my head smacking onto the mattress.

When I stop laughing, I say, "I told you we had the same reasons."

"I didn't expect you to go all description-porn about it."

"Yeah, well, clearly my hormones think I am in desperate need of action." He's silent so long I cram my head into the blankets to look up at him. Even upside down it's impossible to misunderstand his thoughts. So I whack him in the head with my pillow.

My world goes black when he ricochets it back, muffling my laughter as the bed bounces beneath me. By the time I throw the pillow off the bed and take in my first clean breath, I'm surrounded by him, tilting under the weight of his body, and I have to blink twice to take in this new view of him.

His voice is even different. Deeper, commanding. "You said it's the person, right?"

"Jake, I —"

"She's gone, Caroline."

My tongue plasters to the roof of my mouth and my voice comes out hoarse. "She dumped me."

She abandoned me, and I still can't find the things I did wrong. The things that weren't enough to make her stay.

His hand cradles my jaw, thumb brushing over my cheek. "How much time are you going to waste on someone who doesn't deserve it? Stop pretending you don't understand."

His mouth lowers over mine and the wind swells, sending an avalanche of rain against the window, each wave more savage than the last. This is the Jake the other girls talk about. The player. The alpha male. The captain of whatever team is in season.

His tongue delves deep and his hand tangles in my hair, my nape tingling with the tension, and I *do* understand. I understand how he has different versions too, and I wish I knew which one feels right to him, which one makes him feel like he's broken through his own chains.

I don't think it's this one — not for either of us.

My phone trills and we both startle, but as I go to reach for it, Jake's pulling me back to him, his lips hot against my neck. "Ignore it."

"I can't. It's Aubrey."

He pulls back and I don't have time to explain because I'm about to miss her call.

Aubrey's already yelling at me when I get the phone to my ear.

I give Jake a look that says I'm sorry even though I think Aubrey just saved us both, and I grab my jacket from the armchair.

The dryer buzzes so loud my words to Aubrey are completely engulfed, and I tuck the phone against my shoulder, ripping open the dryer door while my half-on coat flops from my arm.

Jake's clothes singe my hands and I barely manage to hold on to them. "Just pull into the driveway and I'll open the garage."

I sprint into the room where Jake is stuck in a state of … shock? Barely constrained rage?

He hasn't moved.

I drop our tangled clothes in a pile near his legs, and he says, "Aubrey is *here*?"

I cover the mouthpiece and nod. "Because of the makeup."

He has no idea what I'm talking about, but I walk out anyway, scrambling to shrug on my coat and cram my bare feet into my boots.

The world beyond the walls of the house is a full-fledged assault. Rain pelts my skin in a thousand pinpricks, and even the sidewalk feels slick beneath my feet. My breath escapes in clouds and tree branches sway and lurch in the wind.

Twin beams of light split the darkness and the steady thump of Aubrey's wipers draws nearer.

Broken concrete shifts and crunches in the space beneath the garage handle, and I remind myself if I make it through this mess I need to send a Mabel email to Dad and tell him someone needs to come look it over. I grab the T-pronged handle with both hands and pull.

My fingers pop free, throbbing and stinging, and I grasp tighter until the handle clicks and the door scrapes open, tilting from the bottom and rising toward the moonless sky.

I duck inside while Aubrey wedges her car in to the empty space next to Mabel's/mine. Her door opens inch by inch, and that's my first clue. The second is her equally slow emergence.

I already learned my lesson with Jake, so I cut her off before she has the chance to stand. "The house belongs to an old lady named Mabel, and I stay here sometimes when I can't stand being anywhere else, and yes it's safe and yes she knows." Most of the time.

Her eyes scan the garage — the oil-stained floor and battered tool benches, the broken window pane — and then inch toward the house. Even through the rain she registers the dented siding on the tiny one-story ranch, the split wood dangling from the side of the deck

Mabel has a habit of asking my dad to hold off on big projects on account of her sensitive, headache-prone ears, and she always knows just how to phrase things so he'll agree.

Three more months, and he'll be free to do whatever he wants.

Aubrey's arms lock over her chest and she nods in a way that's nowhere near agreeable. "Sure. Yeah. Looks totally safe and appropriate for a teenaged girl to hang out in alone."

"Okay. Glad we had this talk. Stuff in the trunk?"

She glares at me but hits the lock button anyway, and it only takes a few minutes to grab all her gear and make another clothes-soaking trek into the house, where Jake has managed to put on his pants but not his shirt, and there's so much silent conversation we may as well be screaming.

I dump Aubrey's makeup cases onto the table and their contents scatter.

There's no time to soothe feelings and craft explanations. Jake is right. It's well past time to stop pretending anything in my life could resemble normal.

Pretending led to leaving a nameless girl in the woods.

But if one thing makes sense, it's that if I want to find Madison, I need to follow the connections the cops won't. Sydney's the closest connection I've got to Chrystal, and if she *is* alive, maybe she knows things — all the things Chrystal promised to tell me about Madison.

I need to find Sydney.

I need to go to The Bricks.

And I need to look the part.

CHAPTER TWENTY-FOUR

Jake veers from the highway and onto the exit ramp, tires bumping over the land mine of potholes, and Aubrey and I say, "This is the wrong exit," in unison.

He taps the steering wheel and clears his throat, shifting uncomfortably in Mabel's driver's seat. "Just have to make a quick stop."

"Jake —"

"Don't be mad —"

"I won't be if you just drive to The Bricks."

"Can't do that."

"*Why* can you not do that?"

Aubrey shrinks further into the back seat as my voice rises, and I'd bet she's regretting her decision to come with us. Jake and I both lobbied for Aubrey staying at Mabel's, which she adamantly refused to do. I would've left and refused to tell her where we're headed, but I need her to drive Jake home, and truth is I don't really want her to leave.

I force my brain to ignore the memory of her sitting across from me, our knees touching, while she studied me. Then she frowned and declared she didn't need to do anything to make me look strung out.

Jake says, "Because you're not royally fucked. At least, you don't have to be."

He rolls Mabel's car into a coffee shop parking lot and my brain is working better than I want it to because I can think of only one reason Jake is stopping for a latte right now.

I stare at the Porsche cooling in a lot flanked by liquor stores. "Jake. I am not talking to your dad again. He's not some magic cure for every situation."

"He can help."

"I don't need help."

He slams the car into park. "You don't — you don't need help? Really? Because we ran from the cops tonight."

Behind me, Aubrey whimpers.

"I can fix this. I just —"

"Caroline." It's the quiet in Jake's voice that gets me to look at him. When I do, his eyes are soft. "He's cool, okay? He came through before. With the lipstick, right? I wouldn't bring you here if he wasn't."

I know he's thinking about all the things I've told him about my parents, how they are definitely not "cool."

"I have makeup on that makes me look like an addict."

"I told him Aubrey was using us as practice." Except he barely let her put any on him.

He glances at his watch, then to the wall of windows and the soft beckoning light beyond them. There's a long pause before he speaks. "If you really want to find Madison, and help Mr. McCormack, maybe you should tell someone the whole story."

He's right. I don't want him to be. I want to spout off some perfectly reasoned argument for why he's wrong, but my brain is a wasteland.

Jake is always my strongest competition in debates, and right now he's proving why.

I'm out of the car, dodging puddles, before he meets me at the front bumper and says, "Aubrey doesn't want to come."

She climbs into the front seat and clicks the locks, giving me a wave that looks like an apology, and then I have nothing to keep me from opening the door and walking through it.

Warmth blankets me as we step inside, scents of buttery pastries and rich roast coffee fighting for domination.

Jake's dad is tucked into a corner table and his fingers fly over his phone screen, shadows playing over the square jaw he shares with his son. Bits of gray tease the dark hair near his temples and a cup of coffee steams in front of him.

As if he senses Jake's presence, his head snaps up and his arms stretch wide. He says, "Hey, buddy!" like Jake's still ten years old.

Jake doesn't seem to mind. There's a weightlessness to him right now, like whatever worries he'd been carrying have vanished.

They hug and I can't watch, can't stop feeling like I'm intruding on something not meant for me.

None of this is meant for me, and an empty place inside me pangs with the realization that I've forgotten what it feels like inside my parents' arms. If there was ever a time I felt weightless in their presence, I can't remember it.

"Caroline!" Mr. Monaghan's thick arm wraps around me in a side-hug, the slight hint of tree bark or something equally manly scenting his cologne.

My arm jerks up to hug him back and Jake nods like mass hugging was all part of his master plan.

Mr. Monaghan releases me and ushers us both to his table where he's got two more coffees waiting. "Jake said lots of sugar and cream."

I nod because I'm too busy wondering when they had time to set up a meeting and discuss my coffee preferences.

Jake slides in next to me and his hand finds my thigh. After what happened in my room, I should tell him to move it, but the heavy weight of it, the heat burning into my skin, makes me feel like we're on the same side. Like I'm a little less lost than I feel.

Mr. Monaghan settles into the chair across from me, pinning his cup between his palms. "It's great to see you again. I wish it was under different circumstances, but I'm glad you're both here."

I can't keep my gaze locked on his. No matter how much I try, it slides away, and Jake gives my knee a reassuring squeeze. I am terribly, horribly aware of the makeup that sits thick on my skin, and the knowledge that it can't cover all the ways I'm going to ignore the reasonable advice Mr. Monaghan is sure to give me. Again.

And I brace for his anger over not having followed it the first time.

He says, "Let's get the formalities out of the way. I'm not your attorney, this isn't a substitute for legal advice, and I still don't have inside knowledge of the ongoing investigation into Madison Bentley's disappearance nor Landon McCormack's alleged involvement. Clear?"

"Mr. McCormack is not involved in Madison's disappearance." The words pop free and Jake's fingers twitch.

Mr. Monaghan holds his palms up. "Okay. But regardless of what you think about his guilt or innocence, you should just let the cops do their job."

Jake says, "The cops *aren't* doing their job though."

Mr. Monaghan nudges Jake's coffee and gives him a small smile. "Did you get a job on the force when I wasn't looking? If you're looking at a career in law, I hear *judge* isn't too bad."

Jake rolls his eyes, not even trying to hide his smile. "Your Dad-jokes game is strong, old man."

"Not too old to beat your ass on the football field."

"Madden football maybe."

Mr. Monaghan's baritone laugh mixes with the hum around us, but then he glances to me and his face goes serious. "So. Jake said there's something he thinks I can help with."

Jake's fingers press hard enough to leave bruises, and I try to do what I came here for. "Mr. McCormack is *not* involved in whatever happened to Madison, and he has never   not ever — done anything to hurt me."

Every word I speak *will* get back to my mom and dad, and when they find out all my secrets, I'll be lucky if I'm ever let out of their sights again. But hopefully, I'm freeing Mr. McCormack. Hopefully, Madison will be home safely before my parents have to read my statement — it's just one more reason I have to follow this to the end. It's not just Madison that needs saving. I need to save myself too.

I tell Mr. Monaghan about me and Willa and The Wayside. About Mr. McCormack and the ride home and the driver's license. About Chrystal knowing something about Madison.

And then, about why my mom can't know about Willa.

Mr. Monaghan pauses, his shoulders slumped. "As a father, I'm extremely saddened you don't feel safe enough with your parents to tell them the truth."

His words knock the breath from my body, and I'm barely recovered when he continues, "As a judge, Caroline, I think you need to tell the detectives everything you've told me."

The gentle pressure of Jake's hand tells me my leg is bouncing beneath the table and I force it still. "I *tried* to tell them. Not everything, but enough."

The glare of headlights splashes through the windows, and I break the eye contact I'm barely making. "They won't believe any of it. Detective Harper made it sound like I'm some lovesick Mr. McCormack groupie."

He slides his coffee aside and leans closer. "I believe you."

I don't deserve his faith in me. His kindness either.

I croak out a thank-you and he continues before I have to say anything else. "Here's how I think I can help. I have a friend who's an attorney. If you'd like, I can have him contact you and you can provide a statement for him to present to the police. Sound good?"

A bit of that weightlessness starts to take hold, until Mr. Monaghan adds, "But, Caroline, I need you to understand something. The police can't search a person's home without probable cause. If they found your license in Mr. McCormack's apartment, they had a reason for being there, and it likely had nothing to do with you."

LIVING THE LIES

There are people who come into our lives to disprove the lies we believe about ourselves.

Sometimes their stays are short — brief collisions as we all tumble through life. The cashier who gives you too much change, leaving you that brief moment to decide if you're truly the honest person you thought yourself to be. The stranger who tests your bravery when they *say* things no one should even *think*.

But those little revelations, they're easy to push down, to ignore or forget.

They're the rumble of thunder, not the deafening roar of our very selves splitting open against the force of an earthquake.

The Larrys were thunder, and contrary to what many of them told me, I was smart. At least smart enough to place in higher-level classes with teachers who understood present circumstances weren't permanent circumstances.

It was in one of those classes that *Brave New World* landed on my worn desk, its cover torn and peeling in the corners, white fibers shredding as they curled toward the middle, the inside stamped with the name of a school that was not mine. I'd long since lost any shame in being grateful for someone else's discards — this time, it meant the tips from one more table went into the stack of bills in the book I'd hollowed out and hidden at home.

The assignment was to choose, just like the characters in the book: Would we rather live in blissful ignorance or suffer under the truth?

I chose truth.

Out of thirty-four students, I was one of two.

It earned me an A and an acknowledgment from my teacher, a silent reassurance he would've chosen the truth too.

I slipped the paper into my bag, careful not to crease its edges or wrinkle its form. It was sacred.

It was proof.

Proof that I was strong, stronger than the rest of them. And it was hope. Hope that I could leave this place and everyone in it one day.

I cemented it into my view of myself, built myself around it.

I chose truth.

Then Livie proved me a liar.

Livie wasn't thunder. Livie was my earthquake.

It only took one moment, seeing her in my trailer, holding my hollowed-out book, and the ground rumbled beneath my feet and my world split apart.

If I trace it back, it was there from the beginning. But that night, when I tried to convince my mom to consider John's deal — that was when it began to unravel. Mom ranted and called me names. "Ungrateful" was the nicest of them. And for once, I didn't cry. Sometimes, when I replay all the moments, I think maybe I smiled.

She wasn't mine to fix.

I'd always mourn the person I needed my mom to be, but I couldn't will her into becoming it no matter how many tears I shed.

I was not my mother's keeper.

I turned and walked out the door.

I didn't pack my things or throw my key onto the table. But even with the absence of grand gestures, I think she knew.

So when I came home from school two days later, I wasn't surprised to see my curtains tangled in my blinds — evidence my mom had ransacked my room. I wasn't shocked by the harsh voices cutting through the thin walls before I'd made it within five feet of the front door. And when I opened that door, I wasn't surprised to see my mom's scowl etched deep on her face, nor the Larry looming over her shoulder.

But Livie's presence felt like a betrayal. A mixing of incompatible worlds. She didn't belong there.

She would never belong to that place.

I didn't want her to see this part of my life, the people in it. I *never* wanted her to see it.

I stumbled back until the step rattled beneath me, and my mom crammed a stack of cash deep into her pocket.

Livie stood, my book clutched to her chest. "I can explain."

"No, you can't."

She rushed forward and tucked my book into my arms. Then her hands framed my face as she said, "I came here to convince her to help the cops, but she was going through your room and she found —" Livie paused, her dark hair wild from the force of the frigid wind. "Don't leave, okay? Please?"

"You don't *belong* here."

Her fingers brushed away my tears. "She was going to take your college money. I couldn't let her do that."

"So you gave her *yours*?"

"Not —" She swallowed. "Not *all* of it. Just enough to make her back off. I've been saving longer than you and —"

She didn't bother with the rest. Didn't continue to say things neither of us would believe.

She gave her money to spare mine. She knew where I lived though I'd never shown her. She couldn't have walked, but her car was absent.

That was the first warning of rumble beneath my feet. Livie knew things she shouldn't, did things she should not have been able to do.

Livie had hidden things from me too.

Her gaze traveled past me to the open door — the one that rhythmically smacked the side of the trailer under the force of the wind. "Your problems are my problems, right? That's the deal."

I nodded because that *was* the deal, but suddenly, the deal didn't feel like truth.

She said, "Don't go, okay?"

She left me there, standing in the middle of a dying lawn with a limping pinwheel speared in its side, and her footfalls thundered back up the steps.

My mom raised her voice, only to fall quiet after a few muttered syllables of Livie's. I hugged my book to my chest as my metal mini-blinds tinkled and popped. If I turned, I'd see them straightened and my curtains untangled at Livie's hands. If I opened my hollowed-out book, I'd see the money I'd saved tucked safely inside, with a few extra included.

I'd built myself around truth. But the money, Livie's presence: these were lies.

Livie's lies.

But then, I had mine too.

In this, we were the same, showing only the parts of ourselves we'd built, the parts that came from the truest places inside us, leaving the things we never asked for. Never wanted.

My *Brave New World* paper sat silently in the backpack resting on my shoulder blades, right where it always was.

I claimed I'd rather suffer through truth than revel in ignorance.

Except that day, when dusk crept over the sun and pulled the veil into night, I waited until Livie emerged from my trailer with a duffel strapped over her shoulder. I didn't question her about the money, about how she knew where I lived. I didn't force the answers to questions I had every right to ask. I didn't apologize for keeping her from this part of me.

Instead, I bathed myself in the truth of who she was. Who I was. The better versions of ourselves we became when we were together.

She was an earthquake, but one that belonged to me. She created fault lines so the light could shine in.

When her forehead came to rest against mine, our heated breaths mingling in soft gasps while the world around us spun, I smiled back.

Our truths change. They stretch and split as we grow, the shedding of them leaving us raw and exposed. If we're lucky, we're surrounded by love in those moments when our tender flesh is still rebuilding. If we're not, we grow scars.

I suffered no scars at Livie's hands, and the ones I bear now hold no truths.

CHAPTER TWENTY-FIVE

The Bricks is not a kind place.

Even though we're deep into the night, there's no peace here. Only restless quiet.

A massive brickyard stands guard over a row of broken houses whose chain-link fences have long since conceded to nature's forces. Uncut grass bows over itself in waves, waiting to be brought to life when spring unfolds. Tumbled bricks gather against the curb, and I'm grateful it's too dark to make out what else might be lying alongside them.

Jake walks with even more determination than normal, as if the meeting with his dad filled him up somehow.

I want to feel what he's feeling — like there's a safety net waiting to catch us all before we leave this entire mess broken and scarred. I want to feel like Mr. Monaghan will help. I'm grateful to him for handling the lipstick, *and* for arranging for his attorney to take my statement so I can tell what I know without my parents hearing me say it. But he also believes Mr. McCormack did something, so I can't trust him.

I don't care what reason the cops had for searching Mr. McCormack's house. Whatever their probable cause was, it's wrong. And I'm going to prove it. The single best way is to fulfill my promise and bring Madison home. If Sydney truly *is* missing, at least I have a lead, some connection to help find Madison. If I find Sydney alive, I have to pray she knows what Chrystal promised to tell me.

Aubrey spent the entire ride in Mabel's car complaining about the smell of moth balls, but she isn't complaining anymore. Moth balls, it seems, are preferable to the pungent smells of vomit, piss, and something that makes me think of burning flesh, still clinging to our clothes even after we've left the first house. And that one was empty.

We wind between weeds that force themselves through the cracked sidewalks while the wind tosses empty bottles to clink against the curb.

The door to the next home is held on by a single hinge that grinds as Jake wrenches it open, and inside the entryway, I step over a literal hole in the floor. A lantern casts a ring of light over peeling wallpaper and rotted floorboards that hold nests of wadded clothing. The faint hint of smoke clouds the air, masking the damp wood and the bite of wind through broken windows.

Aubrey murmurs, "If these walls could talk," like it's something she'd actually like to hear, but whatever stories are buried here are better left unspoken.

The scrape of a lighter cuts through the silence and a flame stretches high, skipping shadows over a couple tucked in the far corner. The girl doesn't look like Sydney, but I'm not sure I could even pick out Jake or Aubrey in this place, let alone a girl I only know through pictures.

I can't escape the feel of this place — desperation that worms beneath your skin, wriggling until it hurts.

I remember it like I remember the singe of searing metal on my palm and the thick press of restraints through my paper-thin gown.

And then I remember the moment the flame in the kitchen took flight and transformed itself into fire. Sometimes burning it down is the only escape.

My fingers twitch with the need to do just that when Jake announces, "We're looking for Sydney," and a hush blankets the house.

I want to shove him down the hole at the front door.

The guy in the corner stretches his legs, jeans pale at the stretched-out knees. "What the fuck for?"

Aubrey steps forward, and she doesn't even look like herself anymore. She stretches every muscle taut, and her arms jerk as she hugs them over her chest, her lips pulled back in a grimace.

There's a moment when I have to remind myself not to be worried, that Aubrey doesn't really want what they have.

Even her voice sounds harder. "What the fuck do you think for?"

It's an unlikely stage, but her performance is even better for it.

He shrugs and says, "We'll share," and then his girlfriend nods toward me and says, "I like your earrings."

My tongue is already moving toward a thank-you when my brain catches up and my hand flies to my earlobe to shield it.

The guy scans over Jake and picks out the one thing that's not negotiable. "Yeah, and I like your watch."

Jake isn't giving up that watch. It's a TAG Heuer and I *should* know the model because Jake's talked about wanting it for years. His dad finally bought it after Jake earned enough credits to graduate with a four-point-something GPA. I should know that too.

Everything about the last several days feels like a lesson in things I should've known. Clues I've missed. All the things I've blinded myself to instead of seeing.

The tendons in Jake's wrist flex, and I can tell he's fighting against the urge to shake his sleeve down, the same way my earring is still hidden behind my hand. But this is my responsibility, and right now it doesn't matter that these earrings are the last present my mom gave me before things were never the same between us.

Madison. I owe her this.

I grasp the diamond and backing and tug them both free, then again on the other side. When I hold them cupped in my palm they sparkle in the moonlight. "What does this get me?"

The guy spreads his arms wide like he's offering us the world, and I can't help but wonder if, to him, it is. His gaze snags on Jake's wrist again. "But it looks like you want what only Syd can get you ..."

My breath hitches. I don't *want* Sydney to be dead, but if she's alive, it means the mystery I've been trying to unravel doesn't exist. It means Madison's disappearance still makes no sense, my only lead is gone and my only hope of vindicating Mr. McCormack is my word. And if that didn't mean enough before, it certainly won't now that I've assaulted cops with Nerf balls and fled the scene.

"Where do we find her?" I hold out my earrings and the girl uncurls from her huddled crouch. Her nails scrape over my palm as she swipes it clean, and somehow, my hand feels heavier.

She jerks her head to the side. "Check next door. She's usually with Max."

Aubrey leads us out and I check my Mr. McCormack phone as we hurry down the steps. I'm almost grateful he hasn't contacted me. The only thing I'd have to tell him is his chance for vindication may lie with a girl who isn't as dead as he needs her to be. If Sydney's alive, there is no other suspect to take Mr. McCormack's place. And if the cops are hunting Mr. McCormack, they couldn't be further from finding Madison.

Aubrey stays in character until we're well past the house, then she spins so fast Jake and I both have to pull up short. She pokes a finger into Jake's chest. "That was awful. I wouldn't trust you to play an inanimate object. It isn't good enough that I made you *look* like an addict if you don't *act* like it."

He starts to respond but she's already storming toward the other house. The short version is Jake should absolutely not speak again, and I am on probationary status.

The front door rushes open and Jake yanks both me and Aubrey backward just before it would've knocked us from the porch. Two guys stream out, muttering insincere apologies as they slip down the steps.

The porch rocks beneath our feet and Aubrey plasters herself to Jake's chest. She looks so tiny in his arms, all the bravado drained now that her audience isn't expecting a show.

They look right together, like if I could replace the background they could be a regular couple.

"Caroline." When my gaze snaps to Jake's it's obvious he's been reading something from me he probably shouldn't have, but all he says is, "Get in the house."

The figures inside move in shadows, skirting the moonlight that spills through from uncovered windows.

We didn't need makeup. No one here looks at anyone else.

The sweet, oily scent of kerosene drifts through the room, but there's no warmth, just cold that presses in from the floor and walls.

Footsteps thunder down the stairs and I move toward them, following the staggered rows of matted footprints in the carpet.

The light brightens with each step, until a kerosene heater comes into view and warmth blasts my skin. I head for the rise and fall of voices on the right, where the hall is punctuated by a series of upright flashlights.

A girl stumbles out the door and into the wall, then she rubs her face even though it was her shoulder that took the brunt of it. She meets my eyes — the first person to since we walked in — and shrugs.

Without word or gesture, she rights herself and blows by me, chin jutted, shoulders back, and I can't get in the room fast enough.

Sydney Hatton lounges on a couch near the back of the room, ankles crossed over her boyfriend's lap. I have to assume he's Max. He jerks his head by way of greeting and I nod back, trying not to be too obvious as I scan the open space and the matte-black safe that dominates the room.

It's not even that big — the size of a microwave — but it's hard not to stare at it, knowing whatever's inside has the power to control lives and disrupt futures. There's life and death behind those heavy metal walls, and plenty that would make you wish there was no time in between.

You can get anything you want in The Bricks. That's what everyone says.

Except if you want answers, because I'm not going to find any here.

Sydney's alive. There is no guy out there kidnapping girls. There's no suspect who's not Mr. McCormack for me to find. There's no secret connection that led Madison to The Wayside — none other than me. And that means Marcel kicking me out — twice — wasn't for any reason other than he wanted me gone.

It means my best friend needed me and I wasn't there, and now she's gone and I don't know how to bring her back.

I don't know how to fix all the things I've broken.

My throat burns with every chemical-laden inhale, and a thin stream of fresh air whistles through a cracked window. The lightbulb flickers, but even with the strobe effect transforming every movement into stop-motion, Sydney's spine stiffens.

By the time I cross the room, her legs are off Max's lap and his casual pose is a bad cover for the sharpness in his eyes.

A shudder rattles through me as I pull a folded piece of paper from my pocket, because it's far too similar to what Detective Brisbane did to me. As it turns out, being on the other side doesn't feel any better.

I unfold it and hold it out to Sydney, but it's obvious she already knows what it is.

She flops back against the ratty couch, throwing up a haze of dust. "You can't blackmail me."

"What? That's your response? Your aunt thinks you're missing!"

"She's supposed to."

My fingers twitch with the need to crumple the paper and

throw it at her. To grab her by the arm and drag her to Chrystal's trailer so she can see her aunt lying in a recliner with a glass of poison beside her.

"Your aunt has a million of these flyers posted trying to find you."

She shrugs, but her lips press together like a flatlined heartbeat. "No one will believe her anyway."

No one will believe her because she's dead. And Sydney clearly doesn't know.

If she doesn't know *that*, odds of her knowing what Chrystal promised to tell me about Madison are next to zero.

I may be leaving this house with nothing, but Sydney deserves to know about her aunt. "There's something you need to know about Chrystal."

Max whispers something in Sydney's ear before easing from the couch, his eyes never leaving Jake, and when he heads toward a smaller room to the left, it's only his nod that reveals another man standing guard.

Sydney smooths her hair from her forehead, creating a dark ring that fades to bottle-blond five inches deep, and then she gathers it high on her head, fanning the nape of her neck with her free hand. "You want to talk, we do it alone."

CHAPTER TWENTY-SIX

Sydney's legs dangle from the sink, rattling the loose cabinet door every time one of her heels strikes it. The strip of light from the cracked bathroom door glares over one side of her face and drapes the other in a veil of black. "Ca-ro-line."

She watches me while she stretches out each syllable, and the comment the guy next door made about things that only Syd can get me feels more ominous with every half-second.

I cross my arms and drop back against the wall. It's too close in here, everything hemmed in by a peeling bathtub and a sink too big for the space. "Your aunt says your mom and stepdad are really worried about you."

She scoffs, either because of the mom and stepdad comment or because I didn't acknowledge she knows my name when she has no reason to. Her dangly earrings jump when she shakes her head. "Now she wants to play mommy? Let *her* be the one to worry for once."

Chrystal's comments ring through my head. About how Sydney's mom had made some mistakes but she was better now. Now, but clearly not soon enough.

I know that feeling, what it's like to live through that moment when you realize you're on your own, that things can never go back, that the people who are supposed to love you will never be what you need.

For all our differences — me, Sydney, and Willa too — we were all burnt by the same fire.

I break the silence. "Are you going to ask me about your aunt?"

Her shoulders lock tight. "She's dead, right?"

When I nod, she says, more to herself than me, "Surprised it took them this long."

"Who —"

"Your girlfriend is gone?"

I still, frozen in place. She knows my name. She knows about Willa.

So this is what Syd can get me. Information. *Secrets.* "She left me."

"Did she?"

"Yes, and that has nothing to do with why I'm here."

"How did she die?"

For a second, I forget to breathe, and my brain stumbles over a few responses before I register she's talking about Chrystal and not Willa. "I think someone poisoned her. I got really sick too. Who is 'them'? Who would want to kill her?"

In a blink, the glaze of tears in her eyes disappears, and she's staring at the rips in her jeans. "She wasn't always such a mess, you know? And for the longest time everyone just treated her like some nut-job conspiracy theorist. The crazy trailer lady who thinks the cops are killing teenaged girls."

"You think the cops killed her?"

"If you spend your life hunting for the bad guys, you're bound to find one."

"Is that what you're doing here? Hunting the bad guys?"

She laughs and her heels thump against the vanity. "Do I

look like I'm hunting bad guys? I don't need to hunt them. They come to me."

"For?"

"Their secrets. Amazing what fine, upstanding citizens will pay to keep their reputation. Nobody expects the crazy trailer lady to keep detailed journals with dates, names and pictures of the men who come slumming down to good ol' West Virginia to have a little fun."

I'm missing a vital clue, but I'm too afraid to admit what I don't know. "So you have the info your aunt collected, and you're blackmailing people."

She hops from the cabinet and her shoes slam into the cracked tile flooring. "I like to call it building my college fund."

"You can't go to college without graduating high school."

"Already have my GED. Now I'm just waiting it out. So what's your plan, Caroline? Gonna rat me out to my mom and stepdaddy?" She grinds her heel into a pile of ceramic that turns to dust beneath her feet. "I wouldn't have let my aunt think I was missing if there was another way, but I'm not going back to that house."

If I missed the undercurrent of threat in her voice, the way she's blocking the only exit would make her point clear. Thing is, as bad as I feel for her mom, I don't *want* to rat Sydney out. I know exactly what it's like to not belong in the place you're supposed to call home, and I know what it's like to do everything necessary to create a place you can.

But for all our similarities, we're not friends, and a rush of anxiety comes over me with the meaning of the words she hasn't spoken.

She knows my name because Chrystal did. Because Chrystal kept records and details and pictures about fine, upstanding men who came slumming down in West Virginia. And one really unfortunate night, Mr. McCormack was stupid enough to order me into his car and drive me home.

I say, "Landon McCormack. He's my teacher, and he didn't do anything wrong, but the cops are trying to pin stuff on him."

Stuff. It's a stupid, inconsequential word that doesn't carry nearly the weight it needs to. I shove my hand in my back pocket and pull out my cash, and I can't escape the irony that I'm paying off Sydney to protect Mr. McCormack from the information I'm using to blackmail him.

I've never bribed anyone before, and judging from Sydney's stare, my thin pile of twenties isn't the going rate.

She takes it anyway. "You don't tell the cops or my mom where I am, or that I'm alive, and I'll make sure any info on your teacher disappears."

It's not good enough. I want to see what info she has and watch her set it on fire.

"What if someone else finds you?"

"Who's looking?"

Fragments of my conversation with Chrystal lodge in my consciousness.

Nobody's looking for Sydney.

They think she ran away.

That's what they always think.

Always.

That word feels too inconsequential too, because it implies

so much more than it is. *Always* means it's happened before. More than once.

And *that* makes sense. If it happened before, it taught Sydney exactly what to do to make her disappearance seem real. Even if it meant making it real enough to fool her aunt, who's apparently devoted her life to uncovering the truth.

I try to summon outrage that Sydney tortured her aunt with her fake disappearance. Instead I can only remember I stole the identity of a dementia patient to cover my own.

I clear my throat and my head spins when I suck in a lungful of kerosene-sweetened air. "*I* was looking. I promised and I meant it. I was looking for you."

She blinks, and even her shadow goes soft around the edges. "I guess you were."

Her gaze drops to the floor. "That teacher of yours, he meets up with some married chick. That's why he comes down here. Not condoning it, but it's better than most of the assholes in Aunt Chrystal's records."

She pauses before she says, "She wasn't crazy."

I wait, my next breath completely dependent on the words she's hinting at speaking, because they may be the only thing that leads me to Madison.

Her fingers throttle the door handle, and the stream of light inches wider. "If you want to find missing girls, start with ones that don't look like you. Or the ones that do, but know not to bring their boyfriend and his ten-thousand-dollar watch to The Bricks."

It's like listening to Chrystal all over again: the Black and

Brown girls, the "white trash." The ones who are nothing like me, nothing like Madison. The ones who pay the price for the life they were born into.

Sydney nods, like she can hear my thoughts. "Start with Rebecca Wilder and Tracy Bast. But I'm not responsible for what happens."

I repeat the names in my head until they don't sound real anymore, and then I finally summon the courage to ask the question I came here for. "My friend is missing. I found a match-book, and it had your aunt's number in my friend's handwriting on it. Your aunt said if I found you, she'd tell me what she knew about her."

"Seems like your friend's got plenty of people looking for her already."

"Not in the right places." I wait until she meets my eyes. "I'm trying to help. I'm looking, not just for Madison, for all of them. Please."

Her sigh is resigned. "I don't know what happened to your friend, but if she got Aunt Chrystal to give up her phone number, I'd bet she found something she shouldn't have. People like that have a habit of disappearing."

I barely manage a nod, because I don't know whether to be sick over what this means for Madison, or grateful I still have a lead to follow.

And because I've got nothing left to lose, I say, "You really think it was the cops who killed your aunt?"

She flings open the door and steps backward into the room, and until my eyes adjust she's just a dark form framed by the flicker of light. "Before Becca disappeared, she told her friends she met an older guy. One who promised to make the petty theft charge against her disappear. You know anyone besides cops who can do that?"

CHAPTER TWENTY-SEVEN

I know everything there is to know about Rebecca Wilder and Tracy Bast. At least everything that's available online.

I fell asleep with the sun spreading into the sky and my laptop heating through the comforter, dragging me into the somber quiet of dreams.

It lied to me though. My dreams weren't quiet.

They swam with pictures of missing girls and unanswered questions. And then reality ripped me awake with a wave of panic and the endless tick of a clock that won't slow its pace no matter how hard I beg. Because time, for Madison, is running out.

It has to be.

I toss aside the covers and press the heels of my hand to my gritty eyes until rainbow spots clog my vision and my stomach rumbles.

Getting Jake and Aubrey out of here made me believe in the power of prayer, because only divine intervention could explain how they left without me shoving them out the door and barricading it behind them.

That, and an appeal to Aubrey's determination when I pointed out she'd miss practice, and to Jake's honor when I reminded him he promised to talk to his dad about drug testing the glass. If the cops are truly involved, I need to know how far they're willing to go.

And based on what I found last night, I need to worry.

Chrystal may have been a bar waitress with a flip phone, but she knew the basics of a computer with internet access. And she certainly knew how to post in forums. Including the details of her daughter Mandy's disappearance four years ago.

She lost her daughter, and then she lost her niece. The cops claimed they both ran away, and right up until the day before Chrystal died, she was posting about how she didn't believe them.

It's a mess of incomplete data, and what I really need — the full scope of everything Chrystal's been collecting for years — is either in her trailer or hidden where I have no hope of finding it.

But between Chrystal's posts about the deaths and disappearances and the Facebook comments from friends and family when Rebecca Wilder and Tracy Bast went missing, I've managed to plaster my wall with notes and comparisons.

Rebecca and Tracy aren't the only girls — they're just the most recent. According to Chrystal, there have been fifteen others. Before my body went on Power Save Mode last night, I proved her wrong on two of the girls. One got picked up for drug charges in Virginia a few months back, and another regularly posts duck-lipped Instagram pics of herself.

Still, that leaves thirteen others. What it doesn't include is any mention of Madison, which leaves me standing at a fork in the road with nothing but a wish that the two paths intersect further up.

My toes curl when they hit the chill of the tile flooring, and the fridge hums and knocks when I grab a water and granola bar. The chocolate chips in it melt deliriously on my tongue, but if I were home, Mom would make pancakes and bacon and

English muffins with just enough butter to pool in the tiny pockets.

And then she'd probably call the cops.

My text to my parents last night claimed I was staying with Aubrey, but given the barrage of messages I've gotten regarding stupid Preston Ashcroft and his enormous mouth telling everyone I was at a party with Jake last night, it's likely they assume I'm with him.

They did the parental duty of insisting Aubrey text to corroborate my story, just like they've done every time I've lied and said I was sleeping over at a friend's.

I don't know if they believe me, or if they're both too scared to call me out on it. Afraid if they call the cops they'll have to admit this isn't the first or hundredth time I haven't slept in my own bed.

Mostly I think they're afraid I'll finally tell each of them all the things the other doesn't want them to know.

Family of secrets. In truth, we've all been blackmailing each other for years.

But Dad did send me three more text messages today before Mom took over — she sent it from his phone, but *Caroline, we expect you home tonight* did *not* come from him. I included her on my response: *I'm fine/safe.*

Nothing they could threaten is worse than the mess I'm in anyway.

It's far too early to leave the house, so I flop onto my bed and wake my laptop, then drag Madison's pile of flash drives next to me.

Thirteen flash drives later my neck is kinked and if I have to look at one more smiling picture of our classmates I'm going to set my computer on fire. Equally irritating and quintessentially Madison: she named the drives, all of them in numerical order, but she didn't bother writing the number on the outside.

They're all useless anyway, unless you're compiling the school yearbook, and I've wasted hours with nothing to show for it. Number ten might've proved useful, but since she either skipped that number or stored that drive somewhere else, it's just another piece of incomplete information.

I jam the next drive in and let number seventeen smack onto my discard pile. Despite my vow not to check, my secret phone says Mr. McCormack still hasn't contacted me.

Pictures bleed onto my screen, an endless collage of smiles and carefree happiness. Snapshots of teammates in celebration and bowed heads of defeat. Girls in the sparkle and shimmer of formal gowns while their dates stand stoically behind them. Students huddled around cherrywood tables that own decades' worth of scratches, laptops perched next to scribbled notebooks.

It's all so painfully familiar and painfully foreign.

I swipe down, down, down until my fingers freeze and my heart goes numb. It's only the last five pictures, but they mean more than the hundreds before.

They're edited. Every one of them.

Every one of them featuring me. Every one of them including Jake.

Him smiling up at me the day I asked him if I could borrow his notes from the class I missed the day before.

Him sliding into a picnic table next to me with his tray of food.

Him staring at me from the stands while I'm on the field.

Us staring at each other during mock debate at Mr. McCormack's class.

And the one of him watching me without smiling, his hand raking through his hair.

I don't like what Madison's insinuating. The narrative she's trying to construct through those five edited shots. I like it even less when I get to the sixth.

It's a picture of the sketch I used — the one that will always remind me of Willa — the night I had its image carved into my skin.

CHAPTER TWENTY-EIGHT

If time had meaning once, it doesn't now.

My life used to revolve around the steady advancement of the clock. Three months until graduation. Three days beyond that until my eighteenth birthday.

Not anymore.

That stopped the second I saw Madison's picture of my sketch — irrefutable evidence she was following me, or at least going through my things. I can't even guess why. Don't *want* to guess why.

That sketch has never left my bag, and if she photographed it, she knows it has meaning. And then there's the lipstick with the iris on it.

I don't *know* if it has anything to do with my sketch, but I can't rule it out.

It's proof though that I'm the thing that led her to Chrystal, to The Wayside, to whatever she was investigating. And whatever she discovered, it was worth enough for Chrystal to give Madison her phone number.

What if she saw something she wasn't supposed to see? Something that got her taken? Since I can't figure out what, I start my search from another angle.

I started the morning by tracking down friends of Rebecca Wilder. Knocking on their doors, begging them to talk to me.

When some relented, I asked about the man who promised to make her theft charges disappear.

And then I got a text from Jake, telling me the when and where of the meeting I agreed to have with Jake's dad's lawyer friend.

I laid my entire story on the table. Signed my name to a paper my parents will definitely see. Inky black letters on stark white paper with a pretentious "Caroline Waverly Lawson" scrawled beneath. I don't know if it will save Mr. McCormack and Madison. I can only wait to see how badly it will destroy me.

I should care more, but my world has tumbled end over end, and the grains inside the hourglass spill minutes until the moment of my expulsion.

My best friend didn't just keep things from me, she spied on me. She held on to the kinds of secrets that could get her kidnapped.

These facts make me look harder, ask more questions when I leave the attorney meeting and talk to more of Becca's friends. But she's been gone far longer than Madison, and no one seems to think she's ever coming home.

So when the growl of an engine roars into my driveway I have to force myself from my room to unlock the door, and I'm turning away before Jake's shoe hits the driveway.

I don't have the headspace to be mad, even though there's a chance the cops are tracking his car, which means he's led them right to me.

His silence sneaks up behind me and hovers, a gasp before the guillotine blade slices down.

Then, "Caroline."

I click and drag a thick red line over the map glaring from my computer screen, stretching it to the matching red pin four miles away.

"Caroline, what is this?"

"A map."

"I see that. What for?"

I stab my finger onto the computer screen, to the map stretching across it. "Each girl gets a different color pin and matching connection lines. School, work, home. See anything interesting?"

If he says no he's a liar.

He spends as much time glancing back at me as he does studying the map. "It looks like there's a group centered around that one area there."

"Yeah. You want to know what's right fucking by there? Chrystal's trailer. And that empty house with the guy that tried to blow our heads off."

He winces and I don't blame him, because that *click slide click* still echoes through my head just when I think I've forgotten it. He says, "There's something I need to —"

"You want to know what else is right by there? Less than ten miles away? Higgins Lake. *The shitty side.* That girl I found *two years* ago? I'm nearly positive that's where I was."

My stomach threatens to revolt every time I think about it. What I could've and should've done. How that day changed everything. Because the day I found that girl was the day I found Willa.

Jake says, "You're *nearly positive*?"

"I wasn't in what you'd call the right frame of mind to be memorizing directions, okay? But even *if* I'm wrong, Preston said —"

"Preston said Madison could've made that call from hundreds of miles away. I googled the cell tower thing, and people call it 'junk science.' There's tons of cases where these 'experts' that claim it works get ripped apart on the stand, or where the FBI hasn't been allowed to testify because it doesn't meet standards. It's bullshit."

"Why are you fighting this so hard?"

"Because *you're* not making sense."

"Just let me finish." I need to speak the words out loud. I need someone to witness them.

Maybe this was how Chrystal felt all these years. Why she made forum posts and kept painstaking records. Maybe silence felt too much like concession.

My finger squeaks against the trackpad when I draw a thick line between "Emily Darby" and "Julie Smith."

I smack my palm against the wall that holds printouts with data from each of the missing girls, and the edges flutter like they're trying to jump free. "All of these girls. From mid-2013 back, make up that other cluster. Including Chrystal's daughter."

He steps closer, hints of cinnamon and leather teasing the air as he studies the screen. "There are outliers."

It's a reasonable counterpoint — there are several pins that aren't anywhere near either group — but that hardly disproves the theory. "I haven't gotten to research all the names yet to see if they're truly missing. Just because Chrystal wasn't right about everything, it doesn't mean she's not right about some things. She posted a list of girls on this forum —"

"You're basing your hypothesis on posts from some conspiracy theory forum?"

"In part, yes. And one of the girls on her list — you remember that teacher from Howard High? The guy that killed himself when he was about to get arrested for murdering a girl? Well, *that girl* was on Chrystal's list. Look at this, Jake, you can't —"

"I need to tell you something."

I shove my laptop to my bed and stand, because if he tells me Madison is dead, I won't have the strength to move again. "What is it?"

"The cops found Chrystal's body. Anonymous tip. Her place was trashed."

It's relief I feel first, followed by guilt. Anger for Chrystal close behind. "So the cops kill her and then ransack her home?"

"You don't know it was the cops."

"You don't know it wasn't." I jerk my arm toward my laptop because evidence is evidence, and when a dozen girls go missing in only a few years and the cops don't notice, there's a reason. "And you weren't the one interviewing friends of Rebecca Wilder today, Jake. Everyone thinks the cops are involved. Her parents were terrible but her friends reported her missing. The cops didn't even try to find her. Ignored everyone when they told them about the guy she met."

"You went out interviewing people?" He paces the room. "Are you trying to get yourself killed?"

"No. I'm trying to save other girls from getting killed. In case you hadn't noticed, the cops are too busy drugging people and —"

"She wasn't drugged." It's only after I've blinked twice that he continues. "I asked my dad to test the glass last night. He agreed to do it on the condition I" — he air quotes — "'not involve myself further.' I lied to him, Caroline. Do you know how hard that was?"

"No."

He's staring at me like he wants me to be lying, but I'm not. "The test was negative."

"So you think I was faking getting sick that night?"

"No, I —"

"You think Chrystal was just … taking a really long fucking nap? Because she's dead now. You just said that."

"Maybe it was something else! Did you eat or drink —"

"No, I —" My thoughts freeze me in place. "Cigarette. She gave me a cigarette."

I blink and he's standing in front of me, his fingers curled around my shoulders, strips of heat melting through the thin fabric of my T-shirt, and his voice goes calm. "Maybe it was the cigarette. Maybe it wasn't. Have you slept at all? Did you eat anything?" My response barely forms before he sighs and says, "Caroline. We don't know that any of this is true."

"Hidden connections."

If time *does* exist, I found a way to stop it. We don't move or speak. We both know what I'm trying to say. Mr. McCormack's walls are covered with quotes from ancient philosophers to modern-day influencers, and they start with Heraclitus: "A hidden connection is stronger than an obvious one."

Jake's hands slip from my shoulders. "Is that what this is about? My ribs are covered in fucking bruises and my dad thinks I'm a criminal and you're hanging out in drug houses and playing Girl Detective and it's all because you're trying to save Mr. McCormack?" The rise in his voice is so gradual I don't realize I'm flinching away until he gets to the end.

"It's *my fault* he's in trouble in the first place! Without me, the cops would never have questioned him. If he didn't have my license, they'd have absolutely nothing to prove their suspicions. And in case you've forgotten, Jake, Madison is still missing and the cops are too busy trying to prove Mr. McCormack is hurting me to actually *look* for her. She is *running out of time.*"

A voice in my head whispers: *If it's not already too late.*

"And these —" I grab a handful of flash drives and fling them at him until they bounce from his chest and scatter onto the floor. "Do you want to know how many pictures she took that you appear in?"

"No."

"I bet not." I storm past him and rip my laptop from the bed and find what I'm looking for. Then I wait for him to register what's on the screen. I went through every single remaining flash drive, and these are still the only six pictures that matter. The only six edited, out of sequence, pictures. "What the fuck *is* this, Jake?"

He won't look at me. His chest heaves and the muscle in his jaw twitches, but he won't look at me. "What do you want me to say?"

"Tell me why she's obsessing over pictures of us. Tell me why and *how* she got a picture of my tattoo sketch."

He shrugs, palms upturned. "I don't know where she got your sketch, and I shouldn't have to tell you about the first part. You're the only person who doesn't know. Or maybe you're just the only person who pretends not to know, because you're too busy throwing yourself at people who don't care about you."

It's a full ten seconds before I manage a strangled "What?"

"I'm not just talking about Mr. McCormack, but him too. If he cared, Caroline. If he cared about you at all, don't you think he would've called on your secret phone?"

His hand jacks upward to cut off my response, but I can't form words anyway when he says, "Your girlfriend too. Here's the thing. Nobody can make it from late breakfast in San Francisco to lunch in L.A. It's a fucking six-hour drive even if you could hovercraft over the twenty goddamn accidents you'd probably pass along the way. And Disneyland? It doesn't have Cinderella's castle. That's Disney World. In Disneyland it's Sleeping Beauty's. And maybe your dad didn't drag you to California a million times when you were growing up, so you wouldn't know whose fucking castle is in the middle of which Disney, but *Jesus*, Caroline. You're one of the smartest people I've ever met and if you *didn't* realize you couldn't drive four hundred miles between breakfast and lunch then you're just *trying* not to see."

I'm too hollowed out to understand any of what he's trying to say. Every word steals a piece of me until I'm nothing.

"She *lied* to you." His hand jerks toward his back pocket and then the stack of Willa's letters spiral as he throws them onto the bed, jagged edges where I ripped open the envelopes catching and snagging on each other. "She's not in California. All of what she wrote is bullshit. She dumped you and couldn't even be honest about it, and I'm *here*. I've *always* been here."

He read Willa's letters. He *took* Willa's letters.

I shovel them into my hands and one of the envelopes slices my palm, a line of sharp heat that swells with each heartbeat.

If I'm the ocean, I can create a flood to destroy everything.

I crumple the mess of letters and torn envelopes to my chest and stumble past him.

Maybe he's right. Maybe I didn't want to see. Maybe she made up the excuse about going to California because she knew I'd say no. Her mom was leaving, she said. She had to go too. Or she'd be stuck with her mom's boyfriend. She had no choice. But I should stay. I needed to stay. My only choice was to not ruin my life.

And maybe hers was to leave me.

I don't bother with a coat. The laces on my shoes flop uselessly, pinging against the tile floor. If Jake doesn't get the fuck out of my driveway I'm going to test the structural integrity of Mabel's sturdy Buick against his front bumper.

The metal handle of the garage door snaps from my hand and fire lances along the top of my ripped-off nail. Blood wells over my middle finger and a fat droplet free falls to the ground where it splatters onto one of Willa's letters that's slipped from my hand.

The ink, the blood, and the puddle the letter's sitting in reach for each other until blue blurs into pink and another droplet of crimson muddles them both.

I leave a smear of red across the garage handle on the second try, and the door arcs toward the mass of grey clouds as I rescue my letter. A drip of water trickles down my arm and tucks itself into the crook of my elbow.

If it's cold out, I can't feel it.

I can't feel anything.

CHAPTER TWENTY-NINE

By the time I make it to St. Francis, Mabel's car is missing a side mirror and it's gained a sizable scrape along the passenger side. It's possible her/my security deposit will go toward fixing the landscaping damage Jake caused. He rushed out of the house just in time to move his car, which was good, because I was fully prepared to run it over.

On the bright side, if I end up dead or imprisoned my parents will have my entire college fund at their disposal and Mabel's yard will look as good as new.

For now though, I'm still alive, hunting the clues Madison's flash drives can't give me. My mouth waters for the bitter relief of a Xanax, but I need to be awake for this. I need to feel everything, the panic and the pain, or it'll be too easy to pretend none of this is real.

Jake wasn't surprised about how many pictures Madison took of him. Not when I showed him Madison's edited pictures either — the ones she took from the unedited masses.

He knew how much she wanted him even if I didn't, just like she knew how he felt about me. I can't stop wondering if he's seen them before, or others like them.

Madison made a habit of telling stories through her camera lens and maybe those stories are out there somewhere. If they are, I'd bet they're on missing drive number ten. And if I'm lucky, they're here too. And what I need is to find every detail of Madison's story.

This is a long shot, but better than breaking into Madison's house and searching for her computer. Much better than searching for a drive that could be anywhere, including Mountain Man's property where I found her lipstick.

My reflection taunts me from the polished floor, bleach and pine filling all the blank spaces where students would be if it weren't the weekend. It's a somber sort of quiet, a breath held before the scream.

I didn't reread Willa's letters.

Later. I'll read them later, when the world stops shaking.

I can't read the words she wrote — my proof that joy exists, my reminder that hope is possible — knowing they're all a lie.

And they won't lead me to Madison.

No matter how much we lied to each other, Madison was still the girl who kept my secret when I was too scared to tell it — the girl whose cold fingers reached for mine that night on her balcony. And I'm still the girl who spent lifetimes next to her, cheering for every success, mourning every failure and laughing through every point in between.

We're the girls whose lives are so entangled there's hardly an event I can't remember her in, millions of moments that built our friendship into something unbreakable.

And we're still the girls who say *I love you* without hesitation.

I mean it, even now. Even knowing the things Madison did.

For that alone, I'd do anything to have her back.

And after Madison, I owe it to Mr. McCormack to clear his name.

I owe the girl at Higgins Lake too. This time, I need to not forget her.

Sunlight fights its way through the glass doors that punctuate the ends of the hallways, but it's dark in the middle. Just me and the empty echo of my footsteps.

The door to the yearbook office sits open, cracked to let the hum of computers spill into the hall.

I swing the door wide and Tabitha Zhao's head pops up from behind a computer monitor across the room.

If I had any doubt as to whether the general school population was aware of the recent chaos of my life, it vanishes with one glance at Tabitha's face.

She forces her mouth closed and swallows. "People were saying you went missing like Madison."

"You mean there are people Preston Ashcroft *didn't* tell he saw me at a party?"

"No, I think he covered the whole school, but like, maybe you went missing after? Everybody's paranoid."

I span my arms wide and shrug. "Here I am. Not missing. Did Madison do any photo editing on these computers?"

"Well, yeah, but —" Her chair screeches against the floor and she circles the desk. She stops just out of lunging distance and fiddles with the bangles on her wrist. "I was a total bitch to you in the bathroom the other day."

"Yep. So, which computer?"

She rolls her eyes. "Can you just let me apologize?"

"If your apology includes telling me which computer Madison used, then yes."

She points into the corner. "That one, with the screen facing the wall."

I'm in the seat so fast it slides across the floor, and the screen has barely blinked to life before Tabitha's leaning over the back of the monitor, chewing on the inside of her cheek like she does when she's not confident about what she's about to do.

Like kiss me.

Or in this instance, say, "Are you in some kind of trouble?"

"I'm in multiple kinds of trouble, so I'd really appreciate it if you didn't tell anyone I was here."

She sighs before swinging around the table and flopping into the seat next to me. "You might as well use my login. As head of the yearbook committee I have total access."

Humility was never one of Tabitha's strong suits, and I'm betting Madison didn't save the pics I'm looking for onto any school-sponsored drive, but I stopped ruling anything out the second Willa's letters tumbled to my bed.

We search the official yearbook drives and find nothing, despite scrolling through more folders than I have time for.

I have a theory, and I wasn't planning to test it while Tabitha watched, but every minute I spend here is one less than I can spare. And Willa's letters are waiting for me, a siren song pulling me under the waves.

Madison is waiting too. I hope.

But I don't think she meant to save those images to the flash drive in my pocket. I think she meant to save them with the other ones. That there *are* other ones is also part of my theory.

The six pictures spanned months of time — one was from shortly after the start of the school year. There's no chance she only took six, especially not when one of them was a pic of my sketch, which never left my backpack.

Also my theory: the school computers have autosave, and

possibly a backup. I just need to find the photos Madison saved without realizing she'd saved them.

Sydney said Chrystal wouldn't have given her phone number to Madison unless she'd found something useful. If Madison documented whatever she was doing with the same level of detail she did *me*, there has to be something here. Some clue. Some lead to follow.

I throw caution to the thick, dry heat spewing from the ancient school furnace and stop pretending I'm not looking for something sketchy.

Beside me, Tabitha is silent but not quiet. The tension in her screams against my skin.

By the time I find what I'm looking for, the outside security lights coat the windows, turning them into mirrors. When the pictures load onto the screen like rows of headstones, I get to see them twice — at least until Tabitha jumps up and lowers the shades, cutting off the outside world's view.

She plops back into her chair and huffs out a breath. "Dude."

Madison may not have constructed an altar to worship Jake at, but these photos are a close second. Colors blur with each flick of my finger as I scan down the screen filled with edited pics, looking for anything that's not "A Day in the Life of Jake."

Soon *my* face starts making an equal appearance.

They're all me and Jake. Talking, laughing, interacting. Plenty where he's looking at me and I'm oblivious.

Tabitha snaps her gum and the scent of mint punctuates every word. "So I guess you can't pretend you don't know he's into you anymore, huh?"

"I wasn't *pretending*. I just didn't really notice, I guess." The words feel like a condemnation, even coming from my own lips. There are so many things I didn't notice. I outfitted myself with a pair of blinders that saw nothing but graduation, freedom and Willa.

But not all of Willa. Not the part where she lied to be rid of me.

Then the next row loads onto the screen and I gasp so loud Tabitha jumps from her chair.

I don't want to see what's in front of me — photographic documentation of my last moments with Willa.

The two of us, framed by beat-up cars as the sun drooped low. The tears streaming down Willa's face and the look of abject pain on mine.

It looks too real to be a lie.

Tabitha's hand flutters to my shoulder then backs away. "I swear I didn't know Mads was, like … stalking you."

I barely recognize my voice. "What was the point?"

"Maybe she was trying to show Jake you were super into your girlfriend?" All she can offer is a shrug at my look of disbelief, but if there's a better explanation, I don't have it.

Her eyes narrow and her teal nail taps against the monitor. "What's up with the creeper over there?"

The picture blurs and focuses as I zoom in, and the profile of a man centers the screen. He's not the focus of the picture and he's partially obscured by both his hat and his hiding spot inside his car. And maybe he's some random guy who left the restaurant and stuck around to watch two girls fight.

But that's not what the pressure on my chest says.

Willa loved me. I was the liar in our relationship, not her.

From the moment I let her find me, sandwiched between cars in her work parking lot, crying fake tears with a bottle of saline drops tucked into my sleeve. Mabel's house that I claimed as my own, the parents I claimed never went to college, the shitty laptop I bought at the pawn shop. All the things I designed to erase the gap between us.

But all of it ended the day I went to visit her mom, to talk to her about cooperating with the cops so Willa could go to college like she wanted. The day I found her mom going through her room, all the money Willa fought to earn piled on her bed.

Then Willa came home and found us both, and there was no pretending anymore. But she loved me, even then. Every part of me.

We sat on the bed at Mabel's house that night, tears shimmering in Willa's eyes. "You lied to me."

"Yes." I wouldn't defend what I did. Couldn't defend it. I could only hope she'd understand.

"That's not okay, Livie." She paused. *"Caroline."*

"It's *not* okay. And I'm sorry, and I won't blame you" — I sucked in a breath, too afraid to let it out — "if you can't forgive me."

I waited, until her eyes met mine. "But I'm still Livie, and you're still Willa."

That hadn't changed. It never would. Those were always the most important parts of us both.

She nodded, her voice soft. "I wouldn't have talked to you, if you were Caroline."

"I know."

Seconds ticked by, the world narrowing to the space between us, and she reached for my hand. "Okay."

And now every bit of doubt I've carried since she left doubles down on me, because I should've destroyed any part of me that questioned what we had. I should've believed in her. In us. Even despite Jake's revelations about her letters. I should have trusted all the things I was too afraid to believe were true.

My gaze travels over the computer screen to the stop-motion depiction of the end. The part where she told me she had to go, that I should stay, and I told her I couldn't come with even though she didn't ask. And then even as I kissed her, one last time, I felt her leaving me.

And I walked away.

Willa's letters to me were real. If she lied in them, it was because she had to.

And that's why I can't breathe. Why Tabitha's voice is a whisper in a wind tunnel and my vision is rimmed in black.

But I can still see.

I can still see the last two pictures in the sequence. The one that shows the second I left the lot in Mabel's Buick, when Willa palmed her phone to dial a number that had to be mine, the man's car door swung open.

And the final one: Willa slipping into the back seat of his car.

CHAPTER THIRTY

My throat burns from the remnants of sickly sweet vomit and every breath threatens to call another wave.

He took her. He took Willa.

That was what Madison knew. The evidence that was enough for Chrystal to hand over her phone number.

Madison *knew*.

And I was *there*.

If I'd stayed, if for once I'd fought instead of flown, we would've left together.

Instead, I'm stopped in a random parking lot, huddled over Willa's letters with my hands shaking too badly to hold them, the black ink of her handwriting stark beneath my phone's flashlight.

If there are clues in these sentences, I can't find them. There are only laughter and memories, joy and light. That's how — even if I didn't know every loop and slant of her handwriting, if I didn't recognize every mention of things only the two of us shared — I know these letters came from Willa.

Willa was always the light in the darkness.

But it's the darkness I can't stop thinking about. Where she is. Whether she's alive.

Whether I'm too late.

Maybe Willa spent her last moments hoping I'd care enough to look for her.

A scream rips from my lungs and doesn't fade until they

ache from lack of breath.

I haven't cried since the day I walked out of conversion therapy, and today is the first day I wish I could.

I gather Willa's letters, smoothing them and pressing them flat to my chest like I can absorb them into my skin.

I replay the words in my head, turning them sideways and upside down, searching out the layers I missed before.

Her pleas for me to move on. *Don't ruin your life, Caroline.* Except what if she meant, "Don't let him *end* your life."

Her insistence she had no choice. *I had to go — for both of us. Your life will be better without me.* Because she didn't want to draw me into whatever danger she'd found.

Her clues, crafted to lead me here, and to keep me safe. *I tried to watch you drive away that last time, but I couldn't.* She couldn't, because someone stopped her.

Sometimes I think about where it all started. The parking lot where we first officially met, the place we said goodbye.

If you let yourself look, you'll find plenty of other girls besides me. Not other girls I might love. Other girls who'd gone missing.

And then.

Promise you won't forget us. Don't forget to let the light in. Love is forever.

Every one of those syllables has a different meaning now. They tell me she had faith. That she believed I would look for her, that I had the strength to save her — and if not her, whatever girls came after.

They're no longer words that tell me it's okay to move on. Sentences that tell me it's okay to be happy without her.

Now I can see them for what they are. A goodbye.

LET HER SLEEP

When I was little, my mom tacked one of those inspirational posters above my bed. It stuck there for years, until the sticky tack started to crumble and the shiny paper fluttered, facedown, onto my pillow. I crumpled it and shoved it into the trash, but even after it was gone, I still saw the words every time I looked at that blank spot above my metal headboard.

"Let her sleep. For when she wakes, she'll move mountains."

I don't think my mom ever meant for me to move mountains.

No one is born with that kind of strength. You only get it through years of training, a gradual resistance built upward from your foundation.

But I'd patched mine in so many places, fought to hold its pieces together for so long, it felt like it would crumble beneath me.

I shouldn't have worried.

I should've trusted in the parts of me that survived despite her.

I know that now too.

I just wish I'd known it sooner.

I wish I'd ignored every word my mom said when she came back from the police station that day.

When she told me they'd asked every "John" in the building — from officer to detective to the meter maids — and none of them admitted to offering a deal to a young girl in a restaurant parking lot. Still, they took my mom's testimony just the same. And she gave enough to secure her own deal.

I wish I could've let it go.

Instead, I'd wait until Livie was deep asleep, her long, even breathing a whisper across my back. I huddled her laptop beneath the warmth of her comforter, and I hunted the man who hunted me.

I wish I'd never tried, but then again, maybe everything would've ended the same.

Maybe John would've found me again instead of me finding him, and we still would've made the same deal. Maybe I still would've tried to end things with Livie. Broke her heart right alongside mine until my willpower nearly failed and I held my phone in hand, a single button from calling her back.

I wish I'd known he'd be watching.

Maybe, if I'd believed myself to be a girl who could move mountains, I wouldn't have accepted his claims that I wasn't good enough for her. I wouldn't have listened when he said she had better options. I would've been strong enough to walk away when he threatened to ruin the deal my mom made. To claim — for once — what I needed, and let my mom figure things out on her own.

I would've questioned it, when he said the world would never miss me.

But now I only wish I had more time.

To have even one more night like the last.

I'd stretched the tightness from my muscles, letting the softness of Livie's bed swallow me, my shower-damp hair pressed against my temple as I filled the conversation with the mundane — school, work, anything but the man from the parking lot, who set me walking away from Livie as the price of my mom's freedom. "Oh, and we found out today that Mikey's coming back to the restaurant."

She dropped her pencil into her lap, its sharp point littering her page of math homework on its descent. Livie was the only person I'd met who could carry on a conversation while figuring out complex math equations without either suffering. "That asshole who beat up his girlfriend? Why is he not in jail?"

The bed shook as I laughed, and then tears welled and I had to whisper an apology to Mikey's girlfriend.

Livie tossed her notebook to the floor and spun to face me. "What's funny about that?"

"Nothing. That's why I apologized. It's just —" I twisted the comforter in my hand, testing my new truths. "Your question was kind of naive."

It took three tries before she could form the words. "The guy puts his girlfriend in the hospital and it's naive to wonder how he's back at work in two weeks?"

I waited, gave her a chance to acknowledge the differences between her world and mine. I waited, without judgment, to show her I understood why she'd lied. "Yes. It *is* naive. The only reason he was even away that long was because it violated his parole, Livie."

"And your boss just thinks it's cool to have him work with you?"

I shrugged. "We complained. My boss gave a bunch of excuses for him and ended it with 'but none of you are his girl-friend so don't worry.'"

"Don't *worry*? What the fuck is wrong with him?"

"Same thing as plenty of other guys."

She jumped from the bed, yanking a sweatshirt over her tank top along the way. Her head popped from the top hole, hair flung in every direction. God, she was beautiful.

She paced the matted carpet and a flush deepened in her pale cheeks. "Well, that's bullshit. And it's all the same, you know? We talk about this in class sometimes. About how girls get in trouble because their skirts are too short and distract the male teachers, or all the assholes who are surprised a girl can be good at math."

She kicked her notebook on the floor, its pages fluttering open. "Calvin Huckabee gets Janie Roberts pregnant junior year and all those asshole parents could talk about was how she couldn't keep her legs closed and not one of them mentioned Calvin keeping his tiny penis to himself. It's all such …"

"Bullshit?" For all our differences, some things were very much the same.

She'd done so much to show me that, to prove the places we came from didn't determine who we were. I should've been angrier that she lied, but I did too. I hid all the parts of my life I didn't think she'd be able to accept.

But here, now, none of that mattered. She was Livie and I was Willa.

I didn't know it at first, not until the pieces started to fall together, but we'd met years ago at a lake — next to a beautiful girl with a necklace of bruises.

When the guilt of my silence got too much for me, I went to the police to report that I found her. That's when I discovered someone else already had, her name scribbled in the detective's notebook, right next to where he wrote mine.

It may not have matched what he inked onto the paper, but even then, we were Livie and Willa.

Even then, our worlds weren't so different. Both of us fighting for a girl no one was trying to find.

Livie paced as I sat huddled in her bed. "Yes. It's absolutely bullshit. It's my world too. And yours. I *exist*. So do you, and Janie Roberts, and Mikey's girlfriend. But it's always the guys that get to make the rules. Why? Why are we supposed to settle for what's best for them?"

She paused, shoulders set. "Who gave them the world to run?"

It was in that moment I knew I could never keep her.

Livie was born to move mountains.

So I'd set her free.

And the next day, when "John" set the rules for me, I'd play by them. I'd end things with Livie, not because I feared him, but because there were mountains out there waiting for Livie to move them.

In the end, there were mountains for me to move too.

But I wish I'd thought it through — why John would go to so much trouble to pretend he was someone he wasn't, why he'd go to such lengths to break me and Livie apart. If I'd paid more attention, I might've considered what else he had to hide.

I might not have been so surprised when I woke to this foreign room and the restraints around my wrists. This room where hazy light streams through the covered windows and settles into the depressions in the plastic sheeting that coats the walls and floors. Where, sometimes, I catch glimpses of a place by the lake that started it all.

He wanted postcards. A tiny rectangle where I'd say things Livie would understand — things she would believe — and I'd sign my name. So she wouldn't look for me, he said. So she'd move on.

The letters I insisted on sending instead were my mountains to move.

I paid for them — for the opportunity to say goodbye, the chance to rewrite his rules, to give Livie the clues that would scream out his name in a final shout of justice.

I paid with my blood and my tears, my pain and my grief. With every last ounce of my life.

I drew upon that place I was born into, that empty, hollowed-out place, and every day I refused to die, I saved another girl that would replace me. I denied him the right to make all the rules. I stripped his power and made it my own.

I fought. I resisted. I paid with everything I had.

And when the end came, it wasn't *his* hands I felt on the curve of my throat, *his* breath that billowed over my skin. I closed my eyes and drifted to a place filled only with me and Livie.

Livie's hands. Soft, gentle, reverent.

Her breath, her lips, against my skin.

Her laughter, sending me home.

I denied him, this monster, the thing he wanted most — my surrender.

And with my dying breath, I moved this mountain.

CHAPTER THIRTY-ONE

The rain sneaks beneath my jacket and trickles down my skin in wandering rivulets, soaking every layer of my clothing along the way. Each blade of grass glistens beneath the sweep of my flashlight.

The last time I came through Mountain Man's property, I had Jake, pepper spray and a tire iron. Today, it's only me and my rage.

Mountain Man knows something. He has to. It wasn't him in that car in the parking lot, but Madison's lipstick was here, and no one guards a decrepit house with a shotgun for no reason. If he wants to kill me for coming back, I'll let him try.

Madison knew too. She watched from that parking lot, taking pictures, while a man took Willa. But she didn't call 911. If she told the cops later, they didn't care. It's been nearly two months since that day.

The lipstick I found here proves she was looking into it, that she knew something was wrong. And Madison's mom said she'd been spending time away from home, using the excuse of some new girl she'd befriended while she was really tracking down Chrystal. Chrystal, who made it her life's mission to find the person responsible for kidnapping her daughter, her niece, and every girl after them.

Girls like Willa. And, when she became too much of a threat, girls like Madison.

That has to be the reason he went after her. Why he strayed from the girls no one would notice to the girl everyone's trying to find. Even with that level of scrutiny — and he had to know there would be — she was more dangerous to him alive.

When I add it all together, I'm walking in Madison's footsteps. She followed the clues and ended up here. Now she's missing, and I can't stop wondering how far her tracks will lead me — and I dread what I'll find when I get to the place where they end.

Objects I can't see or name crunch beneath my feet. It's only when I swallow and pain lances down my throat that I realize I've been yelling.

Shouting a series of challenges for the man with the shotgun to give me what I came here for.

I drop to my knees where I found Madison's lipstick and bite down onto the rubbery flashlight handle so I can use both hands to search. Branches scrape my fingers, the cold rain stinging and soothing in equal measure, but there's nothing here.

The crumbling house stands defiant against the accusing glare of the moon, and I have to blink the rain from my eyes for it to come into focus.

Girls may have died in that house. Madison may be in there right now.

I grab tight to the necklace Willa gave me, the metal warm against my frozen fingertips.

I left her, and it may have gotten her killed.

I spin, scanning the tangles of shrubs and weeds, and I yell again, this time, a demand.

If Mountain Man won't answer me, I'll go to the only place that will.

I follow the crumbling path to the front porch, its moldy pillars opening to a gaping maw of a porch entrance, and I've barely climbed the first step when I hear it.

The *click slide click* I've been waiting for.

The cadence is off though, awkward and stumbling, and when I turn, Mountain Man's bright yellow jacket is glossy with rain. His left arm hangs limp, but that doesn't stop him from leveling the shotgun at me with his right.

He growls, "You here alone?"

I nod and slowly pull my phone from my pocket. I unlock it, my fingers slipping, and Willa's image fills the screen.

It's not my favorite picture of her. That honor is reserved for the one I took the morning after we kissed for the first time, when she woke up tucked into my arms, giggling like we'd just played the ultimate prank on the world.

That picture is mine, and I won't tie it to this.

I hold out my phone, even though Mountain Man is probably too far away to see it clearly. "I'm looking for this girl."

He grunts and his head swivels like he's worried the trees might stretch their branches and reach for him. "Get inside."

I don't hesitate, my feet slamming into the rotted boards of the steps.

If he tells me he killed Willa or Madison, I'll rip his heart out with my bare hands.

He wrenches the door open and the hinges scream, and then I'm following a man into a dying house when there's not a single soul who knows where I am.

Carpet squishes beneath my shoes and Mountain Man flicks on a flashlight, throwing his shadow against the exposed studs where drywall has fallen away. He nods toward the wall behind me. "Where is he?"

"She. I'm looking for a girl. Two girls."

He shakes his head and droplets spray from his matted hair. "Your boyfriend."

"He's not my boyfriend. This girl" — I thrust my phone in his direction — "is my girlfriend. And Madison, she came here. I think they're both —"

My throat closes tight and I can't say what I need to say to make him understand.

In one harsh jerk, he lowers the shotgun and his jaw works, shaggy mustache brushing against his beard below it. "Chrystal's dead."

"I know. I didn't kill her."

He says nothing, but his eyes disappear beneath hooded shadows.

I hold out my phone again, my hand shaking. "This girl. Have you seen this girl? Ever? Have you ever spoken to her? Helped keep her here? Madison's lipstick was in your fucking yard. Chrystal said she knew something about her. Are you working with him? The guy from the picture? *This* girl —"

It's not just my body that's trembling. It's my voice, rising higher with each new sentence.

He turns and stomps away, his heavy boots bouncing sprays of water from the soaked carpet, leaving me in an empty room with the fading light of Willa's picture on my phone.

I scramble to catch him, and before I can ask where he's heading he leads me out the back door.

The rain slows, a miserable drizzle that casts a haze over the thin, trampled path Mountain Man barrels through. More than one creature scrambles at our approach, rustling into shrubs and tall grass bent low from the forces of winter.

Darkness takes on new meaning here, my world reduced to the beam of my flashlight trained on the yellow slicker a few steps ahead.

I don't know how long we walk, how many miles he leads me through clustered trees and open stretches that used to hold homes.

He doesn't turn back to me when he says, "We think he works out here. Found another girl's bracelet along the lakeshore once. Cops came out, said they couldn't prove it was hers. Said maybe someone planted it to make it look like she didn't run away."

I'm silent so long — stunned he said so many words at once — that he glances back to me. I search for a sign he's lying, but there is nothing in his expression, just a muddled blend of sadness and anger, and I almost feel bad about what Jake did to his arm and ribs. "So, what? Now you patrol the woods searching for him?"

He holds a branch high so he can duck beneath it. "Been searching ever since that girl showed us the picture of him. I'd kill him if I could find him here."

Madison. Madison showed Mountain Man a picture — a picture clear enough to identify the killer, one I haven't seen — and he's been hunting him ever since. Waiting.

There's more silence until the scene widens and we step into a small clearing that overlooks a lake. Raindrops ripple the surface and the rising crescent moon seems twice as bright in its reflection.

My mind whirls, trying to splice together the pieces to form a whole story. But I can't get anything to stick. Thoughts slide away before I can make sense of them, because every part of me is focused on the small inlet far in the distance. On the tree that proves everything has come full circle.

Tonight it's a blackened skeleton, lower branches twisting to the frosted ground, but years ago it kept watch over a soft bed of lush green grass filled with a rainbow of wildflowers. And irises.

Those twisted branches made the perfect stepping stones to the higher ones, so easy even a fifteen-year-old girl with a handful of pills could navigate it.

Willa's handwriting is stark in my mind. *Sometimes I think about where it all started.*

I thought she meant the parking lot at her diner, where I pretended to be someone else. A person who had never seen her before.

I never told her I watched from that tree the day she found the girl on the shore. Never told her if she hadn't come along, she would've found me lying in the grass too. Never told her that was the day I fell in love with her — when she showed me there's strength in tenderness, that compassion exists in even the worst of circumstances.

But somehow, she knew. She knew I was there, and in her letters she was trying to tell me.

She was trying to tell me where she was. Where he'd taken her.

And I failed her, from the moment I forgot about the girl we both found. Again when I didn't think to look for her.

Mountain Man's gruff voice thunders through my head,

something about "coming on out of there," and the cold shocks
my legs, water creeping up my thighs. I gasp, flailing backward
until his thick fingers capture my arm and yank me upright.

He drags me from the lake I stumbled into, and I crumple to
the ground, mud sucking at my fingers, my body shuddering.
I'm too late to save her, but I can avenge her.

I can make him sorry.

I drag my gaze up until I meet Mountain Man's eyes. "The
girl on my phone, did you ever see her?" When he shakes his
head no, I say, "And Madison's lipstick? That's because she came
to see you?"

"She came around here on her own, looking for Chrystal."
He works his jaw again, and I can tell he's still debating how
much to tell me. "Near as we can figure, he knew Chrystal was
onto him. We kept thinking it was the cops. Had to be the cops.
All her books pointed to it."

I want to ask questions, but words won't form right and I
struggle to take in everything he's telling me.

"She got a glimpse of him though. That rich girl did. Took
that picture. 'Cept we didn't know who he was, not until we
seen your boyfriend. So we got your name from The Wayside,
found your school, then him."

No. I can't make myself believe Jake killed Willa or Madison.
I can't believe the boy I know, any part of him, is capable of that.

Only …

He followed me. He searched my room. Took Willa's letters.
He swore he didn't hurt Madison.

Mountain Man's jaw ticks, teeth grinding together. "Looks
just like him."

One by one, pieces drop into place like tumblers in a lock.

Madison knew what she captured in her photos — knew *who* she captured.

She suspected and she said nothing.

She found Chrystal instead, sharing part of her knowledge but not all. Not the part about who the man in that car was.

Because of Jake. Not because it was him she captured through her lens, but because it would destroy Jake — and that was more than Madison could handle.

Chrystal and Mountain Man couldn't figure out who the man was — not until they saw Jake.

Looks just like him, but isn't him.

Jake doesn't have the ability to help people avoid their legal problems, and he sure as hell isn't sneaking off campus to kidnap and kill young girls.

But Jake's dad is a judge.

Jake's dad made sure he knew every detail of what we discovered. He held out his palm and watched the only piece of evidence I had tumble into it.

The negative test on Chrystal's glass suddenly makes far more sense.

Everything makes sense. My biggest fear now an inescapable truth.

I'm the link between them all. Between Chrystal and Willa and Madison. I led Thomas Monaghan to all of them.

He took the two people I loved most.

And there's only one I have any hope of saving.

It's too much to process, and my body screams to crawl back

into the cold embrace of the lake and let all of this disappear. All of it.

Then wind kicks through my hair and I swear I can feel the sun against my skin, the faint scent of wildflowers and the reassuring press of pills against my palm.

It's been years, but it's like I've stepped sideways in time until I'm the same girl I was at fifteen.

But I'm not that girl anymore.

I've broken the chains and left them in ragged pieces.

I pull myself from the clammy mud that's coated my hands, my knees, and I stand.

Step One: Confirm Jake's dad is the killer.

Step Two: Determine if Jake is involved.

Step Three: Burn it all down.

CHAPTER THIRTY-TWO

Paper towels crinkle beneath my feet and stick to my soles. Mud streaks the white porcelain of the sink even though I've rinsed it three times, avoiding my reflection so I don't have to look myself in the eyes.

Marcel barely glanced at me before he shuffled me into the women's bathroom and kicked everyone else out.

And now he's standing guard at the door while I change into my spare clothes from his office.

There has to be a line of women waiting to come in and that can't be good for business, but he won't rush me. *You take the time you need, baby girl. Go get yourself right.*

Except there *is* no getting myself right. Not in any way he'd approve of. And that's not what I came here for. I came here for answers. For evidence. For clues.

I won't tell him all the plans forming in my head, all the ways I can get the proof I need and dispense the justice the world won't give. Not after everything he's done for me. I won't let him burn alongside me.

A streak of crimson trickles down my knee. Mom would rush me to the hospital for a tetanus shot the second I admitted I had no idea when or how I cut myself, but wadded paper towel tucked into my jeans will have to do.

My movements feel blurry and foreign, and the harsh fluorescent lighting magnifies every bruise and scrape from my trek through the woods.

The laces of my Chuck Taylors burn against my skin as I yank them tight and I force myself to look at my phone. Willa smiles back at me and I'm solid again.

I leave the safety of the bathroom and emerge into the clamor of the hallway. Spots cloud my vision as my eyes adjust to the loss of light, and the murmured complaints from the crowd in the hallway go silent the second Marcel's heavy hand lands on top of my head. He mutters, "Let's go," and directs me toward his office.

My stomach clamps tight with the knowledge of what he's giving up to do this. He told me to stay away, to lay low, and now I've forced a scene with uncountable witnesses. But he took me in anyway, grasped me from my lowest point and pulled me up, just like the night we met.

And now I'm going to make this right. I'm going to make all of it right.

The door shushes as he closes it behind us — completely closed, even though it's just the two of us, because we're breaking all the rules tonight.

He looks me over and his gaze ends on a heavy sigh that makes the room less empty. His voice cracks when he says, "If I'd known you'd take care of yourself like this, I'd have taken you home with me and *kept* you there."

I shake my head and damp hair brushes my cheek. Somehow, breathing in the soft scent of cardboard and wood polish calms my nerves. "I'm fine."

"You don't *look* fine. You didn't show up here bleeding and covered in mud and looking *fine*."

"I know I'm not supposed to be here, and you shut the door and closed the bathroom for me and —" I force air into my constricted lungs. "I'm not staying, I —"

"No. You're not. Because I'm gonna call those neglectful parents of —"

"No!" My body snaps tight. "You want me to take care of myself? Because that's what I'm trying to do. Willa is —"

I have to close my eyes until I can finish. "Willa is dead."

She has to be, and not just because I feel it, but because it's been months since he took her.

She's not coming back. Not her, or Becca Wilder, or Tracy Bast. Not the girl whose name I never bothered to find out.

He scrubs a massive hand over his bald head, his fingers pressing so hard his skin wrinkles. "Baby girl." That's all he says, and it's an apology and a hug all rolled into the deep timbre of his voice.

"Why did you tell me I couldn't come here anymore?"

"Don't you worry about that now. You —"

I toss my phone onto Marcel's desk so the internet screen-shot of Jake's dad stares up at him. "Tell me, or I'm going to his house and asking him myself."

Truth: I'm not going to his house. I *am* going to his cottage. The one on Higgins Lake. I had to scroll through three years of Jake's social media pictures to find proof.

I need to discover how much Jake knows. If he's an accomplice, or just another victim.

Marcel says, "You're not going anywhere near —"

"Why?"

"Because I know his type. He's a bad man, Caroline."

323

Caroline. He's calling me by my real name, but he's not throwing me out. "I know."

"Then you know why!"

"You're not giving me a choice!"

I barely manage a whisper. "I think he killed Willa. Chrystal's daughter too. All those missing girls — they're gone because of him."

His mouth drops, just the smallest falter of his bottom lip, but for Marcel, it's extreme. "What now?"

I flick through pictures until I get to the ones I had Tabitha send me. The ones from Madison's computer that show Jake's dad sitting in his car while Willa and I fought. Then the one where she climbed into his back seat.

Tabitha found even more after I left. Zoomed in. Clarified. None of them are the version Madison showed Chrystal and Mountain Man. I asked.

I'm terrified that that evidence is gone forever. Maybe it's on missing drive number ten. Maybe it's with Madison, in a place they'll both never be found.

I hold the phone so both Marcel and I can see. "He took her, Marcel. He took her right after I left. And I don't know how he got her to write those letters to me, but Jake —" I swallow. "He said his dad travels to California all the time, so he must've sent them from there. So I need to know if he's the reason you threw me out, and exactly what he said. I need to know everything."

He stares at me so long I'm convinced he's not going to respond. That he's already called my parents and, in one moment, I'm going to hear the terse triple knock Mom uses before she storms into my room without waiting for me to answer.

Instead he tips his chin toward me and says, "He showed up here and threatened me. Said he couldn't have his son with a girl who 'frequented such an establishment.'"

I skip over the idea of Jake's dad thinking we're together before that wary look in Marcel's eyes trips into an information lockdown.

"Was —" I breathe deep and try again. "Was Jake with him?"

He says no and part of the weight on my chest eases. It's not proof, but it's a shred of hope for Jake.

I say, "Threatened you how?"

He rubs at the shoulder he injured in the service and stares over my head. "You remember why we don't shut the door all the way?"

"That's ridiculous. He could claim it all he wants and I'd just say it isn't true."

"Can't put the toothpaste back in the tube, baby girl. Some things, once they're out in the world, they never go away. And that man, he has connections."

He doesn't need to say anything else because he's right. What I say is true doesn't matter. It didn't matter with Mr. McCormack and it won't matter with Marcel either.

And we'd both be on trial. Every bit of my life would be torn to shreds and broadcast to the world. Every decision I've made scrutinized and questioned.

Forget keeping the real version of myself from my parents. There would be no hiding. And no hiding would mean no college. No moving away. It would mean making my house a cage with both parents holding the keys.

It would've destroyed me, and Marcel knew it.

The Honorable Thomas Monaghan. Esteemed judge. Revered father. Killer.

It's the *why* of it that won't stop battering my skull. Why Willa? Why Madison?

And I can't escape that the answer is me.

All of this is because of me.

I shuffle backward toward the door until the cold metal handle presses deep into my spine. "Thank you."

He knows what I mean. *Thank you for everything, including for letting me go.*

He straightens to his full height, a commander readying for battle. "You need help?"

I shake my head and don't offer that I have help — one of my helpers just doesn't know it yet.

Marcel doesn't argue. Doesn't tell me I'm making a mistake or that it's too dangerous. Marcel knows me like Willa knows me.

Knew me.

He's never forgotten that he picked me up on the side of the road after I set fire to a building.

So it's not even a surprise when he says, "Just get out before the smoke hits."

CHAPTER THIRTY-THREE

Wind whips against my back, sending my hair into tendrils that reach toward Jake's family cottage.

Except it's not a cottage at all. There are no quaint welcome mats or swaying porch swings. No creaking wood steps or logs waiting to be chopped for firewood.

It's a towering colonial set on the highest point of the cliff overlooking Higgins Lake, with brick so red it looks black, ivy clinging to its facade, vines twisting to avoid the massive windows that observe the lake. There are balconies for every room, a jacuzzi tub beneath a wood trellis in the backyard and winds that sweep through the surrounding trees, their rustling as permanent as the house itself.

I'm waiting in those trees, hidden, my fingers numb, my body shivering.

I'm waiting for answers.

My car sits well down the street, hidden from view in one of the turnoffs the power company uses, and I kept to the trees as I walked back. It wasn't hard. This is a place you could take a missing girl and not have anyone notice.

Except, all of this feels wrong.

I can picture this house in the daylight, sunlight streaming through those massive windows, spring-scented air ruffling the thick curtains.

It's the right house. A perfect match to the picture Tabitha sent me.

I never would've predicted Tabitha Zhao to be one of my strongest allies, but I can't deny how much she's helped tonight.

Even when it meant giving information on Jake — her friend since kindergarten. But it's her connection that led me here, her pictures from the ninth birthday party Jake's dad threw for him at the cottage. The one Tabitha — head of the yearbook committee even then — made sure appeared in the Holy Redeemer yearbook.

The picture may be over eight years old, but houses are static things.

I'm in the right place, even if everything is telling me I'm not.

Jake's words to me on the outskirts of Mountain Man's property ring in my head. *What if she's here, Caroline? What if she's ten fucking feet away and we left?*

And that's why I need to get inside. I need to see for myself.

I need to end this.

I'm waiting for my second unlikely ally to deliver so I can.

It's twenty-five minutes before Jake's headlights spear the darkness, sweeping the grounds as he navigates the winding path to the cottage.

I hold my breath, waiting for a glimpse of his expression. Something to tell me if he's here because he's worried about me, or if he's worried about me discovering the thing he needs to keep hidden most.

I owe Preston Ashcroft as much as I do Tabitha, even if he doesn't realize it. All it took was a single phone call, an innocent inquiry into whether Preston remembered if Jake's family had a cottage on Higgins Lake. The very lake involved in Preston's theory about Madison's cell pinging the nearby tower. The one Jake was so reluctant to accept.

Figures tumble through my head. How quickly Jake could've gotten here. How long the phone call could've lasted once Preston called Jake to tell him I'd asked about his family cottage — and that simple inquiry was enough, just like I knew it would be, to send Jake here, chasing after me. If Preston's first call was to his brother, the one on Madison's task force, and whether that means I have enough time to find answers on my own — or if his brother will brush the information away like so many before him.

That single phone call feels like it set a clock ticking — every moment I stand here is another one wasted.

There aren't many left, with midnight closing in, threatening to end this day just like the others — with Madison still missing.

I watch from the trees as Jake slams the car into park, and then he's out of it so quickly the interior lights barely have time to flash.

Shadows cling to him, guarding his face as he jogs up the front steps and turns, scanning for something.

For me.

He calls my name and I have to stop myself from yelling back, because I still can't believe he'd be involved in this. I can't reconcile the boy who's tried to help me these past few days — the one who ran after me during the vigil because I seemed upset — I can't mesh that version of him with one that would end the lives of multiple girls.

But maybe those are just the things I want to see. Maybe all this time, my tightrope was still stretched firm beneath my feet, even when I thought I'd jumped from it.

I press myself tight to the tree trunk, bark rough beneath my palms, and Jake shoves his key through the door.

As he swings inside, a robotic voice announces the front door has opened, and I want to scream. I can't sneak in behind him if the alarm system announces when I open the door.

I watch it slam shut, locking me out of the place I need to be most.

Lights spring to life in room after room as Jake walks, then runs, through the house. And then, for the first time, I can see his face.

I just can't read it.

Tension, concern, something close to panic, but none of that tells me why. And it's the why that matters.

Another light, then another, until the cottage glows against the blackness surrounding it and I have to run through the trees to track him, branches raking my skin.

The lights of the far room blaze to life, deep blue walls and dark cherry furniture, and Jake framed by the massive windows, his shoulders rising under the force of his breaths.

Then he goes still and his gaze focuses on the place where I'm standing.

I hate this, the way my heart stammers against my rib cage and my mouth goes dry. I hate that I don't know who I'm supposed to be afraid of.

Mostly I hate that I might be wrong about all of this, and if I am, Madison is waiting for me to finally get it right.

We're five days past forty-eight hours. Past the optimum window for finding a missing person.

Jake's progress through the house becomes a series of flashes through uncovered windows, until a door crashes open on the back porch.

I scramble, praying the rush of wind is enough to muffle the snap of branches beneath my feet. But I'm not sure he's listening for me anyway, not anymore.

It's the set of his shoulders, the confidence in his stride. I know this Jake. It's the one who steps onto the field at every game, the outside world tuned out and the opponent at his mercy.

The beam of his flashlight bounces with every stride, casting a white glow over the frosty ground. It's an eternity of walking, and with every yard, it feels colder, light leaching from the darkening sky as the forest grows dense.

A small cottage — a real one straight from Grimm's fairy tales — rises in the distance, tucked into the woods and overlooking the lake below. The windows are shuttered, the peaked roof littered with twigs and fallen leaves. It looks abandoned and forgotten — except for the heavy deadbolt that glints as the moonlight catches it. And for a moment I can't breathe.

Because everything about this place feels *right*.

Something catches my foot and I go down hard, palms scraping against rocks and branches.

I bite my lip to keep from cursing, waiting every second for Jake to appear above me.

But he doesn't even seem to register the sound.

He doesn't falter until he reaches the door. Even from my spot on the ground, frigid soil bleeding the warmth from my skin, it's impossible to miss the hesitation when he raises his hand to the door. And when his voice rings out, it's not my name he calls out.

He calls for his dad.

I want to tell him I'm sorry. That I know what it's like to discover the people who are supposed to love you the most are the ones who hurt the deepest. I want to tell him he'll survive, but it won't be without cost.

And I want to tell him if he helped hurt Willa, Madison, the girl by the lake or any like her, I'll show him no more mercy than he showed them.

Jake jams his key in the lock but it won't turn. He yanks it free and tries another.

When the third doesn't work, his foot connects with the door hard enough to rattle the frame.

It takes two more kicks to finish the job, until the frame is splintered and the door limps open.

Jake shoves his way inside and I sprint from the woods until I can press myself against the side of the cottage.

My hearing strains for any sign of movement but there's only the rush of wind. Then the door shifts and I freeze, my hands fisted.

Twenty seconds pass and there's no Jake, and I can't stomach waiting any longer. Because if he *is* involved, and Madison is in there, he could be killing her right now.

I creep toward the door until the warmth of the cottage yawns from the gaping frame, carrying the scent of cinnamon and vanilla and, beneath that, something sharper.

I twist inside, my back flat to the wall. The room is barren, the plank-wood floor interrupted only by an iron stove anchoring the corner.

Jake can't be far. And if he comes back, there's nowhere to hide.

It's only six steps to the hallway that leads to a small bathroom on the right, a bedroom beyond that.

The bed is the first sign this cottage is anything more than a forgotten relic, but it's empty. Bedding smoothed and flat.

I don't want to go in that room. I want to run from this place and scrub the feel of it from my skin.

I rush through the hallway, past the kitchen and into the bedroom, but I can't miss the sight of Jake. Can't unsee him crouched near the kitchen floor, his head in hands.

I've barely cleared the edge of the bed when his heavy footsteps echo through the house. There isn't enough time to find a decent hiding spot, so I shove myself beneath the bed, which sits so low I barely fit. The slats hang an inch from my heaving chest, and the slow, suffocating creep of claustrophobia crawls over me.

I squeeze my eyes shut, try not to imagine that this —

This is exactly what a coffin might feel like.

The footsteps stop and I can't see them, but I'd swear they're only inches away.

"Caroline?"

Jake's voice cuts through the darkness and I force my eyes open because if I'm going to die here, I might as well see it coming.

But it's not death that greets me when I do. It's a small box, wedged between the slats.

"Caroline?"

His steps are whisper light. I count them: one, two, then three and four.

A ringtone pierces the silence and I barely stifle my yelp while Jake mutters, "Jesus," and then a second later, "Not now, Preston."

I want to sigh in relief but I'm too afraid to move, even when Jake's voice trails toward the hallway.

"No, she's not here.

"No, and I broke my fucking door down, asshole."

My shoulder blades press into the floor as I shift right, closer to the wood box. I *should* wait until Jake's gone, but I can't stop my hand from reaching, my fingertips brushing over the grooves of worn wood.

"What did she say?

"No, tell me word for fucking word."

I flinch at the anger in his voice, at the feeling of being hunted. I let it sink into me, memorize the feel of it, so when the time comes, I'll remember what it was like for Willa, for Madison, for Becca and Tracy and maybe even the girl by the lake.

I'll remember, so I can make all of this right.

The quiet catches me off guard, and the realization that Jake has stopped talking creeps over me.

I don't know if he's ten feet away or two. I don't know if I should trust him or fear him.

The smallest glow of light spills over the floor, and understanding hits so fast my instincts take over before my brain can finish puzzling out why.

I fumble for the phone in my pocket, jamming the power button just as the first vibration hits.

There's a weighted pause, and then Jake's footsteps echo deeper into the room, every step pushing my heart rate higher.

A closet door creaks, the light flickering on.

Hangers rattle and slide on their metal rod.

And then the door slams shut, and I swear the wood splinters.

The room goes dark and I wait.

I wait until the sound of his presence fades, until it's only silence and the chill of wind rushing through the broken front door.

I wait until I can't any longer, and my fingers grip tight to the hard edges of the box. My hand stings with cuts and scrapes from my fall in the woods, and even in the dark, my palm looks smeared with blood.

I pull and the box slides toward me, grating where it scrapes against the wood slats, but no less stuck.

My fingers travel over the edges, to the top, when they hit a small ridge, and I follow it until it's smothered by the weight of the mattress. It's a stupidly simple design — a flat plank screwed into the lid, the sides extending far enough to rest on the bed slats, holding the box between them.

I wrench my arm to the side and grasp tight to the bottom, twisting with as much force as I can muster, until the left end of the plank holds by just a corner.

I wait again, this time for courage.

Because the longer I lie here, near this place where it all started, the more certain I am I don't want to know what this box holds.

I yank it free, so hard the lid pops open and showers me in gold and silver.

My hand closes around the objects in my palm, and the shapes are unmistakable. The circle of a ring, the sharp point of an earring.

Next to me, Madison's ring glints in the moonlight that bleeds beneath the bed.

Something shifts against my neck, and the second I touch the links and the delicate charm they hold, I know exactly what it is.

Whose it is.

I've memorized every intricate edge and depression, every curve of the iris's downturned petals.

I know what it is, because it matches mine.

CHAPTER THIRTY-FOUR

I know where Madison is.

I know where Madison is and I know where Willa died, and now the box that holds proof bounces in Mountain Man's console as his truck climbs over the back roads that lead to the peninsula with the twisted tree.

To where he'll drop me off before he heads, with evidence in hand, to the police.

They didn't believe me when I called, when Harper answered even though I dialed Brisbane. Condescension seeped through every word as he told me my claims were crazy, when he insinuated I could find myself criminally responsible for filing a false report.

But I didn't make up the five pairs of earrings, four necklaces, and three rings in that box. I didn't *imagine* lying on the floor, gathering them all so I wouldn't leave behind evidence, so I wouldn't deny whoever owned those pieces of jewelry the right to be avenged.

And I didn't pretend to stand in that cabin, clutching that wooden box to my chest, staring at the panel that led to the attic.

I screamed Madison's name. I promised I would bring help.

I shouldn't have promised. Because there's no rope or chain to make the stairs descend. No furniture to move so I can reach. No trees to climb or ladders to scale.

I *know* she's there, even though she never screamed back.

She has to be, because nothing else makes sense.

I couldn't see the twisted tree from the ground floor, but Willa's clues, they led me there, to the place where it all started.

She wouldn't have lied. Willa never lied. Not until the day she told me she had to leave but made up the reasons why.

I stumbled from the cottage, the broken door slamming open and closed in the wind.

I didn't know how much hope I held on to, how much of me still believed Willa was alive, until her necklace touched my skin.

I didn't scream. Definitely didn't cry. I'm nothing but the cold numbness that burrows deeper with every step.

That numbness led me out the door and into the open sky, and just when I thought I'd gotten something wrong, that Madison's ring — his *souvenir* — might be here but she was not, I saw it.

The attic. The dormer in the back. I couldn't see the twisted tree from the ground, but the attic would lift you higher, high enough to see over the cliff's edge.

From there, Willa could see.

Madison can see, if she's still breathing.

But the police aren't coming and I haven't saved her.

But I've given her murderer enough time for Harper to warn him.

And since I can't get to her, I'll bring her murderer to me.

Mountain Man says this is Thomas Monaghan's hunting ground. The side of the lake where girls go missing and no one cares. And out here, there's no one to see even if they did.

We drive instead of walking this time, past empty lots where houses once stood. Crumbling garages and the battered remnants of gravel driveways.

I remember them. Tiny one-story homes and laundry lines in the backyard that were visible from my perch in the tree. Mountain Man says they're all gone now, bought up and torn down.

My dad was furious when some regulatory issue blocked the sale of a string of them years ago because Higgins Lake is actually a reservoir constructed by the US Army Corps of Engineers and owned by the local power company. Now, I think he'd be relieved.

Bad juju, he'd call it. Negative karma or something with his chakra.

I wonder if he's ever realized how close he was to losing me that day, and if he'll ever know Willa was the thing that brought me back.

Mountain Man's truck lurches to a stop and he doesn't even put it in park.

I need to get out of the car. I need to be ready when Aubrey gets here. But my last tie to Willa is in the box that's smeared with my blood.

It holds the last thing she wore, when she was still alive.

A gun appears, lying quietly on Mountain Man's wide palm, blocking my view of the box.

This is part of the agreement. I give him the box to take to the police, he gives me the gun. I don't even know his name and he hasn't offered it.

He talks me through the safety, the trigger, the clip.

If he's got any qualms about teaching a seventeen-year-old girl how to operate a gun, he doesn't show it.

But I don't need the lesson. While Dad sent me to passive-resistance training to learn how to defuse situations, Mom signed me up for Krav Maga self-defense. And then for shooting lessons.

I nod along anyway, until my hand sinks beneath the weight of the gun, and then I jump from the car without looking back.

His headlights bounce away, and then I'm alone in a forest where insects have long since stopped chirping and buzzing, and there's no rustle of leaves where animals scurry past. No one wants to be in the place where a beautiful girl once lay lifeless on the shore.

My hand sags with the solid weight of the gun, the ridges of it cutting into my raw flesh. It feels right, this kind of pain. It feels like living.

I tuck the gun into my back pocket after triple checking the safety like Mountain Man thinks he taught me, and then I text Aubrey before I creep through the fields toward where her car will be soon.

She's been waiting down the road at the liquor store because I wouldn't tell her exactly where to go until I knew Step One was complete. Having her sit in a car near Thomas Monaghan's playground was not an option.

Ten minutes later she eases up the road that once served as someone's driveway. My memory is blurred, but I remember passing an old farmhouse the day my dad sent me to explore while he toured houses with his developer, telling me to come back in an hour. I nodded, even though I had no intention of coming back at all.

But the wooden fence that trails along the property line — broken, bent and failing in some parts, strong and sturdy in others — tells me this may be the same place.

My eyes water at the assault from Aubrey's headlights until she kills them, and she yelps when I knock on her window.

The window slips down and she hisses, "You almost gave me a heart attack," but her expression softens the longer she looks at me.

I hold out my hand. "Give me your keys."

She practically stumbles out of the car and hands them over without protest, which is how I know exactly how terrible I look right now.

Minutes later I've tucked her car into the camouflage of overgrown shrubs and marked the spot with a branch shoved into the dirt.

I hand her back her keys, and mine. "Look for the stick if you need a marker. Your car is facing out so you won't even have to reverse. If something goes wrong and you need a different escape, my car is down the road. Right hand side. Look for the big pile of boulders and go right about five feet. And listen, you'll know when the time is, but you can't stick around, okay? You could get hurt."

I don't look at her. I can't. Aubrey is amazing with makeup, and I don't want to see how accurately she followed my instructions.

But she's looking at me, and I read everything in her voice when she whispers my name.

I shake my head. "It's better if you don't know. C'mon."

I call Jake on the way back to the tree and ask him to meet

me there. I have no idea how long it will take him to get here, or what he may have been doing while I set this all up. And I can't let myself consider I may have figured this out too late. I pretend I don't notice the way he's trying to ask me if I've been to his cabin. If I *know* about his cabin.

If he'd just say he was there, if he'd just be honest, I wouldn't have to do this.

I wouldn't have to be the person who forces him to face the thing he fears most.

But he doesn't. He makes me describe the area three times, the tension in his voice ratcheting higher the longer we talk until he finally resorts to pleading. *I don't understand.* That's what he says more than anything. I don't expect him to.

I don't *want* him to.

If he understands why this place, why now, why I won't just get in my car and go somewhere safe, then he knows all of it. He knows about the box beneath the bed and the attic where girls die. He knows exactly who his dad is, and everything I thought I knew about Jake Monaghan is wrong.

We reach the little clearing and Aubrey's silence is a living thing, and then she says, "Okay." It's more to herself than me. She's given up on trying to get me to explain. "Where do you want me?"

I fixate on the trodden grass, right where I found a discarded girl two years ago. "You'll just need to lie there and …"

"Pretend to be dead."

I nod because I can't do anything else, and her clothes rustle as she lowers herself to the hardened ground.

"Caroline, I need you to tell me if this looks right. If I did a good job with the makeup. I tried to do the bruising like you said, but I'm Brown so they don't look the same, you know?" She pauses. "Caroline?"

She's full of shit. Aubrey doesn't stop in the middle of a production to ask the audience if her performance looks right. And she knows damn well her makeup looks fantastic. She's just forcing me to see her.

My stomach heaves the second I do, the vision of her knocking into me so hard my body folds onto itself.

I *know* she's alive. That she's breathing and touching me and the girl with the bruised neck and sunken eyes is just an act. But it's not an act for Willa, and it's *her* body I see superimposed on Aubrey's when I close my eyes.

Then she's off the ground, tucking my hair behind my ear, her fingers frigid against my skin. "Talk to me. Tell me what's going on. Please, Caroline." Her voice breaks and it's the one thing that can snap me back into focus.

I shoot up straight and do my best family picture day smile. "I'm okay. Don't cry, all right? It'll streak your makeup."

I'm not making her feel better. She's breathing so hard her shoulders show it, and her lips are pulled into a tight line, but she takes her spot on the ground anyway, and within moments she's still.

Jake's Rover rockets up the path, his headlights morphing from a faint flicker to a piercing glare that cuts through the overgrowth. In this silence, I can hear for miles.

I told him to come up the drive that ends far closer to the peninsula. For Step Three to work, his car needs to be visible.

I wait, settling the weight of the gun in my battered palm. The engine dies and a door slams, and then he's running.

He calls my name and I yell back, and then he rounds the corner and skids to a stop on the slippery grass. He's nothing but a shadow, hands in fists and shoulders bunched tight. Twigs snap beneath his feet as he steps forward, so slowly I'm not sure he'll ever get here.

He's close enough I can see his face against the pitch-colored sky, the way his gaze jumps from me to the lake behind me.

He swallows. "What is this, Caroline?"

He follows my outstretched hand to Aubrey's body and his face transforms from concern to abject horror — eyes so wide the whites of them glow in the darkness and his mouth twists into a muttered string of, "Oh fuck. Oh Jesus. Fuck!"

He runs toward Aubrey, his knees hitting the ground before he slides the rest of the way. He cradles her head, his large hands gentle and excruciatingly careful as he lowers his cheek to her mouth. His fingers fly to her throat, pressing softly, and his brows draw down. "She has a pulse!"

He laces his fingers and positions them just right on Aubrey's chest and I scream his name but he's not listening. He's too focused on trying to save a girl who isn't dying. He's too rattled to remember you don't do compressions on someone with a pulse.

And there's not a single part of me that believes he's played a role in the things his father has done.

He locks his elbows, his massive frame looming over Aubrey's body, and I'm too far away to stop him from crushing her ribs with CPR she doesn't need when Aubrey comes to life.

Her heels dig into the dirt and she shoves herself free, and Jake stumbles backward like he's been tased. A string of expletives tumbles from his lips, and then we're all breathing too hard to speak, all too afraid to move.

Step Two complete — the damage from it already forming a forever bruise.

He holds up a single hand, palm out, his voice far steadier than I expect. The words come haltingly, every syllable measured. "What. The fuck. Is this."

I squeeze tight around the butt of the gun and force sound through my ragged throat. "I'm sorry. I didn't think you knew but —"

"Knew *what*?" He jumps to his feet and he's all coiled energy and contained rage. "This was a test? You — you wanted to see if *I* was the one killing all those girls? What the *fuck*, Caroline?"

"No! I didn't — I said I was sorry!"

"You're *sorry*? You thought I was a murderer and you're sorry?"

I step forward, until I'm standing right in the place where Willa knelt beside the girl we found and asked who hurt her. "I didn't think you were a murderer, but you can't blame me for making sure when —"

He pauses, his voice low. "When what?"

Aubrey shuffles back a step, even though I'm not sure she has enough information to piece together what I'm about to say.

Except I still haven't said it, because the words will destroy him. I can almost understand Madison now, why she couldn't be the one to unmask Jake's dad. Almost.

Jake will remember this night, this moment, forever. Just like I remember walking into "therapy" holding my mom's hand, and then the cold emptiness left behind when mine slipped from hers, when my understanding of where we'd really driven settled in.

Jake's life has always been stable, his path clear. I'm going to ruin his life and make him a participant in its destruction. It's not fair to him, but none of this is fair to anyone.

His gaze flickers to Aubrey. "What's going on?" She melts further into the cave of trees, and he focuses back on me. "Caroline?"

It's the tremor in his voice that undoes me, so I raise the gun and level it at him. "I need you to call your dad, Jake. And I need you to make it convincing."

CHAPTER THIRTY-FIVE

Too much time has passed and Jake is still staring at his phone. It's cradled in his open palm, screen lighting his face in a soft glow.

It took minutes for him to stop staring at the gun in my hand, and then at me, silently begging me to give him more than I'm willing to.

This isn't the time to lay out my arguments for why his dad is guilty. He won't believe any of them, and I know Jake. I know that as he's staring at his phone, he's calculating and analyzing. Pulling apart threads of information and weaving them back together.

I wish I knew what pattern he's seeing.

He looks up at me with glossy eyes. "I can't do this."

The gun wavers and I grip it tighter, because I can't shield him from the truth, and trying to could determine whether Madison lives or dies. "There's no other way."

His thumb slams against his phone screen.

He crushes it to his ear and paces in a tight circle.

One step. Two. Turn.

A phone trills and we all jump, but it's not Jake's. Not Aubrey's. Something deep inside my coat buzzes and I scramble to find my Mr. McCormack phone in my pocket.

His name lights the screen, but it's much too late for that.

I hit decline, smearing a line of blood across the screen. Then again when the phone starts all over. This time, I silence it.

Jake stills, a statue in flesh, and says, "Dad?" His gaze follows

Aubrey as she tiptoes back to the empty place where the grass presses flat and lowers herself to the ground.

His entire body trembles as much as his voice. "Dad, I fucked up." A pause. "No. No, I — I didn't mean to do it. It just … got out of hand and —"

My phone rings again and Mr. McCormack is yelling my name before I get it to my ear. I don't give him a chance to talk. I just say, "I'm sorry, about all of this. I'm going to fix it."

The power button cuts into the pad of my finger when I press it tight, and the screen blinks to blackness as I toss it to the ground.

Jake turns, and the moment he sees Aubrey lying there, his knees give out and he's crouched on the soggy ground, hand covering his mouth.

Tears trail over his cheeks and I'm not even holding the gun on him anymore because I'm already doing more damage than any bullet could.

Jake mumbles, "I killed her, Dad. I —"

His face goes blank, and there's only a shushed "Okay" to show he's still thinking and breathing before he ends the call. He drops his hand to his side, and when he stares at me, I recognize everything in his eyes.

I try to say I'm sorry but my voice is buried so I mouth it instead, and he responds, so quiet I strain to hear him, "He's supposed to be out of town."

He doesn't say his dad is on the way, or how long it'll take him to get here if he is.

For all my planning, I didn't count on this variable. I can't kill a man who's not in the state.

Jake says, "He didn't do this," and I shake my head because my words won't convince him. There's only one thing that will.

I don't know what version of myself I am now. Certainly not the student athlete with the four-point-one-three grade point average. Not the one who curls her hair and smiles just right for family photos. Right now I'm not even the girl who stole someone's identity so she could be the person she thought her girlfriend needed her to be.

I'm just the girl with the gun in her scarred hand and enough rage to kill us all.

Time wavers again. Seconds stacking against each other until they become minutes and the moon is the only thing that moves. We're all frozen. Caught in a spell only Thomas Monaghan can break.

He appears without notice or warning.

No car signals his approach, because he knows these woods. It's too quick for him to have come from anywhere other than the cottage — or some other place, hidden in the miles surrounding us.

But if he was nearby, it's been too long. I can't think about what he might have done in the minutes between.

His gaze flickers from Jake to me to the gun in my hand and finally to Aubrey, and his expression never changes.

Jake stumbles back a step, and it's impossible not to compare the reactions of father and son. Impossible not to compare this night to the one before, when they stood in the coffee shop much the same way.

Thomas clasps a thick hand behind Jake's neck, pulling him forward until their foreheads touch and create a mirror image.

Jake's head nods as Thomas speaks. "It's okay, buddy. You were right to call. I can fix this."

And then his voice drops and I can't hear the words he's saying, but I don't need to. This man killed Willa, and he could have Madison wishing for death while he stands there with his hands on my friend.

This man who sat across from me and apologized for my parents not making me feel safe. This man who promised to help. Who looked at me with his soft eyes and gave me hope that parents like him existed.

And now he's touching Jake with the same hands and I want him dead so badly my blood riots and my vision blurs.

The gun's safety is only an impression of a switch beneath my numb fingers, but it doesn't stop me from forcing it off and chambering a round before I train the gun on Jake's dad. This time, my voice is strong. "Get your hands off him."

Thomas's back goes rigid and his hands lift. When he turns toward me, he's not any version of Judge Monaghan I've seen before.

His head cocks as he surveys Aubrey, and then he looks at me when he says, "Aubrey, get up and stand behind me. And don't run."

She obeys without question and I can't blame her. I doubt there are many people who aren't conditioned to obey a judge's orders.

And it's *this* — how he commands and people listen, how we all put our faith in him and he used it against us — this is how he's been able to ruin lives without suffering any consequence.

He steps forward. "Now, Caroline, what's this all about?"

His conversational tone sets my skin on fire. "I know who you are. I know *exactly* who you are."

He sighs. "You're clearly upset —"

"I'm not upset. I'm —"

"You're crying, Caroline."

I blink and heat splashes to my cheek, a searing trail against my numb skin. I'm crying, for the first time in years, in front of the man who took the most important person from my life. And maybe the second.

I grab my phone and the screen flares bright as I hold it out. "Her name is Willa, and you killed her."

"You're not making sense. Now hand over the gun before you hurt someone."

Jake's voice carries on the wind. "He didn't do this."

I can't look at him. I tell myself it's because I can't risk taking my eyes off his dad. "He *did*, Jake."

Mr. Monaghan holds up a hand, and whatever Jake was about to say vanishes. "Listen, I don't know what games you're playing, but this needs to stop. You're all clearly not thinking correctly, and I hate to see any of you kids hurt."

If there was any doubt it's a veiled threat, it disappears when he continues, "Aubrey, think of what would happen to your mom's reputation if people found out you were involved in something like this. With our litigious society, people are looking for reasons to sue prominent surgeons. I'd hate for anyone to see your actions as a reflection on her."

Every word shrinks Aubrey smaller. There's nothing else he could've said that would have had more impact, and he has to know it. This is how he's survived. Preying on the weak and exploiting the vulnerabilities of anyone who dares stand up to him.

I shift the gun to Jake, because he might be Thomas Monaghan's only vulnerability. "Take Aubrey and go."

Jake spits out, "Fuck no," but Aubrey's already at his side, grasping his arm tight, pulling so hard her heels slide on the slick grass, and when Mr. Monaghan issues the command, Jake retreats.

But they're already a vague memory. I remember random details of them but not the whole. Blurred and distant and slow motion.

It's Thomas that's clear to me now. Everything has narrowed to me and him, and there's nothing I can't see. Nothing that isn't in such vibrant focus it hurts to take in. I can't stop staring at his hands, picturing them poisoning Chrystal's drink, encircling Willa's neck.

I blink away new tears and say, "Madison took pictures of you. I have them. I know about your cottage in the woods and the fucking box you keep under your bed."

He doesn't answer. And I know then, his confession is in his stillness.

"No." Jake shrugs Aubrey off and charges forward, until he's standing shoulder-to-shoulder with his dad. "I was *just there*, Caroline! There's nothing there! What the fuck is *wrong* with you?"

Thomas raises both hands in surrender. "I don't want to hurt you, Caroline. I know how much Jake cares about you, and we can get you the help you need. Think of what it will do to your parents to have the world know you've been lying to them for so long. That they've let you live a double life without realizing it. They could be charged with neglect. Jake will have to admit he was so worried about your safety and your mental state he had to bring you to me, twice, for help. No one will believe your story, Caroline. They never have."

"Fuck off, you sadistic piece of shit." Before I can think about what I'm doing, I'm throwing my phone into his chest.

He catches it easily, cradling it in his hands. The hands that brought us all here. "You're not going to shoot me, Caroline. Think of what it would do to Jake. It's dark, you're sobbing, you're more likely to hit Jake or Aubrey than me."

He's wrong.

He's wrong about every single thing he said.

And this — all of this — is because of me. I led Thomas Monaghan into Willa's world. It's because of me that Madison discovered what he'd done. And now, I'll be the thing that rips Jake's life from its foundation.

I'm the connection between everything, and I'm going to set this all right.

I aim and squeeze the trigger, the force rocketing through my outstretched arms, the blast muffling the sounds of Jake's shout and Aubrey's scream.

Jake stares at the space to his left where the ground erupted, and when I level the gun at his head again, I can't bear to see as his expression shifts.

This is the best I can do for him, sparing him the memories of what will happen next.

I say, "Tell Jake to leave," and I barely recognize the calm in my voice.

Thomas whispers to Jake and it sends him back to where Aubrey stands. Where Aubrey *stood*. I can't see her anywhere, and I silently beg her to run. To take her car and leave.

I beg for her to be anywhere but here.

I nod toward the phone and a shudder racks through me at the idea of Willa's image in those hands. "Press the home screen and look at her."

He does, and it's only because of the glare of my phone that I can see the slightest of smiles touch his lips.

It's the rest of his confession, and it's all I need.

The tears come so fast I can't blink them away, and his form blurs as the taste of salt blooms on my tongue. My hands are shaking but I can't feel them. I'm nothing but the heavy piece of metal at the end of my outstretched arms. "How long?"

I don't want to know the answer. I'm not sure I can stomach the answer, but I need to hear it. I owe it to Willa to hear it.

His shoulders drop. Not with shame or remorse, but with the relief of shrugging off the version of himself that doesn't fit. Here, there is no court stenographer, no witnesses, no one to hold him accountable except a seventeen-year-old girl who ran away from home and is a single demerit from getting kicked out of school.

Here, he can be who he really is. He shrugs. "One letter for every day."

My stomach revolts and I swallow the acid that rushes to my tongue. Seven days. One hundred and sixty-eight hours, and the final moments of her life.

He made Willa write letters so I wouldn't think she was missing. He made Madison send a text to Mr. McCormack.

I regrip the gun, my palms slick with sweat and blood, and I ask the question I already know the answer to. "Why her?"

He doesn't pause. "She was in my son's way."

My arms burn beneath the strain of the weight in my hands, but I'll gladly remember this pain. "Why any of them?"

He shrugs. Like that's all they were worth to him. Because he knew his status and power would insulate him, his twisted desire to dominate greater than the value of their lives.

Because he *could*.

I look Thomas in the eyes because I want to be the last thing he sees before he dies. "Tell him you're sorry. At least give him that."

Jake rushes forward again, his father's outstretched arm the only thing holding him back. "Caroline, this is insane! This —"

Jake's gaze catches on something behind me, and his lips part.

It's only then the sound of sirens filters in, wailing in the distance. Only then I see the ripple of flames reflected in his eyes.

It's only then that I know I'm too late. I didn't save Madison. I just hastened the inevitable. And when the wind brings an acrid hint of smoke from the burning cabin, I find myself praying that if she's in there, she's already dead.

Jake whispers, "No," but his voice is strangled. "I was just at the cabin, there is *nothing* —"

"The fucking attic, Jake. You didn't go in the attic."

His gaze snaps to mine and understanding unravels in his eyes. He stares at Thomas, and his voice breaks when he says, "Dad?"

I can't watch this — the moment Jake realizes he's alone, that all the anchors he thought he had in the world were an illusion.

Jake stumbles away, head shaking, and beams of light bounce through trees and shrubs in the distance, faint and growing stronger. Strobes of reds and blues dance over the ground, and the growl of an engine ramps higher.

He stares at the flames behind me, words tumbling from his lips faster than I can piece them together.

But when he whispers he's sorry, it's not me he's apologizing to.

There's only one thing he could feel guilty for.

I barely force the words from my lips. "You told him."

Except it's worse than that. "You *warned* him, and he had time to —"

"No! It wasn't like that!"

But it was. His warning gave his dad enough time to set fire to all the evidence he could. "When did you know, Jake?"

"I didn't!" He can't stop shaking his head and his tears shine in the glow of the flames that rise higher on the cliff above us. "For a minute, I thought maybe — I went home that night, when Preston talked about the cell towers. But then I went to the cottage and —"

"*When*, Jake? When did you know?"

He can't even look at me when he says, "There was another drive, in the safe. It was different." He swallows hard. "It was painted, with nail polish, the pink color she always wore. I knew someone would find the safe eventually, and I knew she was jealous of you, that she was taking pictures, and I knew how you'd react if you found out. I didn't even look at it until —"

His breaths come too heavy to continue, but I don't need him to. He's giving me all the details I don't need, to cover for the things he can't say.

All the things that make sense now.

Madison's mom referenced the visits from people Madison cared about. People like Jake.

Jake knew where Madison's secret safe was. He didn't bother bringing tools to open it at the motel, because he knew he wouldn't need them even if dropping it didn't work — he'd opened that safe before.

He wasn't surprised by the edited images I showed him, because he'd already seen them. And then, missing flash drive number ten — the one that had to hold the pictures Madison showed to Chrystal. The one painted with Madison's pink nail polish. The one Jake took.

But then, Preston mentioned Higgins Lake, and none of it was about me anymore.

That night, Jake went home and looked at the drive that held evidence of the things his dad has done, and he didn't tell. He chose not to believe.

Everything his silence cost him is clear in his eyes.

His voice is barely a whisper. "He's all I have left."

Thomas knocks my response from my mouth as his shoulder rams into my ribs, and the gun jerks from my hands.

I'm weightless just long enough to suck in a lungful of air, and then we slam into the lake, the water so cold it burns.

My head cracks against the rocky lake bed, and whatever chaos exists above the surface can't reach me here. It's just the gurgle of water and the reflection of flames dancing above me.

Thomas's fingers dig into my chest, wrap around my throat, holding me under until my lungs ache and stars dance among the water's ripples.

But then my knee wedges beneath his ribs, my foot on his opposite hip, and when all the self-defense lessons Mom sent me to take over, I don't forget to slam the heel of my hand into his nose. I shove myself from his grasp and into the depths of water just beyond the lake's drop-off.

The force propels me through the water, and then we're a tangle of limbs until I dive deeper. The water is shades of gray and black, and panic surges through me when I don't know if I'm swimming toward the shore or away from it.

But Jake's form stands tall on the edge of the water and I surge toward it, just before the last of my oxygen gives out.

I shove to the surface, gasping, coughing, shivering so hard nothing works right, and blink the water from my eyes. The gun sits just beyond reach, only inches from Jake, black metal on blackened ground.

I claw at the frozen earth, raking the dirt with my fingernails to pull myself forward, but the mucky ground sucks at my shoes beneath the water and I'm still too far.

Too late.

A truck skids to a stop just beyond the peninsula, then two more behind it, and the glow of the headlights creates a halo that surrounds Jake's body.

Thomas's hand closes around my ankle, but before he can pull me under, the gun tumbles over the ground and into my outstretched hand.

I don't even blame Jake when he looks away.

I twist toward his dad, my finger curled around the trigger, and there's a split second where nothing happens, and then the moment when everything does.

The gun jerks in my soaked hands and the shot rips through the eerie silence. Thomas stumbles back, the bullet in his side spilling blood from his stomach and between his fingers.

It's fitting that, in the end, those hands should be covered in blood.

A door slams and voices clamor. Mr. McCormack yells my name. But it's still too late. Too late to stop any of this.

Thomas blinks twice, his gaze flickering up to me as water and blood trail over the cheeks, the jaw, the eyes, which look so much like his son's.

But it's Madison's face I see. Willa's. Tracy, Becca, the girl by the lake and seven others the world may never see.

I'm too late to change that.

Too late to save anyone.

But I'm still the girl with the gun.

Still the girl who's going to keep her promise and set all of this right.

And as my finger squeezes the trigger, I show Thomas Monaghan all the mercy he deserves.

CHAPTER THIRTY-SIX

The steady bong of the grandfather clock in Madison Bentley's marble foyer matches my steps as I climb the stairs to her room.

Beside me, her mom is silent, a smile stretched thin to cover the wild panic that swims in her eyes. It's been two weeks since Madison was found. Two weeks since Thomas Monaghan died.

Two weeks since I killed him, watched him stumble and bleed.

And no matter how many times I replay that moment, it's still not enough.

I'm not sure it will ever be enough.

The only consolation is that he never believed it would happen. That's the only thing that explains why he bothered to torch the cabin and take Madison out of it before he did — no one cares about evidence if they're dead.

They found Madison in the trunk of his car, the one he thought he'd be coming back to. When he could take her body somewhere no one would think to look.

When I lie awake, every night, envisioning all the things I couldn't stop him from doing to Willa, I remember that moment at the lake, when I taught him the true meaning of justice.

We reach the top step, carpet soft and plush beneath my shoes.

I don't want to see Madison. Don't want to see what Jake's dad did to her. Don't want a living example of what Willa went through.

And I don't want to see Madison alive when Willa is dead.

I know she's dead, even though they haven't found her. I should have known it from the beginning.

I've spent the last two weeks reliving every second of missed clues and ignored warnings. Remembering that for all the time I spent searching for Madison, all the times I listened to Chrystal yell about missing girls everyone believed left of their own volition, I never questioned that Willa could be one of them.

She left her life behind, everything she'd worked for, in the middle of her senior year, and I didn't question it. I stood on the St. Francis tightrope, and I didn't look down.

I thought I wasn't like them — the people who'd dismiss a girl going missing, the ones who think there are people who aren't worth looking for.

I know better now.

Madison's mom clears her throat and nudges open the door, a wince clouding her smile. "Well. I'll let you girls talk!"

She mouths, "Thank you for coming," as she gives my shoulder a squeeze, and I nod because I can't smile back.

I step inside Madison's room and my eyes strain to adjust.

The warmth and sweetness of the black-raspberry vanilla candles she loves hover in the air, masking the subtle hint of cleaners and antiseptics.

Madison sits snuggled in the corner, on her favorite chaise, a blanket drawn close. Her knees pull to her chest, her chin resting on arms that circle her legs.

I wait for a smile that doesn't come and it's like a razor to my heart. I don't even recognize this girl, the one who absorbs shadows instead of radiating light. She was the person you went to when you couldn't find the bright side, the one who would leave you laughing through your tears. This is the girl who photoshopped Ryan Reynolds into every picture in the quarterly newsletter just because she knew I'd notice.

But now I'm not supposed to touch her. That's what my mom told me before I came here today. Because the girl that used to hug strangers as an introduction is gone.

Thomas Monaghan created this version of her, and I'll never stop hating him for it.

The only mercy is that he didn't treat Madison like the other girls — not at first. Instead he questioned and interrogated, cataloging every bit of evidence she had and tracing where it might be. She lied to him, about the existence of flash drive number ten. She let him believe he was safe.

He told her that killing her wouldn't be the same as the others.

Mom ran to the bathroom seconds after she told me that.

The smallest strip of light sneaks over the top of Madison's windows, where she couldn't duct tape the curtains to the wall like she did the sides and bottoms.

The sliding glass door I used to break into her room no longer exists — the one with the faulty latch that never locked properly. Now it's a single door.

Heavy steel. The small pane of glass painted black. The deadbolt still shiny brushed chrome.

"I had them change it."

I startle at the sound of her voice, floorboards creaking beneath me. "He's dead."

She nods, just the smallest dip of her chin. "Did you know

at any given time in America, there are between twenty-five and fifty active serial killers? The FBI says they only kill about 150 people per year but lots of stats show that number is way underreported." She sucks in a breath. "Did you know there are currently almost 250 000 girls missing in the US?"

"I can give you one of their names." My voice snaps through the quiet. "I can tell you her birthday and how her eyes looked bluer when she wore certain colors. I can tell you what her laugh sounded like, and I can tell you how many days it took him to —"

"Do you think I don't know that?" Her words shake as violently as her body, tears tracking over her cheeks. "Do you think I haven't thought about *every* decision I made? About everything I did wrong? Do you *think* he didn't love reminding me of what I should've done? Didn't tell me every detail of —"

"Shut up."

"I know, better than anyone, what she went through." She shrugs off her blanket and her legs tumble over the side of the chaise, but she doesn't stand, like she's afraid the world is too unstable to keep her upright. "And I have to live with it."

"You *get* to live with it."

"I tried to help her. I —"

"Bullshit. You watched her get into that car —"

"He didn't force her! How was I supposed to know what —"

"Stop. Tell the cops whatever you want but don't lie to me. You knew. You saw him following her."

"*One* time."

"One too many."

Especially when it happened weeks — maybe months — before Willa went missing. Madison told the cops she saw him in the parking lot of Willa's diner. She told herself it was coincidence, that he was just looking out for me, making sure Willa wasn't "trouble."

Preston Ashcroft told me that, not Mom. Willa is still a thing we don't discuss, like if we don't say her name it'll be like she never existed.

I say, "And then you saw him take her, and you went to a stranger in the hopes they *might* go to the cops because you *knew*."

"Chrystal posted on those forums, and I knew she wouldn't ignore me. I knew she'd try to help. And I kept all my evidence in your locker and I bought that lipstick with the iris —"

"You kept evidence in a locker I haven't opened since I got it and you bought a lipstick? You told Chrystal? Just say it — you did everything you could to pass the responsibility off on someone else. Did it ever occur to you to just *tell* me?"

"I didn't know *how*. I thought maybe you'd find the stuff in the locker or see the lipstick and ask. I know how stupid it sounds now, but we were keeping so many things from each other and if you knew all the things I did —"

Her words come through her sobs. "I was so scared you'd never forgive me."

"How long was it before you realized Willa never came back? When you saw how upset I was and acted like you didn't know why. You knew and you did fucking *nothing*!"

"I couldn't be the one to tell him!" She scrubs her tears and freezes, then shudders as she tugs her sleeve past her wrist, covering whatever scars she left the cottage with.

She retreats into herself again, a closed-tight ball of legs and locked arms. "You don't know what it was like. I've loved

Jake for as long as he's loved you, and I've had to sit and watch. He obviously had feelings for you and you ignored it. You had everything I wanted and you didn't even *care*. And I tried to tell him once — how you were in love with someone else — and he wouldn't listen."

"So you were going to show him? Follow me around taking pictures as proof?"

Her head drops, hair draping over her face to create a wall, a cage, around her eyes. "I thought if he could *see* it, how the two of you were, that he'd finally realize you were never going to love him back. And we were *good* together, me and Jake. I know you, Caroline, and I know him, and I knew the two of you would never work. So yes, I followed you. And then I saw ..."

Her gaze focuses on the empty space where posters used to cover her walls. "And then I saw what I saw, and ..."

She shakes her head. "I went to the police station so many times. Once I even made it inside and then I ... I just couldn't. It couldn't be me. Jake was barely with me, and I couldn't be the one he thought of when he found out who his dad really was."

She was right to be afraid. I'm not sure Jake will ever be able to look at me again. The closest he's gotten is the letter he stuck in my locker — a single folded sheet of paper, the edges jagged and ripped from his notebook — that read *I'm sorry*.

I wanted to write him one back but I can't bring myself to say I'm sorry for killing his dad. I'm not. And I can't make myself forget the things he hid, so I bought him a vape, and cartridges in vanilla and mint. I think he might need it. I don't think he believes I'm the ocean anymore.

"Was it worth it, Madison? Is Jake here now?"

I want to destroy everything in this room. Burn it *all* down. Every memory of what happened on that lake, every moment I held the last belongings of twelve girls in my hands.

My hand lands on the strip of duct tape fastening the curtain tight to the window, eclipsing the light that strains through the cracks in the edges.

It rips free from the wall, clinging to my skin, ripping away layers of my fingerprints. Splotches of paint tear free, ravaging the soft lavender to reveal the deep burgundy layers beneath.

Madison's sobs tell me I should stop but I can't. Can't keep my hands from grasping the other side, the bottom, and finally — as the rod tumbles from the brackets and crashes to the floor — the top.

I don't stop until the tangled mess at my feet goes still and sunshine burns, bright and heavy, into the room.

I force myself to look at her. To see the yellowed bruises and the purple beneath her eyes.

I force myself to witness what Thomas Monaghan has made her into.

And even now, I can't bring myself to tell her that — when faced with evidence that might have saved her — Jake warned his dad instead.

Her sobbed apologies float away like the sprinkles of dust dancing in the rays of light piercing her room, because nothing she says can change anything. No amount of sorry can undo what's been done. And there's nothing in me that can grant her the reprieve she's begging for.

She whispers, "I wish he would've killed me."

She stares at her upturned palms like they might hold

answers. "I let her die. I look at it now and I don't know how. And when I heard you, in the cabin, screaming my name, I swear, Caroline, I prayed you wouldn't find me."

I drop in front of her, my hands on her knees, and I don't remember I'm not supposed to touch her until it's too late. But she doesn't pull away, and for a second, I can see the girl she was before.

I say, "*He* did this. Not you."

I'll never understand how I'm supposed to forgive the unforgivable. I can never forget the things she didn't do for Willa. But I also know what it's like to wish the world would go on without you.

I know what it's like to claw yourself back from that place. And how, sometimes, it takes a display of compassion to show you it's worth it.

It's only because of what Willa taught me that I'm able to squeeze Madison's knee and force her to meet my eyes. "You survived. *You get to live.* You want to atone for what you did?"

I nod toward the window, the glare of the light. "Start with living. Don't let him win."

I need to start living too, and I can't do that here. That hasn't changed.

I whisper, "I love you," and despite everything, the words still come easy.

She nods, her voice so quiet I barely register she's speaking. "I met her."

My hands lift from her knees, and then I'm standing because we're too close for this conversation, and it's too soon for me to hear it.

"When?"

"A few weeks after you guys started dating, I think." She pauses for a fresh onslaught of tears. "You were so happy, and I just wanted to know — I wanted to see what kind of person could transform you like that. I just … I wanted to see what that looked like. To love someone who loved you back."

I hug my arms across my middle, holding myself together so I don't fall apart, because I can't stop wondering if that was the night she saw Thomas Monaghan at the diner. If she smiled at Willa, knowing he was out there. "And?"

"And she talked to me. Even when I acted like a fucking lunatic and asked if she ever felt invisible and even when I started crying. And then as I was walking out —"

I shake my head because I *know* what comes next. The girl I loved — the one that loved me back — would never let someone suffer alone.

She never stopped hoping people could be more than what others thought them to be. And despite the articles and news reports and headlines that reduce her to a numbered victim — a placeholder for any number of girls that could've taken her spot — I know who she was.

She was better than any of us. And I won't let anyone forget her.

I choke out, "She comforted you. She did everything she could to make you, a complete stranger, feel a little less alone, and when she needed you, you *walked away.*"

I'm nearly out the door when Madison's voice slices into me, opening all the wounds that had only begun to scar.

"So did you, Caroline."

CHAPTER THIRTY-SEVEN

I hold tight to the rough concrete of the curb beneath me and close my eyes. The sun warms my skin, bakes into the parking lot surrounding me. There aren't any cars aside from mine. The diner closed so staff could go to the funeral.

Willa's funeral.

It took the cops nearly two months to find her. Some girls and their families haven't been that lucky.

A car rushes by, throwing a roadside puddle into a wave that flows toward the sloped lot, inching closer to my outstretched legs.

My vape rests in my hand, a temptation I don't submit to, no matter how much I want to. Because I'm trying. Because I told Aubrey I would.

Because I want to be a person whose promises are real.

Broken concrete pops beneath the weight of a car entering the lot. Whoever it is, I don't want to see them.

I'm still weeks away from eighteen, and for once, that's worked in my favor, because the police haven't released my name. I'm not facing any charges either. Of everyone, I've come out of this the most unscathed. Cherished and protected in all the ways Willa never was.

Jake's family has done their impressive best to keep details from reaching the public. It hasn't stopped the reporters from trying, and there's no shortage of magazine and newspaper covers bearing Thomas Monaghan's face.

If it weren't for Jake, I'd tell the world about the person Thomas deprived the world of. I'd talk about Willa. Not about Thomas Monaghan and his shocking double life or his professional accomplishments. I'd talk about a world that honors power and influence above twelve girls' existence. I'd show what he did by giving life to the ones he took.

The car engine quiets and a door thumps shut.

Aubrey shuffles forward. "Is it okay that I'm here?"

At my nod, her steps grow bolder, until she's not even pretending not to run, nearly knocking me over when she drops to my curb and smothers me in a hug.

I inhale the sweetness of jasmine like it's a gateway to the night I spent sleeping next to her in her dorm, both of us safe.

Aubrey whispers, "You went away again."

"I know."

"Come back?"

I laugh because I don't think I *can* come back. I can't face what's waiting for me if I move anywhere but forward. "Sure. I'll just join in the Senior Spirit Week festivities and show up to prom and pretend everyone isn't whispering about all the rumors they've heard."

Her mouth twitches into an almost smile. "I heard Tabitha is going to ask you."

"To prom?" My shock overrides everything else, and this time my laugh is genuine. "Hard pass."

"She helped you though, in the end. And she said sorry."

"Still." The truth is I can't look at Tabitha without seeing those pictures.

Silence grows into its own presence, and I roll the vape

between my palms to buy Aubrey time to say whatever's making her fidget and squirm.

Finally, she says, "You could go with me."

"*With you* with you?"

She rolls her eyes. "I don't know, Caroline. Can you just not make this weird? Going with anyone else feels wrong, okay? I don't let just anyone wear my pajamas, you know."

"They are nice pajamas."

"The best." She breathes deep. "Think about it, okay? Let me know?"

I don't know if I'm ready to think about the possibility of anyone else after Willa. If I'll ever be. But maybe Aubrey's not suggesting that at all, or maybe it's exactly why she asked the way she did. "I will. And thanks."

There's another thing I need to thank her for, but if I know Aubrey, she's done her best to forget it. "I didn't know Mountain Man was going to give you the box to take to the cops."

"Nope. Don't go there."

"Will you just let me thank you?"

"No. Because I don't want your 'thank-you' for me being stupid enough to accept some box from a huge dude in full camo, with a *shotgun* and black stuff smeared all over his face. I almost wet myself. 'I'll watch out for your friend. You take this to the cops.' That's what he said to me. He yanked me into the woods and I thought I was going to die and he's just all, 'Hey, can you do this delivery real quick?'"

Her voice squeaks higher. "And I *did*! I just panicked and did what he asked and I was so scared I went fifteen over the speed limit the whole way!"

It's all too horrible to be anything close to funny, but I can't stop my smile. "A whole fifteen over, huh?"

She shoves me and says, "It's not funny," even though she's laughing too.

Until she's not. "I couldn't have done it if I knew what it was."

I tell her I know because I do. Because the feel of that box, the cold circle of Madison's ring against my palm, the weight of Willa's necklace against my chest, they never seem to leave. "I wish you wouldn't have had to, but thank you anyway."

That's the truth too. I would take that away from her if I could, but there's also a part of me that still finds comfort in knowing Mountain Man was out there that night, watching and waiting.

He had justice to seek too.

And I can only hope that Sydney, wherever she is, knows the man who killed her aunt is dead. Thomas Monaghan ruined her life too. Took the one person she had to look out for her. But no one will ever hear about Sydney—no smiling school photo of her next to all of his other victims. That doesn't make her less of one. Apparently, it just makes her one that's even easier to overlook.

Aubrey sucks in a breath and I steel myself for whatever she's about to ask, because I guarantee it's not about prom. "Can I ask —"

"Just do it."

"It's just, you always called her Willa."

"That's who she was to me."

She was Willa and I was Livie, both of us new versions of ourselves, free of the ones that didn't fit.

I didn't lie to her about my name. In that one thing, I was true from the beginning. I close my eyes and I'm back there, on that night that was so unlike this one, when I looked up at her from my spot on the curb, watching as her narrowed eyes warred over whether to trust me ...

Willa's head tilts. "What's your name?"

My lie stalls in my throat. "Well, I don't —"

"You don't know your own name?"

I smile, because in that very moment, I know she's the person I thought she was. "Yes, I know my own name, but I hate it, and it's ... it's not who I am. And I wanted to lie but then I didn't ... want to lie." *I didn't want to lie to you.*

"Well, maybe it's not a lie if it's your truth. So, what's your name?"

I shove off the curb so I can stand closer, so I can reduce everything to the two of us, surrounded by walls of steel and a starlit sky. "I'm Livie."

Some of her wariness gives way to an amused smile. "Okay then. I guess, lovely to meet you, Livie."

"You as well. Now who do you want to be?"

"Oh." All the hardness flees her face, leaving nothing but hopeful wonder. Leaving the girl I met on the shore that day from my place in the twisted tree. "That's not a fair question. I need time to think."

"No you don't."

Her gaze snaps to mine and the understanding in it raises goose bumps over my skin. She breathes out, "Okay. Lovely to meet you, Livie. I'm Willa."

Aubrey clears her throat in a way that tells me we've both

been silent too long, and I answer her question with words that feel inadequate. "When we were together, she was Willa and I was Livie. We both got to be the people we wanted to be, instead of the people we were."

She nods like she understands, but the truth is, there's only two people who truly can. "Without her letters, you wouldn't have known she wasn't really in California, and without those clues, you might never have believed it was really Jake's dad — or known to look for the cabin. She saved Madison's life, you know? And you did too."

I don't tell her what it cost Willa to save Madison's life. I don't tell her Madison might be alive but I'm not sure she's saved.

I haven't visited her again. Maybe one day, when I can erase her voice from my head, reminding me of all the ways I failed.

But I took her picture to Thomas Monaghan's closed-casket funeral and burial.

I took Madison's picture and Willa's and one of each of the other girls.

I wouldn't have gone if Jake had, but since he didn't, I went, and I stayed for every minute. Every minute of eulogies that ignored who Thomas was, all the whispers of "I knew Thomas and he would never ..."

Except he would and he did, and when it was my turn to throw my rose on his grave, I spit on it instead.

I pin my hands between my thighs to warm them. "I've watched a lot of the coverage, the press conferences, and there was this one where the lead detective was making excuses for how this could've gone on so long without anyone noticing. And he said a bunch of stuff about jurisdictions not sharing information and other bullshit, and then he said it was hard to notice a trend of missing girls because Thomas chose so many perfect victims."

I draw my hands into fists to stop them from shaking. "He said they were 'at risk' girls. Girls who'd been in trouble, or whose parents didn't pay attention, or who had run away before. And then he held up a list of missing girls they'd finally taken the time to track down and found alive. Like because those girls actually ran away it was okay to assume the others did too. But —"

My voice trembles. "'Perfect victims.' That's what he called them. And I waited. I waited for anyone to say they were seventeen, or sixteen, or —"

Or, if the murmurs behind my parents' doors are to be believed, even fourteen. They'd yet to confirm her identity.

"I waited for any single one of them to say, 'Hey, detective, do you think maybe it's a problem that one area can produce so many "perfect victims" and no one seems to care?' But no one did. No one even questioned it."

I still don't know the name of the girl by the lake, or if she was one of Thomas's victims. The cops say she was cremated years ago when no one claimed her body. But she has a headstone next to Willa's now, because it doesn't matter how she died. What matters is that someone remembers that she lived.

Aubrey huddles close, her body pressed tight to mine. "There was really no cover-up? They just didn't notice?"

"You remember the detectives responsible for Madison's case? Brisbane and Harper? One was a friend of Thomas Monaghan."

"No shit."

"Yeah, Harper. The same one who picked me up after I broke out of camp years ago." And not that he'd ever admit it, but that part of me I've learned to trust knows that wasn't a coincidence. Not even back then.

Hidden connections.

I stretch my legs in front of me, carving grooves in the dirt beneath the broken concrete. "It's not like Thomas told Harper what was really up. He just asked him to make sure the other detective didn't dig too deep. Thomas told him things went south between Madison and Jake and he was trying to keep Jake out of trouble. And then he had Madison text Mr. McCormack to set him up the night she disappeared."

"Did he think it would actually work?"

"It did once before, I guess. You remember that teacher from Howard High?"

"The one that killed himself?"

"Yeah. The student was on Chrystal's list, and then they found her body and Thomas got scared. He planted evidence in the teacher's house, and apparently it was an easy sell because the guy was coming up on distribution of child porn. Guess who would've been the judge on his case."

She gives a heavy sigh, and it says all the things I'm thinking. That if not for Madison, he would've gotten away with everything. As long as he stuck to the perfect victims, no one would've cared.

Aubrey says, "So I'm volunteering for Project Innocence, to help with Anton Jackson's case," and I nod, because Preston already told the whole school.

"That's great, Aubrey. Really."

Anton's case is one of the many they've started reopening. Cases Thomas Monaghan presided over. Cases he influenced with promises to prosecutors and defense attorneys alike.

Favors granted and barters made. Subtle suggestions to walk away from a case in exchange for a relative's theft charge disappearing, for a recommendation letter. Even the land the cottage sat on was an exchange with a VP at the power company — perfectly secluded and perfectly private.

They're all coming forward, now that they know who he really was. Now that they know he used the court system to troll for victims. Girls who were part of the system. Girls whose parents had enough charges against them to ensure they weren't looking after their daughters.

And Anton Jackson too, whom Thomas Monaghan convicted for the murder of a girl he killed.

He took the system that was supposed to protect them all, and he weaponized it.

Aubrey sucks in a breath and I know she's about to suggest I volunteer too, and then she bails at the last minute and says, "Did you ever ask Mr. McCormack why he didn't call you?"

"Didn't have to. He told me."

He told me everything and I told him everything, cross-referencing our stories so we could fill in each other's blanks.

I told him about the statement I gave to clear his name, all the steps I took to do the same and how they led to finding Madison. He told me about the cops searching his apartment. About how there was no probable cause — he let them in voluntarily because he knew he had nothing to hide.

Except then there was the fake license he meant to take

somewhere to properly shred so it couldn't come back to hurt me. The one he then forgot about, until the cops reminded him.

He wrote me one hell of a recommendation letter for my file.

Aubrey says, "So are you going to tell me what he said, or ...?"

It almost draws a smile. "He said Bianca didn't tell him I came to visit or brought the phone until Marcel called him after I left the Wayside that night. I guess Mr. McCormack played boy scout and gave Marcel his business card the night he drove me home from the bar. Anyway, they went to the cops and used my Mr. McCormack cell to track us down."

I shove off from the curb and my head whirls with the familiarity of the movement. Except this time I'm not moving closer to Willa, because she's gone. "So that's it. That's everything I know, everything Preston has told me, and everything my mom knows according to her texts and the research she's done on her computer."

One day, I'll tell her to start using a password that isn't my name or birthday. One day, when I'm not on virtual house arrest, surrounded by parents who watch from the corners of their eyes.

Dad sold Mabel's house, taking a huge loss in his rush to be rid of it, to pretend it was never there. But we all know it was, and I won't let them forget who I was then and who I am now.

Our secrets don't belong to us anymore. They're out there now. Passed in knowing nods and pointed looks.

They're considering moving — upstate New York somewhere — once I leave for college. Leaving all of this behind. I don't blame them for that. I've waited years to do the same.

It was Mom who stepped in when Dad insisted I stay local. Maybe it was guilt, or maybe it's because of the way she looks at me — like all the versions of me are too much to take in when she's spent so long pretending they weren't there.

But we can't lie to each other anymore.

Aubrey's voice is soft. "Caroline, maybe you should stop looking for information."

"Why? Why should I get off easy? I'm alive. Willa spent seven days dying."

My head throbs, but now, just like before, there won't be any tears. "*Seven days*, Aubrey. And everyone treats her death like some bullshit noble sacrifice to save girls like me and Madison."

"It *was* noble."

"It was murder."

"And she tried to make sure it didn't happen to other people. All the clues you said she tried to put in her letters. When she couldn't save herself she saved —"

"She shouldn't have had to!" My voice is a whip through dead air. *None* of them should've. "Everyone in her life failed her. Including me. And all those other girls. Everyone failed them. And most people won't even remember their names. Where's the nobility in *that*?"

Aubrey's off the curb and standing in front of me before I can blink. "So what are you gonna do about it, Caroline?"

She pauses like I'm supposed to have an answer, but I don't. I'm not certain I even know what she's asking.

"Are you still gonna run away to California when you graduate? Leave everything behind? Are you gonna be Livie or Caroline or someone else who forgets any of this ever happened?"

No new version of myself can forget what happened.

I'm Caroline and I'm Livie. I'm the athlete with the perfect grades who blackmails her teacher. I'm the girl that will always love Willa. And I'm the girl with the gun, pulling the trigger.

I can't run from any of those versions of myself, not without losing who I am now.

Aubrey's hand wraps around my fingers, the warmth of her skin bleeding into mine. "You don't see it, how people listen to you. How you walk into a room and it's like everyone's waiting for you to lead them. You could stay, Caroline. I'm going to Johns Hopkins and you could too. Or somewhere else close."

Except I've spent every day since the night I set fire to that kitchen waiting to be somewhere else. Somewhere nowhere near this place.

I shake free of her hands and flee, over the empty places where Willa will never walk again.

"Caroline!"

Aubrey's voice pulls me to a stop. "What am I supposed to do, Aubrey?"

I've asked myself that question so many times it's lost meaning, but everything feels too big to fix.

She waits, then shrugs. "Hell if I know."

"What?"

"I never said I had answers, but if things are going to change then someone has to change them, right?"

She takes my silence as agreement and continues, "So, change them. My mom has connections. I know she'd help. I'd help. You could do *anything. Something.* I'm here, for whatever you need." Then, softer. "Let me help, Caroline."

No matter how many miles I run from this place, there will always be a piece of me here. I'm not sure I can live with walking away again — not when it cost me so much the last time. And all the things I've learned, they have to be for something. They have to *mean* something, or everything Willa did was for nothing.

Willa fought. I know that with every version of myself. Even when she knew how it would end, even though life had never been fair. She fought.

She fought because no one else would. Because it's never the people who reap the benefits who want to change how the world works. She fought because she was Willa, and she could always find the beauty of things, even amid the damage.

Aubrey stares at me, her breaths heavy and expectant.

Willa fought — now it's my turn.

No more running.

National Suicide Prevention Lifeline
1-800-273-8255
https://suicidepreventionlifeline.org

The Trevor Project
1-866-488-7386
https://www.thetrevorproject.org/get-help-now/#tt

Substance Abuse and Mental Health Services Administration
National Helpline
1-800-662-HELP (4357)
https://www.samhsa.gov/find-help/national-helpline

Rape, Abuse & Incest National Network
800-656-4673
https://www.rainn.org/

For information about the damaging effects of conversion therapy and how to support a ban on the practice, visit https://www.thetrevorproject.org/get-involved/trevor-advoca-cy/50-bills-50-states/about-conversion-therapy/.

AUTHOR'S NOTE

This book will likely always be the hardest one I've ever had to write. I knew the end of it as soon as I knew the beginning, and the truth is, I didn't want to write it. I wanted better for girls like Willa. Girls like Caroline. And all the girls out there who've ever felt forgotten, ignored, unseen. But truths don't disappear just because we refuse to acknowledge them, and as much we need the books that show happily ever afters, we need the books that face the darkness too. I hope I gave a voice to those who rarely get a chance to be heard.

ACKNOWLEDGMENTS

There are so many people who helped make this book a reality.

I owe immeasurable thanks to my fabulous agent, Sarah Davies, whose support and unfailing wisdom made this book possible. And to my editor, Kate Egan, whose calm and thoughtful insight brought even greater depth and honesty to the text. I am so incredibly lucky to be surrounded by women with such knowledge, understanding and integrity, without whom this book wouldn't be what it is today.

Special thanks to the team at KCP Loft, including copy editor Catherine Dorton and cover designer Jennifer Lum.

I have made so many friends in the writing community, and I live in fear of missing someone! But I have to give special thanks to Claribel Ortega, who was with me when this story was just a thought in my head, and who believed in me even when I didn't believe in myself. Andrea Ortega forever. I love you!

To Sonia Hartl and Annette Christie, my Pitch Wars mentors and forever friends. I'll be eternally grateful that they chose me to join their family, for their unwavering encouragement and for truly understanding this book in a way I wasn't sure anyone ever would. It's also because of them that I've gained my extended coven family in Kelsey Rodkey, Auriane Desombre, Rachel Lynn Solomon, Susan Lee and Roselle Lim. I am so fortunate to call these amazingly talented authors my friends, and sharing the good, the bad, and the endless waiting, with their love and humor, makes it all worthwhile.

To my fabulous Pitch Wars Class of 2017. We have such an incredibly special class, and I am still so honored to be part of such a talented and generous group of people. From mutual angst to fierce kettle debates — and maybe even a little vigilante justice — I could not have asked for better classmates. I wish I could name you all, but I do have to give special thanks to my loves Rajani LaRocca and Emily Thiede (maybe I could survive without our group chat, but I wouldn't want to) and Kylie Schachte, Anna Mercier and Kristin Lambert, all of whom have been a constant source of love and support from the very beginning of this wild ride, and I cannot wait to add many more years of friendship.

So many thanks to Susan Gray Foster, whose brilliant critiques have made me a better writer, and who helped shape the earliest version of this book into something worth sharing. And to every reader who gave helpful notes and encouragement: Hoda Agharazi, Julie Christensen, Amelia Diane Coombs, Rachel Simon and Amy Mills.

I also need to thank my fabulous Class of 2K20 Books friends. I've loved watching all of our books debut, and I'm honored to be member of such a fantastic group with such important things to say. I'm going to miss posting FB polls for you all to weigh in on!

And of course, I need to thank my husband and my friends and family, who've watched me pursue this impossible dream without ever questioning whether I'd succeed.

And to my reason for everything — my two girls — for bringing me joy every single day.

And lastly, to all my fellow throwaway girls. I love you. I see you. Go out there and move your mountains.